英語輕鬆學

Speak English Like a Native: Intermediate Level

學好 中級口語

就靠這本！

Preface 序

　　《英語輕鬆學》是一套專門訓練英文口語能力的系列書籍。包含下列
四本：

1 《英語輕鬆學：學好 KK 音標就靠這本！》

2 《英語輕鬆學：學好入門會話就靠這本！》

3 《英語輕鬆學：學好初級口語就靠這本！》

4 《英語輕鬆學：學好中級口語就靠這本！》

　　我們從 KK 音標開始，幫助讀者打好發音基礎，而後三本則各自以最
貼近讀者的生活經驗為主題架構編寫。《英語輕鬆學：學好入門會話就靠
這本！》以日常實用基礎會話為主，《英語輕鬆學：學好初級口語就靠這
本！》、《英語輕鬆學：學好中級口語就靠這本！》除了會話之外，更進階
到題材新穎的短文，讓學習不只輕鬆，還妙趣橫生。

　　內容大題的設計則有以下特點：

1 暖身單元我們結合聽力訓練，以重複聆聽並且搭配關鍵字詞與簡單問
　　題的方式訓練讀者開口說。

2 正文使用中英對照的方式，幫助讀者快速理解內容，其後則列出該課
　　重點單字片語，幫助讀者記憶與運用。

3 會話單元搭配口語新技能，補充英文口語的相關進階說法，後再使用
　　該課相關內容設計聽力簡短對答，幫助讀者同時訓練聽力及口語。

4 短文單元則搭配實用詞句，補充更多相關字詞或文法；並且歸納出該
　　課的重要音標做練習並朗讀課文加強發音。最後鼓勵讀者以自己對課
　　文的印象及該課習得的單字、用語，用自己的話將課文換句話說，測
　　驗自身對課文及相關重點的了解程度，進而活用。

5 最後討論題目的單元，鼓勵讀者與一同學習的夥伴分享自身相關經驗。而全書所有單元皆附參考答案，提供讀者練習、對照。

　　本套書為彩色編排，搭配精美的圖片，讓學習賞心悅目。同時為了讓讀者能更完整且有效率地學習，除了全系列套書附贈免費專業外師朗讀音檔之外，更請本公司王牌講解老師之一奚永慧（Wesley）老師搭配 Stephen、Jennifer 老師，分別錄製講解《英語輕鬆學：學好入門會話就靠這本！》、《英語輕鬆學：學好初級口語就靠這本！》、《英語輕鬆學：學好中級口語就靠這本！》這三本書，歡迎讀者們上「常春藤官方網站」（ivy.com.tw）及「博客來」（books.com.tw）訂購。

　　祝大家學習成功！

Contents 目錄

User's Guide 使用說明

掃描 QR Code 聆聽專業外師朗讀音檔。

暖身單元結合聽力訓練，以重複聆聽並且搭配關鍵字詞與簡單問題的方式訓練讀者開口說。

全書朗讀音檔下載

Lesson 19
A Shopaholic
購物狂

搭配筆記聆聽短文 Listen to the text with the help of the notes given

contentment	滿足
be short of...	缺少……
appliance	家用電器
be no laughing matter	不是鬧著玩的
be prone to...	易於……

再次聆聽並回答問題 Listen again and answer the questions below

Questions for discussion:
1. What does Pam love about shopping?
2. Why might being a shopaholic be a serious problem for some people?
3. What might be the cause of excessive shopping?

實用會話 Dialogue

Ⓐ Welcome to the town! How are you finding the place?
Ⓑ It's more peaceful than the big city! This morning, I saw children playing in the park. I heard birds chirping in the trees. I felt the clean air blowing on my face. I am so relaxed here.
Ⓐ Sounds like you love our little corner of the world. I heard that your family will be joining you soon.
Ⓑ Yes, my wife is arriving next week when our son finishes school.
Ⓐ You'll have to come over for dinner once you're all settled.
Ⓑ Thank you. That sounds lovely.

Ⓐ 歡迎來到鎮上！你覺得這裡怎麼樣呢？
Ⓑ 這裡比大城市還要寧靜！今早我看見孩童在公園嬉戲。我聽見鳥兒在樹上喞啾鳴叫。我感受到乾淨的空氣吹拂腋龐。我在這裡感到很放鬆。

短文聽讀 Text

The other day, my wife was feeling under the weather, so she asked me to take her to the doctor's. The traffic was bad on the way there, so we were late for the appointment. We had to get to the back of the queue and wait for an hour until it was our turn again.

To make matters worse, I got a parking ticket for parking illegally outside the clinic! To be frank, it was my fault; I knew I wasn't supposed to park there. I even saw the sign that told people they would be fined for parking there. However, my wife's health will always be top priority, so I have no regrets.

前幾天，我太太身體不太舒服，所以請我帶她去看醫生。路途上的交通狀況很糟，所以我們比約的診時間還晚到。我們得再排一次隊，等了一個小時才輪到我們看診。

正文使用中英對照的方式，幫助讀者快速理解內容。

單字片語 Vocabulary and Phrases

1 **be / feel under the weather** 身體不適 / 不舒服
Jack is feeling under the weather today.
= Jack is not feeling well today.
= Jack is not feeling good today.
= Jack is feeling ill today.
傑克今天身體不適。

2 **appointment** [əˋpɔɪntmənt] *n.* 預約；會面，約會 (尤指公務)
make / arrange an appointment (with sb) 安排 (與某人) 會面

3 **queue** [kju] *n.* 隊伍 & *vi.* 排隊 (英式用法)
line [laɪn] *n.* 隊伍 & *vi.* 排隊 (美式用法)
stand in a queue 排隊
= stand in line
= queue up
= line up
People stood in a queue in front of the ticket office.
= People stood in line in front of the ticket office.
= People queued up in front of the ticket office.
= People lined up in front of the ticket office.
大家在售票處前排隊。

4 **parking** [ˋpɑrkɪŋ] *n.* 停車 (不可數)
a parking space / lot 停車位 / 停車場
free parking 免費停車位 / 處

5 **ticket** [ˋtɪkɪt] *n.* 罰單，罰款通知
a parking / speeding ticket 違規停車 / 超速駕駛罰單

> 正文後列出該課重點單字片語，幫助讀者記憶與運用。

口語新技能 New Skills

1 表示「特別，尤其」的說法
especially [əˋspɛʃəlɪ] *adv.* 特別，尤其；專門
= particularly [pɚˋtɪkjəlɚlɪ]
= in particular [pɚˋtɪkjələ]
Ted is kind to people, especially to the elderly.
= Ted is kind to people, particularly to the elderly.
= Ted is kind to people, to the elderly in particular.
泰德對大家很和藹，對長輩尤其如此。
This English program is especially designed to suit intermediates.
這個英語課程是專門為中級程度的人設計的。

2 表示「大量的」的說法
◆ 在口語會話中，有許多說法可表示「大量的」，除了常見的 a lot of 或 lots of，亦可使用下列常見說法：
tons of... 大量的……，許多……
= loads of...
= a load of...
= plenty of...
I can't clock out yet; I still have tons of work to do.
= I can't clock out yet; I still have loads of work to do.
= I can't clock out yet; I still have a load of work to do.
= I can't clock out yet; I still have plenty of work to do.
我還不能打卡下班；我還有很多工作要做。

> 會話單元搭配口語新技能，補充英文口語的相關進階說法。

> 使用該課相關內容設計聽力簡短對答，幫助讀者同時訓練聽力及口語。

簡短對答 Quick Response
◆ Make quick responses to the sentences you hear.

討論題目 Free Talk
🖋 Talk on the following topic:
◆ What would you plant in your garden if you had one?

> 討論題目的單元，鼓勵讀者與一同學習的夥伴分享自身相關經驗。

> 會話單元

實用詞句 **Useful Expressions**

❶ 介紹常見的獨立不定詞片語
◆ 獨立不定詞片語具有副詞的功能，通常置於句首以修飾主句。有些獨立
不定詞片語已成了常見的固定用法，如下列：

To make matters worse, ...	更糟的是，……
To be frank (with you), ...	（跟你）坦白說／老實說，……
To be honest, ...	坦白說／老實說，……
To sum up, ...	總結來說，……
To do sb justice, ...	替某人說句公道話，……
To put it simply, ...	簡言之，……
To be brief, ...	簡言之，……
To begin with, ...	首先，……

To be honest, I'm really into hip-hop.
老實說，我非常喜歡嘻哈樂。
To put it simply, a rainbow is the combination
of rain and sunlight.
簡單來說，彩虹就是雨水與陽光的結合。
To begin with, I'd like to introduce our new
recruits to you all.
首先，我想跟大家介紹我們的新聘人員。

❷ 表示「應當」的說法
be supposed to V 應當……
注意
一般而言，此片語與助動詞 should 的
意思相同，但是語氣上較 should 委婉。
You're not supposed to wear jeans in such a fancy restaurant.
你不應該穿牛仔褲到這麼豪華的餐廳。（語氣較委婉）
You shouldn't wear jeans in such a fancy restaurant.
你不應該穿牛仔褲到這麼豪華的餐廳。（語氣較強烈）

短文單元搭配實用詞
句，補充更多相關字
詞或文法。

發音提示 **Pronunciation**

| ❶ [ɔɪ] | avoid [ə`vɔɪd] |
| | join [dʒɔɪn] |

❷ [b]	be [bi]
	vulnerable [`vʌlnərəbḷ]
	club [klʌb]
	basis [`besɪs]

朗讀短文 **Read aloud the text**

🎙 請特別注意 [ɔɪ]、[b] 的發音。

The day when your child leaves home and goes to university
or moves out of the house can leave you feeling down. This
phenomenon is called "empty nest syndrome." Although it is not
a clinical condition, those who experience it may be vulnerable to
depression and marital conflicts. They may experience feelings of
grief, loneliness, or loss of purpose.

To avoid or cope with empty nest syndrome, you can join
clubs and pursue new interests. You can use this as an opportunity
to spend more quality time with your partner. You can also keep
in touch with your child on a regular basis when you live apart.
And the times when your child does come home to visit can be

歸納出該課的重要音
標做練習並朗讀課文
加強發音。

換句話說 **Retell**

🖊 Retell the text with the help of the words and expressions below.

a self-service store, check out, introduce, retailer, redirect,
resource, repetitive, downside, theft, fraud, perception, faceless,
entity, tech-savvy, an honest mistake, -driven, old-fashioned

討論題目 **Free Talk**

🖊 Talk on the following topic:

◆ Would you like to shop in a self-service store?

鼓勵讀者以自己對課
文的印象及該課習得
的單字、用語，用自
己的話將課文換句話
說，測驗自身對課文
及相關重點的了解程
度，進而活用。

短文單元

Chapter 1

運動與健康

Tai Chi
太極拳

搭配筆記聆聽短文 **Listen to the text with the help of the notes given**

an ancient Chinese martial art	古老的中國武術
reduce stress and anxiety	減緩壓力與焦慮
emphasis	強調
combative	打鬥的
center of gravity	重心
utilize	利用

再次聆聽並回答問題 **Listen again and answer the questions below**

🎙 Questions for discussion:

1️⃣ Can old people practice tai chi?

2️⃣ What is one benefit of tai chi?

3️⃣ According to the speaker, is it easy to learn tai chi as a form of self-defense?

Tai chi is an ancient Chinese martial art, which people of all ages across the world do today as a form of exercise. It is regarded as having numerous mental and physical health benefits. It is said that the slow movements and breathing help to reduce stress and anxiety, improve mood, and promote better sleep.

There are also versions of tai chi which place more of an emphasis on its combative side. Students learn how to use their own and their opponent's centers of gravity to their own advantage. The ability to utilize tai chi as a form of self-defense, though, takes thousands of hours of training.

太極拳是一種古老的中國武術，現今世界各地不同年齡層的人會打太極拳來當作一種運動。它被認為有許多促進身心健康上的好處。據說，太極拳的慢速動作及呼吸有助於減緩壓力與焦慮，也可以提振心情並助眠。

此外也有不同類型的太極拳，它們比較強調太極拳打鬥的一面。學生能學會如何運用自己與對手的重心使自己有利。不過，要利用太極拳作為防身術的一種需要數千小時的訓練。

單字片語 Vocabulary and Phrases

❶ martial art 武術
martial [ˋmɑrʃəl] *a.* 武術的；軍事的；戰爭的

❷ numerous [ˋnjumərəs] *a.* 許多的
= plentiful [ˋplɛntɪfəl]

We have worked together on numerous occasions.
我們已經一同共事許多次了。

❸ benefit [ˋbɛnəfɪt] *n.* 好處；利益

❹ movement [ˋmuvmənt] *n.* 動作；行動；(社會或政治) 運動

❺ breathing [ˋbriðɪŋ] *n.* 呼吸 (不可數)
breath [brɛθ] *n.* 呼吸 (可數)
breathe [brið] *vi. & vt.* 呼吸

❻ mood [mud] *n.* 心情
be in a good / bad mood 心情好 / 不好

It seems Dad is in a good mood today.
老爸今天看起來心情挺不錯的。

❼ version [ˋvɝʒən] *n.* 類型，版本

❽ emphasis [ˋɛmfəsɪs] *n.* 強調；重視
place / lay / put emphasis on... 強調……；重視……
= place / lay / put stress on...

We need to place more emphasis on customer service.
我們必須更重視顧客服務。

❾ combative [kəmˋbætɪv] *a.* 打鬥的；好戰的

❿ opponent [əˋponənt] *n.* 對手

4

⑪ **gravity** [ˈɡrævətɪ] *n.* 重力，地心引力

⑫ **advantage** [ədˈvæntɪdʒ] *n.* 優勢；優點；益處
be to sb's advantage　　對某人有利

Luckily, the new policy is to our advantage.
很幸運地，新的政策對我們有利。

⑬ **utilize** [ˈjutəlˌaɪz] *vt.* 利用

We can now utilize sunlight to generate electricity.
我們現在可以利用陽光發電。

＊ generate [ˈdʒɛnəˌret] *vt.* 產生 (電力)

⑭ **self-defense** [ˌsɛlfdɪˈfɛns] *n.* 自衛，防身
defense [dɪˈfɛns] *n.* 防禦；保護

實用詞句　**Useful Expressions**

❶ 表示「將 A 視為 B」的說法
　　regard A as B　　將 A 視為 B
= look upon A as B
= think of A as B
= see A as B
　　After the war, we all regard the solider as a hero.
= After the war, we all look upon the soldier as a hero.
= After the war, we all think of the soldier as a hero.
= After the war, we all see the soldier as a hero.
　　戰爭結束後，我們都視這位軍人為英雄。

❷ 表示「據說」的說法
　　It is said + that 子句　　據說……，謠傳……
= Word has it + that 子句
= Rumor has it + that 子句 (此句中 rumor 為不可數名詞)
= It is rumored + that 子句
　　It is said that Mrs. Brown was very beautiful when she was young.
= Word has it that Mrs. Brown was very beautiful when she was young.

= Rumor has it that Mrs. Brown was very beautiful when she was young.

= It is rumored that Mrs. Brown was very beautiful when she was young.

據說布朗太太年輕時很美麗動人。

發音提示 Pronunciation

❶ [ɛ]	exercise [ˈɛksəˌsaɪz]	better [ˈbɛtə]
	mental [ˈmɛntḷ]	there [ðɛr]
	health [hɛlθ]	emphasis [ˈɛmfəsɪs]
	benefit [ˈbɛnəfɪt]	their [ðɛr]
	help [hɛlp]	center [ˈsɛntə]
	stress [strɛs]	self-defense [ˌsɛlfdɪˈfɛns]
❷ [dʒ]	age [edʒ]	advantage [ədˈvæntɪdʒ]

朗讀短文 Read aloud the text

🔔 請特別注意 [ɛ]、[dʒ] 的發音。

Tai chi is an ancient Chinese martial art, which people of all ages across the world do today as a form of exercise. It is regarded as having numerous mental and physical health benefits. It is said that the slow movements and breathing help to reduce stress and anxiety, improve mood, and promote better sleep.

There are also versions of tai chi which place more of an emphasis on its combative side. Students learn how to use their own and their opponent's centers of gravity to their own advantage. The ability to utilize tai chi as a form of self-defense, though, takes thousands of hours of training.

換句話說 Retell

Retell the text with the help of the words and expressions below.

martial art, numerous, benefit, movement, breathing, mood, version, emphasis, combative, opponent, gravity, advantage, utilize, self-defense

討論題目 Free Talk

Talk on the following topic:

◆ Have you or anyone you know ever learned martial arts before?

朗讀 ▶
Lesson 02

Learning Self-Defense
學習防身術

搭配筆記聆聽會話 **Listen to the text with the help of the notes given**

a self-defense class	防身課
suitable	適合的
concept	概念
defend	防禦
watch out	小心

再次聆聽並回答問題 **Listen again and answer the questions below**

Questions for discussion:

1 Which form of martial arts is the man's favorite?

2 What does the man recommend to the woman?

3 Does the man think the woman is big and strong?

實用會話 Dialogue

🅐 Hey, Barry. I'm thinking about taking a self-defense class, but I'm not sure which one to sign up for.

🅑 Well, I've tried taekwondo, karate, judo, and Brazilian jiu-jitsu, which is my favorite.

🅐 Which do you think would be the most suitable for me?

🅑 I'd say Brazilian jiu-jitsu, too.

🅐 Why's that?

🅑 Because its concept is that even a small person like you can defend yourself against a big, strong opponent.

🅐 Who are you calling "small?"

🅑 Err...

🅐 I'm just kidding. That sounds perfect for me. But you'd better watch out when I start my lessons!

Ⓐ 嘿，貝瑞。我想要上防身課，可是我不知道該報名上哪一種。

Ⓑ 嗯，我有試過跆拳道、空手道、柔道及巴西柔術，我最喜歡巴西柔術。

Ⓐ 你認為哪一個最適合我？

Ⓑ 我認為巴西柔術也會很適合妳。

Ⓐ 為什麼？

Ⓑ 因為它的概念是，即使像妳一樣身材嬌小的人也可以自我防衛抵抗又高又強壯的對手。

Ⓐ 你說誰「嬌小」？

Ⓑ 啊……。

Ⓐ 我只是在開玩笑。那聽起來很適合我。可是我開始上課後你最好小心點！

單字片語 Vocabulary and Phrases

❶ **sign up for...** 報名上……；註冊……
I want to sign up for a yoga class.
我想報名上瑜珈課。

❷ **taekwondo**
[taɪˈkwando / ˌtaɪkwanˈdo] *n.* 跆拳道

❸ **karate** [kəˈrɑtɪ] *n.* 空手道

❹ **judo** [ˈdʒudo] *n.* 柔道

❺ **Brazilian jiu-jitsu** [ˌdʒuˈdʒɪtsu] 巴西柔術
Brazilian [brəˈzɪljən] *a.* 巴西的；巴西人的 & *n.* 巴西人

❻ **suitable** [ˈsutəbḷ] *a.* 適合的；適當的
suit [sut] *vt.* 適合
be suitable for... 適合……
Jeans and sneakers are not suitable for formal occasions.
牛仔褲跟球鞋不適合正式場合。
Your new style suits you perfectly.
你的新風格非常適合你。

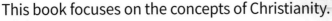

7 concept [ˋkɑnsɛpt] *n.* 概念；觀念

This book focuses on the concepts of Christianity.
這本書聚焦在基督教的觀念。

8 defend [dɪˋfɛnd] *vt.* 防禦，保護

defend oneself against sb/sth 　　保護自己免受某人 / 某事傷害

The police officers were trained to defend themselves against knife attacks.
員警有被訓練保護自己免於刀傷。

口語新技能 New Skills

🔑 表示「小心」的說法

watch out 　　小心，注意；留神

watch out for... 　　注意……；防備……

= look out for...

= be on the lookout for...

= be on the alert for...

Watch out! That car almost hit you.
小心點！那輛車差點撞到你。

Watch out for snakes when you go mountain hiking.

= Look out for snakes when you go mountain hiking.

= Be on the lookout for snakes when you go mountain hiking.

= Be on the alert for snakes when you go mountain hiking.
登山健行時要小心蛇出沒。

 注意

watch out for... 亦可用來表「留意……」或「關注……」。

Watch out for this director's next film. It'll be out next month.
密切關注這位導演的下一部電影。它會下個月上映。

簡短對答 Quick Response

◆ Make quick responses to the sentences you hear.

討論題目 Free Talk

📍 Talk on the following topic:

◆ What form of martial arts would you like to learn?

朗讀 ▶

Lesson 03

Lesson 03

Getting Cold Feet
臨陣退縮

搭配筆記聆聽短文 **Listen to the text with the help of the notes given**

bucket list	願望清單
attach	繫；綁
thrilling	刺激的
get cold feet	臨陣脫逃，怯步
thoroughly	徹底地

再次聆聽並回答問題 **Listen again and answer the questions below**

🎤 Questions for discussion:

1 What is bungee jumping?

2 Does the speaker think bungee jumping is one of the most thrilling activities?

3 According to the speaker, what is the key to bungee jumping?

13

   Bungee jumping is an amazing experience that is on many people's bucket lists. It involves jumping from a tall structure while attached to a long elastic cord. There are few activities more thrilling. However, many people attempt to do it, but end up getting cold feet at the top. It is, therefore, necessary that you think about all aspects carefully.

   It is essential that bungee jumping equipment be thoroughly checked before you jump. If you choose a reputable company, the safety record is likely to be very high. Once you're up there, the key to bungee jumping is to not look down before you jump. It's also important that you not think too much about jumping. Just go for it; you won't regret it!

高空彈跳是個驚奇的體驗，許多人的願望清單上也都有這項活動。高空彈跳是從一個高聳的建築物往下跳，同時會繫上一條既長又有彈性的繩索。很少有比這個更刺激驚險的活動。然而，大部分的人想嘗試玩高空彈跳，最後卻以在高空上怯步收場。因此，仔細地做各方面的考慮是必要的。

在你跳下去之前，徹底檢查高空彈跳的設備是絕對必要的。如果你選擇一間值得信賴的公司，他的安全紀錄應該相當良好。一旦你到了跳臺，玩高空彈跳的關鍵在於跳的時候不要往下看。不要想太多關於跳躍的事也很重要。只要放膽一試；你不會後悔的！

單字片語 Vocabulary and Phrases

1. **bungee** [`ˋbʌndʒi`] **jumping** 　高空彈跳
2. **be on sb's bucket list**
   列入某人（一生中必做的）願望清單
3. **structure** [`ˋstrʌktʃɚ`] *n.* 建築物；結構
4. **attach** [`əˋtætʃ`] *vt.* 繫；綁；貼；固定
   attach A to B　　將 A 繫／綁／貼／固定於 B 上

   The traveler attached a label to his suitcase.
   這名旅客在他的行李箱上貼了標籤。
5. **elastic** [`ɪˋlæstɪk`] *a.* 有彈性的
6. **cord** [`kɔrd`] *n.* 繩索；線
7. **thrilling** [`ˋθrɪlɪŋ`] *a.* 驚險的；令人激動的
8. **attempt** [`əˋtɛmpt`] *vt. & n.* 試圖，嘗試
   attempt to V　　試圖要……
   = try to V
   = make an attempt to V

   The CEO attempted / tried to save the company from going bankrupt.
   = The CEO made an attempt to save the company from going bankrupt.
   執行長設法拯救公司免於破產。

9 **end up + V-ing**　　到頭來……

You should hold the handrail when climbing stairs
or you may end up falling.

爬樓梯時應扶著欄杆，否則你可能會摔下樓去。

10 **get cold feet**　　臨陣退縮，膽怯

Ted was going to ask Lily out but he ended up getting cold feet.

泰德本來要約莉莉出來，結果最後他臨陣退縮。

11 **aspect** [`æspɛkt] *n.* 方面

12 **equipment** [ɪ`kwɪpmənt] *n.* 裝備；設備 (集合名詞，不可數)
a piece of equipment　　一件裝備

13 **thoroughly** [`θɝolɪ] *adv.* 徹底地；仔細地；完全地

14 **reputable** [`rɛpjətəbḷ] *a.* 有信譽的，有聲望的

15 **record** [`rɛkɚd ] *n.* 紀錄 & [ rɪ`kɔrd] *vt.* 記錄；錄 (音 / 影)

16 **go for it**　　放手一試，不遺餘力去做

實用詞句　Useful Expressions

1 necessary、essential 和 important 等形容詞與其修飾的 that 子句的
關係

◆ 某些形容詞，其後接 that 子句時，該子句須使用助動詞 should，而
should 通常予以省略，形成下列固定句構：

It is + 形容詞 + that + 主詞 (+ should) + 動詞原形

◆ 這類形容詞常見有下列八個：
necessary [`nɛsəˌsɛrɪ] *a.* 必要的，必需的
essential [ɪ`sɛnʃəl] *a.* 必要的，不可或缺的
important [ɪm`pɔrtṇt] *a.* 重要的
imperative [ɪm`pɛrətɪv] *a.* 極重要的；緊急的
urgent [`ɝdʒənt] *a.* 緊急的，急迫的
desirable [dɪ`zaɪrəbḷ] *a.* 理想的
recommendable [ˌrɛkə`mɛndəbḷ] *a.* 值得推薦的
advisable [əd`vaɪzəbḷ] *a.* 明智的

It is imperative that everyone (should) follow the guidelines in the manual.

每個人都必須遵照手冊的指導方針，這很重要。

It is urgent that we (should) deal with the problem.

我們迫切需要儘快處理這個問題。

It is advisable that you (should) not carry too much cash with you when traveling in foreign countries.

到國外旅行時，建議你身上不要帶太多現金。

② 常與介詞 to 搭配的名詞

◆ 以下名詞常與介詞 to 並用，to 在此可表「針對」：

key [ki] *n.* 關鍵

answer [ˈænsɚ] *n.* 解答，答案

solution [səˈluʃən] *n.* 解決之道

response [rɪˈspɑns] *n.* 回應

reaction [rɪˈækʃən] *n.* 反應

approach [əˈprotʃ] *n.* 途徑，方法

access [ˈæksɛs] *n.* 接觸

Being optimistic and persistent are the keys to success.

保持樂觀與堅持不懈是成功的關鍵。

Who knows the answer to the question?

誰知道這個問題的答案？

I wrote Jim a letter last week, but there hasn't been any response to my request.

我上星期寫了封信給吉姆，但迄今尚未有任何針對我的請求的回應。

❶ [ɛ]	there [ðɛr]	aspect [ˈæspɛkt]
	however [hauˈɛvɚ]	essential [ɪˈsɛnʃəl]
	attempt [əˈtɛmpt]	check [tʃɛk]
	end [ɛnd]	reputable [ˈrɛpjətəbļ]
	get [gɛt]	record [ˈrɛkɚd]
	therefore [ˈðɛrˌfɔr]	regret [rɪˈgrɛt]
	necessary [ˈnɛsəˌsɛrɪ]	

❷ [t]	tall [tɔl]	top [tɑp]
	attach [əˈtætʃ]	reputable [ˈrɛpjətəbļ]
	to [tu]	safety [ˈseftɪ]
	elastic [ɪˈlæstɪk]	important [ɪmˈpɔrtṇt]
	activity [ækˈtɪvətɪ]	too [tu]
	attempt [əˈtɛmpt]	

朗讀短文 **Read aloud the text**

🎙 請特別注意 [ɛ]、[t] 的發音。

    Bungee jumping is an amazing experience that is on many people's bucket lists. It involves jumping from a tall structure while attached to a long elastic cord. There are few activities more thrilling. However, many people attempt to do it, but end up getting cold feet at the top. It is, therefore, necessary that you think about all aspects carefully.

It is essential that bungee jumping equipment be thoroughly checked before you jump. If you choose a reputable company, the safety record is likely to be very high. Once you're up there, the key to bungee jumping is to not look down before you jump. It's also important that you not think too much about jumping. Just go for it; you won't regret it!

換句話說 Retell

🔖 Retell the text with the help of the words and expressions below.

bungee jumping, be on sb's bucket list, structure, attach, elastic, cord, thrilling, attempt, end up, get cold feet, aspect, equipment, thoroughly, reputable, record, go for it

討論題目 Free Talk

🔖 Talk on the following topic:

◇ Have you or anyone you know ever tried bungee jumping before? How was the experience?

Hitting the Gym
勤上健身房

搭配筆記聆聽會話 **Listen to the text with the help of the notes given**

ripped	有明顯肌肉線條的
bench press	仰臥推舉
stay motivated	保持動力
by comparison	相比之下
addictive	使人上癮的

再次聆聽並回答問題 **Listen again and answer the questions below**

🎙 Questions for discussion:

1 How long has the man been going to the gym?

2 Why did the woman stop working out at home?

3 What will the woman do tomorrow night?

實用會話 Dialogue

🅐 Mike, looks like you've been hitting the gym hard. You look ripped.

🅑 Every day after work for a year now.

🅐 Do you do a lot of weightlifting?

🅑 Yes, I do bench press, dumbbell lifting, and push-ups.

🅐 I tried to work out at home, but so difficult did I find it to stay motivated that I just stopped.

🅑 You should try my gym. Such a good place is it that I have no trouble being persistent.

🅐 I'd like to take you up on that offer, but I'm not sure I can. Your muscles are so big that I'll feel inferior by comparison!

🅑 Ha-ha, don't worry about that. We've all got to start somewhere. I didn't always look as awesome as this, you know.

🅐 Ah, I see the gym has made you modest, too.

B Come with me tomorrow night. So **addictive** will you find it that you'll soon be as ripped—and as modest—as me!

A OK, Mike, you've twisted my arm.

A 麥克，看來你很勤上健身房喔。你的肌肉線條看起來很明顯。

B 我每天下班後都去，現在已經一年了。

A 你做很多舉重運動嗎？

B 對呀，我做仰臥推舉、舉啞鈴還有伏地挺身。

A 我試著在家運動，但我發覺太難保持動力，所以我就停止了。

B 妳該去我的健身房試試。那是個好地方，讓我可以一直堅持下去。

A 我想接受你的提議，但我不確定是否做得到。你的肌肉真大，和你一比讓我覺得自己相形見絀！

B 哈哈，別擔心那個。我們都得從某個地方開始。妳知道的，我並非一直看起來像現在這般好。

A 啊，看來健身房也讓你變謙虛了。

B 明晚和我一起去吧。妳會發現這是件令人上癮的事，因此妳很快便會有和我一樣強壯的肌肉——也會和我一樣謙虛！

A 好了，麥克，你說服我了。

單字片語　Vocabulary and Phrases

1 **hit the gym** 　上健身房
　　hit [hɪt] *vt.* 到達 (三態同形)

2 **ripped** [rɪpt] *a.* 有明顯肌肉線條的

3 **weightlifting** [ˈwetˌlɪftɪŋ] *n.* 舉重 (運動)

4 **bench press** 　仰臥推舉

5 **dumbbell** [ˈdʌmˌbɛl] *n.* 啞鈴

6 **push-up** [ˈpʊʃˌʌp] *n.* 伏地挺身

7 **work out**　健身，鍛鍊
= exercise

8 **motivated** [`motɪ,vetɪd] *a.* 積極的

9 **persistent** [pɚ`sɪstənt] *a.* 堅持不懈的

10 **muscle** [`mʌsḷ] *n.* 肌肉

11 **inferior** [ɪn`fɪrɪɚ] *a.* 較差的

12 **comparison** [kəm`pærəsṇ] *n.* 比較

13 **modest** [`mɑdɪst] *a.* 謙虛的，謙遜的

14 **addictive** [ə`dɪktɪv] *a.* 使人入迷的；使人成癮的

口語新技能　**New Skills**

🔑 表示「說服某人」的說法

twist sb's arm　　說服某人，強迫某人
twist [twɪst] *vt.* 扭轉

注意

本片語原意為「扭某人的手臂」，
因此除了說服的意思之外，亦有
「強迫，威脅」之涵義。

Evan twisted my arm about going
to his girlfriend's birthday party.
伊凡強迫我去參加他女友的生日派對。

比較

pull sb's leg　　(以開玩笑的口吻) 欺騙某人
Did you really win the lottery or are you just pulling my leg?
你是真的中頭獎了還是在跟我開玩笑？

簡短對答 Quick Response

◆ Make quick responses to the sentences you hear.

討論題目 Free Talk

Talk on the following topic:

◆ Do you prefer working out at home or hitting the gym?

Lesson 05

Triathlon
鐵人三項

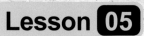

搭配筆記聆聽短文 | **Listen to the text with the help of the notes given**

variation	變化形式
time	計時
a persistent effort	堅定的努力
discipline	訓練；紀律
strive to...	努力要……
surpass	超越

再次聆聽並回答問題 | **Listen again and answer the questions below**

Questions for discussion:

1. What is a triathlon?
2. According to the speaker, what can you do if you want to improve your physical fitness?
3. Why can triathlons reduce the risk of injury?

短文聽讀 **Text**

deniska_ua / Shutterstock.com

A triathlon is a multisport race that consists of three different events: swimming, cycling, and running. While other variations exist, this is by far the most popular combination. If you take part in the Olympic version of a triathlon, you will swim 1.5 km, cycle 40 km, and then run 10 km. All of these events are timed, as are the transitions between the events.

If you want to improve your physical fitness, you can start training for a triathlon. It is a great way to get fit, as it requires a persistent effort to improve in each of the three disciplines. Participants always strive to surpass their previous personal best times in each event. Triathlons also reduce the risk of injury to participants, as the low-impact cycling and swimming compensate for the high-impact running.

　　鐵人三項是一種多項運動競賽，包含了三種不同項目：游泳、騎自行車、長跑。雖然有其他的變化形式，但這是最最受歡迎的組合。如果你參加奧運版本的鐵人三項，你會游泳 1.5 公里、騎自行車四十公里，並跑十公里。這些項目都會計時，項目之間的轉換也會。

　　如果你想要增進你的體適能，你可以開始為鐵人三項訓練。這是變得更健壯的好方法，因為它需要堅定的努力才能分別在三項訓練中進步。參賽者總是會努力超越他們先前在每個項目中個人的最佳時間成績。鐵人三項也可以降低參賽者受傷的機率，因為低衝擊的自行車與游泳彌補了高衝擊的長跑。

單字片語　Vocabulary and Phrases

1 **triathlon** [traɪˋæθlən] *n.* 鐵人三項，三項全能運動

2 **multisport** [ˏmʌltɪˋsport] *a.* 多項運動的

3 **consist of...** 　 由⋯⋯組成
= be made up of...
The committee consists of 20 scholars.
= The committee is made up of 20 scholars.
委員會是由二十位學者組成。

4 **cycling** [ˋsaɪklɪŋ] *n.* 騎自行車
cycle [ˋsaɪkḷ] *vi.* 騎自行車

5 **variation** [ˏvɛrɪˋeʃən] *n.* 變體；變化

6 **combination** [ˏkɑmbəˋneʃən] *n.* 組合；結合

7 **Olympic** [əˋlɪmpɪk] *a.* 奧運的
the Olympic Games　　奧運，奧林匹克運動會

8 **time** [taɪm] *vt.* 計時；為安排時間
The coach timed the swimmers carefully.
教練為游泳選手仔細計時。

9 **transition** [trænˋzɪʃən] *n.* 轉換，轉變，過渡
transition from A to B　　從 A 轉變為 B
The transition from school to full-time work can be difficult.
從上學到全職工作的轉變可能會很難適應。

🔟 **persistent** [pəˋsɪstənt] *a.* 堅持的；持續的

⓫ **effort** [ˋɛfət] *n.* 努力

make an effort to V　　努力要……

Josh made an effort to impress Vicky.
喬許努力要使薇琪印象深刻。

⓬ **discipline** [ˋdɪsəplɪn] *n.* 訓練；紀律

⓭ **participant** [pɑrˋtɪsəpənt] *n.* 參賽者，參與者

participate [pɑrˋtɪsəˏpet] *vi.* 參加

⓮ **surpass** [səˋpæs] *vt.* 超越

Our newest product surpassed everyone's expectations.
本公司最新產品超乎所有人預料。

⓯ **previous** [ˋprivɪəs] *a.* 先前的

⓰ **low-impact** [ˏloˋɪmpækt] *a.* 低衝擊的

high-impact [ˏhaɪˋɪmpækt] *a.* 高衝擊的

impact [ˋɪmpækt] *n.* 衝擊；影響

⓱ **compensate** [ˋkɑmpənˏset] *vi.* 彌補 & *vt.* 補償

compensate for...　　彌補……

compensate sb for sth　　補償某人某物

Hard work can compensate for your lack of experience.
努力工作可以彌補你經驗上的不足。

The company will compensate the workers for any workplace injury.
公司會補償員工任何在工作場所受到的傷害。

實用詞句　Useful Expressions

🔑 by far 的用法

◆ by far 可用來修飾最高級形容詞，表示「程度極大、差距極大」，翻譯時可翻為「最最……」，其用法如下：

by far + the + 最高級形容詞　　最最……

Penny is by far the most hard-working person in our company.
潘妮是我們公司裡最最認真工作的人。

Of the three candidates, Andrew's qualifications are by far the most impressive.
三位應徵者當中，安德魯的資歷是最最令人印象深刻的。

比較

so far　　到目前為止

so far 作副詞用，表「到目前為止」，故句中的動詞時態常使用現在完成式或現在完成進行式。

So far you've done a great job.
到目前為止你都做得很好。

發音提示　Pronunciation

❶ [i]	three [θri]	each [itʃ]
	these [ðiz]	previous [`priviəs]
	between [bɪ`twin]	

❷ [l]（置於母音前）	triathlon [traɪ`æθlɑn]	discipline [`dɪsəplɪn]
	popular [`pɑpjələ]	low [lo]
	Olympic [ə`lɪmpɪk]	

朗讀短文　**Read aloud the text**

📌 請特別注意 [i]、[l]（置於母音前）的發音。

　　A triathlon is a multisport race that consists of three different events: swimming, cycling, and running. While other variations exist, this is by far the most popular combination. If you take part in the Olympic version of a triathlon, you will swim 1.5 km, cycle 40 km, and then run 10 km. All of these events are timed, as are the transitions between the events.

　　If you want to improve your physical fitness, you can start training for a triathlon. It is a great way to get fit, as it requires a persistent effort to improve in each of the three disciplines. Participants always strive to surpass their previous personal best times in each event. Triathlons also reduce the risk of injury to participants, as the low-impact cycling and swimming compensate for the high-impact running.

換句話說　**Retell**

📌 Retell the text with the help of the words and expressions below.

triathlon, multisport, consist of, cycling, variation, combination, Olympic, time, transition, persistent, effort, discipline, participant, surpass, previous, low-impact, compensate

討論題目　**Free Talk**

📌 Talk on the following topic:

◆ Is there any sports competition you would like to participate in?

David Acosta Allely / Shutterstock.com

Lesson 06

A Warning from the Doctor
醫生的警告

搭配筆記聆聽會話 Listen to the text with the help of the notes given

considering	就……而言
smoking habit	抽菸習慣
light a cigarette	點燃一根菸
excluding	除……之外
personally	個人地

再次聆聽並回答問題 Listen again and answer the questions below

Questions for discussion:

1 What does the woman warn the man about?

2 Does the man find it easy to quit smoking?

3 What does the woman like to do for exercise?

實用會話 **Dialogue**

🅐 Hello, Doctor. How were the tests?

🅑 Well, considering your lifestyle, the test results are good. Nevertheless, I think I should give you a warning regarding your smoking habit. You must stop!

🅐 I know, Doctor, but it's difficult.

🅑 Every time you light a cigarette, remember it's taking eleven minutes off your life.

🅐 I will definitely try to quit. Excluding smoking, should I do anything else?

🅑 Make sure you eat healthy food, including a lot of fruit and vegetables. You should also go hiking or jogging on a regular basis. I personally like to go swimming, too; it's great exercise.

🅐 Thanks, Doctor. I'll do my best.

A 醫生，您好。檢查結果怎麼樣呢？

B 嗯，就你的生活方式而言，檢查結果還不錯。
不過，有關你的抽菸習慣，我想我該警告你。你得停止抽菸！

A 醫生，我知道，但這很困難。

B 每當你點燃一根菸時，記得它就從你生命中奪走了十一分鐘。

A 我一定會試著戒菸。除了抽菸之外，還有其他我該做的事嗎？

B 務必要吃健康的食物，包括大量的蔬果。你也應該定期去健行或慢跑。就我
個人而言，我也喜歡去游泳；那是很棒的運動。

A 醫生，謝謝您。我會盡力的。

單字片語 Vocabulary and Phrases

❶ **considering** [kən'sɪdərɪŋ] *prep.* 就……而論；考慮到
Your father is in great health, considering his age.
就年紀而論，你父親算是很健康的了。
Considering the weather, we decided to cancel our trip.
考慮到天氣，我們決定取消旅行。

❷ **lifestyle** ['laɪfˌstaɪl] *n.* 生活方式

❸ **warning** ['wɔrnɪŋ] *n.* 警告，告誡

❹ **smoking** ['smokɪŋ] *n.* 抽菸
smoke [smok] *vi.* & *vt.* 抽菸

❺ **habit** ['hæbɪt] *n.* 習慣

❻ **light** [laɪt] *vt.* 點燃
（三態為：light, lit [lɪt] / lighted, lit / lighted）& *n.* 光，光線（不可數）
light a cigarette / candle　　點燃香菸 / 蠟燭

❼ **cigarette** [ˌsɪgə'rɛt] *n.* 香菸

❽ **quit** [kwɪt] *vt.* & *vi.* 戒除；離開（工作、學校等）（三態同形）
quit smoking / drinking　　戒菸 / 酒
quit one's job　　某人辭掉工作

33

❾ excluding [ɪkˋskludɪŋ] *prep.* 除外

All of us can play the piano, <u>excluding</u> Bob.
= All of us can play the piano, <u>exclusive of</u> Bob.
= All of us can play the piano, Bob <u>excluded</u>.
除了鮑伯以外，我們所有人都會彈鋼琴。

❿ personally [ˋpɝsənlɪ] *adv.* 個人地；親自地

口語新技能 New Skills

❶ 介紹與名詞 basis 相關片語

a on a regular basis　　定期地
= regularly [ˋrɛgjələlɪ]
Frank hits the gym on a regular basis.
法蘭克定期會去健身房。

b on a

daily	basis	每天
weekly		每週
monthly		每月
yearly		每年

Exercising on a daily basis is good
for your health.
每天運動對你的身體健康有益。

c on an hourly basis　　每小時
= every hour
Students at that school take a 10-minute break on an hourly
basis.
那間學校的學生每一小時就有十分鐘的休息時間。

d on a temporary basis　　暫時地
= temporarily [ˋtɛmpəˏrɛrəlɪ]
Kate is working as a teacher on a temporary basis. She hopes to
find a permanent job as a project manager.
凱特目前暫時當老師，她希望可以找到一份當專案經理的永久工作。

2 表示「盡全力」的說法

    do one's best (to V)   某人盡全力 (去做……)

= try one's best (to V)

= do one's utmost (to V)

= do one's level best (to V)

    Lisa will try her best to arrive on time.

    莉莎將會盡全力準時抵達。

簡短對答 **Quick Response**

◇ Make quick responses to the sentences you hear.

討論題目 **Free Talk**

🎤 Talk on the following topic:

    ◇ What kind of exercise do you prefer doing?

Lesson 07

At a New Restaurant
在一間新餐廳

搭配筆記聆聽會話 | **Listen to the text with the help of the notes given**

venison	鹿肉
vegetarian	吃素的人
in that case	那樣的話
give it a shot	試試看某事物
refrain from...	忍住不要……

再次聆聽並回答問題 | **Listen again and answer the questions below**

🔑 Questions for discussion:

1️⃣ When did the restaurant open?

2️⃣ Why doesn't the woman want to try the venison?

3️⃣ What does the man ask the woman not to do?

朗讀

Lesson 07

實用會話 Dialogue

Ⓐ Is this restaurant newly opened?

Ⓑ Yes, ma'am. We opened last week.

Ⓐ What would you recommend?

Ⓑ I recommend that you try our venison. It's very popular.

Ⓐ I'm afraid I'm vegetarian. Sorry, I should have mentioned it before.

Ⓑ In that case, I suggest that you try our vegetarian lasagna.

Ⓐ Sounds good to me. I'll give it a shot.

Ⓑ Can I ask that you refrain from using your cellphone while you're here? We are a "no cellphone" restaurant.

Ⓐ Oh, I've heard about those. What a good idea!

Ⓑ Yes, it's proving very popular with our customers, who can concentrate on the food and the conversation.

Ⓐ More talking; less tapping!

Ⓐ 這是間新開的餐廳嗎？

Ⓑ 是的，女士。我們上週開幕。

Ⓐ 你推薦什麼呢？

Ⓑ 我推薦您試試我們的鹿肉。它十分受歡迎。

Ⓐ 很抱歉我是吃素的。抱歉，我應該先跟你說一聲。

Ⓑ 那樣的話，我推薦您試試我們的素食千層麵。

Ⓐ 聽起來不錯。我想試試看。

Ⓑ 我可以請您在此用餐時不要使用您的手機嗎？我們是「禁用手機」的餐廳。

Ⓐ 喔，我聽過這種餐廳。真是個好點子！

Ⓑ 是的，結果證實這相當受到顧客們的喜愛，他們可以專心用餐和談話。

Ⓐ 多動口；少動手！

單字片語 Vocabulary and Phrases

❶ **venison** [ˋvɛnəzn̩ / ˋvɛnəsn̩] *n.* 鹿肉

❷ **vegetarian** [ˌvɛdʒəˋtɛrɪən] *n.* 素食主義者 & *a.* 素食的
比較
vegan [ˋvigən] *n.* 純素食者 & *a.* 純素的
a vegetarian / vegan restaurant　　素食 / 純素食餐廳

❸ **mention** [ˋmɛnʃən] *vt.* 提到，說起
Cole mentioned that he got married two years ago.
柯爾提到他兩年前結婚了。

❹ **lasagna** [ləˋzɑnjə] *n.* 義大利千層麵 (美式拼法，英式 lasagne)

❺ **give sth a shot**　　嘗試某事
= give sth a try
shot [ʃɑt] *n.* 嘗試
I think I'll give bungee jumping a shot.
= I think I'll give bungee jumping a try.
我想我會去玩看看高空彈跳。

38

6 **refrain** [rɪˋfren] *vi.* 忍耐，抑制
refrain from + N/V-ing　　忍住不……

Please refrain from eating or touching artworks in the gallery.
請勿在藝廊內飲食或觸摸藝術品。

7 **prove** [pruv] *vi.* 證明是，結果是
主詞 + prove (+ to be) + 形容詞 / 名詞　　結果證明……

Ryan's idea proved (to be) a huge success.
結果證明萊恩的點子是個大成功。

8 **concentrate** [ˋkɑnsnˌtret] *vi.* 專注，專心
concentrate on...　　專注於……

= focus on...

The director asked Kelly to concentrate on her work.
經理要凱莉專心工作。

9 **tap** [tæp] *vi.* & *vt.*
(用手指) 輕拍；輕敲 (三態為：tap, tapped [tæpt], tapped)
tap sb on the shoulder / arm　　輕拍某人的肩膀 / 手臂

口語新技能　New Skills

🎤 表示「那樣的話」的說法

In that case, ...　　那樣的話，……
Susan's not feeling well; in that case, we'll cancel the picnic.
蘇珊身體不舒服；那樣的狀況下，我們決定不去野餐。

比較

a in case of + 名詞　　萬一……

In case of a car accident, you should call the police immediately.
萬一發生車禍，你應該馬上打給警方。

b in case + 子句　　如果……，以防……

In case Henry calls while I'm away, please tell him I'll call him back as soon as possible.
如果我不在的時候亨利打電話來，請告訴他我會儘快回電。

c in the case of + 名詞　　關於……；在……情況下

In the case of this proposal, we decided to reject it.

至於這份提案，我們決定將它駁回。

d in any case　　而且，反正

I don't mind not having many friends, and in any case, I prefer being alone.

我不介意沒有很多朋友，況且我比較喜歡獨自一人。

簡短對答　Quick Response

◆ Make quick responses to the sentences you hear.

討論題目　Free Talk

🎤 Talk on the following topic:

◆ Would you be interested in dining at a "no cellphone" restaurant? What do you think about this policy?

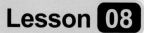

Lesson 08

Kick the Habit
戒除惡習

CH 1 運動與健康

搭配筆記聆聽短文 **Listen to the text with the help of the notes given**

continuously	持續地
cut back on...	減少……
craving	渴望
willpower	毅力
determination	決心

再次聆聽並回答問題 **Listen again and answer the questions below**

🔖 Questions for discussion:

1 What did Jenny realize about her afternoon snacks?

2 What did Jenny want to eat after every meal?

3 How much weight did Jenny lose on the first week of her diet?

41

Jenny drank a lot of soda and was continuously gaining weight. In order to stay fit, she thought that it was about time she kicked the habit of drinking soda. She also found that the afternoon snacks she fondly enjoyed contained too much sugar. Her favorite chocolate cookies, for example, contained 17 g of sugar per "portion." And let's just say she never had only one portion! So, she decided that it was time she cut back on those, too.

It was very hard for Jenny at first: She had sugar cravings after every meal and was desperate for a bar of chocolate! But, through willpower and determination, she managed to stay away from junk food and started to lose weight. In the first week alone, she lost 3 kg. For those of us who drink too much soda and eat too much sugar, maybe it's high time we kicked the habit, too!

珍妮喝很多汽水並持續增胖。為了要保持健康，她認為是時候戒掉喝汽水的壞習慣了。她也發現自己很愛的下午茶點心含糖量過高。例如，她最喜歡的巧克力餅乾每「份」就有十七克的糖。而且她從不只吃一份而已！所以，她也決定是時候少吃那些餅乾了。

起初，這對珍妮來說很困難：每餐飯後她都會生起想吃糖的渴望，而且特別想來一條巧克力！不過憑著毅力和決心，她成功地遠離垃圾食物並開始瘦下來了。光是第一個禮拜，她就減了三公斤。我們這些喝太多汽水和攝取過多糖分的人，或許也是時候戒除那些壞習慣了！

單字片語　Vocabulary and Phrases

❶ continuously [kən`tɪnjʊəslɪ] *adv.* 持續地，連續地

❷ stay fit　　保持健康
= stay healthy
　fit [fɪt] *a.* 健康的

❸ kick the habit (of...)　　戒除 (⋯⋯的) 壞習慣
= break the habit (of...)
　be in the habit of...　　有⋯⋯的習慣

The doctor suggested that Jack kick / break the habit of smoking.
醫生建議傑克戒掉抽菸的壞習慣。

❹ fondly [`fɑndlɪ] *adv.* 喜愛地，喜歡地

❺ contain [kən`ten] *vt.* 含有 (某種成分)
Lemons contain lots of vitamin C.
檸檬含有大量的維生素 C。

❻ portion [`pɔrʃən] *n.* (食物的) 一份
a (generous) portion of roast beef　　一 (大) 份烤牛肉

❼ cut back on sth　　減少某物
For the past few weeks, I've been cutting back on the sugar in my diet.
過去幾個星期來，我一直在減少飲食中糖的攝取量。

8 craving [ˋkrevɪŋ] *n.* 渴望
= longing [ˋlɔŋɪŋ]
  have a craving / longing for...　渴望……

9 desperate [ˋdɛsp(ə)rɪt] *a.* 極度渴望的
  be desperate for sth　　對某事物很渴望
  be desperate to V　　極度渴望做……

10 bar [bɑr] *n.* 條；塊；根
  a chocolate bar　　一條巧克力，巧克力棒

11 willpower [ˋwɪl͵paʊɚ] *n.* 毅力 (不可數)

12 determination [dɪ͵tɝməˋneʃən] *n.* 決心 (不可數)

13 stay away from sb/sth　　遠離某人 / 某事物
= keep away from sb/sth

  Visitors are told to stay / keep
  away from the beehives.
  遊客被告知要遠離蜂巢。

實用詞句 Useful Expressions

1 表示「該是……的時候了」的說法

It is	time	
	about time	+ 過去式的 that 子句　　該是……的時候了
	high time	

It is time (that) we decided whether to hold a press conference or not.
該是我們決定是否召開記者會的時候了。

It is about time (that) Sophie started to exercise on a regular basis.
該是蘇菲開始規律運動的時候了。

After a long day at work, it is high time (that) you took a rest.
歷經漫長的一天工作後，該是你休息的時候了。

注意

使用上列句構時，that 子句的時態須為過去式，且可省略關係代名詞
that。上列句構亦可將 that 子句改為不定詞片語，如下：

	time		
It is	about time	(+ for sb) + to V	該是 (某人)⋯⋯的時候了
	high time		

故上述三個例句可改寫成：

→ It is time for us to decide whether to hold a press conference or not.

→ It is about time for Sophie to start to exercise on a regular basis.

→ After a long day at work, it is high time for you to take a rest.

2 表示「假設⋯⋯」的說法

Let's (just) say (+ that 子句)　　假設 (⋯⋯)

= say (+ that 子句)

注意

此句型常用於說話者要舉例或建議時，且通常為較隨意的語氣。

Let's say / Say (that) it takes three months to complete the task; then, we'd better start now.

假設這項任務要花三個月完成，那麼我們最好現在就開工。

發音提示 Pronunciation

❶ [ɔɪ]	enjoy [ɪn'dʒɔɪ]	

❷ [ɚ]	order ['ɔrdɚ]	never ['nɛvɚ]
	afternoon ['æftɚ͵nun]	after ['æftɚ]
	sugar ['ʃugɚ]	willpower ['wɪl͵pauɚ]
	per [pɚ / pɝ]	

朗讀短文 Read aloud the text

🎙 請特別注意 [ɔɪ]、[ɚ] 的發音。

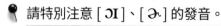

Jenny drank a lot of soda and was continuously gaining weight. In order to stay fit, she thought that it was about time she kicked the habit of drinking soda. She also found that the afternoon snacks she fondly enjoyed contained too much sugar. Her favorite chocolate cookies, for example, contained 17 g of sugar per "portion." And let's just say she never had only one portion! So, she decided that it was time she cut back on those, too.

It was very hard for Jenny at first: She had sugar cravings after every meal and was desperate for a bar of chocolate! But, through willpower and determination, she managed to stay away from junk food and started to lose weight. In the first week alone, she lost 3 kg. For those of us who drink too much soda and eat too much sugar, maybe it's high time we kicked the habit, too!

換句話說 Retell

🎙 Retell the text from "the perspective of Jenny" with the help of the words and expressions below.

continuously, stay fit, kick the habit of, fondly, contain, portion, cut back on, craving, desperate, bar, willpower, determination, stay away from

討論題目 Free Talk

🎙 Talk on the following topic:

◆ Do you often crave snacks? What do you usually do about your cravings?

Lesson 09

A Fish Out of Water
如魚離水

搭配筆記聆聽會話 | **Listen to the text with the help of the notes given**

senior	高年級生
freshman	一年級生
take things step by step	一步一步慢慢來
learn one's lesson	（某人）記取教訓
You don't have to ask me twice!	我十分贊成！

再次聆聽並回答問題 | **Listen again and answer the questions below**

Questions for discussion:

1 Did the boy perform well in the basketball game?

2 What did the woman forget to bring to the supermarket?

3 What does the woman suggest in the end?

實用會話 **Dialogue**

🄰 How was the basketball game, Eric?

🄱 Not good, Mom. I asked to play in the game for seniors.

🄰 But you're only 15 years old.

🄱 I know. But I'm the best player on the freshman team, so I thought I would be OK.

🄰 What happened?

🄱 No sooner had I started playing than I knew I had made a mistake. I was too young and too small. I was no match for those older boys. I felt like a fish out of water.

🄰 You should stick to the freshman team and take things step by step.

🄱 I've learned my lesson, Mom. How was your day?

A I went grocery shopping, but I forgot my purse.
No sooner had I arrived at the supermarket than
I realized I couldn't pay for anything!

B So neither of us has had a successful day, then!

A As we've got no groceries, how about we go out for pizza?

B You don't have to ask me twice!

A 艾瑞克，籃球比賽打得怎麼樣呢？

B 不太順利，老媽。我要求加入高年級組的比賽。

A 但你才十五歲而已。

B 我知道。但我是一年級隊伍中最棒的球員，所以我當時認為沒問題。

A 發生了什麼事呢？

B 我一開始比賽就知道我做了錯誤的決定。我年紀太輕，身材又小。我根本比不上那些年紀較大的男生。我就像是一隻離開水裡的魚，很不自在。

A 你應該要留在一年級隊伍並且一步一步慢慢來。

B 老媽，我已經記取教訓了。那妳過得如何呢？

A 我去採買食品雜貨，但忘了帶皮包。我到了超市才發現我買不了任何東西！

B 看樣子我們今天都不太順利！

A 由於我們沒有任何食物，我們出去吃披薩怎麼樣呢？

B 我十分贊成！

單字片語 Vocabulary and Phrases

1 **game** [gem] *n.* 比賽，競賽
a baseball game　　棒球比賽
a big game　　　　重大賽事

2 **senior** [ˈsinjɚ] *n.*
（高中或大學）最高年級的學生

3 freshman [ˈfrɛʃmən] *n.*
(高中或大學) 一年級的學生 (複數為 freshmen)

4 stick [stɪk] **to sth**　　堅守某事物
The story of the successful athlete inspired me to stick to my dream.
那名成功運動員的故事激勵我堅持自己的夢想。

5 step by step　　逐步地，按部就班地

6 learn a / one's lesson　　(某人) 記取教訓

7 grocery [ˈɡrosərɪ / ˈɡrosɚɪ] *n.* 食品雜貨 (常用複數)
a grocery store　　食品雜貨店

8 You don't have to ask me twice!　　我十分贊成！(於口語中使用時，表示說話者相當樂意接受對方的提議、邀約等)

口語新技能　New Skills

🔑 表示「如魚離水」的說法

(be / feel) like a fish out of water　　如魚離水 (形容一個人在不熟悉的環境中感到不自在)
I always feel like a fish out of water in new environments.
我在新的環境總是會感到不自在。

注意
(take to sth) like a duck to water　　如魚得水 (形容一個人做某事十分自然，如同天生一般)
Although he only started playing, James took to golfing like a duck to water.
雖然詹姆士才剛開始打高爾夫球，但他打得很上手。

簡短對答 Quick Response

◇ Make quick responses to the sentences you hear.

討論題目 Free Talk

🎙 Talk on the following topic:

◇ Have you ever felt like a fish out of water? What happened?

Reasons to Be Vegetarian
成為素食主義者的理由

搭配筆記聆聽短文 **Listen to the text with the help of the notes given**

estimate	估計
figure	數據
diabetes	糖尿病
global warming	全球暖化
a developing country	發展中國家
emission	排放物

再次聆聽並回答問題 **Listen again and answer the questions below**

Questions for discussion:

1. Why are more and more people becoming vegetarian?
2. What is one of the health benefits of being vegetarian?
3. What will happen to the climate if we eat less meat?

短文聽讀 **Text**

Wishing to be healthier, more and more people are becoming vegetarian. In the USA, for example, it's estimated that around 8% of adults are vegetarian, and in some countries, such as Germany, the figure is more than 10%. There are many benefits of being vegetarian. It can reduce the risk of heart disease and certain cancers, as well as type 2 diabetes.

It can also help the environment by reducing global warming. Though being a great source of food and income in developing countries, raising animals could worsen climate change. The less meat we eat, the greater the reduction in climate-changing emissions. When deciding whether to be a vegetarian or not, you could treat these facts as food for thought!

　　愈來愈多人因為希望更健康而成為素食主義者。舉例來說，在美國估計有大約 8% 的成人是素食主義者，在一些國家如德國，該數據則高於 10%。當素食主義者有許多好處。吃素可以降低罹患心臟病與某些癌症以及第二型糖尿病的風險。

　　吃素也可以減緩全球暖化而有利於環境。儘管在發展中國家是一大食物與收入的來源，養殖動物會使氣候變遷惡化。我們吃愈少肉，使氣候變遷的排放量減少幅度就愈多。當你在思考要不要成為素食主義者時，可以將這些事實納入考慮！

單字片語 Vocabulary and Phrases

1. **vegetarian** [ˌvɛdʒəˈtɛrɪən] *a.* 素食的 & *n.* 素食者
   vegan [ˈvigən] *a.* 全素的 & *n.* 吃全素的人

2. **figure** [ˈfɪgjɚ] *n.* 數字；身材

3. **benefit** [ˈbɛnəfɪt] *n.* 好處；利益 & *vt.* 有益於 & *vi.* 獲益
   benefit from...　　　從……中獲益

   Convenience is a great benefit of mobile payment.
   方便性是行動支付的一大好處。

   How can we benefit from this deal?
   我們可以如何從這筆交易中獲利？

4. **diabetes** [ˌdaɪəˈbitiz] *n.* 糖尿病

5. **global warming**　　　全球暖化

6. **income** [ˈɪnˌkʌm] *n.* 收入
   a source of income　　　收入來源

7. **developing** [dɪˈvɛləpɪŋ] *a.* 開發中的，發展中的
   developed [dɪˈvɛləpt] *a.* 已開發的，先進的
   a developing country　　　發展 / 開發中國家
   a developed country　　　已發展 / 開發國家

8. **worsen** [ˈwɝsn̩] *vt.* & *vi.* (使) 惡化

   The situation worsened when the politician interfered.
   當那位政客介入時，情況惡化了。

⑨ **reduction** [rɪˋdʌkʃən] *n.* 減少

⑩ **emission** [ɪˋmɪʃən] *n.* 排放物（常用複數）；排放（不可數）

⑪ **food for thought** 值得考慮的事，值得深思的事

The speech has given me some food for thought.

這場演講發人省思。

實用詞句　**Useful Expressions**

🔑 介紹「the + 比較級…, the + 比較級…」的用法

the + 比較級…, the + 比較級…　　愈……就愈……

ⓐ The less meat we eat, the greater the reduction…
　　　　　(1)　　　　　　　　　(2)

(1) 為副詞子句。此處句首的 The 為副詞連接詞，引導副詞子句。但The 亦可視為副詞，修飾其後的副詞 less。

(2) 為主句。此處句首的 the 為副詞，修飾其後的比較級形容詞 greater。

ⓑ 使用此句型時須注意，若句中的主詞為代名詞或專有名詞，且其後的動詞為 be 動詞時，該 be 動詞不可省略；但若主詞為一般名詞時，be 動詞則可省略。

The older you are, the more responsibilities you have.
　　　　代名詞

你年紀愈大，要負的責任就愈多。

The hotter the weather (is), the more people there are on the beach.
　　　　一般名詞

天氣愈熱，海灘上就愈多人。

VesiBoycheva / Shutterstock.com

❶ [ʌ]	become [bɪˋkʌm]	such [sʌtʃ]
	adult [əˋdʌlt]	income [ˋɪnˌkʌm]
	some [sʌm]	reduction [rɪˋdʌkʃən]
	country [ˋkʌntrɪ]	

❷ [r] (置於母音前)	vegetarian [ˌvɛdʒəˋtɛrɪən]	reduce [rɪˋdjus]
	risk [rɪsk]	raise [rez]
	environment [ɪnˋvaɪrənmənt]	reduction [rɪˋdʌkʃən]

朗讀短文 **Read aloud the text**

📌 請特別注意 [ʌ]、[r] (置於母音前) 的發音。

Wishing to be healthier, more and more people are becoming vegetarian. In the USA, for example, it's estimated that around 8% of adults are vegetarian, and in some countries, such as Germany, the figure is more than 10%. There are many benefits of being vegetarian. It can reduce the risk of heart disease and certain cancers, as well as type 2 diabetes.

It can also help the environment by reducing global warming. Though being a great source of food and income in developing countries, raising animals could worsen climate change. The less meat we eat, the greater the reduction in climate-changing emissions. When deciding whether to be a vegetarian or not, you could treat these facts as food for thought!

換句話說 Retell

📌 Retell the text with the help of the words and expressions below.

vegetarian, figure, benefit, diabetes, global warming, income, developing, worsen, reduction, emission, food for thought

討論題目 Free Talk

📌 Talk on the following topic:

◆ Are you or anyone you know a vegetarian? What was the reason for being a vegetarian?

Chapter 2

旅遊與購物

Lesson 11

Traveling on a Budget
旅遊預算有限

搭配筆記聆聽短文 **Listen to the text with the help of the notes given**

car rental	租車
accommodation	住宿
endless	永無止境的
budget-friendly	經濟實惠的，價格親民的
a budget airline	廉價航空
a national carrier	國家航空公司
hostel	青年旅館

再次聆聽並回答問題 **Listen again and answer the questions below**

🎙 Questions for discussion:

1 According to the speaker, where should you stay to save more money?

2 Does the speaker recommend dining at fancy restaurants?

3 According to the speaker, is it possible to travel on a low budget?

Most people want to travel the world, but traveling can be expensive. Flights, car rental, accommodations, entrance tickets to attractions, food and drink... The list of costly items can seem endless.

Are you wondering what you can do to make traveling more budget-friendly? Here are a few tips! You can travel on budget airlines instead of national carriers. You can travel by public transportation instead of renting a car. You can stay in cheap hostels instead of hotels. You can pre-book entrance tickets at cheaper prices. You can eat street food instead of dining at fancy restaurants. Whatever your budget is, you can still travel the world.

大多數人都想要環遊世界，但旅行是件挺花錢的事。班機、租車、住宿、觀光景點的門票、飲食……。這張記錄昂貴物品的清單看似永無止境。

你正在思考可以做些什麼來讓旅行變得更經濟實惠嗎？這裡有些訣竅！你可以選擇廉價航空公司而非國家航空公司。你可以搭乘大眾運輸交通工具而非租車。你可以住在便宜的青年旅館而非飯店。你可以用較便宜的價格事先訂好門票。你可以吃街邊小吃而非到高級餐廳用餐。不論你的預算有多少，你都可以環遊世界。

單字片語 Vocabulary and Phrases

1 flight [flaɪt] *n.* 班機，航班；航程，飛行
book / catch a flight 預訂航班 / 趕搭飛機

2 car rental 汽車出租
a car rental company 汽車出租公司

3 accommodation [əˌkɑməˈdeʃən] *n.* 住宿 (英式用法，不可數)
注意

accommodation 在英式英語中為不可數名詞，但在美式英語則常用複數，成 accommodations。

accommodate [əˈkɑməˌdet] *vt.* 提供膳宿；容納

This hotel can accommodate at least 3,000 tourists.
這間飯店最少可以提供三千名遊客住宿。

4 an entrance ticket 門票
entrance [ˈɛntrəns] *n.* 進入 (權)；入口

5 attraction [əˈtrækʃən] *n.* 吸引人的事物
a tourist attraction 觀光景點

6 costly [ˈkɔstlɪ] *a.* 昂貴的
= expensive [ɪkˈspɛnsɪv]

7 endless [ˈɛndləs] *a.* 無止境的

8 budget-friendly [ˌbʌdʒɪtˈfrɛndlɪ] *a.* 不昂貴的，價格親民的
-friendly [ˈfrɛndlɪ] *suffix* 適合……使用的；對……無害的
user-friendly [ˌjuzəˈfrɛndlɪ] *a.* 易於使用的
eco-friendly [ˈikoˌfrɛndlɪ] *a.* 環保的，不傷害環境的

9 **tip** [tɪp] *n.* 祕訣，竅門；小費
a handy / useful tip 　實用祕訣
give sb a tip 　給某人建議；給某人小費

10 **You can travel on budget airlines instead of national carriers.**
= You can travel on budget airlines rather than national carriers.
你可以選擇廉價航空公司而非國家航空公司。

G Tipene / Shutterstock.com

11 **a budget airline** 　廉價航空，低成本航空公司
= a low-cost airline / carrier
airline [ˈɛrˌlaɪn] *n.* 航空公司

12 **a national carrier** 　國家航空公司
= a flag carrier
carrier [ˈkærɪɚ] *n.* 航空公司

13 **pre-book** [ˌpriˈbuk] *vt.* 事先預訂

14 **street food** 　街邊小吃

實用詞句　Useful Expressions

1 字首 pre- 的用法

◆ 字首 pre- 可置動詞或名詞前，形成複合詞。

pre- [pri] *prefix* 先於……，在……前
pre-order [ˌpriˈɔrdɚ] *vi. & vt.* 預訂，預購
pre-game [ˌpriˈgem] *a.* (體育) 比賽前的
pre-teen [ˌpriˈtin] *n.* (青春期前的) 兒童

比較

post- [post] *prefix* 在……之後
post-war [ˌpostˈwɔr] *a.* 戰後的
post-industrial [ˌpostɪnˈdʌstrɪəl] *a.* 後工業化的

2 副詞連接詞 whatever 的用法

◆ 本文中的 whatever 為副詞連接詞，表「不論什麼」，相當於 no matter what，其所引導的副詞子句與主要句子之間要有逗點相隔。

whatever [(h)wɑtˈɛvɚ] *conj.* 不論什麼，無論如何

Whatever you say, Clara won't change her mind.

= No matter what you say, Clara won't change her mind.

不論你說什麼，克萊拉都不會改變心意。

Whatever task is assigned, Mark completes it with efficiency.

= No matter what task is assigned, Mark completes it with efficiency.

不論馬克被指派哪種任務，他都會很有效率地完成。

比較

whoever [huˈɛvɚ] *conj.* 不論誰

= no matter who

Whoever did it, he or she should apologize to Mrs. Anderson.

= No matter who did it, he or she should apologize to Mrs. Anderson.

不論是誰做了這件事，他或她都該向安德森女士道歉。

Whoever wins the game, he will be awarded a trophy.

= No matter who wins the game, he will be awarded a trophy.

不論是誰贏得這場比賽，他都會被授予一個獎盃。

發音提示 Pronunciation

❶ [ʌ]	but [bʌt]	budget [ˈbʌdʒɪt]
	wonder [ˈwʌndɚ]	public [ˈpʌblɪk]

❷ [f]	flight [flaɪt]	few [fju]
	food [fud]	fancy [ˈfænsɪ]
	friendly [ˈfrɛndlɪ]	

朗讀短文 **Read aloud the text**

📍 請特別注意 [ʌ]、[f] 的發音。

Most people want to travel the world, but traveling can be expensive. Flights, car rental, accommodations, entrance tickets to attractions, food and drink... The list of costly items can seem endless.

Are you wondering what you can do to make traveling more budget-friendly? Here are a few tips! You can travel on budget airlines instead of national carriers. You can travel by public transportation instead of renting a car. You can stay in cheap hostels instead of hotels. You can pre-book entrance tickets at cheaper prices. You can eat street food instead of dining at fancy restaurants. Whatever your budget is, you can still travel the world.

換句話說 **Retell**

📍 Retell the text with the help of the words and expressions below.

flight, car rental, accommodation, entrance tickets, attraction, costly, endless, budget-friendly, tip, a budget airline, a national carrier, pre-book, street food

討論題目 **Free Talk**

📍 Talk on the following topic:

◆ Have you ever traveled on a budget before? What did you do to make traveling more budget-friendly?

Lesson 12

Tips on Tipping
給小費的訣竅

搭配筆記聆聽短文 **Listen to the text with the help of the notes given**

optional	選擇性的
mandatory	義務性的，強制的
dilemma	兩難的狀況
taxing	費神的
customary	慣例的
be considered an insult	視為侮辱

再次聆聽並回答問題 **Listen again and answer the questions below**

Questions for discussion:

1 How much should you tip the hotel maid in the United States?

2 Are tipping cultures the same in every country?

3 Should you give tips when traveling in Japan?

How much should you tip when you travel abroad? Is it optional or mandatory? This is a dilemma faced by most travelers, who are unsure of the rules. So, here are a few general tips to make tipping less taxing!

In the United States, the standard tip for most restaurant services is 15%. For hotel staff, it's customary to tip $1 or $2, especially to those who help carry your luggage or clean your room. The tipping culture varies in different countries. For instance, tipping is optional in Australia and the UK, while in Canada and Mexico, tips are expected. In Japan, meanwhile, tipping is actually considered an insult!

　　你出國旅遊時應該要給多少小費？給小費是選擇性還是強制的？這是大部分旅客不甚了解規定而會面對的兩難問題。所以，在此有一些普遍的小祕訣，讓給小費這件事沒那麼費神！

在美國，大多數餐廳服務的標準小費是給 15%。針對飯店員工，慣例上會給一美元或兩美元的小費，特別是給那些幫你提行李或打掃房間的人。小費文化因不同國家而異。舉例來說，在澳洲與英國，給小費是選擇性的，然而在加拿大與墨西哥會期待收到小費。同時，在日本給小費其實是被視為侮辱！

單字片語 Vocabulary and Phrases

1 **tip** [tɪp] *vi.* & *vt.* 給小費
（三態為：tip, tipped [tɪpt], tipped）& *n.* 小費；祕訣

I tipped the taxi driver $5 for his service.
我給計程車司機五美元小費以感謝他的服務。

Thanks for giving me tips on skiing.
謝謝你告訴我滑雪的祕訣。

2 **optional** [ˈɑpʃənl̩] *a.* 可選擇的
option [ˈɑpʃən] *n.* 選擇

Are these classes optional?
這些課是選修嗎？

3 **mandatory** [ˈmændətɛrɪ / ˈmændətɔrɪ] *a.* 義務的，強制的

It is mandatory for passengers to wear seat belts.
乘客有義務要繫安全帶。

4 **dilemma** [dəˈlɛmə] *n.* 進退兩難
be in a dilemma　　處於進退兩難之境

Linda is in a dilemma about which job offer to accept.
琳達不知道要接受哪個工作邀約而處於兩難之境。

5 **be unsure of...**　　不清楚……；不確定……
unsure [ʌnˈʃʊr] *a.* 不清楚的，不了解的；不確定的

Adam is always unsure of what to do.
亞當總是不確定要做什麼。

6 **taxing** [ˈtæksɪŋ] *a.* 費勁的；繁重的

7 **standard** [ˈstændəd] *a.* 標準的 & *n.* 標準

We need to follow the standard procedure.
我們必須遵守標準程序。

8 **customary** [ˈkʌstəmˌɛrɪ] *a.* 慣例的；合乎習俗的
custom [ˈkʌstəm] *n.* 習俗

9 **vary** [ˈvɛrɪ] *vi.* 變化 (三態為：vary, varied [ˈvɛrɪd], varied)
vary in...　　在……有所不同

The company's products vary considerably in quality.
該公司的產品品質差異很大。

10 **insult** [ˈɪnsʌlt] *n.* 侮辱 & [ɪnˈsʌlt] *vt.* 侮辱，辱罵

What you said is an insult to my culture.
你所說的話對我的文化是種侮辱。

Riley was mad because a boy
insulted her.
萊莉因為有個男孩辱罵她而生氣。

實用詞句　**Useful Expressions**

1 關係代名詞 who 與 whom 的用法

◆ 關係代名詞有連接詞的功能，用來引導形容詞子句。關係代名詞 who 與 whom 用來代替人，主詞使用 who，即在引導的形容詞子句中作主詞；受詞則使用 whom，即在引導的形容詞子句中作受詞。

關係代名詞	主詞	受詞
代替人	who	whom

People who believe in themselves are more likely to succeed.
相信自己的人會更有機會成功。

John is a man whom everyone looks up to.
約翰是大家都景仰的人。

注意

現今在日常的口語會話上關係代名詞 whom 較少使用，常會以主詞的 who 取代，如下列例句：

Kevin is a person whom I enjoy working with.
→ Kevin is a person who I enjoy working with.
凱文是我喜歡一同共事的人。
但須注意,受詞 whom 仍為合乎文法的使用方式,
因此在書寫或正式場合的會話中宜使用 whom。

2 表示「同時」的說法
meanwhile [ˈminˌ(h)waɪl] *adv.*
& *n.* 同時
= meantime [ˈminˌtaɪm]
= in the meanwhile
= in the meantime
I'll make dinner; meanwhile, you can set the table.
= I'll make dinner; in the meanwhile, you can set the table.
= I'll make dinner; in the meantime, you can set the table.
我會煮晚餐;在此同時,你可以擺好餐桌。

比較

for the meantime　　暫時
I don't have enough money to buy a car, so for the meantime, I'm
taking the bus to work.
我沒有足夠的錢買車子,所以我暫時都搭公車上班。

發音提示 **Pronunciation**

❶ [u]	rule [rul]	united [juˈnaɪtɪd]
	few [fju]	who [hu]
	to [tu]	room [rum]

❷ [w]	when [(h)wɛn]
	while [(h)waɪl]
	meanwhile [ˈminˌ(h)waɪl]

朗讀短文 Read aloud the text

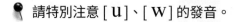

📌 請特別注意 [u]、[w] 的發音。

How much should you tip when you travel abroad? Is it optional or mandatory? This is a dilemma faced by most travelers, who are unsure of the rules. So, here are a few general tips to make tipping less taxing!

In the United States, the standard tip for most restaurant services is 15%. For hotel staff, it's customary to tip $1 or $2, especially to those who help carry your luggage or clean your room. The tipping culture varies in different countries. For instance, tipping is optional in Australia and the UK, while in Canada and Mexico, tips are expected. In Japan, meanwhile, tipping is actually considered an insult!

換句話說 Retell

📌 Retell the text with the help of the words and expressions below.

tip, optional, mandatory, dilemma, be unsure of, taxing, standard, customary, vary, insult

討論題目 Free Talk

📌 Talk on the following topic:

◆ Do you think the practice of tipping should exist? Why or why not?

Lesson 13
When in Rome, Do As the Romans Do
入境隨俗

搭配筆記聆聽會話 **Listen to the text with the help of the notes given**

toast	向……敬酒
turn... down	拒絕……
lose count	數不清
loads of...	很多……
soak up...	吸乾……

再次聆聽並回答問題 **Listen again and answer the questions below**

Questions for discussion:

1 What happened to the man at the farewell party?

2 What is the drinking tradition in Russia?

3 Does the man remember how much he drank?

實用會話 Dialogue

Ⓐ How was your trip to Russia? You look exhausted!

Ⓑ I've still not recovered from my final night. My friends hosted a farewell dinner party for me. On the table was a big bottle of vodka.

Ⓐ I thought you like vodka.

Ⓑ I do. But it's tradition there to toast everyone and everything until the bottle is empty! I don't think I'll ever drink vodka again!

Ⓐ Oh, dear. Couldn't you have turned it down?

Ⓑ Well, I didn't want to be rude. In Russian culture, toasting is very important. And, you know, when in Rome, do as the Romans do!

Ⓐ I think those "Romans" might have had a bit more practice at downing vodka than you! How many shots did you drink?

Ⓑ After the ninth or tenth, I lost count.

Ⓐ Ha-ha. Was there food at this dinner party, or just vodka?

B On the menu were beef stroganoff, meatballs, pickled cabbage, and loads of bread.

A Just not enough to soak up that vodka!

A 你的俄羅斯之旅怎麼樣呢？你看起來累斃了！

B 我還沒從最後一個晚上回神過來。我朋友為我辦了一場歡送晚餐派對。桌上有一大瓶伏特加。

A 我以為你喜歡喝伏特加。

B 我的確喜歡。但那裡有個傳統是要向每個人、每件事敬酒，直到酒瓶空了為止！我想我絕對不會再喝伏特加了！

A 喔，親愛的。你沒辦法拒絕這麼做嗎？

B 嗯，我不想失禮。敬酒在俄羅斯的文化中非常重要。你也知道的，要入境隨俗！

A 我想那些「俄羅斯人」可能比你更會喝伏特加！你喝了幾杯酒？

B 我在第九或十杯後就數不清了。

A 哈哈。這場晚餐派對有食物嗎？還是只有伏特加？

B 菜單上有俄羅斯酸奶牛肉、肉丸子、酸菜還有很多麵包。

A 那些都不足以讓你喝完那瓶伏特加還不會醉！

單字片語 Vocabulary and Phrases

1 **exhausted** [ɪgˋzɔstɪd] *a.* 精疲力盡的

2 **vodka** [ˋvɑdkə] *n.* 伏特加

3 **toast** [tost] *vt.* 向……敬酒 & *n.* 敬酒，乾杯；吐司
toast sb/sth 　　向某人 / 某事敬酒
= make / propose a toast to sb/sth

4 **turn... down / turn down...** 　　拒絕……
Johnson's application for more funds was turned down by the company.
該公司拒絕了強森要求更多經費的申請。

⑤ **down** [daʊn] *vt.* 大口喝下；快速吃下

Jack downed the soda in one gulp.

傑克一口喝下汽水。

⑥ **shot** [ʃɑt] *n.* (烈酒的) 少量，一小口 (為量酒的單位，常用以代指單一杯的烈酒)

⑦ **lose count**　不記得數目，數不清

⑧ **beef stroganoff** [ˈstrɔgəˌnɔf]　俄羅斯酸奶牛肉

⑨ **meatball** [ˈmitˌbɔl] *n.* 肉丸子

⑩ **pickled cabbage**　酸菜

pickled [ˈpɪkḷd] *a.* 醃漬的

⑪ **loads of...**　許多的……

口語新技能　New Skills

❶ 表示「入境隨俗」的說法

When in Rome, do as the Romans do.　入境隨俗。(諺語)

◆ 本句諺語若直譯為：「在羅馬時，做羅馬人在做的事。」文中便用這句諺語表示他到了俄羅斯就要遵循俄羅斯人的傳統，因此 "I think those 'Romans' ...",此句話中的 Romans 並非真的指羅馬人，而是巧妙地用諺語中的 Romans 來代指前文提及的俄羅斯人。

❷ Just not enough to soak up that vodka!　那些都不足以讓你喝完那瓶伏特加還不會醉！

soak up sth / soak sth up　吸乾某物

Ted used a sponge to soak up the water spilled on the table.

泰德用一塊海綿來吸乾灑在桌面上的水。

注意

文中的 "Just not enough to soak up that vodka!" 直譯為：「不足以吸光那瓶伏特加！」，作者用 soak up 來比喻吸乾伏特加的酒精，意即不會喝醉。

75

簡短對答 Quick Response

◆ Make quick responses to the sentences you hear.

討論題目 Free Talk

Talk on the following topic:

◆ What is the drinking culture in your country?

Lesson 14

朗
讀
▶
Lesson 14

A Self-Service Store
無人自助商店

搭配筆記聆聽短文 **Listen to the text with the help of the notes given**

check out	結帳
retailer	零售商
repetitive	重複的
downside	缺點
entity	實體
tech-savvy	精通科技的

再次聆聽並回答問題 **Listen again and answer the questions below**

🔑 Questions for discussion:

1 Are there any sales assistants in a self-service store?

2 What do customers need to use to check out in a self-service store?

3 According to the speaker, what is one downside of self-service stores?

短文聽讀 **Text**

Would you like to shop in a self-service store where there are no sales assistants and you have to use your smartphone to check out? Increasing numbers of stores, from EasyGo in China to Amazon Go in the US, are introducing this technology. Retailers like it because they can redirect resources from the repetitive checkout process to actual customer service, where they are most needed.

What about the downsides? For the retailer, these include the risk of theft and fraud, as well as the perception that the retailers are faceless entities. For the customer, particularly those who are older or less tech-savvy, there is the risk of confusion and the possibility of making honest mistakes. Retailers need to strike the right balance between tech-driven efficiency and old-fashioned customer care.

你會想在一個沒有店員而且你必須用你的智慧型手機結帳的無人自助商店購物嗎？從中國的 EasyGo 到美國的 Amazon Go，有愈來愈多商店引進這類科技。零售商很喜歡無人自助商店，因為他們得以將資源從反覆的結帳手續重新導向實際的顧客服務，而顧客服務也最需要資源。

那無人自助商店的缺點是什麼？對零售商來說，這些包含偷竊和詐騙的風險，以及顧客可能會認為這些零售商是無名的實體。對顧客來說，特別是那些較年邁或較不善於使用科技的人，有可能會有些混亂，以及犯下無心之過的可能。零售商需要在科技驅動的效率及舊式的顧客服務之間取得正確的平衡。

CH 2 旅遊與購物

單字片語　Vocabulary and Phrases

❶ a self-service store　無人自助商店
self-service [ˌsɛlfˈsɝvɪs] *a.* 自助的

❷ check out　結帳；退房
check in　辦理入住手續

Please go to the counter to check out.
結帳請到櫃檯。

❸ introduce [ˌɪntrəˈdjus] *vt.* 引進；介紹；推出
introduce A to B　將 A 介紹給 B

New policies will be introduced to improve the situation.
新的政策會被推行以改善現況。

Kevin introduced his new girlfriend to us.
凱文將他的新女友介紹給我們認識。

❹ retailer [ˈritelɚ] *n.* 零售商
retail [ˈritel] *n.* & *vt.* 零售

❺ redirect [ˌridəˈrɛkt] *vt.* 使重新導向；使改變方向
Resources will be redirected to support our campaign.
資源會被重新調配以支援我們的活動。

❻ resource [ˈrisɔrs / rɪˈsɔrs] *n.* 資源（常用複數）
natural resources　自然資源

7 **repetitive** [rɪˋpɛtɪtɪv] *a.* 重複的

8 **downside** [ˋdaʊnˏsaɪd] *n.* 缺點，壞處
upside [ˋʌpˏsaɪd] *n.* 優點，好處

9 **theft** [θɛft] *n.* 偷竊，竊盜

10 **fraud** [frɔd] *n.* 詐欺，欺騙

11 **perception** [pɚˋsɛpʃən] *n.* 看法；觀點
perceive [pɚˋsiv] *vt.* 認為；察覺

perceive A as B　　把 A 認為是 B

The words of the dictator were perceived as a threat.
那位獨裁者的話被認為是個威脅。

＊ dictator [ˋdɪkˏtetɚ] *n.* 獨裁者

12 **faceless** [ˋfesləs] *a.* 無臉的；無特徵的

13 **entity** [ˋɛntətɪ] *n.* 實體

14 **tech-savvy** [ˏtɛkˋsævɪ] *a.* 精通科技的
savvy [ˋsævɪ] *a.* 有見識的

15 **an honest mistake**　　無心之過
honest [ˋɑnɪst] *a.* 誠實的；坦白的
mistake [mɪsˋtek] *n.* 錯誤

16 **-driven** [ˋdrɪvən] *suffix* ⋯⋯驅使
driven [ˋdrɪvən] *a.* 奮發向上的；執著的

Our company relies heavily on the market-driven economy.
本公司極度仰賴市場驅使的經濟。

Rachel is driven when it comes to work.
談到工作，瑞秋很奮發向上。

17 **old-fashioned** [ˏoldˋfæʃənd] *a.* 過時的；老式的

1 介紹連接詞 as well as 的使用方法

as well as...　　以及……

◆ 連詞 as well as 為對等連接詞,可連接對等的單字、片語或子句。

Sam as well as Gary is interested in producing music.

(as well as 連接兩個對等的主詞)

山姆和蓋瑞都對製作音樂有興趣。

Annie came to the US to learn English, as well as to know more about its culture.

(as well as 連接兩個對等的不定詞片語)

安妮來到美國是為了學習英語,也是為了更了解美國文化。

Fiona is popular because she is easygoing, as well as because she loves making new friends.

(as well as 連接兩個對等的副詞子句)

費歐娜人緣好是因為她很隨和,也因為她很喜歡結交新朋友。

注意

as well as 連接主詞時,該句的動詞要依據第一個主詞做變化。

Tom as well as I is in charge of this project.

湯姆和我都負責該企畫。

2 表示「在 A 與 B 間維持平衡」的說法

strike a balance between A and B　　在 A 與 B 間維持平衡

(strike 的三態為:strike, struck [strʌk], struck)

balance [ˋbæləns] *n.* 平衡

It's difficult to strike a balance between work and leisure.

要在工作與休閒之間取得平衡十分困難。

CH 2 旅遊與購物

❶ [i]	increase [ɪnˋkris]	resource [ˋrisɔrs]
	easy [ˋizɪ]	these [ðiz]
	retailer [ˋritelɚ]	need [nid]
	redirect [ˏridəˋrɛkt]	between [bɪˋtwin]

❷ [tʃ]	check [tʃɛk]
	China [ˋtʃaɪnə]
	checkout [ˋtʃɛkˏaʊt]

朗讀短文 **Read aloud the text**

🎤 請特別注意 [i]、[tʃ] 的發音。

Would you like to shop in a self-service store where there are no sales assistants and you have to use your smartphone to check out? Increasing numbers of stores, from EasyGo in China to Amazon Go in the US, are introducing this technology. Retailers like it because they can redirect resources from the repetitive checkout process to actual customer service, where they are most needed.

What about the downsides? For the retailer, these include the risk of theft and fraud, as well as the perception that the retailers are faceless entities. For the customer, particularly those who are older or less tech-savvy, there is the risk of confusion and the possibility of making honest mistakes. Retailers need to strike the right balance between tech-driven efficiency and old-fashioned customer care.

換句話說 Retell

📍 Retell the text with the help of the words and expressions below.

a self-service store, check out, introduce, retailer, redirect, resource, repetitive, downside, theft, fraud, perception, faceless, entity, tech-savvy, an honest mistake, -driven, old-fashioned

討論題目 Free Talk

📍 Talk on the following topic:

◇ Would you like to shop in a self-service store?

Shuang Li / Shutterstock.com

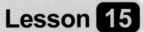

Lesson 15

Making Ends Meet
收支平衡

搭配筆記聆聽短文 Listen to the text with the help of the notes given

basic needs	基本需求
income	收入
household bill	家庭帳單
turn to...	向……求助
work out a budget	列出預算
raise	加薪

再次聆聽並回答問題 Listen again and answer the questions below

Questions for discussion:

1. What do people often seek help from?
2. What is usually the first step in saving money?
3. What is one thing a person can do to earn more money?

Nowadays, many families and individuals struggle to make ends meet; that is, they find it difficult to earn enough money to provide for their basic needs. Often, incomes don't rise as fast as the cost of rent, gas, electricity, food, and numerous other household bills.

People often turn to the internet to look for ideas of how to save money. Usually, the first step is to work out a budget. That's how you can see how much you should spend and know where to cut costs. But there is another area you can focus on: earning more money. You could get a part-time job, ask for a raise or promotion at work, sell unwanted items online, or even become a dog walker!

現今，許多家庭或個人努力要維持生計；意思是，他們發現要賺足夠的錢以供基本需求很困難。收入增加的速度往往不如房租、油錢、電費、食物價錢以及許多其他家庭帳單。

　　大家經常會求助於網路以找尋省錢的方法。通常，第一步是列出預算。這樣你會了解你應該要花多少錢，並知道應該要在哪些方面減少支出。不過，有另外一個部分你可以注意：賺更多錢。你可以找個兼職工作、在工作上要求加薪或升遷、在網路上販賣不想要的物品，或甚至成為專門遛狗的人！

單字片語　Vocabulary and Phrases

❶ make ends meet　收支平衡
end [ɛnd] *n.* 端點，末端
注意
本片語的由來眾說紛紜，有一說表示 ends (兩端) 是指記帳時，帳目中的總收入與總支出，而要讓這兩筆金錢相符，故衍伸出 make ends meet 表「收支平衡」之意。

How do you manage to make ends meet?
你是如何成功達到收支平衡的？

❷ basic needs　基本需求

❸ income [ˋɪnˌkʌm] *n.* 收入

❹ household [ˋhaʊsˌhold] *a.* 家庭的；家喻戶曉的
a household name　家喻戶曉的人物

❺ bill [bɪl] *n.* 帳單
pay the bill　付帳

Have you paid the phone bill?
你繳電話帳單了嗎？

❻ turn to sth/sb　求助於某事物 / 某人
Wendy lives alone in a foreign country, so she has no one to turn to for help.
溫蒂獨自住在國外，所以她無法向任何人尋求幫助。

❼ budget [ˋbʌdʒɪt] *n.* 預算 & *vt.* 編列預算
on a (tight) budget　預算緊縮

The couple is living on a tight budget.
那對夫妻生活的預算吃緊。

We have budgeted $200 for a short vacation.
我們列了兩百美元的預算去微度假。

8 **earn** [ɝn] *vt.* 賺得；贏得
earn a living　　維生
= make a living

Sam is earning $70,000 a year.
山姆的年薪是七萬美元。

9 **part-time** [ˌpɑrtˈtaɪm] *a.* 兼職的 & *adv.* 兼職地
full-time [ˌfʊlˈtaɪm] *a.* 全職的 & *adv.* 全職地
a part-time / full-time job　　兼職 / 全職工作

10 **raise** [rez] *n.* 加薪

11 **promotion** [prəˈmoʃən] *n.* 升遷
promote [prəˈmot] *vt.* 升遷
be promoted to + 職位　　被提升為……

Karen was promoted to general manager after years of hard work.
經過多年的努力，凱倫被晉升為總經理。

實用詞句　**Useful Expressions**

1 副詞 nowadays 的用法
nowadays [ˈnaʊəˌdez] *adv.* 現今
= these days
= today
= now

注意
副詞 nowadays 可置句首，亦可置句尾。

Nowadays, you can sell your used goods online.
= You can sell your used goods online nowadays.
= These days, you can sell your used goods online.

= Today, you can sell your used goods online.
= Now, you can sell your used goods online.
現今，你可以在網路上販賣你的二手物品。

2 表示「也就是說」的說法
that is (to say)...   也就是說……；更確切地說……
注意
本片語表「也就是說……」時，等於 in other words；表「更確切地說……」時，等於 to clarify ['klærə,faɪ] 或 to specify ['spɛsə,faɪ]。
I think the manager has some doubts about our project; that is (to say), I don't think he'll approve it.
= I think the manager has some doubts about our project; in other words, I don't think he'll approve it.
我認為經理對我們的企畫有些存疑；也就是說，我不認為他會批准。

Our sales representative will arrive before noon; that is (to say), around 11 o'clock.
= Our sales representative will arrive before noon; to specify, around 11 o'clock.
我們的業務員會在中午前抵達；更確切地說，大約十一點鐘。

發音提示 **Pronunciation**

	individual [,ɪndə'vɪdʒʊəl]	should [ʃʊd]
❶ [U]	look [lʊk]	could [kʊd]
	usually ['juʒʊəlɪ]	

	struggle ['strʌgl̩]
	gas [gæs]
❷ [g]	get [gɛt]
	dog [dɔg]

🔖 請特別注意 [ʊ]、[g] 的發音。

Nowadays, many families and individuals struggle to make ends meet; that is, they find it difficult to earn enough money to provide for their basic needs. Often, incomes don't rise as fast as the cost of rent, gas, electricity, food, and numerous other household bills.

People often turn to the internet to look for ideas of how to save money. Usually, the first step is to work out a budget. That's how you can see how much you should spend and know where to cut costs. But there is another area you can focus on: earning more money. You could get a part-time job, ask for a raise or promotion at work, sell unwanted items online, or even become a dog walker!

換句話說 **Retell**

🔖 Retell the text with the help of the words and expressions below.

make ends meet, basic needs, income, household, bill, turn to, budget, earn, part-time, raise, promotion

討論題目 **Free Talk**

🔖 Talk on the following topic:

◆ What do you usually do to make ends meet? What do you do to reduce costs or increase income?

Living from Paycheck to Paycheck
月光族

搭配筆記聆聽會話 | **Listen to the text with the help of the notes given**

monthly expenses	每月開銷
paycheck	薪資
cut back on...	減少……
non-starter	無成功希望的主意
doable	可行的

再次聆聽並回答問題 | **Listen again and answer the questions below**

Questions for discussion:

1 What does the woman say they need to do?

2 What does the woman suggest?

3 When will the man and woman start making a budget?

實用會話 **Dialogue**

A We need to reduce our monthly expenses, Pete.

B Why?

A We're living from paycheck to paycheck and not saving any money.

B Do you have any ideas how we can cut back on our spending?

A Drink less beer?

B Buy fewer shoes?

A Well, I think we can agree those are both non-starters.

B Absolutely.

A Let's create a budget. That way, we can see exactly what we're spending our money on. Then we can think about how we can save more. That's how my sister managed to put more money aside.

B That's doable. We can start tomorrow.

A Actually, there's a shoe sale tomorrow.

B And a beer festival.

A Let's start next month!

A 彼特，我們需要減少每月開銷。

B 為什麼？

A 我們每個月都把錢花光了，而且沒有存什麼錢。

B 你對於我們要如何減少開銷有什麼想法嗎？

A 少喝啤酒？

B 少買鞋子？

A 嗯，我想我們會同意這兩個主意成功的機率都不大。

B 沒錯。

A 咱們來擬出預算吧。如此一來，我們可以確切了解我們錢都花在哪。然後我們可以思考如何存更多錢。我姊姊是這樣成功存更多錢的。

B 聽來可行。我們可以明天開始。

A 其實，明天有場鞋子特賣會。

B 還有啤酒節。

A 咱們下個月再開始吧！

單字片語 Vocabulary and Phrases

① **expense** [ɪkˋspɛns] *n.* 花費，開銷

② **live from paycheck to paycheck**　月底就將當月薪水花光
paycheck [ˋpetʃɛk] *n.* 薪資
I can't lend you any money. I'm living from paycheck to paycheck myself.
我不能借你錢。我自己就是月光族。

③ **spending** [ˋspɛndɪŋ] *n.* 花費，開銷 (不可數)

④ **non-starter** [ˏnɑnˋstɑrtɚ] *n.* 無成功希望的想法 / 計畫 (非正式用法)

5 spend [spɛnd] *vt.* & *vi.* 花費
（三態為：spend, spent [spɛnt], spent）

spend + 金錢 + on sth　　花若干金錢在某事物上
spend + 時間 + on sth　　花若干時間在某事物上
spend + 時間 + V-ing　　花若干時間做某事

Ivan spent half of his monthly salary on video games.
艾凡將他月薪的一半花在電動遊戲上。

Irene spends most of her time writing novels.
愛琳花大部分的時間寫小說。

6 put sth aside / put aside sth　　存 (錢)；空出 (時間)

Heather plans to put $300 aside each month.
海瑟計劃每個月存三百美元。

Benny tries to put aside more time to be with his family.
班尼試圖空出更多時間陪家人。

7 doable [ˋduəbl̩] *a.* 可行的，可做的
= feasible [ˋfizəbl̩]

Everyone agreed that Tina's plan is more doable than Simon's.
所有人都認同蒂娜的計畫比賽門的可行。

口語新技能　New Skills

🔑 表示「減少」的說法

◆ 本課使用動詞 reduce 與片語動詞 cut back on 以表示「減少」。其中，
reduce 在書面及口語上皆可使用，而 cut back on 則較常用於非正式
的口語會話中。

a reduce [rɪˋdjus] *vt.* 使減少
Exercising regularly can help reduce stress.
定期運動有助於減輕壓力。

b cut back (on)...　　減少……
= cut down (on)...
You should cut back on your
spending.
你應該要減少開銷。

93

The government recently enacted a law to cut down on pollution.
政府最近立法以降低汙染。

簡短對答 Quick Response

◆ Make quick responses to the sentences you hear.

討論題目 Free Talk

🎙 Talk on the following topic:

◆ What do you spend the most on every month?

Lesson 17

At the Flea Market
在跳蚤市場

CH 2 旅遊與購物

搭配筆記聆聽短文 **Listen to the text with the help of the notes given**

vendor	小販
whomever	任何……的人
second-hand goods	二手物品
haggle	討價還價
reasonable	合理的
auction	拍賣會

再次聆聽並回答問題 **Listen again and answer the questions below**

🎙 Questions for discussion:

1. What can vendors sell at a flea market?
2. Can you offer a cheaper price to the seller at a flea market?
3. How much was the Chinese bowl sold for at first?

95

A flea market is a place where people can buy and sell goods. Vendors can sell whatever they want to whomever they choose. It's a good place to buy second-hand goods, antiques, collectibles, and cheap items. Usually, the prices are not fixed and you can haggle, meaning you can offer whatever price you think is reasonable for the things you like.

There's also a slim chance that you might get very lucky. For instance, a Chinese bowl bought for $3 in New York turned out to be from the 11th century and was sold at an auction years later for $2.2 million! And an original copy of the US Declaration of Independence, which was discovered inside a $4 painting, was later sold for $2.4 million!

　　跳蚤市場是人們可以買賣物品的地方。小販可以賣他們想要的任何東西給他們所選的任何人。這是一個購買二手物品、古董、收藏品以及便宜貨的好地方。通常，價格並不固定，你可以討價還價，也就是說你可以針對你喜歡的東西提出任何你認為合理的價格。

　　此外，有很微小的機率你可能會非常幸運。舉例來說，一個來自中國的碗在紐約以三美元的價錢被買下，結果這個碗竟是出自十一世紀，且在多年後的一場拍賣會中以兩百二十萬美元售出！另外，一份美國獨立宣言的正本在一幅價值四美元的畫中被發現，它後來以兩百四十萬美元售出！

CH
2
旅遊與購物

單字片語　Vocabulary and Phrases

1 **a flea market**　　跳蚤市場
flea [fli] *n.* 跳蚤

2 **vendor** [ˋvɛndɚ] *n.* 小販

3 **second-hand** [ˌsɛkəndˋhænd] *a.* 二手的
second-hand smoke　　二手菸

4 **antique** [ænˋtik] *n.* 古董 & *a.* 古董的
antique furniture　　古董傢俱

5 **collectible** [kəˋlɛktəb!] *n.* 收藏品 (= collectable，常用複數)

6 **fixed** [fɪkst] *a.* 固定的，不變的
The items are sold at a fixed price.
商品都以定價販賣。

7 **haggle** [ˋhæg!] *vi.* 討價還價
haggle with sb over sth　　就某物跟某人討價還價
The tourists are haggling with the vendor over the price of the souvenirs.
那些觀光客在為紀念品的價格與攤販討價還價。

8 **offer** [ˋɔfɚ] *vt. & vi.* 提議，提出 & *n.* 提議
offer sb + 金額 + for sth　　向某人出價某金額買某物
John offered me $9,000 for my used car.
約翰出價九千美元購買我的二手車。

97

9 **reasonable** [`rizṇəbl] *a.* 合理的
unreasonable [ʌn`rizṇəbl] *a.* 不合理的

10 **slim** [slɪm] *a.* 微小的；稀薄的；苗條的

11 **turn out (to be...)** 結果 (是……)

The rumor turned out to be true.
那則謠言結果是真的。

12 **auction** [`ɔkʃən] *n.* 拍賣會 & *vt.* 拍賣

13 **copy** [`kɑpɪ] *n.* 一份 & *vt.* & *vi.* 影印；模仿
(三態為：copy, copied [`kɑpɪd], copied)

an original copy   正本
make a copy of sth   影印某物

Could you make ten copies of this document for the meeting?
你可以為會議將這份文件影印十份嗎？

14 **the Declaration of Independence**   (美國) 獨立宣言
declaration [ˌdɛklə`reʃən] *n.* 宣言，宣告
independence [ˌɪndɪ`pɛndəns] *n.* 獨立

實用詞句　Useful Expressions

🔑 介紹複合關係代名詞的用法

◆ 複合關係代名詞是由下列兩個詞類組成：
先行詞 (如 anyone、the thing、anything) + 關係代名詞
複合關係代名詞共有下列五個：

代替人	**whoever** = anyone who / that 任何……的人
	whomever = anyone whom / that 任何……的人
代替物	**whatever** = anything which / that 所……的任何東西
	what = the thing(s) which / that 所……的東西

| 代替人或物 | 三者以上 | whichever = any one that
同一類的任何一個…… |
| | 兩者 | whichever = either that
同一類的任何一個…… |

<u>Whoever</u> buys a purse today will receive a 10% discount.

= <u>Anyone who</u> buys a purse today will receive a 10% discount.
任何今天購買手提包的人將獲得九折優惠。

You may invite <u>whomever</u> you like to the party.

= You may invite <u>anyone whom</u> you like to the party.
（whom 為動詞 like 的受詞，可省略）
你可以邀請任何你喜歡的人來參加派對。

<u>Whatever</u> you choose is on the house.

= <u>Anything that</u> you choose is on the house.
你所選的任何東西都由店家免費招待。

<u>What</u> James said turned out to be true.

= <u>The things that</u> James said turned out to be true.
結果詹姆士說的話是真的。

The shirt comes in <u>three</u> colors. <u>Whichever</u> you choose will go great with your jacket.

= The shirt comes in <u>three</u> colors. <u>Any one that</u> you choose will go great with your jacket.
這件襯衫有三種顏色。你挑選的任何一個顏色都會與你的夾克很搭。

We have <u>two</u> rooms available. You may take <u>whichever</u> you want.

= We have <u>two</u> rooms available. You may take <u>either that</u> you want.
我們有兩間空房。你可以挑選任何你想要的。

❶ [j]	usually [ˈjuʒʊəlɪ]	York [jɔrk]
	you [ju]	year [jɪr]
	New [nju]	

❷ [k]	market [ˈmɑrkɪt]	lucky [ˈlʌkɪ]
	can [kæn]	York [jɔrk]
	second-hand [ˌsɛkəndˈhænd]	auction [ˈɔkʃən]
	antique [ænˈtik]	discover [dɪsˈkʌvɚ]
	collectible [kəˈlɛktəbl̩]	copy [ˈkɑpɪ]
	fixed [fɪkst]	declaration [ˌdɛkləˈreʃən]
	like [laɪk]	

朗讀短文 **Read aloud the text**

🖊 請特別注意 [j]、[k] 的發音。

A flea market is a place where people can buy and sell goods. Vendors can sell whatever they want to whomever they choose. It's a good place to buy second-hand goods, antiques, collectibles, and cheap items. Usually, the prices are not fixed and you can haggle, meaning you can offer whatever price you think is reasonable for the things you like.

There's also a slim chance that you might get very lucky. For instance, a Chinese bowl bought for $3 in New York turned out to be from the 11th century and was sold at an auction years later for $2.2 million! And an original copy of the US Declaration of Independence, which was discovered inside a $4 painting, was later sold for $2.4 million!

換句話說　Retell

📌 Retell the text with the help of the words and expressions below.

a flea market, vendor, second-hand, antique, collectible, fixed, haggle, offer, reasonable, slim, turn out to be, auction, copy, the Declaration of Independence

CH
2
旅遊與購物

討論題目　Free Talk

📌 Talk on the following topic:

◆ Have you ever been to a flea market before? Did you find anything interesting there?

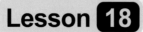

Lesson 18

Drive a Hard Bargain
極力殺價

搭配筆記聆聽會話 **Listen to the text with the help of the notes given**

bargain	划算品
be willing to...	願意……
drive a hard bargain	極力殺價
split the difference	妥協
a vinyl record	黑膠唱片

再次聆聽並回答問題 **Listen again and answer the questions below**

Questions for discussion:

1 How much does the man want to sell the vase for at first?

2 How much is the woman paying for the vase in the end?

3 Besides vases, what else is the woman looking for?

Ⓐ How much are the vases?

Ⓑ I have three vases. Which one would you like to buy?

Ⓐ I'd like whichever is the cheapest.

Ⓑ This one is the cheapest at $20.

Ⓐ That's more than I expected. Can you do better?

Ⓑ How about $18? It's a bargain at that price.

Ⓐ Well, I'm willing to pay $15 for it.

Ⓑ You drive a hard bargain. Why don't we split the difference and call it $16.50?

Ⓐ You've got a deal. Do you know which stall has the best quality old vinyl records?

🅑 You can choose whichever stall you like; they're all good quality here.

🅐 Thanks for your help!

🅐 這些花瓶多少錢？

🅑 我有三個花瓶。妳想要買哪一個？

🅐 我想要最便宜的那個。

🅑 這個二十美元最便宜。

🅐 那比我預期的高。你可以給更好的價格嗎？

🅑 十八美元如何？它在這個價格很划算了。

🅐 嗯，我願意付十五美元買它。

🅑 妳真會殺價。我們何不兩邊都退讓，妥協在十六又五十毛美元呢？

🅐 成交。你知道哪個攤位有品質最佳的老黑膠唱片嗎？

🅑 妳可以選擇任何一個妳喜歡的攤位；在這裡，它們的品質都很好。

🅐 謝謝你的幫忙！

單字片語 Vocabulary and Phrases

❶ vase [ves / vɑs] *n.* 花瓶

❷ bargain [ˋbɑrgɪn] *n.* 划算品（可數）& *vi.* 議價，討價還價
bargain with sb　　與某人討價還價

The piece of furniture I bought yesterday was a real bargain.
我昨天買到的傢俱實在很划算。

The union is bargaining with the employer for better wages.
工會正與雇主商討取得更好的薪資。

＊ union [ˋjunjən] *n.* 工會

❸ willing [ˋwɪlɪŋ] *a.* 願意的
be willing to V　　願意……

Sally is willing to help her brother with his homework.
莎莉願意幫她弟弟寫作業。

4 **stall** [stɔl] *n.* 攤位

5 **quality** [ˈkwɑlətɪ] *n.* 品質
be of high / poor quality
品質好 / 不好

The bags that this brand sells
are of high quality.
這品牌賣的包包品質都很好。

Rainbow Bkk / Shutterstock.com

6 **vinyl** [ˈvaɪnl̩] *n.* 乙烯基，塑膠

7 **record** [ˈrɛkəd] *n.* 唱片

口語新技能 New Skills

1 表示「極力討價還價」的說法
drive a hard bargain　　極力討價還價，很會殺價
= strike a hard bargain
The customer drove a hard bargain, but we eventually made a deal.
= The customer struck a hard bargain, but we eventually made a deal.
那位客人很極力討價還價，但我們最終達成協議。

注意
此片語除了用於買賣東西時客人與店家兩方議價的情形，亦可用於表示職場
上兩方談判或交涉時難以達成協議。

Our company representative drove a hard bargain at the meeting.
本公司的代表在會議中寸步不讓。

2 表示「妥協，讓步」的說法
split the difference　　妥協，讓步
split [splɪt] *vt.* 分裂，分割 (三態同形)
Let's split the difference and come
to an agreement.
我們雙方讓步並達成共識吧。

下列為與「妥協，讓步」相關的片語：

meet sb halfway　　與某人妥協

I'm willing to meet you halfway and offer $10.

我願意與你妥協並出價十美元。

簡短對答　Quick Response

◆ Make quick responses to the sentences you hear.

討論題目　Free Talk

📍 Talk on the following topic:

◆ If you had the chance to be a vendor at a flea market, what would you like to sell?

Sirima Silver / Shutterstock.com

Lesson 19

A Shopaholic
購物狂

CH
2
旅遊與購物

contentment	滿足
be short of...	缺少……
appliance	家用電器
be no laughing matter	不是鬧著玩的
be prone to...	易於……

🔑 Questions for discussion:

1 What does Pam love about shopping?

2 Why might being a shopaholic be a serious problem for some people?

3 What might be the cause of excessive shopping?

Pam is a shopaholic. She can't go through one day without shopping. She loves the feelings of happiness and contentment that shopping provides. Crowded as her closet is, she still thinks it's short of one more pair of shoes. Packed as her kitchen is, she always believes it could do with one more appliance. Luckily, Pam earns a lot of money, so she can afford all of this stuff. And, if she ever loses her job, she's got plenty she can sell!

However, for some people, being a shopaholic is no laughing matter. While Pam earns enough money to cover her splurges, others might spend much more than they can afford. High as their credit card bills are, they always add more to the balance. Shopaholics often shop as a result of a stressful situation in their lives, or to deal with feelings of depression. They are also prone to damage their personal relationships through their behavior—much like any other addiction.

Those who think shopping is taking over their lives should always ask for help.

　　潘姆是個購物狂。她沒辦法忍受一天不買東西。她熱愛購物帶給她的快樂與滿足感。儘管她的衣櫥已經很滿了，她仍認為還少一雙鞋。儘管她的廚房很擁擠，她總覺得還可以再多放一臺家電。幸好，潘姆賺很多錢，所以可以負擔購買這些東西。再者，如果她失業了，她還可以賣掉很多東西！

　　不過對某些人來說，身為一個購物狂可不是鬧著玩的。潘姆賺的錢足以支付她的揮霍，但有些人花的錢可能會超過他們能負擔的數目。就算他們的信用帳單金額已高到驚人，他們總會繼續增加債務。生活中的壓力，或是為了紓解抑鬱感經常是造成購物狂購物的原因。他們也容易因為這種行為而破壞人際關係 —— 如同其他成癮症一樣。認為購物已操控自己生活的人都該尋求協助。

單字片語　Vocabulary and Phrases

1. **shopaholic** [ˌʃɑpəˈhɔlɪk] *n.* 購物狂
   -aholic [əˈhɔlɪk] *suffix* 對……沉迷的人，有……癮症的人
   workaholic [ˌwɝkəˈhɔlɪk] *n.* 工作狂
   bookaholic [ˌbukəˈhɔlɪk] *n.* 讀書狂

2. **go through...**　　經歷 / 遭受……
   Our family has gone through many ups and downs, but we stick together.
   我們家歷經許多起起落落，但我們總是緊密扶持。

3. **contentment** [kənˈtɛntmənt] *n.* 滿意，滿足

4. **be short of...**　　缺少……
   short [ʃɔrt] *a.* 缺少的
   be short of time / money　　時間 / 錢不夠

5. **packed** [pækt] *a.* 非常擁擠的

6. **appliance** [əˈplaɪəns] *n.*
   家用器具，家用電器

109

7 **be no laughing matter**
不是鬧著玩的，沒有在開玩笑的

Being overweight is no laughing matter. It can lead to chronic diseases.
體重過重這件事是很嚴重的。它有可能導致一些慢性病。

8 **splurge** [splɜdʒ] *n.* & *vt.* & *vi.* 亂花錢，揮霍

9 **balance** [ˈbæləns] *n.* (債務的) 餘款

10 **be prone to...**　　易於……，傾向……
= be apt to...
= be inclined to...
= tend to...

People are prone to drink too much at happy events such as weddings.
人們往往會在婚禮這類快樂的活動上喝太多酒。

11 **personal relationships**　　人際關係

12 **take over (sth)**　　取得對 (某物) 的控制；接管 (某物)

Jim instead of Tim will take over my job.
是吉姆而非提姆將接管我的工作。

實用詞句 **Useful Expressions**

🔖 以 as 取代 though 的句型

◆ 當副詞連接詞 though (儘管) 所引導的副詞子句屬於下列五種句構時，though 可被副詞連接詞 as (儘管) 取代，並形成倒裝句構。

a though + 主詞 + be 動詞 + 形容詞
→ 形容詞 + as / though + 主詞 + be 動詞

Though / Although Heidi is pretty, she doesn't photograph well.

→ Pretty as / though Heidi is, she doesn't photograph well.
= As pretty as Heidi is, she doesn't photograph well.
雖然海蒂很漂亮，卻不上相。

b though + 主詞 + be 動詞 + 名詞

→ 名詞 + as / though + 主詞 + be 動詞

注意

當名詞前有不定冠詞 a / an，移至句首時，一定要將 a / an 刪除。

Though / Although it was a joke, some people found it offensive.

→ Joke as / though it was, some people found it offensive.

儘管這只是個玩笑，有些人卻覺得這很無禮。

c though + 主詞 + 動詞 + 副詞

→ 副詞 + as / though + 主詞 + 動詞

Though / Although Ed showed up late, we were glad he made it.

→ Late as / though Ed showed up, we were glad he made it.

= As late as Ed showed up, we were glad he made it.

儘管艾德很晚才到，我們仍很高興他趕上了。

d though + 主詞 + 動詞 + 受詞

→ Much as / though + 主詞 + 動詞 + 受詞

注意

though 引導的副詞子句若無副詞，改寫時可在句首置副詞 much（很），再接 as 或 though。

Though / Although my parents want me to study medicine, all I want to do is be a writer.

→ Much as / though my parents want me to study medicine, all I want to do is be a writer. (Much though... 現在較少用)

= As much as my parents want me to study medicine, all I want to do is be a writer.

雖然我父母很想要我學醫，但我只想成為一名作家。

e though + 主詞 + may + 動詞原形

→ 動詞原形 + as / though + 主詞 + may

注意

though 引導的副詞子句有助動詞 may 時，改寫時可將原句中的動詞原形置句首，再接 as 或 though。

Though you may try, it's difficult to change Mark's mind.

→ Try as you may, it's difficult to change Mark's mind.

你儘管試試，要改變馬克的心意很困難。

發音提示　**Pronunciation**

❶ [e]	day [de]	relationship [rɪˈleʃənʃɪp]
	always [ˈɔlwez]	behavior [bɪˈhevjɚ]
	situation [ˌsɪtʃuˈeʃən]	take [tek]

❷ [j]	behavior [bɪˈhevjɚ]

朗讀短文　**Read aloud the text**

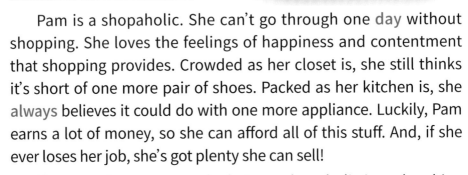

📌 請特別注意 [e]、[j] 的發音。

　　Pam is a shopaholic. She can't go through one day without shopping. She loves the feelings of happiness and contentment that shopping provides. Crowded as her closet is, she still thinks it's short of one more pair of shoes. Packed as her kitchen is, she always believes it could do with one more appliance. Luckily, Pam earns a lot of money, so she can afford all of this stuff. And, if she ever loses her job, she's got plenty she can sell!

　　However, for some people, being a shopaholic is no laughing matter. While Pam earns enough money to cover her splurges, others might spend much more than they can afford. High as their credit card bills are, they always add more to the balance. Shopaholics often shop as a result of a stressful situation in their lives, or to deal with feelings of depression. They are also prone to damage their personal relationships through their behavior—much like any other addiction. Those who think shopping is taking over their lives should always ask for help.

換句話說 Retell

🔑 Retell the text "from the perspective of Pam" with the help of the words and expressions below.

shopaholic, go through, contentment, be short of, packed, appliance, be no laughing matter, splurge, balance, be prone to, personal relationships, take over

討論題目 Free Talk

🔑 Talk on the following topic:

◆ Do you consider yourself a shopaholic?

朗讀 ▶ Lesson 20

At a Thrift Store
在二手商店

搭配筆記聆聽會話 **Listen to the text with the help of the notes given**

browse	(在商店) 隨便看看
connoisseur	鑑賞家
offer a discount	提供折扣
drive a hard bargain	拼命討價還價
shade	色調

再次聆聽並回答問題 **Listen again and answer the questions below**

🎙 Questions for discussion:

❶ How much discount did the man get for the table in the end?

❷ Do the chairs go with the table?

❸ Will the man buy the chairs as well?

Robinotof / Shutterstock.com

Ⓐ Good afternoon. How may I help you, sir?

Ⓑ I'm just browsing. Is this table made of mahogany?

Ⓐ Yes, it is. Good eye, sir. Old as it is, it's a really good piece of hand-carved furniture.

Ⓑ Good as it may be, it's too expensive.

Ⓐ How about 20% off for a connoisseur like yourself?

Ⓑ Hmm... How about 50% off?

Ⓐ I'm sorry, sir. Generous as I am, I can't afford to offer a discount like that.

Ⓑ OK. Make it 30% off and you've got a deal.

Ⓐ You do drive a hard bargain! OK, sir. It's a deal.

Ⓑ Do those chairs go with the table?

A They don't come as a set. They're actually a slightly different shade of mahogany.

B Different as they are, I don't think a blind man on a galloping horse would notice.

A If you're interested in them, I could offer the same 30% discount as the table.

B OK, I'll take them, too. So much for just browsing!

A 午安。先生,有什麼我可以為您服務的嗎?

B 我只是隨意看看。這張桌子是紅木製成的嗎?

A 是的,沒錯。先生,您眼力真好。雖然它很舊了,但它真的是很優質的手工雕刻傢俱。

B 它固然很好,但太貴了。

A 那給像您這樣的鑑賞家八折優惠怎麼樣呢?

B 嗯……。五折怎麼樣呢?

A 抱歉,先生。儘管我很慷慨,但我無法負擔提供那樣的折扣。

B 好吧,如果妳打七折,我就跟你買。

A 您真的很會討折扣!好吧,先生。就這麼說定了。

B 購買桌子也會附贈那些椅子嗎?

A 它們不是一套的。事實上,它們是些微不同色調的紅木。

B 就算它們不一樣,但我覺得一般人根本不會注意到。

A 如果您對這些椅子也有興趣,我也可以給您跟桌子一樣的七折折扣。

B 好,我也要買椅子。只是隨便看一下就買了這麼多!

單字片語　Vocabulary and Phrases

❶ browse [brauz] *vi.* (在商店) 隨便看看

We still have enough time to browse around the souvenir shop.
我們仍有足夠的時間隨意逛逛紀念品店。

2 **be made of...** 由……製成的

3 **mahogany** [mə'hagənɪ] *n.* 紅木，桃花心木

4 **have a (good) eye for sth** 對某事物有好眼力

5 **connoisseur** [ˌkanə'sɝ / ˌkanə'sur] *n.* 鑑賞家，鑑定家

6 **drive a hard bargain (over sth)** (為某物) 拼命討價還價
bargain ['bargɪn] *n.* 便宜貨，減價品

7 **shade** [ʃed] *n.* 色調；差別
many shades of opinion 各種不同觀點

8 **..., I don't think a blind man on a galloping horse would notice.** ……，我覺得一般人根本不會注意到。
本句話直譯為：「我不認為騎在奔馳的馬上的盲眼男子會注意到。」意即差別之處過於細微，一般人根本不會注意到。

口語新技能 New Skills

🔑 表示「好眼力」的說法

Good eye. 好眼力。/ 有眼光。
have a good eye for... 對……有好眼力 / 好眼光
= have an eye for...
Betty has an eye for detail.
貝蒂觀察敏銳，很擅長注意細節。

比較

Good ear. 好聽力。/ 好鑑賞力。
have a good ear for... 對……很有鑑賞力
= have an ear for...
Kate has a good ear for music.
= Kate has an ear for music.
凱特對於音樂很有鑑賞力。

簡短對答 Quick Response

◇ Make quick responses to the sentences you hear.

討論題目 Free Talk

🔖 Talk on the following topic:

◇ Have you ever bargained at a thrift shop before?

Chapter 3

日常生活

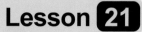

Lesson 21

朗讀
▶
Lesson 21

A Newcomer to the Town
鎮上新來的人

搭配筆記聆聽會話 **Listen to the text with the help of the notes given**

peaceful	寧靜的
chirp	(鳥) 啾啾叫
relaxed	感到放鬆的
come over	來訪
settle	安頓

再次聆聽並回答問題 **Listen again and answer the questions below**

🔍 Questions for discussion:

1. Does the man like the town?
2. Is the man's family with him?
3. When will the man's wife and son join him?

A Welcome to the town! How are you finding the place?

B It's more peaceful than the big city! This morning, I saw children playing in the park. I heard birds chirping in the trees. I felt the clean air blowing on my face. I am so relaxed here.

A Sounds like you love our little corner of the world. I heard that your family will be joining you soon.

B Yes, my wife is arriving next week when our son finishes school.

A You'll have to come over for dinner once you're all settled.

B Thank you. That sounds lovely.

A 歡迎來到鎮上！你覺得這裡怎麼樣呢？

B 這裡比大城市還要寧靜！今早我看見孩童在公園嬉戲。我聽見鳥兒在樹上啁啾鳴叫。我感受到乾淨的空氣吹拂臉龐。我在這裡感到很放鬆。

A 聽起來你很喜歡我們這個在世界一角的小地方。
我聽說你家人即將過來與你相聚。

B 是的，我兒子學期結束後，我太太下週就會抵達。

A 待你安頓好一切後，一定要來我家吃晚餐。

B 謝謝你。聽起來不錯。

單字片語 Vocabulary and Phrases

1 **peaceful** [`pisfəl] *a.* 寧靜的，安靜的

2 **chirp** [tʃɝp] *vi.* (鳥) 發出啾啾叫聲
I love waking up to the sound of birds chirping in the morning.
我喜歡早上隨著啾啾的鳥叫聲醒來。

3 **corner** [`kɔrnɚ] *n.* 角落

4 **come over**　　來訪，拜訪
Come over to my place if you're available this Friday.
如果你這週五有空，來我家吧。

5 **settle** [`sɛtḷ] *vt. & vi.* 安頓，定居
settle down　　安頓下來；安定下來
Has everything been settled yet?
一切都安頓好了嗎？
Have you settled down in your new apartment yet?
你在新的公寓安頓下來了嗎？

6 **lovely** [`lʌvlɪ] *a.* 令人愉快的；美好的；漂亮的

口語新技能 New Skills

1 How are you finding the place?　　你覺得這裡怎麼樣呢？
◆ 句中的 find 並非表一般常見的意思「發現，找到」，而是表「覺得，認為」，用於表示對某事的感受、看法等。
find [faɪnd] *vt.* 覺得，認為 (三態為：find, found [faʊnd], found)

🄐 How are you finding Tokyo / Paris / Lisbon?
🄑 I find it interesting / charming / amazing.
🄐 你覺得東京 / 巴黎 / 里斯本怎麼樣呢？
🄑 我覺得這座城市很有趣 / 迷人 / 令人驚喜。

❷ 介紹連綴動詞
◆ 連綴動詞共有五個，皆可譯為「……起來」，其後一律置形容詞或可作形容詞用的分詞作補語，惟須注意，若要在此類連綴動詞後與名詞並用，須加上介詞 like（像）。

🄐 連綴動詞後接形容詞

sound	+ 形容詞	聽起來……
look		看起來……
smell		聞起來……
taste		嚐起來……
feel		感覺起來……

The guy with a microphone over there looks handsome.
那邊那個拿著麥克風的男生看起來很帥。

This dish smells nasty but tastes great.
這道菜聞起來很糟但很好吃。

🄑 連綴動詞後接名詞

sound	+ like + 名詞	聽起來像……
look		看起來像……
smell		聞起來像……
taste		嚐起來像……
feel		感覺起來像……

It tastes like cinnamon.
它嚐起來像肉桂。

This texture feels like silk.
這質地感覺像絲綢。

簡短對答 Quick Response

◆ Make quick responses to the sentences you hear.

討論題目 Free Talk

🔑 Talk on the following topic:

◆ Do you prefer living in a big city or a small town? Why?

Lesson 22

At a Housewarming Party
喬遷派對

搭配筆記聆聽會話 **Listen to the text with the help of the notes given**

especially	特別，尤其
bloom	(花朵) 盛開
put a lot of effort into...	花很多心思在……
exhausting	令人精疲力盡的
garden furniture	花園傢俱

再次聆聽並回答問題 **Listen again and answer the questions below**

🔑 Questions for discussion:

1️⃣ Whose house are the man and woman in?

2️⃣ What did the woman buy for the garden?

3️⃣ Will the man come again next week?

🅐 Welcome to the party, Brandon.

🅑 Thank you, Debbie. Your house is beautiful. I especially love your garden. The flowers are blooming! Everything looks so colorful.

🅐 Thank you. We put a lot of effort into the garden. Last week, we bought tons of soil and planted all the flowers. It was exhausting!

🅑 It looks like it was worth the effort.

🅐 Next week, we're picking up some garden furniture to complete the look. I think we'll get a garden swing and a few chairs for relaxing.

🅑 I'll be visiting next week, too, then!

🅐 布蘭登,歡迎你來派對。

🅑 黛比,謝謝妳。妳家真漂亮。我特別喜歡妳的花園。花朵都盛開了!一切看起來都很繽紛。

A 謝謝。我們花了很多心思在花園上。我們上週買了很多土，並種下所有的花。真是讓我精疲力盡！

B 看起來一切辛苦都值得。

A 我們下週要去買些花園傢俱來讓整體看起來更完整。我想我們會去弄個鞦韆和幾張休憩用座椅。

B 那我下週會再來玩！

單字片語　Vocabulary and Phrases

❶ bloom [blum] *vi. & n.* (尤指觀賞用的植物的花) 盛開；開花
be in (full) bloom 　（花朵）盛開，綻放

Flowers in the park are blooming in profusion.
公園裡百花齊放。

* profusion [prəˋfjuʒən] *n.* 充分，豐富
in profusion 　大量地

比較
blossom [ˋblasəm] *vi. & n.* (尤指果樹的花) 盛開；開花
be in (full) blossom 　（花朵）盛開，綻放

The apple trees in the yard blossomed yesterday.
院子裡的蘋果樹昨天開花了。

❷ colorful [ˋkʌləfəl] *a.* 色彩繽紛的，顏色鮮豔的

❸ put effort into + N/V-ing 　花很多心思在 / 努力……

To master a new language, you have to put lots of effort into it.
要精通一個新語言，你必須下很多功夫。

❹ exhausting [ɪgˋzɔstɪŋ] *a.* 令人精疲力竭的
exhausted [ɪgˋzɔstɪd] *a.* 感到精疲力竭的

❺ pick up sth / pick sth up 　購買某物

John picks up a newspaper from the newsstand every morning.
約翰每天早晨都在報攤上買份報紙。

6 **furniture** [`ˈfɝnɪtʃɚ`] *n.* 傢俱（集合名詞，不可數）

故「一件傢俱」不可說：

a furniture（×）

→ a piece of furniture（✓）

7 **swing** [swɪŋ] *n.* 鞦韆

play on the swing　　盪鞦韆

口語新技能　New Skills

1 表示「特別，尤其」的說法

especially [əˈspɛʃəlɪ] *adv.* 特別，尤其；專門

= particularly [pəˈtɪkjələlɪ]

= in particular [pəˈtɪkjələ]

Ted is kind to people, especially to the elderly.

= Ted is kind to people, particularly to the elderly.

= Ted is kind to people, to the elderly in particular.

泰德對大家很和藹，對長輩尤其如此。

This English program is especially designed to suit intermediates.

這個英語課程是專門為中級程度的人設計的。

2 表示「大量的」的說法

◆ 在口語會話中，有許多說法可表示「大量的」，除了
常見的 a lot of 或 lots of，亦可使用下列常見說法：

tons of...　　大量的……，許多……

= loads of...

= a load of...

= plenty of...

I can't clock out yet; I still have tons of work to do.

= I can't clock out yet; I still have loads of work to do.

= I can't clock out yet; I still have a load of work to do.

= I can't clock out yet; I still have plenty of work to do.

我還不能打卡下班；我還有很多工作要做。

簡短對答 Quick Response

◆ Make quick responses to the sentences you hear.

討論題目 Free Talk

🔑 Talk on the following topic:

◆ What would you plant in your garden if you had one?

Lesson 23

Weather Forecast
氣象預報

搭配筆記聆聽會話 **Listen to the text with the help of the notes given**

scorcher	大熱天
boiling hot	炎熱的
mercury	水銀（溫度計）
venture outside	外出
outlook	展望

再次聆聽並回答問題 **Listen again and answer the questions below**

🔑 Questions for discussion:

❶ According to the woman, what will the weather be like tomorrow?

❷ What should people do if they go outside tomorrow?

❸ Does the man enjoy the hot weather?

實用會話 Dialogue

🅐 So, Shirley, is it going to be another scorcher tomorrow?

🅑 It certainly is, Kent. We're in for another boiling hot day, with the mercury set to rise to 38 degrees Celsius.

🅐 Wow. It sounds like the air-conditioners will be working hard again!

🅑 You're right about that, Kent. If you do venture outside, please remember to wear sunscreen lotion and avoid the midday sun.

🅐 That's great advice, Shirley. And what's the outlook for the rest of the week?

🅑 Well, it looks like the sweltering temperatures are here to stay.

🅐 Oh, it's too hot for me!

🅐 雪莉，所以明天又會是個大熱天嗎？

🅑 肯特，鐵定是的。隨著溫度計上的水銀上升至攝氏三十八度，我們又將度過炎熱無比的一天。

A 哇。聽起來冷氣又要辛苦運轉了！

B 你說得對，肯特。如果你真的得到外面去，請記得擦防曬乳，並避開正中午的太陽。

A 雪莉，那真是很棒的建議。這週接下來的天氣怎麼樣呢？

B 嗯，看起來酷暑難耐的高溫還會持續一陣子。

A 喔，我真的覺得太熱了！

單字片語 Vocabulary and Phrases

❶ scorcher [ˋskɔrtʃɚ] *n.* 大熱天
It's a real scorcher today.
今天真的熱極了。

❷ certainly [ˋsɝtn̩lɪ] *adv.* 當然地，毫無疑問地

❸ be in for...　　即將遭遇……（尤指令人不太愉快的事）
Andy is in for trouble because he broke his neighbor's window.
安迪即將遭遇麻煩，因為他打破了鄰居的窗戶。

❹ boiling [ˋbɔɪlɪŋ] *adv.* & *a.* 沸騰地 / 的
be boiling hot　　如滾燙般熱的，極熱的

❺ mercury [ˋmɝkjərɪ] *n.* 水銀，汞（不可數）

❻ rise [raɪz] *vi.* 上升，增加（三態為：rise, rose [roz], risen [ˋrɪzn̩]）
The interest rate rose by 0.5% yesterday.
昨天利率上升了 0.5%。

❼ Celsius [ˋsɛlsɪəs] *n.* 攝氏
Fahrenheit [ˋfærənˏhaɪt] *n.* 華氏

❽ air-conditioner [ˋɛrkənˏdɪʃənɚ] *n.* 冷氣機（亦可寫為 air conditioner）
比較
air-conditioning [ˋɛrkənˏdɪʃənɪŋ] *n.*
冷氣，空調（不可數）
（亦可寫為 air conditioning）

9 **venture** [ˈvɛntʃɚ] *vi.* 冒險

Nothing ventured, nothing gained.

不入虎穴，焉得虎子。(諺語)

10 **sunscreen** [ˈsʌnˌskrin] **(lotion)** 防曬乳

11 **midday** [ˈmɪdˌde] *n.* 正午 (= noon [nun])

12 **outlook** [ˈautˌluk] *n.* 展望 (與介詞 for 並用，常用單數)

13 **sweltering** [ˈswɛltərɪŋ] *a.* 熱得要命的

口語新技能　New Skills

🔑 形容天氣氣溫的常見說法

◆ 形容天氣炎熱或寒冷，除了用 hot (熱的) 與 cold (冷的) 之外，亦可使用下列常見說法：

a 形容天氣炎熱

It's | blazingly hot | today.
　　| boiling hot |
　　| sizzling hot |
　　| sweltering |

= It's a real scorcher today.

今天真的熱極了。

b 形容天氣寒冷

It's | freezing cold | today.
　　| biting cold |
　　| bitterly cold |

今天天氣非常冷。

簡短對答 **Quick Response**

◆ Make quick responses to the sentences you hear.

討論題目 **Free Talk**

🔑 Talk on the following topic:

◆ Do you prefer hot weather or cold weather? Why?

A Parking Ticket
一張違規停車罰單

搭配筆記聆聽短文 **Listen to the text with the help of the notes given**

feel under the weather	身體不舒服
appointment	約診
queue	排隊
illegally	違規地
be fined for...	因……被罰款
top priority	首要考量

再次聆聽並回答問題 **Listen again and answer the questions below**

Questions for discussion:

1 Why are the speaker and his wife going to the doctor's?

2 What did the speaker receive for parking illegally?

3 Does the speaker regret parking illegally?

The other day, my wife was feeling under the weather, so she asked me to take her to the doctor's. The traffic was bad on the way there, so we were late for the appointment. We had to get to the back of the queue and wait for an hour until it was our turn again.

To make matters worse, I got a parking ticket for parking illegally outside the clinic! To be frank, it was my fault; I knew I wasn't supposed to park there. I even saw the sign that told people they would be fined for parking there. However, my wife's health will always be top priority, so I have no regrets.

前幾天，我太太身體不太舒服，所以請我帶她去看醫生。路途上的交通狀況很糟，所以我們比約診時間還晚到。我們得再排一次隊，等了一個小時才輪到我們看診。

雪上加霜的是，我因為在診所外違規停車，所以被開了一張罰單！坦白說，這的確是我的錯；我知道我不該在那裡停車的。我甚至有看到告示牌上寫著在那裡停車可能會被罰款。不過，我太太的健康一直都會是我的首要考量，所以我不後悔。

單字片語 Vocabulary and Phrases

❶ be / feel under the weather 身體不適 / 不舒服

Jack is feeling under the weather today.
= Jack is not feeling well today.
= Jack is not feeling good today.
= Jack is feeling ill today.
傑克今天身體不適。

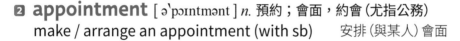

❷ appointment [ə`pɔɪntmənt] *n.* 預約；會面，約會 (尤指公務)
make / arrange an appointment (with sb) 安排 (與某人) 會面

❸ queue [kju] *n.* 隊伍 & *vi.* 排隊 (英式用法)
line [laɪn] *n.* 隊伍 & *vi.* 排隊 (美式用法)
stand in a queue 排隊
= stand in line
= queue up
= line up

People stood in a queue in front of the ticket office.
= People stood in line in front of the ticket office.
= People queued up in front of the ticket office.
= People lined up in front of the ticket office.
大家在售票處前排隊。

❹ parking [`pɑrkɪŋ] *n.* 停車 (不可數)
a parking space / lot 停車位 / 停車場
free parking 免費停車位 / 處

❺ ticket [`tɪkɪt] *n.* 罰單，罰款通知
a parking / speeding ticket 違規停車 / 超速駕駛罰單

6 **illegally** [ɪˈligḷɪ] *adv.* 違規地，違法地
   illegal [ɪˈligḷ] *a.* 違規的，違法的

7 **clinic** [ˈklɪnɪk] *n.* 診所

8 **fault** [fɔlt] *n.* 錯誤，過錯
   be sb's fault   某人的過錯

9 **fine** [faɪn] *vt. & n.* 罰款
   be fined for...   因……被罰款

10 **top priority** [praɪˈɔrətɪ]   首要考量

11 **regret** [rɪˈgrɛt] *n. & vt.* 後悔，悔恨；遺憾

實用詞句 **Useful Expressions**

1 介紹常見的獨立不定詞片語

◆ 獨立不定詞片語具有副詞的功能，通常置句首用以修飾主句。有些獨立不定詞片語已成了常見的固定用法，如下列：

To make matters worse, ...	更糟的是，……
To be frank (with you), ...	(跟你) 坦白說 / 老實說，……
To be honest, ...	坦白說 / 老實說，……
To sum up, ...	總結來說，……
To do sb justice, ...	替某人說句公道話，……
To put it simply, ...	簡言之，……
To be brief, ...	簡言之，……
To begin with, ...	首先，……

To be honest, I'm really into hip-hop.
老實說，我非常喜歡嘻哈樂。

To put it simply, a rainbow is the combination of rain and sunlight.
簡單來說，彩虹就是雨水與陽光的結合。

To begin with, I'd like to introduce our new recruits to you all.
首先，我想跟大家介紹我們的新聘人員。

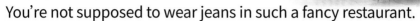
Alex Colom / Shutterstock.com

2 表示「應當」的說法

be supposed to V　　應當……

注意

一般而言，此片語與助動詞 should 的
意思相同，但是語氣上較 should 委婉。

You're not supposed to wear jeans in such a fancy restaurant.

你不應該穿牛仔褲到這麼豪華的餐廳。（語氣較委婉）

You shouldn't wear jeans in such a fancy restaurant.

你不應該穿牛仔褲到這麼豪華的餐廳。（語氣較強烈）

發音提示　Pronunciation

1 [æ]	ask [æsk]	an [æn]
	traffic [ˈtræfɪk]	matter [ˈmætɚ]
	bad [bæd]	frank [fræŋk]
	had [hæd]	that [ðæt]
	back [bæk]	have [hæv]
	and [ænd]	

2 [ð]	the [ði / ðə]	there [ðɛr]
	other [ˈʌðɚ]	that [ðæt]
	weather [ˈwɛðɚ]	they [ðe]

朗讀短文　Read aloud the text

🔑 請特別注意 [æ]、[ð] 的發音。

　　The other day, my wife was feeling under the weather, so she asked me to take her to the doctor's. The traffic was bad on the way there, so we were late for the appointment. We had to get to the back of the queue and wait for an hour until it was our turn again.

To make matters worse, I got a parking ticket for parking illegally outside the clinic! To be frank, it was my fault; I knew I wasn't supposed to park there. I even saw the sign that told people they would be fined for parking there. However, my wife's health will always be top priority, so I have no regrets.

換句話說 Retell

🔑 Retell the text with the help of the words and expressions below.

feel under the weather, appointment, queue, parking, ticket, illegally, clinic, fault, fine, top priority, regret

討論題目 Free Talk

🔑 Talk on the following topic:

◆ Have you ever been fined before? If yes, what happened?

140

Got Pickpocketed
被扒了

搭配筆記聆聽會話 Listen to the text with the help of the notes given

beyond description	難以形容
concentrate on...	專注於……
a petty crime	輕微的犯罪
not necessarily	未必
a lost cause	沒希望的事

再次聆聽並回答問題 Listen again and answer the questions below

🔑 Questions for discussion:

1 What happened to the man?

2 What does the woman suggest to the man?

3 Does the man want to report the crime?

141

實用會話 **Dialogue**

🅐 Hey, Tim. You look like you've had a bad day.

🅑 I got pickpocketed. I'm furious beyond description.

🅐 Oh, no! What happened?

🅑 I think my wallet and phone must've been taken at the concert. The only time that I wasn't concentrating on my surroundings was when they played my favorite song.

🅐 You should inform the police.

🅑 That's the last thing that I would do. They won't be interested in such a petty crime.

🅐 I still think you should report it. It's not necessarily a lost cause.

🅑 The fact that I have no evidence won't help.

🅐 There may be CCTV evidence. Don't give up!

🅐 嘿，提姆。你看起來好像今天過得很糟。

🅑 我被扒了。我氣到難以形容的地步。

🅐 喔，不！發生了什麼事？

🅑 我認為我的錢包和手機一定是在演唱會被偷走的。我唯一沒有注意週遭環境的時候是當他們在表演我最喜歡的歌時。

🅐 你應該要通知警方。

🅑 那是我最不想做的事。他們不會對這麼輕微的犯罪有興趣。

🅐 我還是認為你應該要舉報這件事。這未必沒希望。

🅑 我沒有任何證據，而這個事實幫不了我。

🅐 監視器上可能會有證據的。別放棄！

單字片語　Vocabulary and Phrases

❶ **pickpocket** [ˈpɪkˌpɑkɪt] *vt.* 扒竊，偷竊 & *n.* 扒手

❷ **furious** [ˈfjʊrɪəs] *a.* 極為憤怒的
be furious about / at...　　對……極為憤怒

Mr. Miller was furious about his son's pranks.
米勒先生對於他兒子的惡作劇感到非常生氣。

❸ **wallet** [ˈwɑlɪt] *n.* 皮夾，錢包

❹ **concentrate** [ˈkɑnsṇˌtret] *vi. & vt.* 注意；集中
concentrate on...　　專注於……
= focus on...

We need to <u>concentrate on</u> the matter at hand.
= We need to <u>focus on</u> the matter at hand.
我們必須專注在眼前的問題上。

❺ **surroundings** [səˈraʊndɪŋz] *n.*
週遭環境 (恆用複數)

❻ **inform** [ɪnˈfɔrm] *vt.* 通知，告知
= notify [ˈnotəˌfaɪ]
inform sb of sth　　通知某人某事
= notify sb of sth

The travel agency informed us of a change of schedule.

= The travel agency notified us of a change of schedule.

旅行社通知我們關於行程上的一項異動。

7 **petty** [`pɛtɪ] *a.* 輕微的，瑣碎的，不重要的

Shoplifting is usually considered a petty crime.

順手牽羊通常被視為輕罪。

＊ shoplifting [`ʃɑpˌlɪftɪŋ] *n.*
順手牽羊，在商店行竊

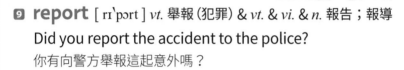

8 **crime** [kraɪm] *n.* 犯罪案件

commit a crime 犯罪

9 **report** [rɪ`pɔrt] *vt.* 舉報 (犯罪) & *vt.* & *vi.* & *n.* 報告；報導

Did you report the accident to the police?

你有向警方舉報這起意外嗎？

10 **necessarily** [`nɛsəˌsɛrəlɪ / ˌnɛsə`sɛrəlɪ] *adv.* 必然地

not necessarily 不必然，未必

Expensive things aren't necessarily better.

昂貴的東西未必比較好。

11 **a lost cause** 沒希望的事；註定失敗的事

cause [kɔz] *n.* 目標，理想

Trying to convince William to be interested in baseball is a lost cause.

試圖讓威廉對棒球有興趣是不可能的事。

12 **evidence** [`ɛvədəns] *n.* 證據 (集合名詞，不可數)

an evidence (✕)

→ a piece of evidence 一項證據 (✓)

13 **CCTV** 監視器；閉路電視 (為 closed-circuit television 的縮寫)

circuit [`sɝkɪt] *n.* 電路，線路

口語新技能  New Skills

1 介詞 beyond 搭配名詞的用法

◆ 介詞 beyond 字面上表示「遠於，超過」，可與名詞搭配，進而表示「難以……」或「無法……」。本課即與名詞 description（形容，描述）搭配使用。

beyond description　　非筆墨所能形容，難以形容

= beyond words

description [dɪˋskrɪpʃən] *n.* 形容，描述

The view from the mountaintop is beautiful beyond description.

= The view from the mountaintop is beautiful beyond words.

山頂上的風景美不勝收。

◆ 其他常與介詞 beyond 搭配的用法如下：

beyond belief	難以置信
beyond repair	無法修復
beyond recognition	難以辨識

2 The fact that I have no evidence won't help.

我沒有任何證據，而這個事實幫不了我。

◆ the fact 後常接 that 引導的子句，作 the fact 的同位語。本句中，子句 that I have no evidence（我沒有任何證據）即為 the fact 的同位語。而 the fact 與其後接之 that 所引導的子句除了可作主詞之外，亦可作動詞或介詞的受詞。

The fact that Sam has lost his job is bitter news.

山姆失去了工作是個令人難過的消息。（the fact 作主詞）

It is hard for Anna to accept the fact that her husband has cheated on her.

安娜難以接受她老公外遇的事實。（the fact 作動詞受詞）

Harry was disappointed about the fact that he had failed the exam.

哈利對於考試不及格感到沮喪。

（the fact 作介詞受詞）

145

◆ Make quick responses to the sentences you hear.

🎙 Talk on the following topic:

◆ If you were the man, would you report the crime to the police?

Empty Nest Syndrome
空巢症候群

搭配筆記聆聽短文 **Listen to the text with the help of the notes given**

phenomenon	現象
a clinical condition	臨床疾病
be vulnerable to...	易受……的傷害
grief	悲傷
keep in touch with...	與……聯絡
on a regular basis	定期

再次聆聽並回答問題 **Listen again and answer the questions below**

🔑 Questions for discussion:

1️⃣ Is empty nest syndrome a clinical condition?

2️⃣ What might people with empty nest syndrome feel?

3️⃣ What is one way to cope with empty nest syndrome?

147

The day when your child leaves home and goes to university or moves out of the house can leave you feeling down. This phenomenon is called "empty nest syndrome." Although it is not a clinical condition, those who experience it may be vulnerable to depression and marital conflicts. They may experience feelings of grief, loneliness, or loss of purpose.

To avoid or cope with empty nest syndrome, you can join clubs and pursue new interests. You can use this as an opportunity to spend more quality time with your partner. You can also keep in touch with your child on a regular basis when you live apart. And the times when your child does come home to visit can be treasured even more.

你的孩子離家念大學或搬出家門的那天可能會讓你心情低落。這現象被稱為「空巢症候群」。雖然這並不是一個臨床疾病，但經歷空巢症候群的人可能容易有抑鬱症與婚姻衝突。他們可能會感到悲傷、孤獨或失去目標。

你可以加入社團並從事新嗜好以避免或應付空巢症候群。你可以利用這作為與另一伴好好相處的機會。你也可以與孩子分開住之後定期聯絡。你孩子回家探望的時光會更被珍惜。

單字片語 Vocabulary and Phrases

1 phenomenon [fə`namə,nan] *n.* 現象
（複數為 phenomena [fə`namənə]）

2 empty nest syndrome　　空巢症候群
nest [nɛst] *n.* 巢，窩
syndrome [`sɪn,drom] *n.* 症候群

3 clinical [`klɪnɪkḷ] *a.* 臨床的
clinical trial　　臨床試驗

4 condition [kən`dɪʃən] *n.* 疾病；狀況；條件

5 vulnerable [`vʌlnərəbḷ] *a.* 易受傷的；脆弱的
be vulnerable to sth　　易受某事物的傷害

Women are more vulnerable to
domestic violence than men.
女性比男性更容易遭受家暴。

6 marital [`mærətḷ] *a.* 婚姻的
marital conflicts　　婚姻衝突

7 grief [grif] *n.* 悲傷，悲痛
grieve [griv] *vt. & vi.* 悲痛

8 spend quality time with sb　　與某人好好相處
quality [`kwɑlətɪ] *a.* 優質的，很好的

The busy father wishes to spend more quality time with his
children.
那位忙碌的父親希望多花一些時間好好地陪伴他的小孩。

9 keep in touch with sb 　　與某人保持聯絡

= keep in contact with sb

I keep in touch / contact with Leah through social media.
我透過社群媒體與莉雅保持聯絡。

10 on a regular basis 　　定期

Oliver goes jogging on a regular basis.
奧利佛會定期慢跑。

實用詞句　Useful Expressions

介紹不定詞片語表示「目的」的用法

不定詞片語 (to + 動詞原形) 作副詞時，可用來表示「目的」。

◆ 此時不定詞片語通常置句尾，但也可以移至主詞前，並在片語後加上逗點，如本課句子：

To avoid or cope with empty nest syndrome, you can join clubs and pursue new interests.

= You can join clubs and pursue new interests to avoid or cope with empty nest syndrome.
你可以加入社團並從事新嗜好以避免或應付空巢症候群。

注意

表示「目的」的副詞不定詞片語亦可用下列片語改寫：

You can join clubs and pursue new interests | to
　　　　　　　　　　　　　　　　　　　 | in order to
　　　　　　　　　　　　　　　　　　　 | so as to

avoid or cope with empty nest syndrome.

發音提示 Pronunciation

❶ [ɔɪ]	avoid [əˈvɔɪd]
	join [dʒɔɪn]

❷ [b]	be [bi]
	vulnerable [ˈvʌlnərəbl̩]
	club [klʌb]
	basis [ˈbesɪs]

朗讀短文 Read aloud the text

🔑 請特別注意 [ɔɪ]、[b] 的發音。

The day when your child leaves home and goes to university or moves out of the house can leave you feeling down. This phenomenon is called "empty nest syndrome." Although it is not a clinical condition, those who experience it may be vulnerable to depression and marital conflicts. They may experience feelings of grief, loneliness, or loss of purpose.

To avoid or cope with empty nest syndrome, you can join clubs and pursue new interests. You can use this as an opportunity to spend more quality time with your partner. You can also keep in touch with your child on a regular basis when you live apart. And the times when your child does come home to visit can be treasured even more.

換句話說 Retell

🎙 Retell the text with the help of the words and expressions below.

phenomenon, empty nest syndrome, clinical condition, vulnerable, martial, grief, spend quality time with, keep in touch with, on a regular basis

討論題目 Free Talk

🎙 Talk on the following topic:

◈ Have you ever left home for school or work before? How did you feel?

When It Rains, It Pours
禍不單行

搭配筆記聆聽會話 Listen to the text with the help of the notes given

check	檢查
phrase	成語，片語
pour	下大雨
give... a call	打電話給……
lend	借給

再次聆聽並回答問題 Listen again and answer the questions below

Questions for discussion:

1 Is this the first time the man has lost his things?

2 What does the woman suggest to the man?

3 Does the woman want to lend the man her phone?

153

Ⓐ What's wrong, Tony?

Ⓑ I can't find my keys. I've lost them again!

Ⓐ Are you sure you have **checked** everywhere?

Ⓑ Yes. I've checked in my jacket, under the **sofa**, and even in the **refrigerator**!

Ⓐ Why are you always losing things?

Ⓑ Old age, maybe? If I were to **receive** a dollar every time I lost something, I'd be a rich man by now.

Ⓐ If I were to receive a dollar every time you said that **phrase**, I'd be even richer! Why don't you call your wife? Maybe she has your keys.

Ⓑ I can't. I've lost my phone, too.

Ⓐ Oh, my! When it rains, it pours.

B Could I borrow your phone to give my wife a call?

A If I lend you my phone, you will probably lose it!

A 東尼，怎麼了？

B 我找不到我的鑰匙。我又把鑰匙弄丟了！

A 你確定你每個地方都檢查過了嗎？

B 對。我檢查過我的外套、沙發底下，甚至冰箱裡面！

A 為什麼你總是會弄丟東西？

B 可能是年紀大？如果我每次弄丟東西可以獲得一美元，我現在會是個有錢人。

A 如果我每次聽到你講這句話時可以獲得一美元，我會比你更有錢！為什麼不打電話給你老婆呢？或許你的鑰匙在她那邊。

B 沒辦法。我也弄丟我的手機了。

A 喔，我的天！真是禍不單行啊。

B 我可以借妳的手機打電話給我老婆嗎？

A 如果我借你我的手機，你八成也會把它搞丟！

單字片語 Vocabulary and Phrases

1 **check** [tʃɛk] *vt. & vi.* 檢查

Before you start your road trip, be sure to check the tires.
你的公路旅行開始前，務必要檢查輪胎。

2 **sofa** [ˋsofə] *n.* 長沙發
= couch [kaʊtʃ]

3 **refrigerator** [rɪˋfrɪdʒəˏretɚ] *n.* 冰箱
= fridge [frɪdʒ]

4 **receive** [rɪˋsiv] *vt.* 收到，獲得

Sarah received a bonus for her excellent performance at work.
莎拉工作表現傑出所以獲得獎金。

155

5 **phrase** [frez] *n.* 成語；片語

6 **borrow** [`bɑro] *vt.* 借用

borrow sth from sb　　向某人借某物

Zack asked to borrow some money from his parents.

查克向他爸媽詢問能不能借點錢。

7 **lend** [lɛnd] *vt.* 借給 (三態為：lend, lent [lɛnt], lent)

lend sth to sb　　借給某人某物

= lend sb sth

The boy's parents are unwilling to lend money to their son.

= The boy's parents are unwilling to lend their son money.

那位男孩的爸媽不願意借錢給他們的兒子。

口語新技能　New Skills

🔑 表示「禍不單行」的說法

When it rains, it pours.　　禍不單行。

pour [pɔr] *vi.* & *vt.* 下大雨

注意

下列說法亦可用來表示「禍不單行」：

It never rains but it pours.　　　不雨則已，一雨傾盆。

Misfortunes never come singly.　　災難從不單獨發生。

＊misfortune [mɪs`fɔrtʃən] *n.* 厄運；災難

　　singly [`sɪŋglɪ] *adv.* 單獨地

簡短對答 Quick Response

◇ Make quick responses to the sentences you hear.

討論題目 Free Talk

🔑 Talk on the following topic:

◇ Do you often lose your things?

Lesson 28

Tidying Up
整理乾淨

搭配筆記聆聽會話 **Listen to the text with the help of the notes given**

tidy	整理
hang up	掛上
litter	亂丟
pretend	假裝
talk back	頂嘴

再次聆聽並回答問題 **Listen again and answer the questions below**

🔑 Questions for discussion:

1️⃣ What does the woman tell the boy to do?

2️⃣ Why are there clothes on the floor?

3️⃣ What was the boy doing with the toys?

Ⓐ Your room is a mess, Jamie. Please tidy it up.

Ⓑ It is tidy, Mom.

Ⓐ No, it isn't. The clothes lying on the floor need to be hung up in your closet. The toys under the bed need to be put in your toy box. The trash littered everywhere needs to be thrown away. Should I continue?

Ⓑ The clothes are on the floor because I was getting changed. The toys are under the bed because I was pretending to be in a cave. And that's not trash; those are paper airplanes.

Ⓐ Don't talk back, young man! Do as your mother says!

Ⓑ OK. I'm sorry, Mom. I'll tidy it up now.

Ⓐ Thank you.

A 傑米，你的房間亂七八糟。請你整理一下。

B 它很乾淨了，媽媽。

A 不，才沒有。地上的衣服需要掛在你的衣櫃裡。床底下的玩具需要放到你的玩具箱裡。亂丟滿地的垃圾需要丟掉。我要繼續嗎？

B 衣服放在地上是因為我在換衣服。玩具在床底下是因為我假裝在山洞裡。然後那些不是垃圾；那些是紙飛機。

A 年輕人，別頂嘴！你媽媽叫你做什麼就做什麼！

B 好。對不起，媽媽。我現在會來整理。

A 謝謝。

單字片語 Vocabulary and Phrases

❶ **tidy** [`ˋtaɪdɪ`] *vt.* 整理（三態為：tidy, tidied [`ˋtaɪdɪd`], tidied）& *a.* 整潔的

tidy up(...) 　將（……）整理乾淨

Please tidy up your desk.
請將你的書桌整理乾淨。

❷ **trash** [`træʃ`] *n.* 垃圾（不可數，美式用法）

= garbage [`ˋgɑrbɪdʒ`]（美式用法）

= rubbish [`ˋrʌbɪʃ`]（英式用法）

注意

trash、garbage 及 rubbish 皆為不可數名詞。

a trash / garbage / rubbish 　一件垃圾（×）

→ a piece of trash / garbage / rubbish（✓）

Tom volunteered to pick up trash on the beach.
湯姆自願去撿海灘上的垃圾。

3 **litter** [ˋlɪtɚ] *vt. & vi.* 亂丟 & *n.*
(被扔在公共場所地面上的) 垃圾 (不可數)

Bottles and cans were littered everywhere after the concert.
演唱會過後瓶瓶罐罐的垃圾被丟得到處都是。

4 **continue** [kənˋtɪnju] *vt.* 繼續
continue + V-ing 繼續……
= continue to V
= go on + V-ing
= keep on + V-ing
Sam continued complaining about his job all night.
= Sam continued to complain about his job all night.
= Sam went on complaining about his job all night.
= Sam kept on complaining about his job all night.
山姆一整晚一直在抱怨他的工作。

5 **pretend** [prɪˋtɛnd] *vi. & vt.* 假裝
pretend to V 假裝要……
pretend + that 子句 假裝……

The little girl is pretending to have an afternoon tea party.
那位小女孩在假裝辦一場下午茶派對。

George pretended that he was sick so he didn't have to go to school.
喬治假裝他生病了，這樣他就不必去上學。

CH
3
日常生活

口語新技能 New Skills

🔑 表示「向某人頂嘴」的說法

talk back (to sb) 向 (某人) 頂嘴 / 回嘴
Don't talk back to your teacher!
別向老師頂嘴！

比較

a talk down to sb 以居高臨下的語氣對某人說話
James likes to talk down to his colleagues because he is the
most senior worker.
詹姆士喜歡用居高臨下的語氣對同事講話，因為他是最資深的員工。

b talk around sth　　拐彎抹角地說某事

My boss hates it when people talk around issues.

我老闆很討厭以拐彎抹角的方式討論問題。

c talk sth over / talk over sth　　討論 / 商量某事

I need to talk things over with my manager before making any decision.

我在做任何決定前需要先與經理商量一下。

d talk sth out / talk out sth　　商談以消除……（分歧 / 誤會）

Fred and George should talk out their differences before working together.

佛萊德與喬治一同合作前應該要好好談談以消除分歧。

e talk (sb) through sth　　（向某人）解釋清楚某事

The professor talked me through the process of the experiment.

教授向我清楚說明實驗的步驟。

f talk sth up / talk up sth　　熱烈地討論某事物

The movie was talked up by the press.

這部電影受到媒體大肆宣傳。

簡短對答　Quick Response

◆ Make quick responses to the sentences you hear.

討論題目　Free Talk

🔑 Talk on the following topic:

◆ Have you ever talked back to your parents? What happened?

Lesson 29

Getting Out of Bed
起身下床

搭配筆記聆聽短文 **Listen to the text with the help of the notes given**

a morning person	習慣早起的人
tempting	誘人的
the snooze button	(鬧鐘上的) 貪睡按鈕
covers	被單
disrupt	擾亂

再次聆聽並回答問題 **Listen again and answer the questions below**

🔑 Questions for discussion:

1 Why did Chris' wife wake him up?

2 What do most sleep experts say about going back to sleep?

3 What does the speaker say you should do when the alarm goes off?

163

短文聽讀 **Text**

Chris was awoken from his deep sleep by his wife, Hannah. She told him it was already 6 a.m., and that he had to get up now lest he miss his train. Chris couldn't bring himself to leave his nice, warm bed, though, so he slept until 7 a.m. As one would expect, he didn't catch his early train. Maybe he should have booked a later train. Or maybe he should have listened to his wife and gotten out of bed sooner!

Getting out of bed in the morning is not an easy thing to do, especially if you are not a morning person. It can be tempting to keep pressing the snooze button so that you get a few more precious minutes under the covers. However, most sleep experts agree that going back to sleep can disrupt the body clock even more. So, when the alarm goes off, get straight out of bed, lest you fall back asleep!

克里斯的妻子漢娜把他從熟睡中叫醒。她告訴他已經早上六點了,他得現在起床,免得錯過火車。但是克里斯沒辦法起身離開他那美好又溫暖的床,所以他一直睡到早上七點。正如預料,他並沒有趕上早班火車。也許他該訂班次晚一點的火車。又或許他該聽妻子的話,早點起床!

早上起身離開床從來就不是件容易的事,對不習慣早起的人來說更是如此。繼續按下鬧鐘的貪睡按鈕挺誘人的,這可以讓你多得幾分鐘與床溫存的寶貴時光。然而,大部分的睡眠專家都同意睡回籠覺更容易打亂你的生理時鐘。因此,鬧鐘響了就要立即起身,以免你又睡著了!

單字片語 Vocabulary and Phrases

1 awake [ə`wek] *vt.* & *vi.* (使) 醒來
(三態為:awake, awoke [ə`wok ], awoken [ ə`wokən]) & *a.* 醒著的

stay awake   保持清醒
keep sb awake   讓某人清醒

It was raining outside when Dylan awoke.
狄倫醒來時,外頭正在下雨。

2 catch [kætʃ] *vt.* 趕上 (三態為:catch, caught [kɔt], caught)
catch a train / bus   趕上搭火車 / 公車

Jerry rushed to the airport to catch his flight.
傑瑞趕往機場以趕上他的班機。

3 a morning person   習慣早起的人;在早上充滿活力的人
= an early bird
a night owl   習慣晚睡的人;夜貓子

4 tempting [`tɛmptɪŋ] *a.* 誘人的,吸引人的
It is tempting to V   (從事)……很吸引人
sb + be tempted to V   某人想要 (從事)……

It is tempting to have a second slice of cake.
再吃第二塊蛋糕是件誘人的事。

I'm tempted to have a second slice of cake.
我想要吃第二塊蛋糕。

5 **snooze** [snuz] **button** （鬧鐘上的）貪睡按鈕，延時按鈕

= snooze alarm

6 **precious** [ˋprɛʃəs] *a.* 珍貴的，寶貴的

7 **covers** [ˋkʌvɚz] *n.* 被單；床罩；床毯 (恆用複數)

8 **expert** [ˋɛkspɝt] *n.* 專家

9 **disrupt** [dɪsˋrʌpt] *vt.* 擾亂

Patrick's pet dog disrupted his sleep several times last night.
派翠克的寵物狗昨晚吵醒他好幾次。

實用詞句 **Useful Expressions**

🔑 副詞連接詞 lest 的用法

◆ 副詞連接詞 lest 引導的副詞子句須使用助動詞 should，而 should 通常予以省略，保留其後的動詞原形。

    lest + 主詞 (+ should) + 動詞原形　　以免 / 免得……

= for fear that + 主詞 + | may + 動詞原形 (表現在或將來的狀況) |
                  | might + 動詞原形 (表過去的狀況) |

= for fear of + V-ing

   Put on a coat lest you (should) catch a cold.

= Put on a coat for fear that you may catch a cold.

= Put on a coat for fear of catching a cold.
   穿上外套吧，免得感冒了。

   Sheila drank lots of coffee lest she (should) fall asleep at work.

= Sheila drank lots of coffee for fear that she might fall asleep at work.

= Sheila drank lots of coffee for fear of falling asleep at work.
   席拉喝了很多咖啡，以免在工作時睡著。

注意

副詞連接詞 lest 後的子句可省略助動詞 should，但若使用 for fear 加 that 子句的句構，其後的助動詞 may 或 might 不可省略。

❶ [ə]	awake [əˋwek]	alarm [əˋlɑrm]
	especially [əˋspɛʃəlɪ]	asleep [əˋslip]
	precious [ˋprɛʃəs]	

❷ [ɝ]	early [ˋɝlɪ]
	expert [ˋɛkspɝt]

朗讀短文 **Read aloud the text**

🎙 請特別注意 [ə]、[ɝ] 的發音。

    Chris was **awoken** from his deep sleep by his wife, Hannah. She told him it was already 6 a.m., and that he had to get up now lest he miss his train. Chris couldn't bring himself to leave his nice, warm bed, though, so he slept until 7 a.m. As one would expect, he didn't catch his **early** train. Maybe he should have booked a later train. Or maybe he should have listened to his wife and gotten out of bed sooner!

    Getting out of bed in the morning is not an easy thing to do, **especially** if you are not a morning person. It can be tempting to keep pressing the snooze button so that you get a few more **precious** minutes under the covers. However, most sleep **experts** agree that going back to sleep can disrupt the body clock even more. So, when the **alarm** goes off, get straight out of bed, lest you fall back **asleep**!

CH
3

日
常
生
活

167

換句話說 Retell

📍 Retell the text from "the perspective of Chris" with the help of the words and expressions below.

awake, catch, a morning person, tempting, snooze button, precious, covers, expert, disrupt

討論題目 Free Talk

📍 Talk on the following topic:

◇ Do you consider yourself a morning person?

Saving the Planet
拯救地球

搭配筆記聆聽會話 **Listen to the text with the help of the notes given**

a community cleanup (或 clean-up)	社區清潔活動
zombie	殭屍
a reusable cup	可重複使用的杯子
consumption	消費
energy-efficient	節能

再次聆聽並回答問題 **Listen again and answer the questions below**

🎙 Questions for discussion:

1 What does the woman say they can do after they move to their new apartment?

2 Does the man want to drink less coffee?

3 According to the woman, what should the man do before leaving the house?

Ⓐ What can we do to save the planet?

Ⓑ We can bike more and drive less. Once we move to our new apartment, we can volunteer for community cleanups.

Ⓐ What else?

Ⓑ See that iced latte you're drinking? Buy fewer of those!

Ⓐ As soon as I leave home, I need my morning coffee! When I don't drink it, I'm a zombie for the rest of the day.

Ⓑ At least use a reusable cup. We need to reduce our consumption and create less trash.

Ⓐ Anything else?

Ⓑ Before you leave the house, you should always take a reusable shopping bag. When you clean your teeth, turn off the faucet. Also, you should always use energy-efficient light bulbs.

🅐 Those ones that take ages to light up?

🅑 Yep, those ones.

🅐 我們可以做什麼來拯救地球？

🅑 我們可以多騎單車、少開汽車。我們一搬到新的公寓就可以自願參加社區清潔活動。

🅐 還有什麼？

🅑 你看到你在喝的那杯冰拿鐵嗎？少買一些！

🅐 我一出門就需要我的早晨咖啡！我不喝咖啡的話一整天會像殭屍一樣。

🅑 至少用可重複使用的杯子。我們需要減少消費並製造更少垃圾。

🅐 還有其他嗎？

🅑 你出門前應該要拿一個可以重複使用的購物袋。你刷牙時要關掉水龍頭。還有，你應該使用節能的燈泡。

🅐 要花很久時間才會亮的那種燈泡嗎？

🅑 沒錯，就是那些。

CH
3
日常生活

單字片語 Vocabulary and Phrases

❶ **planet** [ˋplænɪt] *n.* 行星
the planet 地球

❷ **volunteer** [ˏvɑlənˋtɪr] *vi.* 自願 & *n.* 志工
volunteer for... 自願……
volunteer to V 自願從事……

The young boy volunteered for the army.
那位年輕的男孩自願從軍。

❸ **community** [kəˋmjunətɪ] *n.* 社區

❹ **cleanup** (或 **clean-up**) [ˋklinʌp] *n.*
清掃，清潔

❺ **latte** [ˋlɑte] *n.* 拿鐵

❻ **zombie** [ˋzɑmbɪ] *n.* 殭屍

7 **reusable** [rɪˋjuzəbḷ] *a.* 可重複使用的
reuse [riˋjuz] *vt.* 重複使用
a reusable cup　　可重複使用的杯子

These containers can be reused.
這些容器可以被重複使用。

8 **consumption** [kənˋsʌmpʃən] *n.* 消費；消耗 (不可數)
consume [kənˋs(j)um] *vt.* 消費；消耗

My new car consumes less energy.
我的新車消耗較少能源。

9 **faucet** [ˋfɔsɪt] *n.* 水龍頭 (美式用語)
= tap [tæp] (英式用語)

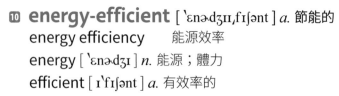

注意
表示「打開 / 關掉水龍頭」不可說：
open / close the faucet (✗)
應說 turn on / off the faucet (✔)

10 **energy-efficient** [ˋɛnəʤɪˏfɪʃənt] *a.* 節能的
energy efficiency　　能源效率
energy [ˋɛnəʤɪ] *n.* 能源；體力
efficient [ɪˋfɪʃənt] *a.* 有效率的

To cut costs, our office will be installing energy-efficient lighting.
為了減少支出，我們辦公室會安裝節能的照明設備。

11 **bulb** [bʌlb] *n.* 電燈泡
= light bulb

口語新技能　New Skills

🎤 once、when、as soon as 等副詞連接詞構成的純條件句

◆ 使用純條件句時，下列副詞連接詞可構成條件句：
once (一旦)　　　　　　　unless (除非)
when (當)　　　　　　　　before (在……之前)
as soon as (一旦)

◆ 本課句子：

a Once we move to our new apartment,
we can volunteer for community cleanups.
我們一搬到新的公寓就可以自願參加社區清潔活動。
(once 引導的副詞子句中使用現在式動詞 move，主句使用助動詞
can)

b Before you leave the house, you should always take a
reusable shopping bag.
你出門前應該要拿一個可以重複使用的購物袋。
(before 引導的副詞子句中使用現在式動詞 leave，主句使用助動詞
should)

c When you clean your teeth, (you should) turn off the faucet.
你刷牙時要關掉水龍頭。
(when 引導的副詞子句中使用現在式動詞 clean，主句為祈使句，
省略了主詞 you 及助動詞 should)

簡短對答　Quick Response

◆ Make quick responses to the sentences you hear.

討論題目　Free Talk

🎙 Talk on the following topic:

◆ In your daily life, what do you do that contributes to saving the
planet?

173

Notes

Chapter 4

網路與社交

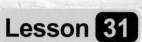

Lesson 31

Online Dating
線上約會

朗讀
▶
Lesson 31

搭配筆記聆聽短文 **Listen to the text with the help of the notes given**

widely accepted	普遍可接受的
a wealth of...	許多……
take sensible precautions	採取明智的預防措施
reveal	透漏

再次聆聽並回答問題 **Listen again and answer the questions below**

🎙 Questions for discussion:

❶ What do supporters of online dating say about it?

❷ What does the speaker think people should do when using an online dating app?

❸ What should you do when someone asks you to do something on an online dating app?

SWIPE LEFT or SWIPE RIGHT!

In recent years, online dating has become a widely accepted way of meeting new people. Indeed, one in five relationships now begins online. Supporters of online dating say it allows you to meet people you probably never would have met in real life. There are a wealth of dating apps available, such as the famous "swipe right" of Tinder.

Whichever app you choose, though, it is important to take sensible precautions, such as not revealing too much personal information. Whatever someone asks you to do or send, make sure you are comfortable with the situation. And whomever you choose to meet, make sure they are who they say they are!

近幾年，線上約會已經成為認識新朋友普遍可接受的方式。確實，現在交往關係中五個就有一個起始於網路。線上約會的支持者表示這讓你認識你現實生活中可能永遠不會認識的人。市面上有許多與約會相關的應用程式，例如Tinder 知名的「往右滑」。

不過，無論你選擇哪個應用程式，採取明智的預防措施如不要透漏太多個人資訊是很重要的。無論別人叫你做什麼或傳什麼資訊，確定你在該情形下是自在的。無論你選擇與誰見面，確定他們的確是他們所說的那個人！

單字片語 Vocabulary and Phrases

1 online dating 線上約會

2 a wealth of... 大量的／許多的……
Eileen has a wealth of experience in marketing.
愛琳有許多行銷經驗。

3 available [əˋveləbḷ] *a.* 可使用的；可得到的
The meeting room is available this afternoon.
會議室今天下午可以使用。

loocmill / Shutterstock.com

4 swipe [swaɪp] *vi. & vt.* (在觸控螢幕上) 滑動；刷 (卡)
For more information, simply swipe left.
只要向左滑就可以獲得更多資訊。

5 sensible [ˋsɛnsəbḷ] *a.* 明智的

6 precaution [prɪˋkɔʃən] *n.* 預防措施 (可數)
take precautions 採取預防措施
On such a hot day, you should take precautions and put on sunblock.
在這麼熱的一天，你應該要採取預防措施並塗抹防曬霜。

7 reveal [rɪˋvil] *vt.* 透漏，揭露
reveal a secret 洩漏祕密

8 personal information 個人資訊
personal [ˋpɝsənḷ] *a.* 個人的，私人的

實用詞句 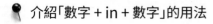 **Useful Expressions**

🖊 介紹「數字 + in + 數字」的用法

數字 + in + 數字　　幾個……中有幾個；幾分之幾
= 數字 + out of + 數字
Studies show that the chances of having this disease are one in a thousand.
= Studies show that the chances of having this disease are one out of a thousand.
研究指出感染這疾病的機率是千分之一。

◆ 下列為與「數字 + in + 數字」相關的常見片語：
one in a million　　可能性極小的；萬中挑選的；獨一無二的
注意
million [ˈmɪljən] 表「百萬」，而 one in a million 字面上即表「百萬分之一」，因此用於形容某事情發生的機率極小，或是某人或事物是獨一無二、萬中挑選的。

The chances of anything going wrong is one in a million.
出問題的可能性是微乎其微的。

Fanny has the voice of an angel. She is truly one in a million!
芬妮的歌聲如天使般，她真是獨一無二！

發音提示 **Pronunciation**

❶ [æ]	has [hæz]	as [æz]
	have [hæv]	ask [æsk]
	app [æp]	and [ænd]

❷ [ɛ]	wealth [wɛlθ]

朗讀短文 **Read aloud the text**

📌 請特別注意 [æ]、[ɛ] 的發音。

In recent years, online dating has become a widely accepted way of meeting new people. Indeed, one in five relationships now begins online. Supporters of online dating say it allows you to meet people you probably never would have met in real life. There are a wealth of dating apps available, such as the famous "swipe right" of Tinder.

Whichever app you choose, though, it is important to take sensible precautions, such as not revealing too much personal information. Whatever someone asks you to do or send, make sure you are comfortable with the situation. And whomever you choose to meet, make sure they are who they say they are!

換句話說 **Retell**

📌 Retell the text with the help of the words and expressions below.

online dating, a wealth of, available, swipe, sensible, precaution, reveal, personal information

討論題目 **Free Talk**

📌 Talk on the following topic:

◆ Are you interested in using online dating apps? Why or why not?

Lesson 32

Meeting an Online Friend
與網友見面

朗讀 ▶ Lesson 32

搭配筆記聆聽會話 **Listen to the text with the help of the notes given**

in person	親自地
public	公共的；公開的
take a walk	散步
use up...	用光……
in real life	在現實生活中

再次聆聽並回答問題 **Listen again and answer the questions below**

🔑 Questions for discussion:

1 Have the man and the woman met in person before?

2 What does the man suggest they do?

3 When will the man and the woman meet?

181

(using an online dating app)

🅐 So, we've been **chatting** for a couple of weeks now. Would you like to meet **in person**?

🅑 Um... sure. Wherever we meet, though, I want it to be a **public** place.

🅐 How about the café in St. Mary's Park? We could have a coffee, and then take a walk.

🅑 That sounds nice. Are you free on Saturday afternoon?

🅐 Yes. How's 2 p.m.?

🅑 Perfect. Now all I have to do is choose what to wear!

🅐 Whatever you wear, I'm sure you'll look beautiful.

🅑 Hey, don't use up all your best **lines** before we see each other in real life.

🅐 Oh, don't worry; I've got thousands of those!

（使用線上約會應用程式）

🅐 所以，我們已經聊了好幾個禮拜。妳想要見面嗎？

🅑 啊……好。不過，無論我們在什麼地方見面，我希望是公共場所。

🅐 聖瑪麗公園裡的咖啡廳如何？我們可以喝杯咖啡，然後散步。

🅑 那聽起來不錯。你星期六下午有空嗎？

🅐 有。下午兩點如何？

🅑 太棒了。現在我要做的是挑選該穿什麼衣服！

🅐 無論妳穿什麼，我相信妳都會看起來很美。

🅑 嘿，別在我們在現實生活中見面前就用完你的甜言蜜語了。

🅐 喔，別擔心；我有好幾千條甜言蜜語！

單字片語　Vocabulary and Phrases

1 chat [tʃæt] *vi.* & *n.* 聊天（三態為：chat, chatted [ˈtʃætɪd], chatted）
chat with sb　　與某人聊天
= have a chat with sb

I chatted with my mom on the phone last night.
= I had a chat with my mom on the phone last night.
我昨晚與我媽媽用電話聊天。

2 in person　　親自地
= personally [ˈpɝsn̩lɪ]

The CEO greeted the new employees in person.
= The CEO greeted the new employees personally.
執行長親自迎接新進員工。

3 public [ˈpʌblɪk] *a.* 公共的；公開的；公眾的 & *n.* 公眾
in public　　公開地
= publicly [ˈpʌblɪklɪ]
the public　　社會大眾

It is against the law to smoke in public places.
在公共場所抽菸是違法的。

CH
4
網路與社交

183

Gary will perform his song <u>in public</u> for the first time.

= Gary will perform his song <u>publicly</u> for the first time.

蓋瑞將首次公開地表演他的歌曲。

4 **line** [laɪn] *n.* 話語，臺詞 (在此指搭訕的話或甜言蜜語)

a pick-up line　　搭訕話語

Stefan Rotter / Shutterstock.com

口語新技能　New Skills

1 How's 2 p.m.?　　下午兩點如何？

= How about 2 p.m.?

= How does 2 p.m. sound?

在表示「……如何？」時，「How about...?」與「How does... sound?」為較常見的說法。

A What should we have for dinner?

B How about pizza?

= How does pizza sound?

A 我們晚餐要吃什麼？

B 吃披薩如何？

2 表示「用光某物」的說法

use up sth / use sth up　　用光 / 用完某物

Can you lend me some money? I used up all my savings.

你可以借我一點錢嗎？我花光所有積蓄了。

◆ 下列為意思相近的常見片語：

a run out of sth 　用光 / 用完某物

We ran out of gas on our way home.
我們在回家的路上車子沒油了。

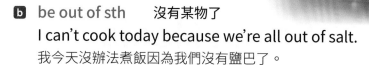

b be out of sth 　沒有某物了

I can't cook today because we're all out of salt.
我今天沒辦法煮飯因為我們沒有鹽巴了。

簡短對答 　Quick Response

◆ Make quick responses to the sentences you hear.

討論題目 　Free Talk

🔑 Talk on the following topic:

◆ Have you or anyone you know met an online friend in person before?

朗讀 ▶ Lesson 33

Social Media
社群媒體

搭配筆記聆聽短文 Listen to the text with the help of the notes given

billion	十億
nowadays	現今
source	來源
manage to...	設法 / 成功做到……
frown on...	不贊同……
inevitably	無可避免地

再次聆聽並回答問題 Listen again and answer the questions below

🔑 Questions for discussion:

1 How many people use social media around the world?

2 Aside from sharing photos and opinions, what can social media also be used for?

3 How long does a person spend on social media per day on average?

Vasin Lee / Shutterstock.com

Despite being less than twenty years old, social media now has over 3 billion users around the globe. Some of the most popular social media sites, with over 1 billion users, are YouTube, WhatsApp, and WeChat. Nowadays, social media is used not only to share our photos and opinions, but also as a source of news and information.

In spite of the fact that most of us lead busy lives, we still manage to find time to spend on social media. On average, a person spends almost two hours a day on social media. Some of this is during our commute to and from work. And, despite the fact that many companies frown on social media use at the office, some of it inevitably takes place during work time.

雖然存在的時間不到二十年，社群媒體目前在全球已有超過三十億用戶。
YouTube、WhatsApp 及微信擁有超過十億用戶，是一些最受歡迎的社群媒體

網站。現今，社群媒體不僅是用來分享我們的照片與想法，也是新聞與資訊的一種來源。

　　儘管大多數人生活忙碌，我們仍能法找到時間花在社群媒體上。平均而言，一個人一天中花將近兩個小時在社群媒體上。有些時間是在我們上下班的通勤上。還有，儘管許多公司反對在辦公室使用社群媒體，有些使用社群媒體的時間無可避免地發生於上班時。

單字片語　Vocabulary and Phrases

1 social media　社群媒體
social [`soʃəl] *a.* 社交的；社會的
media [`midɪə] *n.* 媒體

2 billion [`bɪljən] *n.* 十億

3 globe [glob] *n.* 地球；地球儀
around the globe　在全球
= around the world

4 source [sɔrs] *n.* 來源，出處
Sunlight is a great source of energy.
陽光是一個很好的能量來源。

5 manage [`mænɪdʒ] *vt.* 設法
manage to V　設法 / 成功做到……
How did you manage to finish everything by yourself?
你是如何能設法自己完成所有事？

6 average [`ævərɪdʒ] *n.* 平均 & *a.* 平均的；一般的
On average, ...　平均而言，……
On average, I work 40 hours per week.
平均而言，我一週工作四十個小時。

7 commute [kə`mjut] *n.* & *vi.* 通勤
commute between A and B　在 A 與 B 之間來回通勤

Tony commutes between Brooklyn and Manhattan by subway every day.
東尼每天坐地鐵在布魯克林與曼哈頓之間來回通勤。

8 **frown** [fraʊn] *vi.* & *n.* 皺眉頭
frown on / upon sth　　反對某事，不贊同某事
frown at sb　　對某人皺眉頭

Smoking in public is often frowned upon.
在公開場合抽菸常常是不樂見的。

Sally frowned at the little boy for crying and screaming.
莎莉因為那位小男孩又哭又叫而對他皺了眉頭。

9 **inevitably** [ɪnˋɛvətəblɪ] *adv.* 不可避免地
= unavoidably [ˌʌnəˋvɔɪdəblɪ]
inevitable [ɪnˋɛvətəbl̩] *a.* 不可避免的，必然的

實用詞句　**Useful Expressions**

🔑 despite 與 in spite of 的用法

despite...　　儘管 / 雖然……
= in spite of...

a in spite of 為介詞片語，而 despite 為介詞，其後須接名詞或動名詞作受詞。

◆ 本課句子：

<u>Despite</u> <u>being</u> less than twenty years old, social media now has over 3 billion users around the globe.
= <u>In spite of</u> <u>being</u> less than twenty years old, social media now has over 3 billion users around the globe.
雖然存在的時間不到二十年，社群媒體目前在全球已有超過三十億用戶。
（介詞 despite 後接動名詞 being，despite 亦可與 in spite of 替換）

b in spite of 與 despite 後面不可直接接 that 子句作受詞，因為 that 所引導的名詞子句不可作介詞的受詞。使用時，須先加上 the fact 作 in spite of 或 despite 的受詞，再接that 子句。此時，that 子句為 the fact 的同位語。

In spite of the fact + that 子句   儘管 / 雖然……
= Despite the fact + that 子句
In spite of the fact that I was exhausted, I had
trouble falling asleep.
= Despite the fact that I was exhausted, I had trouble falling
asleep.
雖然我很疲倦，但我難以入睡。

發音提示 Pronunciation

❶ [aɪ]	despite [dɪˋspaɪt]	lives [laɪvz]
	site [saɪt]	find [faɪnd]
	spite [spaɪt]	time [taɪm]

❷ [n] （置於母音前）	now [naʊ]	manage [ˋmænɪdʒ]
	nowadays [ˋnaʊəˏdez]	many [ˋmɛnɪ]
	opinion [əˋpɪnjən]	company [ˋkʌmpənɪ]
	news [n(j)uz]	inevitably [ɪnˋɛvətəblɪ]

朗讀短文 Read aloud the text

🎤 請特別注意 [aɪ]、[n]（置於母音前）的發音。

Despite being less than twenty years old, social media now
has over 3 billion users around the globe. Some of the most
popular social media sites, with over 1 billion users, are YouTube,
WhatsApp, and WeChat. Nowadays, social media is used not only
to share our photos and opinions, but also as a source of news and
information.

In spite of the fact that most of us lead busy lives, we still manage to find time to spend on social media. On average, a person spends almost two hours a day on social media. Some of this is during our commute to and from work. And, despite the fact that many companies frown on social media use at the office, some of it inevitably takes place during work time.

換句話說 Retell

🎙 Retell the text with the help of the words and expressions below.

social media, billion, globe, source, manage, average, commute, frown, inevitably

討論題目 Free Talk

🎙 Talk on the following topic:

◆ Are you a heavy user of social media?

CH
4

網路與社交

朗讀 ▶ Lesson 34

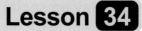

Lesson 34

What Did I Tell You?
我告訴你什麼？

搭配筆記聆聽會話 **Listen to the text with the help of the notes given**

run out of gas	沒油了
run low on fuel	快沒油了
morning routine	早晨作息
recollection	回憶
attitude	態度

再次聆聽並回答問題 **Listen again and answer the questions below**

🔑 Questions for discussion:

❶ What does the woman want the man to do?

❷ What did the man tell the woman yesterday?

❸ Why didn't the woman want to listen to the man?

Ⓐ Hi, honey. Can you come pick me up and take me to work? My car ran out of gas.

Ⓑ What did I tell you yesterday? I said you need to fill up your car because it's running low on fuel.

Ⓐ I don't remember you telling me that.

Ⓑ It was during that whole conversation about our morning routine and how we need to get out of bed earlier.

Ⓐ I have no recollection of that conversation.

Ⓑ If you had listened to me, you would have gotten to the office by now.

Ⓐ If you had said it with a better attitude, I might have listened.

Ⓑ How do you know I didn't say it with a good attitude if you don't remember me telling you?

Ⓐ Err...

Ⓐ 嗨，親愛的。你可以來接我並送我去上班嗎？我的車沒油了。

Ⓑ 我昨天告訴妳什麼？我說妳得幫妳的車加油因為它快沒油了。

Ⓐ 我不記得你告訴我這件事。

Ⓑ 是在我們討論我們的早晨作息以及如何早點起床時。

Ⓐ 我完全不記得那段對話。

Ⓑ 如果妳當時聽了我講的話，或許現在就會到辦公室了。

Ⓐ 如果你當時說話態度好一點，我或許就會聽了。

Ⓑ 如果妳不記得我告訴你這件事，妳怎麼知道我沒有用好的態度講話？

Ⓐ 呃……。

單字片語　Vocabulary and Phrases

❶ **fuel** [ˈfjuəl] *n.* 燃料

❷ **routine** [ruˈtin] *n.* 慣例；例行公事 & *a.* 例行的
daily routine　　每日例行公事，日常作息

Exercising in the morning is part of my daily routine.
早上運動是我日常作息的一部分。

A routine inspection will be conducted tomorrow.
明天會執行一場例行檢查。

❸ **recollection** [ˌrɛkəˈlɛkʃən] *n.* 回憶
recollect [ˌrɛkəˈlɛkt] *vt.* 回憶
= remember [rɪˈmɛmbɚ]
= recall [rɪˈkɔl]
have no recollection of sth　　不記得某事物

Oddly, Harry has no recollection of what happened last night.
很奇怪的是，哈利不記得昨晚發生的事。

Dean recollects seeing Lydia at the party.
迪恩記得在派對上見到莉蒂亞。

❹ **attitude** [ˈætətjud] *n.* 態度

口語新技能 New Skills

❶ 表示「用光某物」的說法

run out of sth　　用光某物

run out of gas / money / time　　沒油 / 錢 / 時間了

Unfortunately, we ran out of gas in the middle of the desert.

很不幸地，我們的車在沙漠中沒油了。

比較

run low on sth　　快用光某物

I asked Sam to go to the supermarket because we're running low on milk.

我請山姆去一趟超市，因為我們的牛奶快沒了。

❷ by now 的用法

by now　　到現在為止

注意

本片語常與「would / should / could / ought to + have + 過去分詞」（應當已經……）並用。

Teresa should have arrived by now.

泰瑞莎現在應該已經到了。

比較

for now　　暫時

= for the time being

Let's just leave the discussion here <u>for now</u>.

= Let's just leave the discussion here <u>for the time being</u>.

我們暫時討論到這邊吧。

簡短對答 Quick Response

◆ Make quick responses to the sentences you hear.

討論題目 Free Talk

Talk on the following topic:

◆ What would you do if someone talked to you with a bad attitude?

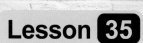

Lesson 35

Virtual Reality
虛擬實境

搭配筆記聆聽短文 **Listen to the text with the help of the notes given**

interactive	有互動的
simulated	虛擬的
sensory	感官的
application	應用
endless	無限的

CH 4
網路與社交

再次聆聽並回答問題 **Listen again and answer the questions below**

🔑 Questions for discussion:

1️⃣ What is virtual reality?

2️⃣ According to the speaker, how can virtual reality be used for education?

3️⃣ According to the speaker, how can virtual reality be applied in medical training?

197

Virtual reality (VR) is an interactive computer-generated experience taking place within a simulated environment. Typically, users wear a VR headset, which generates sounds and images that take them on a sensory journey. They can then move around and interact with their new "world."

VR could be the future of gaming. Depending on the game you play, you can feel as though you are in a place similar to the real world or a complete fantasy world. You can be whoever you want to be, and do whatever you want to do.

However, VR also has many more practical applications. It can be used to train astronauts, so they can feel as though they were in space. It can be used for education, so children can experience life in the past. And it can be used for medical training, so surgeons can act as if they were in real-life situations. The possibilities are endless.

虛擬實境 (VR) 是一個有互動性的電腦成像體驗，發生在一個虛擬的環境裡。一般而言，使用者穿戴虛擬實境的頭戴裝置，這個裝置會產生聲音與畫面帶領使用者踏上一趟感官旅程。使用者可以接著移動並與新的「世界」互動。

虛擬實境有機會成為電玩遊戲的未來。根據你所玩的遊戲，你會感覺彷彿身在與現實世界相似的地方，或是完全虛幻的世界。你可以成為任何你想要成為的人，做任何你想做的事情。

不過，虛擬實境也有許多實際應用之處。它可以被用來訓練太空人，讓他們感覺彷彿就在太空。它可以被用在教育上，讓學童體驗過去的生活。它也可以被用在醫療訓練上，讓外科醫生可以模仿現實生活的情況。虛擬實境有無限的可能性。

單字片語　Vocabulary and Phrases

1 **virtual reality**　虛擬實境 (常縮寫為 VR)
virtual [ˋvɝtʃʊəl] *a.* 虛擬的
reality [rɪˋælətɪ] *n.* 現實

2 **interactive** [͵ɪntɚˋæktɪv] *a.* 互動的

3 **simulated** [ˋsɪmjə͵letɪd] *a.* 模擬的
simulate [ˋsɪmjə͵let] *vt.* 模擬，模仿
simulation [͵sɪmjəˋleʃən] *n.* 模擬，模仿

4 **headset** [ˋhɛd͵sɛt] *n.* 頭戴裝置；耳機

5 **generate** [ˋdʒɛnə͵ret] *vt.* 產生

Roman Kosolapov / Shutterstock.com

The newest technology generated a lot of interest.
最新的科技引起很多興趣。

6 **sensory** [ˋsɛnsərɪ] *a.* 感官的，感覺的

7 **interact** [͵ɪntɚˋækt] *vi.* 互動
interact with...　與……互動

The little girl interacts well with other children at school.
那位小女孩在學校裡與其他小孩互動良好。

8 **depend** [dɪˋpɛnd] *vi.* 視……而定；依賴
depend on...　視……而定

Where we will go on the weekend depends on the weather.
我們週末要去哪裡端看氣象而定。

9 **fantasy** [`fæntəsɪ] *n.* 幻想

10 **practical** [`præktɪkḷ] *a.* 實際的；實務的
This candidate has five years of practical experience.
這位應徵者有五年的實務經驗。

11 **application** [ˌæplə`keʃən] *n.* 應用；申請

12 **surgeon** [`sɜdʒən] *n.* 外科醫師
physician [fɪ`zɪʃən] *n.* 內科醫師

13 **possibility** [ˌpasə`bɪlətɪ] *n.* 可能性
possible [`pasəbḷ] *a.* 可能的

14 **endless** [`ɛndlɪs] *a.* 無限的，無數的
= unlimited [ʌn`lɪmɪtɪd]
= limitless [`lɪmɪtlɪs]
= infinite [`ɪnfənɪt]

I have an endless list of things to do.
我有數不清的事情要做。

實用詞句 Useful Expressions

🔖 介紹「彷彿」的用法

◆ as if 與 as though 皆為副詞連接詞，引導副詞子句，表示「彷彿」。使用時，as if 與 as though 可與三種時態搭配：

a 副詞子句的動詞使用一般時態以表示發生的可能性極大。
It looks as if / as though it is going to rain.
看起來好像要下雨了。

b 副詞子句的動詞使用過去式以表示與現在事實相反。
John talks as if / as though he were the boss.
約翰講話好像他是老闆一樣。

注意

表示與現在事實相反時，be 動詞過去式在書寫上一律使用 were 而非 was。

c 副詞子句的動詞使用過去完成式以表示與過去事實相反。

Vicky acted <u>as if / as though</u> she <u>had done</u> nothing wrong.

薇琪的行為舉止就像她沒有犯任何錯一樣。

注意

除了副詞子句外，as if 與 as though 亦可接不定詞片語、分詞片語或介詞片語。

The manager raised his eyebrows as if <u>to disapprove of the</u>

不定詞片語

<u>idea.</u>

那位經理抬起眉毛好像表示不同意該想法。

The child screamed as though <u>seeing a ghost.</u>

分詞片語

那個小孩尖叫得好像看見鬼一樣。

The street performer made the card disappear as if <u>by magic.</u>

介詞片語

那位街頭表演者就像變魔術般地讓卡片消失。

CH
4

網路與社交

發音提示 **Pronunciation**

❶ **[U]**	virtual [`vɝtʃʋəl]	
	could [kʋd]	

❷ **[l]** （置於母音後）	virtual [`vɝtʃʋəl]	also [`ɔlso]
	typically [`tɪpɪkḷɪ]	practical [`præktɪkḷ]
	world [wɝld]	children [`tʃɪldrən]
	feel [fil]	medical [`mɛdɪkḷ]
	real [`riəl]	

201

🎙 請特別注意 [ʊ]、[l]（置於母音後）的發音。

　　Virtual reality (VR) is an interactive computer-generated experience taking place within a simulated environment. Typically, users wear a VR headset, which generates sounds and images that take them on a sensory journey. They can then move around and interact with their new "world."

　　VR could be the future of gaming. Depending on the game you play, you can feel as though you are in a place similar to the real world or a complete fantasy world. You can be whoever you want to be, and do whatever you want to do.

　　However, VR also has many more practical applications. It can be used to train astronauts, so they can feel as though they were in space. It can be used for education, so children can experience life in the past. And it can be used for medical training, so surgeons can act as if they were in real-life situations. The possibilities are endless.

換句話說 Retell

🎙 Retell the text with the help of the words and expressions below.

virtual reality, interactive, simulated, headset, generate, sensory, interact, depend, fantasy, practical, application, surgeon, possibility, endless

討論題目 Free Talk

🎙 Talk on the following topic:

◇ Have you ever experienced VR before? If not, would you like to try it?

Keep Your Head Up
打起精神

搭配筆記聆聽會話 | **Listen to the text with the help of the notes given**

considerate	貼心的，體貼的
claim	聲稱
deserve	應得，應該
fall ill	生病
thoughtful	體貼的

CH 4
網路與社交

再次聆聽並回答問題 | **Listen again and answer the questions below**

🔑 Questions for discussion:

1 What happened to the man?

2 What did the man's girlfriend say about him?

3 What will the man do if he gets another girlfriend?

🅐 What's the matter, Tom? You look like you need a hug.

🅑 My girlfriend broke up with me.

🅐 Oh, no! What happened?

🅑 She said I'm not considerate enough. She claimed that I never asked her how her day was.

🅐 And is that true?

🅑 Were it true, I would deserve to be dumped.

🅐 Did she give any other reasons?

🅑 Well, she also mentioned that I never went to the hospital to visit her mom when she fell ill. Had she told me about this earlier, I could've done something about it.

🅐 Keep your head up. Maybe you can learn something from this for the future. Had you been more thoughtful, you might still have a girlfriend.

B Should I get another girlfriend, I'll try to be more considerate. Now, where's that hug?

A 湯姆,你怎麼了?你看起來像是需要一個擁抱。

B 我的女朋友跟我分手了。

A 喔,不!發生了什麼事?

B 她說我不夠貼心。她聲稱我從來沒問過她過得如何。

A 那是真的嗎?

B 如果是真的,我被分手真是罪有應得。

A 她有說其他理由嗎?

B 嗯,她也有提到她媽媽生病時我從未去醫院探望她。如果她早點告訴我這件事,我就會有所作為。

A 打起精神。或許你可以從這學到什麼以作未來參考。如果你當時更體貼,你或許現在仍會有女朋友。

B 要是我有交到新的女朋友,我會努力變得更貼心。來,那個擁抱呢?

單字片語 Vocabulary and Phrases

1 **considerate** [kənˋsɪdərɪt] *a.* 體貼的 (= thoughtful)
It is considerate of you to hold the door for me.
你幫我擋門很體貼。

2 **claim** [klem] *vt.* 聲稱;主張
claim + that 子句　　聲稱……
claim to V　　聲稱……

The scientist claimed that he had found the cure for the disease.
= The scientist claimed to have found the cure for the disease.
那位科學家聲稱他已經找到治療那個疾病的方法。

3 **deserve** [dɪˋzɝv] *vt.* 應得,值得
deserve to V　　應 / 值得……
deserve + N　　應 / 值得……

We all agree that Sarah deserves to win.
我們都同意莎拉應得勝利。

4 dump [dʌmp] *vt.* 分手 (非正式用語)
dump sb   與某人分手，甩掉某人

Patrick dumped Yvonne yesterday.
派翠克昨天與伊芳分手了。

5 thoughtful [ˈθɔtfəl] *a.* 體諒的

口語新技能 **New Skills**

1 表示「分手」的說法
   break up (with sb)   (與某人) 分手
= dump sb (dump 較指甩了對方，一方弱勢，一方強勢)
= ditch sb (ditch 較指甩了對方，一方弱勢，一方強勢)
   Nancy just broke up with her boyfriend.
= Nancy just dumped her boyfriend.
= Nancy just ditched her boyfriend.
   南西剛和她的男朋友分手。

◆ 本片語亦有下列意思：

a be breaking up   (電話中) 聲音斷斷續續
   I can't hear you. You're breaking up.
   我聽不到你講話。你的聲音斷斷續續的。

b break sth up / break up sth   將……拆開
   Frank broke the candy bar up and gave each child a piece.
   法蘭克將這塊糖果掰開，分給每個小孩一人一塊。

c Break it up!   別打架了！
   Break it up, you two!
   你們兩個別打架了！

2 表示「打起精神」的說法

Keep your head up.　打起精神 / 不要灰心。

= Keep your chin up.

= Hold your head high.

Keep your head up, and don't lose your faith.

打起精神，別失去信心。

簡短對答 Quick Response

◆ Make quick responses to the sentences you hear.

討論題目 Free Talk

Talk on the following topic:

◆ Have you or your friend ever been through a break-up before?

In a Long-Distance Relationship
遠距離戀愛

搭配筆記聆聽會話 **Listen to the text with the help of the notes given**

in person	親自地
cost an arm and a leg	貴得要命，極昂貴
grab a coffee	買杯咖啡
time difference	時差
That's the spirit!	這樣想就對了！

再次聆聽並回答問題 **Listen again and answer the questions below**

🔑 Questions for discussion:

1 Where is the man's girlfriend?

2 Why can't the man visit his girlfriend?

3 Why can't the man's girlfriend come visit him?

實用會話　Dialogue

🅐 So, how's your relationship with your girlfriend these days?

🅑 It's tough. As you know, Shelley and I are in a long-distance relationship.

🅐 Yeah, I bet it's hard. London's not exactly close to LA!

🅑 We talk on the phone a lot. Hardly do we ever see each other in person, though.

🅐 Maybe it's time for you to visit England again.

🅑 I'd like to, but the flight tickets cost an arm and a leg. I don't have enough money now.

🅐 Can Shelley not come over here?

🅑 She's snowed under with coursework for her MBA. Hardly does she have the time to grab a coffee, never mind fly eleven hours to come and see me.

🅐 Then there's the time difference, I guess.

🅑 Well, yeah, that doesn't help. Still, there's only another six months to go and we'll be back together.

🅐 That's the spirit!

🅐 你最近和女友的關係還好嗎?

🅑 很難熬。如妳知道的,雪麗跟我現在是遠距離戀愛。

🅐 是呀,我敢肯定一定不容易。倫敦跟洛杉磯的距離根本不近!

🅑 我們很常講電話。但是,我們幾乎無法親自見到對方。

🅐 或許是時候你再去一趟英國了。

🅑 我也想,但是機票貴得要命。我現在沒有足夠的錢。

🅐 雪麗沒辦法來這裡嗎?

🅑 她正為企業管理碩士的課業忙得不可開交。她幾乎連買杯咖啡的時間都沒有,更別說要坐十一個小時的飛機過來看我了。

🅐 而且,我想還有時差。

🅑 嗯,是的,那更是幫倒忙。儘管如此,只要再過六個月,我們就可以團聚了。

🅐 這樣想就對了!

單字片語 Vocabulary and Phrases

❶ **tough** [tʌf] *a.* 艱難的,棘手的

❷ **long-distance** [ˋlɔŋˋdɪstəns] *a.* 長距離的,長途的
a long-distance flight　　長途班機

❸ **bet** [bɛt] *vt.* 敢肯定 & *vt.* & *vi.* 打賭 (三態同形)
I bet that Miranda is still in the office.
我打賭米蘭達還在辦公室。

❹ **in person**　　親自地
= **personally** [ˋpɝsənlɪ]

5 **cost an arm and a leg**　　極昂貴；花一大筆錢
= cost a fortune

6 **be snowed under (with sth)**　　(因某事) 忙得不可開交
Susan is completely snowed under with the project now.
蘇珊現在正因為該計畫忙得不可開交。

7 **coursework** [ˈkɔrsˌwɝk] *n.* 課業 (不可數)

8 **MBA**　　企業管理碩士 (為 Master of Business Administration 的縮寫)

9 **grab** [græb] *vt.* (因忙碌) 趕緊吃 / 睡 (三態為：grab, grabbed [græbd], grabbed)
grab a bite to eat　　趕緊吃點東西

10 **time difference**　　時差

11 **一段時間 + to go**　　還剩下⋯⋯的時間
three days / weeks / months to go　　還剩下三天 / 三週 / 三個月

12 **That's the spirit!**　　這樣(做 / 想) 就對了！(此句話於口語中使用時，代表說話者贊同對方的態度、想法或行為)

口語新技能 `New Skills`

🔑 表示「更不用說」的說法

never mind...　　更不用說⋯⋯
= let alone...
I don't think I can walk 10 km, never mind run that far.
= I don't think I can walk 10 km, let alone run that far.
我不認為我可以走十公里，更別提跑那麼遠了。
本課句子可改寫如下：
Hardly does she have the time to grab a coffee, never mind fly eleven hours to come and see me.
= Hardly does she have the time to grab a coffee, let alone fly eleven hours to come and see me.
她幾乎連買杯咖啡的時間都沒有，更別說要坐十一個小時的飛機過來看我了。

CH
4
網路與社交

211

注意

"never mind" 亦有下列常見意思：

a never mind (about...)   沒關係；別擔心

Never mind about the mistake. Just be careful next time.

別太擔心你犯的那個錯誤。下次小心點就好了。

b never mind + N/V-ing   不用管……

Never mind the money. I can lend you some.

不用管錢的問題。我可以借你一些。

簡短對答 Quick Response

◆ Make quick responses to the sentences you hear.

討論題目 Free Talk

📌 Talk on the following topic:

◆ Do you think you can maintain long-distance relationships well? Why or why not?

Lesson 38

朗讀
▶
Lesson 38

Me and My Big Mouth
我真多嘴

搭配筆記聆聽短文 Listen to the text with the help of the notes given

main course	主餐
offend	冒犯
talkative	健談的
let slip a secret	把祕密說溜嘴
miscarriage	流產

CH
4
網路與社交

再次聆聽並回答問題 Listen again and answer the questions below

🔑 Questions for discussion:

1 Why was Dana offended?

2 What did Stan tell the speaker?

3 How long do most couples wait
   until they reveal they're pregnant?

短文聽讀 **Text**

I went for dinner with my friend, Dana, the other evening. Dana had a real glow about her and she ate a lot: two starters, a main course, and two desserts! "Eating for two?" I asked her. No sooner had I said those words than I was overwhelmed with regret. Dana was really offended. She was not pregnant, she informed me. I guess she was just hungry. Me and my big mouth!

Then, last night, I went for a few drinks with Dana's husband, Stan. After several beers, Stan got very talkative and let slip a secret: He and his wife are expecting a baby! So, Dana *is* pregnant! No sooner had he told me than I became very confused. Why did Dana hide the fact that she is pregnant? Stan informed me that most couples wait until 12 weeks to reveal their news, as this is when the chance of miscarriage significantly decreases. At least now I don't feel as bad about me and my big mouth!

前幾天晚上我和我的朋友黛娜一起去吃晚餐。黛娜容光煥發而且吃了很多：兩道開胃菜、一道主餐還有兩道甜點！我問她：「一人吃兩人補嗎？」一說完那些話，我就後悔不已。黛娜感到被冒犯了。她告訴我她並沒有懷孕。我猜她只是剛好餓了。我真是多嘴！

　　然後，昨晚我與黛娜的老公史丹去小酌幾杯。幾杯啤酒下肚後，史丹變得很健談還把祕密說溜了嘴：他和他老婆要生小孩了！所以，黛娜確實懷孕了！他一講完我就感到十分困惑。為什麼黛娜要隱瞞她懷孕的事情呢？史丹告訴我大部分的夫妻會等到第十二週後才會揭曉這個消息，因為這是流產機率大幅降低的時候。至少現在我不用為自己多嘴一事感到愧疚了！

單字片語　**Vocabulary and Phrases**

1. **glow** [glo] *n.* 容光煥發，紅潤光澤
2. **starter** [`stɑrtɚ] *n.* 開胃菜
3. **a main course**　　主餐，主菜
4. **overwhelm** [ˌovɚˈ(h)wɛlm] *vt.* (強烈的感情) 充溢，使不知所措
   be overwhelmed with...　　對……招架不住

   Nancy was overwhelmed with joy when she found her missing dog.
   南西找回失蹤的狗狗時內心喜不自勝。
5. **offend** [əˈfɛnd] *vt.* & *vi.* 冒犯，使生氣
6. **pregnant** [`prɛgnənt] *a.* 懷孕的
7. **inform** [ɪnˈfɔrm] *vt.* 通知，告知
8. **Me and my big mouth!**　　我真多嘴！
   big mouth　　多嘴的人
9. **talkative** [`tɔkətɪv] *a.* 健談的；多話的
10. **let slip sth / let sth slip**　　洩漏某事，把某事說漏嘴
11. **be expecting (a baby)**　　即將生小孩；有孕在身
    = be pregnant (with a baby)
12. **reveal** [rɪˈvil] *vt.* 揭露；透漏
    reveal the truth　　揭開真相

⑬ **miscarriage** [ˌmɪsˈkærɪdʒ] *n.* 流產
⑭ **significantly** [sɪgˈnɪfəkəntlɪ] *adv.* 顯著地；重大地
⑮ **decrease** [dɪˈkris] *vi. & vt.* (使) 變小，(使) 減少

實用詞句 Useful Expressions

🔖 否定副詞置句首的倒裝句：No sooner... than...

◆ no sooner 為否定副詞，置句首時其後接過去完成式的主句 (主詞與助動詞須倒裝) 及 than 引導的過去式副詞子句。

No sooner + had + 主詞+ 過去分詞 + than 引導的過去式副詞子句
一……就……

= Hardly / Scarcely + had + 主詞+ 過去分詞 + when / before引導的過去式副詞子句

注意

現在的英文多使用 "Hardly / Scarcely... when..."，較少使用 "Hardly / Scarcely... before..."。

ⓐ no sooner、hardly、scarcely 置句首時，其後的主詞與助動詞須倒裝：

No sooner had I gotten on the train than I saw Alex.
(助動詞 had 與主詞 I 須倒裝)

= Hardly had I gotten on the train when I saw Alex.
= Scarcely had I gotten on the train when I saw Alex.
我一上火車就看見艾力克斯。

No sooner had Ricky heard the news than he cried.
(助動詞 had 與主詞 Ricky 須倒裝)

= Hardly had Ricky heard the news when he cried.
= Scarcely had Ricky heard the news when he cried.
瑞奇一聽到該消息就哭了。

ⓑ no sooner 亦可置句中，此時主詞與助動詞不須倒裝，故上面的例句可改寫如下：

I had no sooner gotten on the train than I saw Alex.

= I had hardly gotten on the train when I saw Alex.

= I had scarcely gotten on the train when I saw Alex.

我一上火車就看見艾力克斯。

Ricky had no sooner heard the news than he cried.

= Ricky had hardly heard the news when he cried.

= Ricky had scarcely heard the news when he cried.

瑞奇一聽到該消息就哭了。

發音提示　Pronunciation

	glow [glo]	so [so]
❶ [O]	no [no]	most [most]
	overwhelm [ˌovɚˈ(h)wɛlm]	don't [dont]

	dessert [dɪˈzɝt]	his [hɪz]
❷ [Z]	those [ðoz]	confused [kənˈfjuzd]
	was [wɑz]	news [njuz]
	husband [ˈhʌzbənd]	

朗讀短文　Read aloud the text

🎙 請特別注意 [O]、[Z] 的發音。

　　I went for dinner with my friend, Dana, the other evening. Dana had a real glow about her and she ate a lot: two starters, a main course, and two desserts! "Eating for two?" I asked her. No sooner had I said those words than I was overwhelmed with regret. Dana was really offended. She was not pregnant, she informed me. I guess she was just hungry. Me and my big mouth!

CH 4
網路與社交

217

Then, last night, I went for a few drinks with Dana's husband, Stan. After several beers, Stan got very talkative and let slip a secret: He and his wife are expecting a baby! So, Dana *is* pregnant! No sooner had he told me than I became very confused. Why did Dana hide the fact that she is pregnant? Stan informed me that most couples wait until 12 weeks to reveal their news, as this is when the chance of miscarriage significantly decreases. At least now I don't feel as bad about me and my big mouth!

換句話說 Retell

Retell the text with the help of the words and expressions below.

glow, starter, a main course, overwhelm, offend, pregnant, inform, Me and my big mouth! talkative, let slip, be expecting a baby, reveal, miscarriage, significantly, decrease

討論題目 Free Talk

Talk on the following topic:

◆ Are you usually cautious about what you say?

Lesson 39

A Woman of Many Talents
多才多藝的女子

朗讀
▶
Lesson 39

搭配筆記聆聽會話 **Listen to the text with the help of the notes given**

version	版本
outfit	服裝
single	單身的
There's plenty more fish in the sea.	天涯何處無芳草。
bet	打賭

再次聆聽並回答問題 **Listen again and answer the questions below**

🔑 Questions for discussion:

1 What song did the woman's sister play at the concert last night?

2 What instrument can the woman's sister play?

3 What does the man want to know about the woman's sister?

🅐 Your sister is a really good piano player, Nancy.

🅑 Thanks, Jack. Yes, she is.

🅐 I loved that version of Beethoven's *Moonlight Sonata* she played at the concert last night.

🅑 Me, too. She can play other instruments as well.

🅐 Oh, really! What else can she play?

🅑 Well, not only can she play the piano, but she can also play the violin and the flute.

🅐 She's a woman of many talents! And not only is she talented, but she's also very beautiful. I loved that outfit she was wearing at the concert. Do you mind me asking… "Is she single?"

🅑 Jack! That's my sister you're having those thoughts about!

🅐 That doesn't answer my question, Nancy.

Ⓑ Sorry, Jack. Not only does she have a husband, but she also has two kids.

Ⓐ Oh, that's a shame.

Ⓑ Don't worry. There's plenty more fish in the sea.

Ⓐ I bet they can't play the piano as well as your sister...

Ⓐ 南西，妳姊姊真的是很棒的鋼琴演奏家。

Ⓑ 謝啦，傑克。是呀，她真的很棒。

Ⓐ 我喜歡她昨晚在音樂會上彈奏貝多芬《月光奏鳴曲》的那個版本。

Ⓑ 我也是。她也會演奏其他樂器。

Ⓐ 喔，真的嗎！她還會什麼樂器？

Ⓑ 嗯，她不僅會彈鋼琴，還會拉小提琴跟吹長笛。

Ⓐ 她真是多才多藝！而且她不只有天賦，還長得很漂亮。我喜歡她在音樂會上穿的服裝。妳介意我問……「她單身嗎？」

Ⓑ 傑克！你竟敢對我姊姊有非分之想！

Ⓐ 南西，妳沒有回答我的問題。

Ⓑ 抱歉，傑克。她不只有老公，還有兩個小孩。

Ⓐ 噢，那真可惜。

Ⓑ 別擔心。天涯何處無芳草。

Ⓐ 我敢說她們的鋼琴一定不如你姊姊彈得好……。

單字片語 Vocabulary and Phrases

❶ **version** [ˈvɝʒən] *n.* 版本
the latest / original version　最新 / 原始的版本

❷ **Beethoven**　貝多芬（出生於 1770 年的德國鋼琴家、作曲家，全名為 Ludwig van Beethoven）

❸ *Moonlight Sonata*　《月光奏鳴曲》（貝多芬最著名的作品之一）
sonata [səˈnɑtə] *n.* 奏鳴曲

❹ **instrument** [ˈɪnstrəmənt] *n.* 樂器

221

5 **a man / woman of many talents**　　多才多藝的人
talent [ˈtælənt] *n.* 天賦，才能

6 **talented** [ˈtæləntɪd] *a.* 有天賦的
= **gifted** [ˈgɪftɪd]

7 **outfit** [ˈaʊtˌfɪt] *n.* 全套服裝

8 **single** [ˈsɪŋɡl̩] *a.* 單身的，未婚的
married [ˈmærɪd] *a.* 已婚的

9 **There's plenty more fish in the sea.**
天涯何處無芳草。(口語)
= There're plenty of fish in the sea.（嚴謹的語法）
plenty [ˈplɛntɪ] *n.* 充足，眾多，大量

口語新技能 **New Skills**

動詞 mind 的用法

mind [maɪnd] *vt.* & *vi.* 介意，在意
mind + V-ing　　介意做……
Would you mind turning the volume down? I'm studying.
你介意把音量關小嗎？我正在念書。

◆ 下列為與動詞 mind 相關的片語：

a if you don't mind　　如果你不介意的話
I think I'll go home now, if you don't mind.
如果你不介意的話，我想我現在要回家了。

b Do you mind?　　(不耐煩且有點惱怒地說) 可以請你停止嗎？
Do you mind? I'm trying to sleep here.
可以請你停止嗎？我在睡覺耶。

c Don't mind me.　　不用在意我。
Don't mind me. I'm just going through here.
不用在意我。我只是經過這裡而已。

d mind you　　請注意，提醒你 (英式用法)
I'd love to play basketball with you.
Mind you, I used to be a professional player.
我很樂意跟你一起打籃球。不過提醒你，我以前是職業球員。

簡短對答　Quick Response

◆ Make quick responses to the sentences you hear.

討論題目　Free Talk

🔑 Talk on the following topic:

◆ If you could choose to be talented in something, what would you choose?

Lesson 40

Like Father, Like Son
有其父必有其子

搭配筆記聆聽短文 **Listen to the text with the help of the notes given**

mechanic	技師
wrench	扳手
trade	事業
partnership	合夥關係
profitable	有營收的，有利潤的

再次聆聽並回答問題 **Listen again and answer the questions below**

Questions for discussion:

1. How did Manny's father learn to be a mechanic?

2. What happened to Manny while he was cycling by the river?

3. How did Manny's grandfather feel about Manny fixing his own bike?

Manny's father is a mechanic. Manny likes to go to the garage when his father is working there. Like father, like son, he enjoys playing with machines and tools. If his father picks up a wrench, so does Manny. If his father checks a tire, so does Manny. He has learned a lot from his father. This is also how Manny's father learned to be a mechanic: from his own father.

One day, Manny's bike broke down while he was cycling by the river. Instead of calling his father, he studied what was wrong with the bike and successfully fixed it himself. He was very proud of himself, and so was his father when he came home. Even prouder was Manny's grandfather, who was delighted to see his trade being passed down to the next generation.

They decided to form a partnership and set up Delgado & Sons Garage to serve the needs of the local community. The residents of

the town loved seeing all three Delgado men working hard on their cars. The business was immensely popular, and also profitable.

曼尼的爸爸是個技師。當他爸爸在汽車修理廠工作時,曼尼也喜歡去那裡。有其父必有其子,他也喜歡玩機器和工具。如果他爸爸拿一個扳手,曼尼也會拿。如果他爸爸在檢查輪胎,曼尼也會照做。他向他爸爸學習了很多。這也是曼尼的爸爸怎麼學會做一個技師的:從他自己的爸爸身上學習。

有一天,曼尼在河邊騎自行車時,他的自行車壞了。他沒有打電話給他爸爸,反而是自己研究自行車的問題,並成功地靠著自己修好了自行車。他十分自豪,當他回家後,他爸爸也感到非常驕傲。曼尼的爺爺更是引以為傲,他很樂見他的事業可以被傳承到下一代。

他們決定要合夥並成立德爾加多父子汽車修理廠,為在地街坊提供服務。鎮裡的居民也喜歡看到德爾加多家的三位男士很努力地修車。這家公司很受歡迎也有不錯的營收。

單字片語 　Vocabulary and Phrases

❶ **mechanic** [məˋkænɪk] *n.* 技師

❷ **garage** [gəˋrɑʒ] *n.* 汽車修理廠;車庫

❸ **Like father, like son.** 　　有其父必有其子。(諺語)
　 Like mother, like daughter. 　有其母必有其女。(諺語)

❹ **wrench** [rɛntʃ] *n.* 扳手

❺ **break down** 　(車輛等)故障,拋錨
　 Our car broke down on our way to Manhattan.
　 我們的車在去曼哈頓的途中拋錨了。

❻ **cycle** [ˋsaɪkḷ] *vi.* 騎自行車

❼ **trade** [tred] *n.* 生意;行業,交易;手藝

❽ **pass sth down (to sb)** 　把某物往下傳承(給某人)

This antique vase was passed down to me from my grandmother.
這個古董花瓶是我奶奶傳給我的。

9 **partnership** [`partnɚˌʃɪp] *n.* 合夥關係，合作關係

10 **set up...** 建立……

= establish...

The manager proposed that a branch office be set up in London.
經理提議在倫敦開設一家分公司。

11 **serve** [sɝv] *vt.* & *vi.* 服務

12 **immensely** [ɪˈmɛnslɪ] *adv.* 非常，極

13 **profitable** [`prɑfɪtəbḷ] *a.* 有利潤的；有益的

實用詞句 **Useful Expressions**

🔑 簡應句

◆ 英文中的簡應句 (short response)，若為肯定句會用副詞 so、too 表「也……」，且使用 so 時，其後須採倒裝句構；若為否定句會使用副詞 neither、either 表「也不……」，若使用 neither，其後亦須採倒裝句構。在簡應句中使用上述四個副詞時須注意，句中一定要置對等連接詞來連接兩個句子。否定簡應句也可使用 nor (也不)，其後亦採倒裝句構，惟 nor 本身是連接詞，故使用時無須在其前置 and。

a 句中有 be 動詞
肯定句：
The living room is spacious, and so is the dining room.

= The living room is spacious, and the dining room is, too.
客廳很寬敞，飯廳也是。

否定句：
The living room isn't spacious, and neither is the dining room.

= The living room isn't spacious, and the dining room isn't, either.

= The living room isn't spacious, nor is the dining room.
客廳不寬敞，飯廳也不寬敞。

b 句中有助動詞

肯定句：

Jacob might join the hiking club, and so might Lucy.

= Jacob might join the hiking club, and Lucy might, too.
雅各可能會加入健行社，露西可能也會。

否定句：

Jacob might not join the hiking club, and neither might Lucy.

= Jacob might not join the hiking club, and Lucy might not, either.

= Jacob might not join the hiking club, nor might Lucy.
雅各可能不會加入健行社，露西可能也不會。

c 句中有一般動詞

肯定句：

Mary always makes plans beforehand, and so does Andy.

= Mary always makes plans beforehand, and Andy does, too.
瑪麗總會預先做好計畫，安迪也會。

否定句：

Mary never makes plans beforehand, and neither does Andy.

= Mary never makes plans beforehand, and Andy doesn't, either.

= Mary never makes plans beforehand, nor does Andy.
瑪麗從不會預先做好計畫，安迪也不會。

d 特殊情況

若在對話中使用簡應句，且兩句指的是同一人／物時，不論是肯定句或否定句，均使用 so 引導，且其後的句子不倒裝。此時 so 相當於 indeed (的確)。

Ⓐ This movie is thought-provoking.

Ⓑ So it is.

= Indeed it is.

Ⓐ 這部電影發人省思。

Ⓑ 它的確是。

A ou can't play basketball well.
B So I can't.
= Indeed I can't.
A 你不太會打籃球。
B 我的確不太會。

發音提示 Pronunciation

❶ [aʊ]	how [haʊ]	
	down [daʊn]	
	proud [praʊd]	
	town [taʊn]	

❷ [dʒ]	enjoy [ɪnˈdʒɔɪ]	
	generation [ˌdʒɛnəˈreʃən]	

朗讀短文 Read aloud the text

🔑 請特別注意 [aʊ]、[dʒ] 的發音。

Manny's father is a mechanic. Manny likes to go to the garage when his father is working there. Like father, like son, he enjoys playing with machines and tools. If his father picks up a wrench, so does Manny. If his father checks a tire, so does Manny. He has learned a lot from his father. This is also how Manny's father learned to be a mechanic: from his own father.

One day, Manny's bike broke down while he was cycling by the river. Instead of calling his father, he studied what was wrong with the bike and successfully fixed it himself. He was very proud of himself, and so was his father when he came home. Even prouder was Manny's grandfather, who was delighted to see his trade being passed down to the next generation.

229

They decided to form a partnership and set up Delgado & Sons Garage to serve the needs of the local community. The residents of the town loved seeing all three Delgado men working hard on their cars. The business was immensely popular, and also profitable.

換句話說 **Retell**

📌 Retell the text from "the perspective of Manny" with the help of the words and expressions below.

mechanic, garage, Like father, like son. wrench, break down, cycle, trade, be passed down to, partnership, set up, serve, immensely, profitable

討論題目 **Free Talk**

📌 Talk on the following topic:

◆ Do you think you and your father or mother are alike? If yes, in what ways are you alike?

Chapter 5

職場與交通

Lesson 41

A Job Offer
工作機會

Lesson 41

搭配筆記聆聽短文 Listen to the text with the help of the notes given

submit an application	遞交申請信
to no avail	徒勞無功
desperate	絕望的
interview	面試
portfolio	作品集

再次聆聽並回答問題 Listen again and answer the questions below

Questions for discussion:

1 What was Gordon looking for?

2 What should Gordon bring to the interview?

3 Does Gordon want to work at the company?

232

Gordon has been looking for a new job for a long period of time. He has submitted many applications to numerous companies, but to no avail. He was becoming desperate and was worried about how to pay the bills.

That was until today! He was offered an interview with a large advertising company. An e-mail was sent to him asking him to bring his advertising portfolio to show the account director. It's a famous advertising firm, and Gordon has always dreamed of working there. During the interview, Gordon impressed the account director so much that he was offered a job on the spot!

高登找新工作找了很久。他遞出了多封申請信給很多公司，但都徒勞無功。他逐漸感到絕望，並擔憂該如何支付帳單費用。

直到今天才有轉機！他獲得到大型廣告公司面試的機會。他收到了一封電子郵件請他攜帶向客戶經理展示的廣告作品集。這是間知名廣告公司，高登也一直夢想在那裡工作。在面試途中，高登讓客戶經理印象非常深刻，他當場給了高登工作邀約！

單字片語　**Vocabulary and Phrases**

❶ **period** [ˈpɪrɪəd] *n.* 一段時間
a period of time　　一段時間
a trial period　　　試用期間

❷ **submit** [səbˈmɪt] *vt.* 遞交
（三態為：submit, submitted [səbˈmɪtɪd], submitted）
The teacher told the students to submit an English composition at the end of the class.
老師告訴學生們在這節課結束時要繳交一篇英文作文。

❸ **application** [ˌæpləˈkeʃən] *n.* 申請 (書)
a job application　　　求職信
an application form　　申請表

❹ **numerous** [ˈnjumərəs] *a.* 許多的

❺ **desperate** [ˈdɛspərɪt] *a.* 絕望的；極度渴望的；奮不顧身的

❻ **offer** [ˈɔfɚ] *vt.* & *n.* 提供
offer sb sth　　提供某人某物
= offer sth to sb
This college offers the students lots of practical computer courses.
= This college offers lots of practical computer courses to the students.
這所大學提供學生多種實用電腦課程。

❼ **advertising** [ˈædvɚˌtaɪzɪŋ] *n.* 廣告 (業) (不可數)
radio / TV / newspaper advertising　　廣播 / 電視 / 報紙廣告

❽ **portfolio** [pɔrtˈfolɪˌo] *n.* 作品集

⑨ an account director 客戶經理

⑩ firm [fɜm] *n.* 公司 (= company [ˈkʌmpənɪ]) & *a.* 堅定的

⑪ dream [drim] *vi.* & *vt.* 夢想，希望
（三態為：dream, dreamed / dreamt [drɛmt], dreamed / dreamt）
dream of / about + N/V-ing　　夢想 / 希望 (從事)……
dream + that 子句　　　　　　夢想 / 希望……

Vicky dreamed of studying at Harvard University.
薇琪夢想就讀哈佛大學。

Vicky dreamed that one day she'd study at Harvard University.
薇琪夢想有一天能就讀哈佛大學。

實用詞句　Useful Expressions

❶ 表示「徒勞無功」的說法
　　to no avail　　徒勞無功，白費功夫
= to no purpose
= in vain
　　avail [əˈvel] *n.* 效用 (不可數)
　　vain [ven] *a.* 徒勞的，無用的；虛榮的
　　Blaire tried to avoid sunburn, but to no avail.
= Blaire tried to avoid sunburn, but to no purpose.
= Blaire tried to avoid sunburn, but in vain.
　　布萊兒試著避免被曬傷，但卻白費功夫。

　　We tried to convince Tommy to stop smoking, but to no avail.
= We tried to convince Tommy to stop smoking, but to no purpose.
= We tried to convince Tommy to stop smoking, but in vain.
　　我們曾試圖說服湯米戒菸，但是沒有用。

❷ 表示「當場」的說法
　　on the spot　　當場
　　spot [spɑt] *n.* 地點，場所；圓點
　　Jim was fired on the spot for stealing.
　　吉姆因為偷竊而當場遭到開除。

下列為與 spot 相關的片語：

put sb on the spot　　讓某人難堪 / 為難

Mary was put on the spot when her boyfriend proposed to her in front of a huge crowd.

瑪麗因為男朋友在眾多人面前求婚而感到難堪。

發音提示　**Pronunciation**

❶ [aɪ]	time [taɪm]
	advertising [ˈædvɚˌtaɪzɪŋ]

❷ [j]	new [nju]
	numerous [ˈnjumərəs]
	during [ˈdjurɪŋ]
	interview [ˈɪntɚˌvju]

朗讀短文　**Read aloud the text**

🎤 請特別注意 [aɪ]、[j] 的發音。

　　Gordon has been looking for a new job for a long period of time. He has submitted many applications to numerous companies, but to no avail. He was becoming desperate and was worried about how to pay the bills.

　　That was until today! He was offered an interview with a large advertising company. An e-mail was sent to him asking him to bring his advertising portfolio to show the account director. It's a famous advertising firm, and Gordon has always dreamed of working there. During the interview, Gordon impressed the account director so much that he was offered a job on the spot!

換句話說 Retell

📍 Retell the text with the help of the words and expressions below.

period, submit, application, numerous, desperate, offer, advertising, portfolio, an account director, firm, dream

討論題目 Free Talk

📍 Talk on the following topic:

◇ What is your dream job?

In a Video Conference
在視訊會議當中

搭配筆記聆聽會話 Listen to the text with the help of the notes given

quote	報價單
terms	條款
confirm	確定
That's good to hear.	真高興聽到這個消息。
forward	轉寄

再次聆聽並回答問題 Listen again and answer the questions below

Questions for discussion:

1 Did the man receive the quote?

2 Is the man's boss happy with the terms?

3 What will the man do with the signed document?

實用會話 Dialogue

Ⓐ Good morning, Brian. The quote was sent to you last night. Did you receive it?

Ⓑ Yes, Joyce, it was received at 7 p.m. It was given to my boss this morning.

Ⓐ Excellent. Is he happy with the terms?

Ⓑ Yes, I can confirm that we're happy with everything.

Ⓐ That's good to hear. Please sign the document and forward it to us.

Ⓑ Sure thing. When will we receive the items?

Ⓐ The goods will be supplied to you as soon as we receive the signed document.

Ⓑ I'll return it to you now.

Ⓐ Thank you.

Ⓐ 布萊恩，早安。報價單昨晚寄給你了。你有收到嗎？

Ⓑ 有的，喬伊絲，晚上七點收到的。我今早把它拿給我老闆了。

Ⓐ 太好了。他對條款還滿意嗎？

Ⓑ 是的，我可以確定我們對一切都很滿意。

Ⓐ 真高興聽到這個消息。請簽署文件後再轉寄給我們。

Ⓑ 沒問題。我們會在什麼時候收到貨品呢？

Ⓐ 我們一收到簽署過的文件便會馬上供貨給你們。

Ⓑ 我現在就寄還文件給妳。

Ⓐ 謝謝。

單字片語 Vocabulary and Phrases

❶ **quote** [kwot] *n.* 報價單 & *vt.* 報價；引用

❷ **be happy with...**　　對……感到滿意的
happy [ˋhæpɪ] *a.* 感到滿意的

We worked on the book for six months and are happy with the results.
我們撰寫這本書歷時六個月，並對結果感到很滿意。

❸ **term** [tɝm] *n.* 條款 (恆用複數)；期限；學期

❹ **confirm** [kənˋfɝm] *vt.* 確定；確認 (安排或日期等)
confirm + that 子句　　確定……
confirm a booking / reservation　　確認預訂

The manager confirmed that we had reached an agreement with that company.
經理證實我們已與那間公司達成協議。

I'm calling to confirm my dinner reservation for tomorrow night.
我打電話來是要確認明晚的晚餐預約資訊。

5 **forward** [`fɔrwəd] *vt.* 轉寄 (信件)
forward an e-mail　　轉寄電子郵件

6 **Sure thing.**　　當然，沒問題。
= No problem.
= Of course.

7 **supply** [sə`plaɪ] *vt.* 供應，供給，提供
（三態為：supply, supplied [sə`plaɪd], supplied）
supply sb with sth　　提供某人某物

The factory promised to supply us with everything we need.
該工廠保證會提供我們一切所需。

口語新技能 New Skills

🔔 表示對某消息感到高興的說法

That's good to hear.　　真高興聽到這個消息。

◆ 本句話常用於回應聽到某個令人感到高興、開心的消息時，亦有下列幾
種說法：
That's great to hear.
= It's good / great to hear that.
= I'm glad / happy to hear that / it.

Ⓐ Our school's baseball team won the game.

Ⓑ That's good to hear!

Ⓐ 我們學校的棒球隊贏得比賽了。

Ⓑ 真高興聽到這個消息！

簡短對答 Quick Response

◆ Make quick responses to the sentences you hear.

Talk on the following topic:

◆ Have you ever been in a video conference before?

Cut Me Some Slack
別刁難我

搭配筆記聆聽會話 **Listen to the text with the help of the notes given**

deadline	期限
pick up the pace	加快速度
urgent	緊急的
hold sb up	耽誤某人
deal	交易

再次聆聽並回答問題 **Listen again and answer the questions below**

🔑 Questions for discussion:

1 Is the woman done with the report?

2 Where did the woman go to do research?

3 When will the visitors arrive?

21　22　23

Deadline
Today!

28　31

🅐 Have you finished the report yet, Patricia?

🅑 Not yet, Mike. It'll be finished today, which was the agreed deadline.

🅐 Please pick up the pace, though. It's urgent.

🅑 I know. I had to do some research in the library, which is on the other side of the city. And I got stuck in a traffic jam, which held me up on my way back to the office. Cut me some slack, please.

🅐 I understand. I'm just nervous about the deal. Our visitors, who arrive tomorrow, will be expecting professionalism and perfection.

🅑 And they'll get it. Just give me a couple more hours.

🅐 派翠莎，妳完成報告了嗎？

🅑 還沒，麥克。報告會在今天完成，這是說好的期限。

🅐 但請加快速度。這很緊急。

B 我知道。我必須去圖書館做一些研究，圖書館在本市的另外一邊。而且我被堵在車陣中，這使我在回辦公室的路上耽誤了。請不要刁難我。

A 我了解。我只是對這筆交易感到很緊張。我們的訪客明天會到，他們期望看到專業與完美的水準。

B 他們會看到的。只要再給我幾個小時。

單字片語 Vocabulary and Phrases

1 agreed [əˈgrid] *a.* 商定的，一致同意的
What is the agreed price?
商定好的價錢是多少？

2 deadline [ˈdɛdˌlaɪn] *n.* 期限，截止日
meet the deadline　　趕上期限
miss the deadline　　錯過期限

3 pace [pes] *n.* 速度；進度；步調
pick up the pace　　加快速度
keep pace with...　　跟上……
= keep up with...
Carol finds it hard to keep pace with the times.
= Carol finds it hard to keep up with the times.
卡蘿認為要跟上時代很難。

4 urgent [ˈɝdʒənt] *a.* 緊急的，急迫的
urgency [ˈɝdʒənsɪ] *n.* 緊急 (不可數)
an urgent matter　　緊急事件
= a matter of urgency
Please tell Eric to call me back. It's an urgent matter.
麻煩請艾瑞克回電給我。這是緊急事件。

5 hold sb/sth up　　耽誤某人 / 某事
I was held up at the airport due to the snowstorm.
我因為暴風雪而在機場被耽誤了。

6 **deal** [dil] *n.* 交易；協議 & *vi.* 交易；處理（與介詞 with 並用）
（三態為：deal, dealt [dɛlt], dealt）

It's a deal.　　一言為定。

make a deal　　約定

You're practically making a deal with the devil by borrowing money from him.
你跟他借錢根本就是在跟惡魔做交易。

＊ practically [ˈpræktɪk!ɪ] *adv.* 幾乎，差不多；實際地

7 **professionalism** [prəˈfɛʃən!ɪzəm] *n.* 專業水準
professional [prəˈfɛʃən!] *a.* 專業的 & *n.* 專家

8 **perfection** [pɚˈfɛkʃən] *n.* 完美
perfect [ˈpɚfɪkt] *a.* 完美的
perfectly [ˈpɚfɪktlɪ] *adv.* 完美地

= to perfection

The desserts were made to perfection.

= The desserts were made perfectly.
這些甜點做得十分完美。

9 **a couple**　　一些，幾個
a couple of...　　一些……，幾個……

I'll stay at my friend's house for a couple more days.
我會在我朋友家裡多住個幾天。

John had a couple of friends over for a few drinks.
約翰邀請一些朋友來他家小酌幾杯。

口語新技能　**New Skills**

🔊 表示「不要刁難某人」的說法

cut sb some slack　　放某人一馬，不刁難某人
slack [slæk] *n.* 繩子鬆弛的部分

注意

a 本片語字面上的意思為「剪給我一些繩子鬆弛的部分」，意即希望可以鬆綁嚴格的規定，之後才衍伸出「放某人一馬，不刁難某人」之意。

b 下列片語的意思與「別刁難某人，放某人一馬」相似：

get off sb's back　　　　　別再嘮叨某人了
don't give sb a hard time　別為難某人
= stop giving sb a hard time
　Cut me some slack! I'm doing the best I can.
= Get off my back! I'm doing the best I can.
= Stop giving me a hard time! I'm doing the best I can.
　放我一馬吧！我已經盡全力了。

簡短對答　Quick Response

◆ Make quick responses to the sentences you hear.

討論題目　Free Talk

🎙 Talk on the following topic:

◆ How do you handle the pressure of meeting a deadline?

Being Multilingual
多國語能力

Lesson 44

搭配筆記聆聽短文 | **Listen to the text with the help of the notes given**

translator	翻譯員
fluent	流利的
export	出口
travel far and wide	到世界各地旅遊
indispensable	不可或缺的

再次聆聽並回答問題 | **Listen again and answer the questions below**

🎙 Questions for discussion:

1️⃣ What languages can Olivia speak fluently?

2️⃣ Why is the job at the car manufacturer ideal for Olivia?

3️⃣ Where will Olivia travel to next week?

Olivia, who is a translator, is multilingual. She can speak fluent English, French, Spanish, and Japanese. She works for a famous car manufacturer in Detroit. The company exports cars all over the world. Olivia, despite being new to the company, gets to travel far and wide with her job. This is an ideal job for Olivia because she can put her skills to good use.

Last week, when she was in Paris, she translated five important contracts so that deals worth millions of dollars could be secured. Next week, she will be traveling to London, Toronto, and back to Detroit. Olivia, through her intelligence and diligence, has quickly made herself indispensable to the company.

奧莉薇亞是一位翻譯員，她會說多國語言。她的英語、法語、西班牙語和日語都很流利。她任職於底特律的一間知名汽車製造商。該公司出口車子至世

界各地。儘管奧莉薇亞才剛進公司不久，她便有機會藉工作到世界各地旅行。這對奧莉薇亞來說是份理想的工作，因為她可以充分發揮她的所學。

　　奧莉薇亞上週在巴黎時翻譯了五份重要的合約，如此一來便能確保價值上百萬美元的交易到手。下週，她將會到倫敦、多倫多然後再回到底特律。奧莉薇亞憑藉她的才智與勤奮，已快速地讓自己成為公司中不可或缺的一員。

單字片語　Vocabulary and Phrases

1 translator [trænsˈletɚ] *n.* 翻譯員
　 interpreter [ɪnˈtɝprɪtɚ] *n.* 口譯員

2 multilingual [ˌmʌltaɪˈlɪŋgwəl / ˌmʌltɪˈlɪŋgwəl] *a.* 會說 / 寫多國語言的
　 bilingual [baɪˈlɪŋgwəl] *a.* 會說 / 寫雙語的

3 fluent [ˈfluənt] *a.* 流利的
　 be fluent in + 語言　　流利使用某語言

　 English is Kevin's native language, but he is more fluent in Spanish.
　 英語是凱文的母語，但是他西班牙語比較流利。

4 manufacturer [ˌmænjəˈfæktʃərɚ] *n.* 製造商

5 export [ɪksˈpɔrt] *vt.* 出口 & [ˈɛkspɔrt] *n.* 出口；出口商品
　 import [ɪmˈpɔrt] *vt.* 進口 & [ˈɪmpɔrt] *n.* 進口；進口商品

6 far and wide　　四處，各處

　 Airplanes enable us to travel far and wide.
　 飛機讓我們得以到各地旅行。

7 put sth to (good) use　　(充分) 利用 / 發揮某物

　 Chloe has put the information to good use.
　 克蘿伊充分地使用了這個資訊。

8 translate [trænsˈlet] *vt. & vi.* 翻譯
　 translate A into B　　將 A 翻譯為 B

　 I translated this short passage into English.
　 我將這篇短文翻譯成英語。

9 contract [ˈkɑntrækt] *n.* 合約

⑩ **deal** [dil] *n.* 交易，協定

⑪ **secure** [sɪˈkjʊr] *vt.* 獲得，得到
The team secured a place in the finals.
該隊伍取得進入決賽的席位。

⑫ **intelligence** [ɪnˈtɛlədʒəns] *n.* 智力，智慧 (不可數)

⑬ **diligence** [ˈdɪlədʒəns] *n.* 勤奮，勤勉 (不可數)

⑭ **indispensable** [ˌɪndɪˈspɛnsəbḷ] *a.* 必需的，不可或缺的
be indispensable to sb/sth　　對某人 / 某物是不可或缺的

實用詞句　Useful Expressions

🔖 介紹插入語

◆ 通常為了對一句話做補充、強調或引起對方注意，會在句子中間插入一
些單字、片語或子句，這些字詞或子句稱作「插入語」，且插入語並不會
影響到原句的文法結構，就算將插入語拿掉，也不會改變句子本來的結
構。插入語有諸多形式，列舉幾個常見的如下：

ⓐ 介詞片語作插入語
如本課第一段第五句：
Olivia, <u>despite being new to the company,</u> gets to travel far
　　　　　　　　插入語
and wide with her job.
儘管奧莉薇亞才剛進公司不久，她便有機會藉工作到世界各地旅
行。
及本課第二段最後一句：
Olivia, <u>through her intelligence and diligence,</u> has quickly
　　　　　　　　　插入語
made herself indispensable to the company.

奧莉薇亞憑藉她的才智與勤奮，已快速地讓自己
成為公司中不可或缺的一員。

b 副詞作插入語

Everyone says Lauren is nice. I, <u>however,</u> don't like her.

　　　　　　　　　　　　　插入語

大家都說蘿倫人很好。但是，我不喜歡她。

c 獨立分詞片語作插入語

Danny, <u>generally speaking,</u> is not as bad as I thought.

　　　　　　插入語

總之，丹尼不如我想得那麼壞。

d 獨立不定詞片語作插入語

Money is important, <u>to be sure,</u> but it's not everything.

　　　　　　　　插入語

可以肯定的是，金錢很重要，但它並非萬能。

e 子句作插入語

You can, <u>if (it is) necessary,</u> use my car.

　　　　　插入語

如有必要，你可以開我的車。

f 特殊情況

由「主詞＋表認知的動詞（例：believe、think、guess、suppose
等）」形成的插入語，於關係子句中使用時，其前後不會置任何標點
符號，且關係代名詞亦不受插入語影響。

Rachel is a woman who <u>I believe</u> can deal with tough problems.

　　　　　　　　　　　　插入語

我相信瑞秋是個可以解決困難問題的人。

（上述句中，who 作為原關係子句中的主詞，不會因加了插入語
I believe 而變成 whom。）

	car [kɑr]	was [wɑz]
① [ɑ]	far [fɑr]	dollar [ˈdɑlɚ]
	job [dʒɑb]	Toronto [təˈrɑnto]

	multilingual [ˌmʌltɪˈlɪŋgwəl]
② [m] （置於母音前）	famous [ˈfeməs]
	manufacturer [ˌmænjəˈfæktʃərɚ]
	million [ˈmɪljən]
	make [mek]

朗讀短文 **Read aloud the text**

🔑 請特別注意 [ɑ]、[m]（置於母音前）的發音。

Olivia, who is a translator, is multilingual. She can speak fluent English, French, Spanish, and Japanese. She works for a famous car manufacturer in Detroit. The company exports cars all over the world. Olivia, despite being new to the company, gets to travel far and wide with her job. This is an ideal job for Olivia because she can put her skills to good use.

Last week, when she was in Paris, she translated five important contracts so that deals worth millions of dollars could be secured. Next week, she will be traveling to London, Toronto, and back to Detroit. Olivia, through her intelligence and diligence, has quickly made herself indispensable to the company.

換句話說 Retell

Retell the text from "the perspective of Olivia" with the help of the words and expressions below.

translator, multilingual, fluent, manufacturer, export, far and wide, put sth to good use, translate, contract, deal, secure, intelligence, diligence, indispensable

討論題目 Free Talk

Talk on the following topic:

◆ Are you multilingual? If not, what are the languages you would like to learn?

朗讀 ▶
Lesson 45

Timely Help
及時的協助

Lesson 45

搭配筆記聆聽短文 **Listen to the text with the help of the notes given**

a marketing specialist	行銷專員
pay the bills	支付帳單
an advertising campaign	廣告活動
relevant experience	相關經驗
on schedule	準時

再次聆聽並回答問題 **Listen again and answer the questions below**

🔑 Questions for discussion:

1️⃣ What does Jasmine do for a living now?

2️⃣ What was Jasmine asked to do for work?

3️⃣ Why was Jasmine worried about the assignment?

CH 5 職場與交通

255

Jasmine was thrilled to find a job as a marketing specialist. She had been looking for work for a few months, and had started to worry about how she was going to pay the bills. But for this new job, she might have had to borrow money from her parents. Even better, the work proved to be exciting and challenging, and she liked all her colleagues.

During her second week on the job, Jasmine was asked to complete a very difficult assignment—plan an entire advertising campaign for a big client. She had never done that before, so she was worried that she didn't have the relevant experience to complete the task by the deadline. Thankfully, her coworker, Amy, was nice enough to give her some assistance so that she could finish the work on schedule. But for Amy's timely help, she never would have finished it on time.

潔絲敏很興奮終於找到行銷專員的工作。她已經找工作找了幾個月，並開始擔心她要如何支付帳單。要不是有這份新工作，她可能需要向她的爸媽借錢。更好的是，結果這份工作內容令人興奮又有挑戰性，她也很喜歡每位同事。

　　在她上班的第二週，潔絲敏被要求完成一項非常艱難的任務——幫一位重要客戶規劃一整場的廣告活動。她從未做過那種事，所以很擔心她並沒有相關的經驗可以在期限內完成工作。幸好，她的同事艾咪人很好，給了她一些協助讓她得以準時完成工作。要不是艾咪的及時協助，她不可能準時完成工作。

單字片語　Vocabulary and Phrases

1 thrill [θrɪl] *vt.* 使興奮 & *n.* 興奮

Tim was thrilled to meet the movie star in person.
提姆很興奮能見到那位電影明星本人。

2 marketing [ˋmɑrkɪtɪŋ] *n.* 行銷；促銷 (不可數)

3 specialist [ˋspɛʃəlɪst] *n.* 專員；專家 (= expert [ˋɛkspɝt])

4 look for...　　尋找……

Larry has spent an hour looking for his lost wallet.
賴瑞已經花了一個小時尋找他遺失的錢包。

5 challenging [ˋtʃælɪndʒɪŋ] *a.* 有挑戰性的

6 colleague [ˋkɑlig] *n.* 同事 (= coworker [ˋko͵wɝkɚ])

7 assignment [əˋsaɪnmənt] *n.* 任務，工作 (= task [tæsk])

8 advertising [ˋædvɚ͵taɪzɪŋ] *n.* 廣告 (不可數)
advertisement [͵ædvɚˋtaɪzmənt / ˋædvɚ͵taɪzmənt] *n.* 廣告

9 campaign [kæmˋpen] *n.* 活動；運動

10 relevant [ˋrɛləvənt] *a.* 相關的，有關的

Do you have any relevant experience in this field?
你有這領域的相關經驗嗎？

11 deadline [ˋdɛd͵laɪn] *n.* 期限，截止日期
meet the deadline　　趕在截止日前完成

⓬ **on schedule** 準時，按進度
ahead of schedule 進度超前
behind schedule 進度落後

Beth is so efficient that she always
finishes her work on schedule.
貝絲很有效率，她總是會準時完成工作。

⓭ **timely** [ˈtaɪmlɪ] *a.* 及時的，適時的
Thanks to his timely warning, we were able to avoid the traffic.
由於他適時的警告，我們得以避開車潮。

實用詞句 Useful Expressions

❶ 表示「要不是……」的說法

◆ 本課旨在介紹 but for 的用法。but for 表示「要不是」或「若非」，之後須
接名詞，只能使用於下列兩種情況中：

Ⓐ 與現在事實相反的假設語氣

But for + 名詞, 主詞 + | could | + V
                       | would
                       | might
                       | should
                       | ought to |

要不是 / 若非……就……

注意

本句型可用「If it were not for + 名詞, ...」替換。

But for your company, I would be bored and lonely.
= If it were not for your company, I would be bored and
lonely.
要不是你的陪伴，我會既無聊又寂寞。

258

b 與過去事實相反的假設語氣

But for + 名詞, 主詞 + | could | + have + p.p.
| would |
| might |
| should |
| ought to |

要不是 / 若非當時……就……

注意

本句型可用「If it had not been for + 名詞, ….」替換。

But for my parents' support, I would have given up.

= If it had not been for my parents' support, I would have given up.

要不是我父母當時的支持，我或許就會放棄。

2 Thankfully, her coworker, Amy, was nice enough to give her some assistance...　幸好，她的同事艾咪人很好，給了她一些協助……。

本句使用下列句型：

形容詞 / 副詞 + enough to + V　夠……以致於能……

注意

本句型中，enough 為副詞，表示「足夠」，修飾其前的形容詞或副詞。

John is old enough to stay home by himself.

約翰年紀夠大，可以自己待在家。

Tina is not tall enough to ride the roller coaster.

蒂娜不夠高，不能搭雲霄飛車。

He finished his work quickly enough to meet the deadline.

他夠快完成工作，能趕上期限。

發音提示 Pronunciation

❶ [æ]

Jasmine [ˈdʒæsmɪn]	plan [plæn]
as [æz]	advertising [ˈædvɚˌtaɪzɪŋ]
have [hæv]	campaign [kæmˈpen]
and [ænd]	task [tæsk]
challenging [ˈtʃælɪndʒɪŋ]	thankfully [ˈθæŋkfəlɪ]
ask [æsk]	

❷ [ŋ]

marketing [ˈmɑrkɪtɪŋ]	challenging [ˈtʃælɪndʒɪŋ]
looking [ˈlʊkɪŋ]	during [ˈdjʊrɪŋ]
going [ˈgoɪŋ]	advertising [ˈædvɚtaɪzɪŋ]
exciting [ɪkˈsaɪtɪŋ]	thankfully [ˈθæŋkfəlɪ]

朗讀短文 Read aloud the text

🔑 請特別注意 [æ]、[ŋ] 的發音。

Jasmine was thrilled to find a job as a marketing specialist. She had been looking for work for a few months, and had started to worry about how she was going to pay the bills. But for this new job, she might have had to borrow money from her parents. Even better, the work proved to be exciting and challenging, and she liked all her colleagues.

During her second week on the job, Jasmine was asked to complete a very difficult assignment—plan an entire advertising campaign for a big client. She had never done that before, so she was worried that she didn't have the relevant experience to complete the task by the deadline. Thankfully, her coworker, Amy, was nice enough to give her some assistance so that she could finish the work on schedule. But for Amy's timely help, she never would have finished it on time.

換句話說 Retell

📌 Retell the text from "the perspective of Jasmine" with the help of the words and expressions below.

thrill, marketing, specialist, look for, challenging, colleague, assignment, advertising, campaign, relevant, deadline, on schedule, timely

討論題目 Free Talk

📌 Talk on the following topic:

◆ What was the most challenging task you were asked to do for your job?

You're a Lifesaver
你真是救星

搭配筆記聆聽會話 **Listen to the text with the help of the notes given**

headlight	車頭燈
overnight	整晚
Don't mention it.	別客氣。
check out...	檢查……
injury	傷害

再次聆聽並回答問題 **Listen again and answer the questions below**

🎤 Questions for discussion:

1 What is wrong with the woman's car?

2 What will the man do for the woman?

3 What happened to the woman's mom?

A I don't believe it. My car won't start.

B What's the problem?

A The battery is dead. I think I left my headlights on overnight. I'm supposed to be taking my mom to the hospital this morning.

B Don't worry. I'll take her. I'll just inform the office that I'll be late for work today.

A Thank you. You're a lifesaver. But for you, I wouldn't know what I should do.

B Don't mention it. It's nothing serious with your mom, I hope?

A Not really. She sprained her ankle while dancing last night, so she just needs to get it checked out. But for this injury, she would be in perfect health.

B I hope I'm as fit as your mom when I'm 80!

A 太難以置信了。我的車發動不了。

B 怎麼了？

A 電池沒電了。我猜想車頭燈整晚都開著。我今天早上應該
要帶我媽媽去醫院的。

B 別擔心。我會帶她去。我只需要告訴公司我今天上班會晚到。

A 謝謝。你真是救星。要不是你，我不知道我該怎麼辦。

B 別客氣。妳媽媽沒生什麼嚴重的病，是嗎？

A 還好。她昨晚去跳舞的時候扭傷腳踝，所以她只需要去檢查一下。若非這個
傷，她會非常健康。

B 我希望我八十歲的時候跟妳媽媽一樣健朗！

單字片語 Vocabulary and Phrases

❶ **headlight** [ˈhɛdˌlaɪt] *n.* 車頭燈（因為車頭燈有兩個，故常用複數）

❷ **overnight** [ˌovəˈnaɪt] *adv.* 整晚；一夕之間
I stayed at my friend's house overnight.
我在朋友家待了整晚。

❸ **be supposed to V**　　理應……
Kevin was supposed to organize next week's meeting.
凱文應該要安排下週的會議。

❹ **lifesaver** [ˈlaɪfˌsevə] *n.* 救星；救命的人 / 物
Seat belts are real lifesavers when it comes to car accidents.
談到車禍，安全帶真的是救星。

❺ **sprain** [spren] *vt.* 扭到 & *n.* 扭傷
Michael sprained his ankle while playing basketball.
麥可打籃球的時候扭傷他的腳踝。

❻ **injury** [ˈɪndʒərɪ] *n.* 傷害
injure [ˈɪndʒə] *vt.* 傷害

❼ **fit** [fɪt] *a.* 健壯的，健康的

口語新技能 New Skills

🎙 表示「檢查某事物」的說法

check out sth / check sth out　檢查某事物

The doctor checked out the patient's arm to see if anything was broken.

醫生檢查那位病患的手臂看看是否有任何骨頭斷裂。

注意

◆ 本片語亦有下列意思：

ⓐ check sth out　看一看（某活動、演唱會、電影等）

A new restaurant just opened. Let's go check it out.

新的餐廳剛開幕。咱們去看看吧。

ⓑ check out sth / check sth out　查證／核實某事物

The police need to check out the suspect's alibi.

警方需要查證嫌犯的不在場證明。

＊ alibi [ˈæləˌbaɪ] *n.* 不在場證明

ⓒ check out sth / check sth out　（在圖書館）借書

Kate checked out some books from the library.

凱特從圖書館借了一些書。

CH
5
職場與交通

簡短對答 Quick Response

◆ Make quick responses to the sentences you hear.

討論題目 Free Talk

🎙 Talk on the following topic:

◆ Have you ever helped someone when they're in a desperate situation?

The Glass Ceiling Effect
玻璃天花板效應

搭配筆記聆聽短文 **Listen to the text with the help of the notes given**

metaphor	比喻
minority	少數族群
middle management	中階管理
an invisible barrier	隱形的障礙
an unconscious prejudice	隱性偏見

再次聆聽並回答問題 **Listen again and answer the questions below**

Questions for discussion:

1 What is the glass ceiling effect?

2 What groups of people are affected by the glass ceiling effect the most?

3 What is one of the reasons that caused the glass ceiling effect?

短文聽讀 **Text**

We use the glass ceiling metaphor to describe the phenomenon where certain groups of people are unable to reach the top in an organization. In most cases, these people are women (or minorities) who can only rise to the level of middle management in a company. They can see the top and they hope they can reach it. But, in fact, there is an invisible barrier that keeps them from getting there. We all wish that there were no glass ceiling; unfortunately, however, it's still quite common.

But what causes it? One reason is that, because many senior management positions in companies are already occupied by men, there is an unconscious prejudice against women joining their "boys' club." Another possible reason is that women have more family commitments, so are less likely to compete for higher-paying jobs with better perks. We must all work together and hope that the glass ceiling can be shattered soon!

我們用玻璃天花板來比喻某些群體在某組織中無法晉升到高階職位的現象。大部分的情況中,這些人是女性(或少數族群),她們只能在公司晉升到中階管理職位。她們可以望見高階職位,也期許自己能攀升上去。但事實卻是有一道隱形的障礙阻攔她們升遷。我們都期望沒有玻璃天花板這種現象;然而不幸的是,它仍普遍存在。

那是什麼因素造成的呢?其中一個原因是,因為公司內大多的高階管理職位已由男性擔任,而這些人對於女性加入他們的「男子俱樂部」產生隱性偏見。另一個可能的原因為女性在家庭照顧上有更多責任,所以不太會去爭取待遇更好的高薪工作。我們一定要一起努力,並冀望可以早日打破玻璃天花板的現象!

單字片語 Vocabulary and Phrases

❶ the glass ceiling (effect)　　玻璃天花板(效應)
ceiling [ˈsilɪŋ] *n.* 天花板
effect [ɪˈfɛkt] *n.* 效應;影響;結果

❷ metaphor [ˈmɛtəˌfɔr] *n.* 隱喻,暗喻
simile [ˈsɪmrlɪ] *n.* 明喻

❸ top [tɑp] *n.* (公司、組織中) 最重要的職位;最高的地位

❹ minority [maɪˈnɔrətɪ] *n.* 少數民族 / 群體;少數

❺ middle management　　中階管理階層
management [ˈmænɪdʒmənt] *n.* 管理階層

❻ invisible [ɪnˈvɪzəbḷ] *a.* 無形的;肉眼看不見的
visible [ˈvɪzəbḷ] *a.* 顯而易見的;肉眼可見的

❼ barrier [ˈbærɪr] *n.* 障礙 (物)
the language barrier　　語言障礙
be a barrier to...　　是……的障礙 / 絆腳石
= be an obstacle to...
= be a hindrance to...

Being too arrogant is the biggest barrier to success.
過於自傲是成功最大的絆腳石。

8 senior management　　高階管理階層

= top management

senior [`sɪnjɚ] *a.* 地位較高的

9 occupy [`ɑkjəˌpaɪ] *vt.* 擔任（職位）；占據
（三態為：occupy, occupied [`ɑkjəˌpaɪd], occupied）

Mr. White occupies an important position in the company.
懷特先生在該公司身居要職。

10 unconscious [ʌn`kɑnʃəs] *a.* 未意識到的；不省人事的

11 prejudice [`prɛdʒədɪs] *n.* 偏見，成見
have a prejudice against...　　對……有偏見

12 commitment [kə`mɪtmənt] *n.* 承諾要做的事；必須要做的事
family / work commitments　　家庭義務 / 工作承諾

13 compete [kəm`pit] *vi.* 競爭
compete (with sb) for sth
（與某人）競爭某物

An estimated 200 contestants will
compete for the championship.
預估將有兩百名參賽者角逐冠軍。

dvphotoworld / Shutterstock.com

14 shatter [`ʃætɚ] *vt. & vi.* (使) 粉碎，(使) 破碎

Jonathan dropped the picture frame by accident and shattered the
glass.
強納森不小心把相框摔在地上，打碎了玻璃。

實用詞句　**Useful Expressions**

1 動詞 wish 的用法

◆ wish 作及物動詞表「希望」，其後可接 that 子句作受詞，亦可接不定詞
片語作受詞。

CH
5

職場與交通

a 接 that 子句

wish 後接 that 子句時，會形成假設語氣。故表與「現在事實相反」時，子句要用過去式；若表與「過去事實相反」則要用過去完成式。切記，wish 後的 that 子句時態沒有現在式。

1) 與現在事實相反

   I wish (that) I can go scuba diving with you. (×)

→ I wish (that) I could go scuba diving with you. (✓)

   我真希望能跟你一起去潛水。

2) 與過去事實相反

   I wished (that) I could go scuba diving with you. (×)

→ I wished (that) I could have gone scuba diving with you. (✓)

   我真希望當時能跟你一起去潛水。

b 接不定詞片語（此時用法等同於 hope）

   Kathy wishes to travel to outer space one day.

= Kathy hopes to travel to outer space one day.

   凱西希望有朝一日能到外太空旅遊。

2 動詞 hope 的用法

◇ hope 作及物動詞亦表「希望」，其後可接 that 子句或不定詞片語作受詞，惟接 that 子句時，用法與 wish 不同。

a 接 that 子句

hope 後接 that 子句時，that 子句可使用一般時態。

1) 表現在的狀況，使用現在式

   Elisa hopes that she can save enough money for a new cellphone.

   伊莉莎希望她可以存夠錢買一臺新手機。

2) 表將來的狀況，使用未來式

   I hope that I will be able to travel around Europe in the future.

   我希望將來可以遊遍歐洲。

3) 表進行的狀況，使用現在進行式

   I hope that Matt is feeling better.

   我希望麥特身體好點了。

4) 表完成的狀況，使用現在完成式

Mom hopes that we <u>have</u> already <u>cleaned</u> our bedrooms.

老媽希望我們已經把房間清理乾淨。

b 接不定詞片語（此時用法等同於 wish）

Jonas once hoped <u>to become</u> a veterinarian.

= Jonas once wished <u>to become</u> a veterinarian.

喬納斯曾經希望成為一名獸醫。

發音提示　**Pronunciation**

❶ [ɑ]	phenomenon [fə`nɑmə͵nɑn]	
	top [tɑp]	
	common [`kɑmən]	
	occupy [`ɑkjə͵paɪ]	
	unconscious [ʌn`kɑnʃəs]	
	possible [`pɑsəbḷ]	
	job [dʒɑb]	

❷ [ʃ]	organization [͵ɔrgənə`zeʃən]	
	wish [wɪʃ]	
	position [pə`zɪʃən]	
	unconscious [ʌn`kɑnʃəs]	
	shatter [`ʃætɚ]	

CH
5

職場與交通

271

朗讀短文 Read aloud the text

📍 請特別注意 [ɑ]、[ʃ] 的發音。

　　We use the glass ceiling metaphor to describe the phenomenon where certain groups of people are unable to reach the top in an organization. In most cases, these people are women (or minorities) who can only rise to the level of middle management in a company. They can see the top and they hope they can reach it. But, in fact, there is an invisible barrier that keeps them from getting there. We all wish that there were no glass ceiling; unfortunately, however, it's still quite common.

　　But what causes it? One reason is that, because many senior management positions in companies are already occupied by men, there is an unconscious prejudice against women joining their "boys' club." Another possible reason is that women have more family commitments, so are less likely to compete for higher-paying jobs with better perks. We must all work together and hope that the glass ceiling can be shattered soon!

換句話說 Retell

📍 Retell the text with the help of the words and expressions below.

the glass ceiling, metaphor, top, minority, middle management, invisible, barrier, senior management, occupy, unconscious, prejudice, commitment, compete, shatter

討論題目 Free Talk

📍 Talk on the following topic:

◇ Do you agree that women can be good leaders?

Lesson 48

Working Overtime
加班

搭配筆記聆聽會話 **Listen to the text with the help of the notes given**

work week	一週的工作時間
otherwise	不然,否則
workload	工作量
lighten	減輕
figure	想,認為

再次聆聽並回答問題 **Listen again and answer the questions below**

Questions for discussion:

1. Why can't the man join the woman?
2. Is the man happy with his salary?
3. What does the woman suggest the man do?

CH
5
職場與交通

273

🅐 Ready for that beer, Jim?

🅑 Sorry, Kate. I've still got a few more hours' work to do.

🅐 You're working late again? They must be paying you well!

🅑 I wish. I'm getting lousy pay for a 60-hour work week. They just keep piling it on.

🅐 They must have thought you didn't have enough work to do; otherwise they wouldn't have given you more.

🅑 They may have thought so, but I can barely handle my original workload.

🅐 You should tell your supervisors. Maybe they can lighten your workload by employing another person.

🅑 Ha! You must have never met my boss! There's more chance of me winning the lottery.

Ⓐ Can I give you a hand, then?

Ⓑ You must have something better to do on a Friday night, Kate.

Ⓐ I figured the quicker you finish, the quicker we can go for that beer!

Ⓐ 吉姆，準備好去喝杯啤酒了嗎？

Ⓑ 凱特，抱歉。我還得花幾個小時工作。

Ⓐ 你又要加班了嗎？他們給你的薪水一定不錯！

Ⓑ 但願如此。我一週工作六十小時卻只拿到一丁點薪水。他們只是不停地增加我的工作。

Ⓐ 他們一定認為你的工作還不夠多；不然他們不會給你更多工作。

Ⓑ 或許他們是這麼想的，但我快要處理不來原先的工作量了。

Ⓐ 你應該告訴你的經理。他們也許可以僱用另外一個人來減輕你的工作量。

Ⓑ 哈！妳一定沒有見過我的老闆！我中樂透的機會還比較大。

Ⓐ 那麼，我可以幫你嗎？

Ⓑ 凱特，妳週五晚上一定有更好的事情可以做。

Ⓐ 我想你愈快完成工作，我們就愈快可以去喝杯啤酒！

單字片語 Vocabulary and Phrases

❶ work week　　一週的工作時間（美式用法）
= workweek
= working week（英式用法）
　a 40-hour work week　　一週工作四十小時

❷ pile sth on / pile on sth　　增加／積累（壓力、工作等）
The teacher piled on the pressure by giving her students yet another test.
這位老師又給她的學生一份考試，讓他們壓力增加。

❸ otherwise [ˈʌðɚˌwaɪz] adv. 否則，要不然

❹ barely [ˈbɛrlɪ] adv. 幾乎不，勉強

Jack can barely pay his rent, much less buy a new car.
傑克連房租都快付不出來，更別說要買一臺新車了。

5 handle [`hændl̩] *vt.* 處理
= deal with...
= cope with...

Holly <u>handled</u> the problem calmly and quickly.
= Holly <u>dealt with</u> the problem calmly and quickly.
= Holly <u>coped with</u> the problem calmly and quickly.
荷莉冷靜且快速地處理了這個問題。

6 workload [`wɝk͵lod] *n.* 工作量
a heavy workload　　工作繁重

7 supervisor [`supɚ͵vaɪzɚ] *n.* 經理；監督者

8 lighten [`laɪtn̩] *vt.* 減輕，減少
lighten the burden / workload　　減輕負擔 / 工作量

9 win the lottery　　中樂透
lottery [`lɑtərɪ] *n.* 樂透
a lottery ticket　　一張彩券

10 figure [`fɪgjɚ] *vt.* 認為，想
We figured that it was impossible to cross the fast-flowing river.
我們認為想橫渡那條湍急的河流是不可能的。

口語新技能　**New Skills**

1 表示「幫助某人」的說法
give sb a (helping) hand　　幫助某人
Blaire kindly gave me a hand when I ran into trouble.
布萊兒在我遇上麻煩時好心對我伸出援手。

注意

◆ 下列片語亦可表示「幫助某人」：

a lend sb a (helping) hand　　幫助某人
Could you lend me a hand with this box?
你可以幫我搬這個箱子嗎？

b do sb a favor　　幫某人忙

Could you do me a favor by opening the window?

你可以幫我開個窗嗎？

c assist sb in + V-ing　　幫忙某人……

I assisted Mom in doing chores last night.

我昨晚協助媽媽做家事。

2 I figured the quicker you finish, the quicker we can go for that beer!

我想你愈快完成工作，我們就愈快可以去喝杯啤酒！

◆ 本句使用下列固定句構：

the + 比較級..., the + 比較級...　　愈……，就愈……

The hotter the weather is, the fewer people will go to a hot spring.

天氣愈熱，就愈少人會去泡溫泉。

簡短對答　Quick Response

◆ Make quick responses to the sentences you hear.

討論題目　Free Talk

Talk on the following topic:

◆ What would you do if your workload were too heavy?

CH 5 職場與交通

277

Lesson 49

Cycling to Work
騎自行車上班

搭配筆記聆聽會話 Listen to the text with the help of the notes given

lest	免得
get beyond a joke	(情況已超越玩笑的程度) 令人惱怒的
congestion	(交通) 擁擠，堵塞
build up...	增強……
in no time	馬上

再次聆聽並回答問題 Listen again and answer the questions below

Questions for discussion:

1 What is the woman wearing?

2 Why doesn't the woman want to drive to work?

3 What does the woman suggest to the man?

A Good morning, Pam. Why are you going to work wearing bike shorts?

B I've decided to cycle to work instead of driving, lest I be stuck in traffic again.

A Yeah, the traffic jams are getting beyond a joke. There's so much congestion. You should have done this a long time ago.

B I know. It's also good for my health.

A Not to mention it's good for the environment. I should have done it, too.

B How about we start cycling to work together, then?

A Well, I'm not a very fast cyclist. I think I'd have to set off at 5 a.m. lest I be late every morning!

B Don't worry; it just takes a bit of practice. Come out with me in the evenings and you'll build up your speed in no time.

A Thanks, Pam. I may take you up on that offer!

A 潘姆，早安。為什麼妳穿著自行車短褲去上班？

B 我決定要騎自行車而非開車去上班，免得我又被困在車陣中。

A 是呀，交通堵塞真的很惱人。太多堵車的情況了。妳老早就該這麼做了。

B 我知道。這也有益於我的健康。

A 更不用說這對環境良好。我也早該這麼做。

B 那麼我們開始一起騎自行車上班怎麼樣呢？

A 喔，我自行車騎得不快。我想我得要清晨五點出發，免得我每天早上都遲到！

B 別擔心；只要練習一下就好。傍晚的時候和我一起出去，你馬上就可以騎得很快了。

A 謝啦，潘姆。我可能會接受你的提議！

單字片語　**Vocabulary and Phrases**

① **cycle** [ˈsaɪkl̩] 騎自行車 (英式用法)
= bike [baɪk] (美式用法)

② **be / get stuck in traffic**
被困在車陣中
stuck [stʌk] *a.* 卡住的，無法動彈的

③ **a traffic jam**　　交通堵塞，塞車

④ **get beyond a joke**　　(情況已超越玩笑的程度) 令人惱怒的
I used to think Ryan was funny, but his teasing is getting beyond a joke.
我之前認為萊恩很風趣，但他的揶揄開始令人感到惱怒。

⑤ **congestion** [kənˈdʒɛstʃən] *n.* 擁擠現象 (不可數)
traffic congestion　　交通擁擠現象

6 **cyclist** [ˈsaɪklɪst] *n.* 騎自行車的人，自行車騎士
= biker [ˈbaɪkɚ]

7 **set off / out**　　出發，啟程
set off / out for + 地方　　出發前往某地
= depart for + 地方
= leave for + 地方

As soon as Karen finished reading the novel, she got the urge to set off for Provence.
凱倫一讀完那本小說後，她就有股想出發去普羅旺斯的衝動。

8 **build up...**　　增強 (體力)；增進 (情感)
(三態為：build [bɪld], built [bɪlt], built)
build up one's strength　　增強某人的體力
build up trust　　建立信任

9 **in no time**　　很快地

10 **take sb up on sth**　　接受某人提出的某事
take sb up on an offer / a suggestion　　接受某人的提議 / 建議

I'll take you up on that advice.
我會接受你給予的建議。

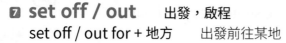

口語新技能　New Skills

🔑 表示「更不用說」的說法

Not to mention...　　更不用說……
= Not to speak of...
= To say nothing of...

注意

"Not to speak of..." 與 "To say nothing of..." 後需要接 the fact 作介詞 of 的受詞，才能接 that 子句作 the fact 的同位語。

Not to mention (that) it's good for the environment.
= Not to speak of the fact that it's good for the environment.
= To say nothing of the fact that it's good for the environment.
更不用說這對環境良好。

簡短對答 **Quick Response**

◆ Make quick responses to the sentences you hear.

討論題目 **Free Talk**

🎤 Talk on the following topic:

◆ How do you usually commute? Would you like to try a different way?

Self-Driving Cars
自動駕駛汽車

搭配筆記聆聽短文 Listen to the text with the help of the notes given

investment	投資
convince	說服
transport	交通工具
unregulated	無規範的
hack	(駭客) 入侵電腦系統

再次聆聽並回答問題 Listen again and answer the questions below

Questions for discussion:

1 What is a self-driving car?

2 What does the speaker say about the self-driving car industry?

3 What are self-driving cars vulnerable to?

283

A self-driving car is a car that can drive with little or no human input. It's such a safe form of driving that it's estimated thousands of lives would be saved each year if everyone used self-driving cars. However, more investment is needed so that companies can produce more self-driving cars. And the public needs to be convinced of their safety so that they are more willing to buy them.

No form of transport can be completely safe, but what are the specific concerns related to self-driving cars? The industry is currently unregulated, which means that there are no established safety standards. The transition from manual cars to self-driving cars could be chaotic, as there would be a mixture of vehicles on the road. And self-driving cars could be vulnerable to hacking and computer malfunctions. These safety issues need to be addressed so that the potential safety benefits can be unleashed. Only when this is done can self-driving cars possibly be the future of driving.

自動駕駛汽車（自駕車）是一種幾乎不需要人力操縱的汽車。這是一種很安全的駕駛模式，因此假若大家都開始使用自動駕駛汽車，估計每年可以挽回好幾千條性命。然而，這需要更多投資，如此一來企業才能生產更多自動駕駛汽車。而且它們的安全性必須讓大眾信服，這樣大家才會有更高的購買意願。

沒有一種交通工具是百分百安全的，但是與自動駕駛汽車相關的疑慮是什麼呢？這種產業目前沒有規範，這意味著沒有已建立完善的安全標準。從手動開車到自動駕駛的過度期可能會很混亂，因為路上會參雜各種車輛。自動駕駛汽車也可能容易受到駭客入侵和電腦故障的影響。這些安全問題需要被解決，才能使潛在的安全好處發揮作用。唯有這麼做，自動駕駛汽車才有可能是未來的開車方式。

單字片語 Vocabulary and Phrases

❶ self-driving [ˌsɛlfˈdraɪvɪŋ] *a.* 自動駕駛的
a self-driving car　　自動駕駛汽車

❷ input [ˈɪnˌpʊt] *n.* 投入，貢獻

❸ investment [ɪnˈvɛstmənt] *n.* 投資

❹ transport [ˈtrænsˌpɔrt] *n.* 交通工具（英式用法，美式用法為 transportation）

❺ unregulated [ʌnˈrɛgjəˌletɪd] *a.* （政府或法律）無規範的

❻ established [ɪˈstæblɪʃt] *a.* 已建立的

❼ standard [ˈstændəd] *n.* 標準，水準
safety standards　　安全標準
a high / low living standard　　高 / 低生活水準

❽ transition [trænˈzɪʃən] *n.* 過度，轉變
transition from A to B　　從 A 轉變為 B

❾ manual [ˈmænjʊəl] *a.* 用手操作的；靠人工的

❿ chaotic [keˈɑtɪk] *a.* 毫無秩序的，紊亂的

D Busquets / Shutterstock.com

⑪ mixture [ˈmɪkstʃɚ] *n.* 混合 (物)
a mixture of A and B　　A 和 B 的混合 (物)

⑫ vulnerable [ˈvʌlnərəbḷ] *a.* 易受攻擊的；脆弱的
be vulnerable to sth　　易受某事的攻擊或傷害

⑬ hack [hæk] *vi.* & *vt.* 入侵電腦系統
hack into...　　入侵 (電腦系統)

⑭ malfunction [mælˈfʌŋkʃən] *n.* 故障，失靈

⑮ address [əˈdrɛs] *vt.* 解決，處理
address the issue / problem　　解決問題

⑯ potential [pəˈtɛnʃəl] *a.* 潛在的，可能的

⑰ unleash [ʌnˈliʃ] *vt.* 釋放

實用詞句　**Useful Expressions**

🔑 句型：such... that...、so... that...、so that...

◇ 本課將介紹以下三種句型：

ⓐ such + 不可數名詞 / 複數名詞 / a(n) 單數可數名詞 + that...
如此……，以致於……

This is such tasty <u>spaghetti</u> that I can't
　　　　　　　　不可數名詞

help but keep eating it.
這份義大利麵是如此美味，使得我忍
不住一直吃。

These are such <u>great books</u> that I
　　　　　　　複數名詞

recommend you read them.
這些書是那麼地棒，因此我建議你讀讀看。

Tom is such <u>a considerate man</u> that everyone likes him.
　　　　　　　單數可數名詞

湯姆是如此貼心的人，因此大家都很喜歡他。

b so + 形容詞 + (a(n) + 單數可數名詞) + that...
如此……，以致於……

注意

在 so... that... 句型中，so 作為副詞，其後須置形容詞，使 so 可修飾該形容詞。若要置名詞，亦可加在形容詞後，惟 so... that... 的句型中，只能置單數可數名詞，故上列第一、二個例句無法更改如下：

This is so tasty spaghetti that I can't help but keep eating it. (×)

These are so great books that I recommend you read them. (×)

上列第三個例句可改寫如下：

Tom is so considerate (a man) that everyone likes him. (✔)

c so that 表「為了；因此」，視為連接詞，可連接兩個子句

so that   為了，以便；因此，所以

= so [so]

We should listen to wise counsel so (that) we can make proper decisions.
我們應該要聽從明智的忠告，以便能做出適當的決定。

We used transparent packaging so (that) customers can see what is inside the box.
我們使用透明材質包裝，因此顧客看得見盒子裡面的東西。

發音提示 **Pronunciation**

❶ [ju]	human [ˈhjumən]	computer [kəmˈpjutɚ]
	use [juz]	future [ˈfjutʃɚ]
	produce [prəˈdjus]	

2 **[v]**	drive [draɪv]	investment [ɪnˈvɛstmənt]
	lives [laɪvz]	convince [kənˈvɪns]
	save [sev]	vehicle [ˈviɪkl̩]
	everyone [ˈɛvrɪˌwʌn]	vulnerable [ˈvʌlnərəbl̩]
	however [haʊˈɛvɚ]	

朗讀短文　Read aloud the text

🎙 請特別注意 [ju]、[v] 的發音。

　　A self-driving car is a car that can drive with little or no human input. It's such a safe form of driving that it's estimated thousands of lives would be saved each year if everyone used self-driving cars. However, more investment is needed so that companies can produce more self-driving cars. And the public needs to be convinced of their safety so that they are more willing to buy them.

　　No form of transport can be completely safe, but what are the specific concerns related to self-driving cars? The industry is currently unregulated, which means that there are no established safety standards. The transition from manual cars to self-driving cars could be chaotic, as there would be a mixture of vehicles on the road. And self-driving cars could be vulnerable to hacking and computer malfunctions. These safety issues need to be addressed so that the potential safety benefits can be unleashed. Only when this is done can self-driving cars possibly be the future of driving.

換句話說 Retell

📌 Retell the text with the help of the words and expressions below.

self-driving, input, investment, transport, unregulated, established, standard, transition, manual, chaotic, mixture, vulnerable, hack, malfunction, address, potential, unleash

討論題目 Free Talk

📌 Talk on the following topic:

◆ Do you believe that self-driving cars will be the future of driving?

Notes

Chapter 6

性格特點

Lesson 51

A Magician Never Reveals His Secrets
魔術師從不揭露他的祕密

搭配筆記聆聽會話 **Listen to the text with the help of the notes given**

prop	道具
speaking of which	說到這個
be curious about...	好奇……
No can do.	不行。(= No, I can't do it.)
reveal	揭露

再次聆聽並回答問題 **Listen again and answer the questions below**

🔑 Questions for discussion:

1️⃣ Did the woman enjoy the man's magic show?

2️⃣ What is the woman curious about?

3️⃣ Does the man work alone?

實用會話 **Dialogue**

Ⓐ What's in your bag, Stan?

Ⓑ The bag contains some of the props for my magic show. It's full of playing cards, magic wands, ropes, saws, and juggling balls!

Ⓐ Speaking of which, your show was spectacular. I loved the parts with the animals. I'm curious about how you made the rabbit disappear.

Ⓑ I can't tell you.

Ⓐ Come on. I'm your biggest fan!

Ⓑ No can do, sorry. A magician never reveals his secrets.

Ⓐ At least tell me how you got that beautiful magician's assistant to work with you.

Ⓑ Now that really was magic!

CH
6

性
格
特
點

A 史丹，你包包裡有什麼？

B 我包包裡有一些我表演魔術的道具。全都是撲克牌、魔術棒、繩子、鋸子和雜耍球！

A 說到這個，你的表演真令人驚豔。我喜歡和動物一起的那些橋段。我很好奇你怎麼把兔子變不見。

B 我無可奉告。

A 快說吧。我是你的頭號粉絲耶！

B 抱歉，我不能說。魔術師從不揭露他的祕密。

A 那至少告訴我你是如何讓那位美麗魔術師助理和你一起共事。

B 那真的是靠變魔術了！

單字片語 Vocabulary and Phrases

❶ **contain** [kənˈten] *vt.* 裝有；包含
This album contains all of my favorite photos.
這本相簿裡裝著所有我最愛的照片。

❷ **prop** [prɑp] *n.* 道具（常用複數）
stage props　　舞臺道具

❸ **playing cards**　　撲克牌

❹ **a magic wand** [wɑnd]　　魔術棒；魔杖
wave a (magic) wand　　揮動魔術棒

❺ **juggling balls**　　雜耍球
juggle [ˈdʒʌgḷ] *vi. & vt.* 玩雜耍
Vivian can juggle nine balls at the same time.
薇薇安可以同時拋接九顆球。

❻ **spectacular** [spɛkˈtækjələ] *a.* 令人驚豔的；壯觀的
a spectacular view　　壯麗的景緻

❼ **curious** [ˈkjʊrɪəs] *a.* 好奇的
be curious about...　　對⋯⋯感到好奇
Being too curious about the affairs of others can lead to trouble.
對他人的私事太過好奇會惹來麻煩。

8 reveal [rɪˋvil] *vt.* 揭露，透露

Trust me. I won't reveal your secret to others.
相信我。我不會把你的祕密洩漏給其他人。

9 assistant [əˋsɪstənt] *n.* 助理

口語新技能　New Skills

🔑 表示「說到這個」的說法

Speaking of which, ...　　說到這個／對了，……
= By the way, ...

注意

ⓐ speaking of which 的 which 指稱的是前面提到的事情，通常用於有上下文的對話中。

ⓑ 片語 by the way 除了用於對話中提到某件事進而開啟另一個話題的情形，也可用於說話者想要轉移話題或改變主題的狀況。
Speaking of which, have you seen Iris recently?
= By the way, have you seen Iris recently?
對了，你最近有見到艾莉絲嗎？

簡短對答　Quick Response

◆ Make quick responses to the sentences you hear.

討論題目　Free Talk

🔑 Talk on the following topic:

◆ If you had a magic wand, what would you do with it?

CH
6
性格特點

Helicopter Parents
直升機父母

搭配筆記聆聽短文 **Listen to the text with the help of the notes given**

feel sorry for sb	為某人感到惋惜
hover	盤旋
coordinate	協調
interfere in...	介入／干預……
no doubt	無庸置疑
do sb a favor	幫某人忙

再次聆聽並回答問題 **Listen again and answer the questions below**

🎙 Questions for discussion:

1 What is one thing helicopter parents might do?

2 What problem might children with helicopter parents face in the future?

3 Does the speaker think helicopter parents are good for children?

    I feel sorry for children whose parents organize every aspect of their lives. These parents are called helicopter parents because they always "hover" over their children. They coordinate their social events, arrange endless extracurricular activities, and interfere in every part of their educational life.

    I'm sure these parents are just showing love for their children, and no doubt some children are happy with this situation. But it can actually leave children less able to cope when they become adults. They don't know how to manage their own time or make their own decisions, because their parents have always done it for them. So, helicopter parents aren't necessarily doing their children any favors by treating them this way.

我為那些父母會安排所有生活大小事的孩子感到惋惜。這些父母被稱為直升機父母，因為他們總是在孩子的上空「盤旋」。這些父母協調孩子的社交活動、安排無止盡的課外活動，且介入孩子教育生活的每一部分。

　　我相信這些父母只是對他們的孩子表現愛意，而且無疑地，有些孩子對於這個情況感到很開心。然而這其實會讓孩子長大成人後更難以處理問題。他們不知道如何安排自己的時間或自己做出決定，因為他們的父母總會幫他們做這些事。因此，直升機父母如此對待孩子未必對孩子是好事。

單字片語 Vocabulary and Phrases

❶ aspect [ˈæspɛkt] *n.* 方面

❷ helicopter parents 直升機父母

helicopter [ˈhɛlɪˌkɑptɚ] *n.* 直升機

注意

「直升機父母」是指過分干預孩子生活或過度保護孩子的家長。這些父母的行為猶如直升機在孩子周圍盤旋著，故稱為「直升機父母」。

❸ hover [ˈhʌvɚ] *vi.* (直升機或鳥) 盤旋

hover over... 在……上空盤旋

The vultures hovered over the dying animal.

禿鷹在瀕死的動物上空盤旋著。

❹ coordinate [koˈɔrdnˌet] *vt.* 協調，安排

= organize [ˈɔrgəˌnaɪz]

❺ endless [ˈɛndlɪs] *a.* 無止盡的，不斷的

My father's endless nagging really annoys me.

我老爸無止盡的嘮叨真的很煩。

❻ extracurricular [ˌɛkstrəkəˈrɪkjələ] *a.* 課外的

extracurricular activities 課外活動

❼ interfere [ˌɪntɚˈfɪr] *vi.* 干預；妨礙

interfere in... 干預……

interfere with... 妨礙……

Religion should not interfere in politics.
宗教不應該干預政治。

Molly's anxiety is interfering with her performance at work.
茉莉的焦慮症影響到她在工作上的表現。

8 cope [kop] *vi.* 處理，應付
cope with...　　處理……
= deal with...
= handle...

How do you cope with stress?
= How do you deal with stress?
= How do you handle stress?
你是如何處理壓力？

9 favor [ˋfevɚ] *n.* 恩惠；青睞；贊成 & *vt.* 贊成
do sb a favor　　幫某人忙

My professor did me a favor by writing a letter of recommendation.
我的教授幫我寫了一封推薦信。

實用詞句　Useful Expressions

1 表示「為某人感到惋惜」的說法
feel sorry for sb　　為某人感到惋惜 / 可惜 / 難過
= feel bad for sb
I feel sorry for the children who lost their fathers in the war.
我為那些因為戰爭而失去父親的孩子們感到難過。

比較
feel sorry for oneself　　為自己感到忿忿不平
= feel bad for oneself
Tom was drinking and feeling sorry for himself.
湯姆當時在喝酒並為自己的遭遇感到不平。

2 表示「無庸置疑」的說法
no doubt　　無庸置疑，毫無疑問（用於發表自己相當肯定的想法或意見）
doubt [daʊt] *n.* 懷疑，疑慮

注意

a no doubt 常置於句首，修飾整個主句。

Teaching is no doubt a difficult job. (較少用)

= No doubt teaching is a difficult job. (較常用)
教書毫無疑問是份很艱難的工作。

b 下列說法亦可用於表示「無庸置疑」：

without (a) doubt
無疑地，確實 (用於發表自己極為肯定的想法或意見)

undoubtedly [ʌnˈdaʊtɪdlɪ] *adv.*
無庸置疑地 (用於發表自己極為肯定的想法或意見)

上列例句亦可改寫如下：

Teaching is without (a) doubt a difficult job.

= Teaching is undoubtedly a difficult job.
教書確實是份很艱難的工作。

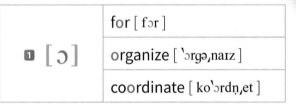

發音提示 Pronunciation

1 [ɔ]	for [fɔr]	
	organize [ˈɔrgəˌnaɪz]	
	coordinate [koˈɔrdnˌet]	

2 [ʃ]	social [ˈsoʃəl]	show [ʃo]
	educational [ˌɛdʒʊˈkeʃənl]	situation [ˌsɪtʃʊˈeʃən]
	sure [ʃʊr]	

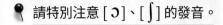

📍 請特別注意 [ɔ]、[ʃ] 的發音。

I feel sorry for children whose parents organize every aspect of their lives. These parents are called helicopter parents because they always "hover" over their children. They coordinate their social events, arrange endless extracurricular activities, and interfere in every part of their educational life.

I'm sure these parents are just showing love for their children, and no doubt some children are happy with this situation. But it can actually leave children less able to cope when they become adults. They don't know how to manage their own time or make their own decisions, because their parents have always done it for them. So, helicopter parents aren't necessarily doing their children any favors by treating them this way.

換句話說 **Retell**

📍 Retell the text with the help of the words and expressions below.

aspect, helicopter parents, hover, coordinate, endless, extracurricular, interfere, cope, favor

討論題目 **Free Talk**

📍 Talk on the following topic:

◆ Do you think your parents are helicopter parents?

CH
6

性格特點

301

Making a Vlog
製作影片部落格

搭配筆記聆聽會話 **Listen to the text with the help of the notes given**

blog	部落格
as soon as	一……就……
edit	編輯
get into...	開始對……感興趣
look forward to...	期待……

再次聆聽並回答問題 **Listen again and answer the questions below**

📍 Questions for discussion:

1️⃣ What is the woman doing?

2️⃣ What is the woman's video about?

3️⃣ When will the woman show the man the video?

Ⓐ What are you doing with your camera, Kathy?

Ⓑ I'm making a vlog, Greg. I'm a vlogger.

Ⓐ What's a vlogger?

Ⓑ A vlogger is a person that makes a blog with video content. I'm making a vlog that shows all my friends and family my first day at university.

Ⓐ That sounds interesting. Can I see it?

Ⓑ Sure. As soon as I finish editing the clip, I'll show you.

Ⓐ Great, thanks! How did you get into vlogging?

Ⓑ I was spending a lot of time watching TikTok videos that weren't very professional. I thought, "I can do better than this!"

Ⓐ Cool. I'll look forward to seeing it then!

Ⓐ 凱西，妳在用妳的相機做什麼？

Ⓑ 我在製作影片部落格，葛瑞格。我是一名影片部落客。

Ⓐ 什麼是影片部落客？

Ⓑ 影片部落客是用影片內容製作部落格的人。我正在製作一個影片部落格，讓我所有的朋友家人看看我上大學的第一天。

Ⓐ 聽起來挺有趣的。我可以看看嗎？

Ⓑ 當然。我一修剪完片段就給你看。

Ⓐ 太棒了，謝謝！妳怎麼對影片部落格感興趣？

Ⓑ 我花很多時間看了抖音影片，這些影片並不是很專業。我想：「我可以做得比這好！」

Ⓐ 真酷。那我很期待看到妳的影片！

單字片語　Vocabulary and Phrases

❶ vlog [vlɑg] *n.* 影片部落格
vlogger [ˋvlɑgɚ] *n.* 影片部落客
注意
vlog 一字是由 blog [blɑg]（部落格）演變而來，即 video blog 或 video weblog，指「影片部落格」，是一種以影像為主要形式的部落格。

❷ content [ˋkɑntɛnt] *n.* 內容（不可數）；內容物（常用複數）
The content of this novel is quite ordinary.
這本小說的內容很普通。
The customs official asked to check the contents of my luggage.
海關官員要求檢查我行李的內容物。

❸ edit [ˋɛdɪt] *vt.* 編輯，剪輯
Tom edited the video down to two minutes.
湯姆將影片剪短到兩分鐘。

❹ clip [klɪp] *n.* 片段

❺ get into sth 開始對某事物感興趣；參加某活動
Andrew got into weightlifting recently.
安德魯最近開始對重訓感興趣。

⑥ look forward to N/V-ing 期待……

I look forward to seeing you soon.
我期待很快與您相見。

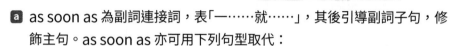

🔑 副詞連接詞 as soon as 的用法

ⓐ as soon as 為副詞連接詞，表「一……就……」，其後引導副詞子句，修飾主句。as soon as 亦可用下列句型取代：

As soon as + 主詞 + 動詞, 主句　　一……就……
= The instant + 主詞 + 動詞, 主句
= The moment + 主詞 + 動詞, 主句
= Upon + N/V-ing, 主句
= On + N/V-ing, 主句

注意

upon 或 on 之後只能加名詞或動名詞，而非子句。

As soon as Kevin finished the job, he went home.
= The instant Kevin finished the job, he went home.
= The moment Kevin finished the job, he went home.
= Upon finishing the job, Kevin went home.
= On finishing the job, Kevin went home.
凱文一做完工作就回家了。

ⓑ 本課中，as soon as 用來表示未來的狀況，此時形成條件句，且 as soon as 可用 once 取代。該表示條件的副詞子句時態須採現在式或現在完成式，而主句則採用未來式，即：

As soon as + 主詞 + 現在式 / 現在完成式動詞, 主詞 + will + 動詞原形
As soon as Ron comes back, we'll go out for dinner.
= Once Ron comes back, we'll go out for dinner.
榮恩一回來我們就會去吃晚餐。
本課句子：
As soon as I finish editing the clip, I'll show you.
= Once I finish editing the clip, I'll show you.
我一修剪完片段就給你看。

◇ Make quick responses to the sentences you hear.

討論題目 **Free Talk**

🎙 Talk on the following topic:

◇ What would you film about if you were making a vlog?

306

Lesson 54

Becoming a Minimalist
成為極簡主義者

搭配筆記聆聽短文 Listen to the text with the help of the notes given

donate	捐獻
pass on... to...	傳……給……
occupy	使忙碌
de-clutter	整理
re-assess	重新評估
re-evaluate	重新評斷

再次聆聽並回答問題 Listen again and answer the questions below

🔖 Questions for discussion:

1 What do minimalists usually do with the clothes that are never worn?

2 What can minimalist parents do about their kids' toys?

3 What can being a minimalist do for you spiritually?

CH
6

性格特點

307

Many people seeking a simpler life are becoming minimalists. The clothes hanging in the closet that are never worn are thrown out or donated to charity. The books and DVDs sitting on the shelf that are gathering dust are given to a friend or recycled. The kids' toys piled up in the bedroom are passed on to other parents to occupy their little ones.

But being a minimalist is about more than just getting rid of your unwanted possessions. It is also about de-cluttering your mind, re-assessing your goals, and re-evaluating your ambitions. What are your priorities in life? What is important to you? Maybe it's time to try out the lifestyle of a minimalist and minimize your life!

許多追求更簡約生活的人成為極簡主義者。掛在衣櫥裡從來都沒穿過的衣服都被丟掉或是捐給慈善機構。放在架子上積灰塵的書本與 DVD 都送給朋友或拿去回收了。堆積在臥房裡的兒童玩具送給其他家長給他們的小孩玩了。

但當個極簡主義者不只是丟掉你不要的物品。這也是關於整理你的思緒、重新評估你的目標，並重新評斷你的志向。你生活中的首要之務是什麼？對你來說什麼是重要的？或許該是時候嘗試看看極簡主義者的生活，使你的生活變得更簡約！

單字片語 Vocabulary and Phrases

❶ minimalist [`mɪnɪml̩ɪst] *n.* 極簡主義者
minimalism [`mɪnɪmə͵lɪzəm] *n.* 極簡主義

❷ donate [`donet] *vt.* 捐獻；捐贈
donate sth to...　　將某物捐給……

Tina donates some of her clothes to the homeless shelter every year.
蒂娜每年都會捐一些衣服給遊民庇護所。

❸ recycle [ri`saɪkl̩] *vt.* 回收，重複利用

❹ pile up　　堆積，累積

Work piles up easily if you're not efficient enough.
如果你效率不佳，工作很快就會堆積起來。

❺ pass on sth to sb / pass sth on to sb　　將某物傳給某人

I'll pass on this book to you once I'm done with it.
我一看完這本書就會給你。

❻ occupy [`ɑkjə͵paɪ] *vt.* 使忙碌；占據
(三態為：occupy, occupied [`ɑkjə͵paɪd], occupied)

The board game will occupy the children for hours.
那個桌遊會讓孩子們玩好幾個小時。

❼ get rid of...　　丟棄……；擺脫……

We got rid of some unwanted furniture.
我們丟掉了一些不要的傢俱。

CH
6
性格特點

309

I couldn't get rid of that persistent salesman.
我無法擺脫那位糾纏不休的推銷員。

8 clutter [ˈklʌtɚ] *vt.* 散亂，塞滿
= clutter up

There are too many boxes cluttering up the storage room.
太多箱子堆滿儲存室了。

9 assess [əˈsɛs] *vt.* 評估

We should assess the situation before making the decision.
我們應該在做出決定前先評估情況。

10 evaluate [ɪˈvæljuˌet] *vt.* 評估

Employees' performance will be evaluated towards the end of the year.
員工績效會在接近年底時評估。

11 ambition [æmˈbɪʃən] *n.* 抱負，野心

12 priority [praɪˈɔrətɪ] *n.* 優先的事物
one's top / first priority　　某人的首要之務

Our top priority is to improve our customer service.
我們的首要之務是改善顧客服務。

13 lifestyle [ˈlaɪfˌstaɪl] *n.* 生活方式

14 minimize [ˈmɪnəˌmaɪz] *vt.* 使減到最少；使降到最低
maximize [ˈmæksəˌmaɪz] *vt.* 使增到最多

Regular exercise and a healthy diet can help minimize the risk of heart disease.
規律運動與健康的飲食習慣有助於將罹患心臟病風險降到最低。

實用詞句 Useful Expressions

🔑 字首 de- 與 re- 的用法

◆ 本文中的 de-cluttering、re-assessing 及 re-evaluating 分別使用字首 de- 與 re-。字首 de- 有「除去；減少」，而 re- 則有「重新；重複」的意思。字首可置於動詞、名詞、形容詞或副詞字首，用以修飾該單字。英語有許多字首，以下介紹一些常見的字首：

常見的字首	意思	與該字首搭配的常見單字
anti-	反對；防（止）	anti-war　反戰的 anti-aging　抗老的
co-	共同，一起	co-write　合寫 coworker　同事
de-	除去；減少	debug　排除錯誤 devalue　貶值
ex-	前任；以前	ex-wife　前妻 ex-con　坐過牢的人
inter-	之間；中間	international　國際的 interpersonal　人際的
pre-	之前；預先	pre-war　戰前的 preset　預先設定
re-	重新；重複	remarry　再婚 reuse　重複利用
un-	否定；相反	unable　不能 unhappy　不開心的

	clothes [kloz]	donate [ˈdonet]
1 [o]	thrown [θron]	goal [gol]

	donate [ˈdonet]	bedroom [ˈbɛdˌrum]
2 [d]	dust [dʌst]	rid [rɪd]
	friend [frɛnd]	de-clutter [ˌdiˈklʌtɚ]
	kid [kɪd]	mind [maɪnd]

朗讀短文　**Read aloud the text**

請特別注意 [o]、[d] 的發音。

Many people seeking a simpler life are becoming minimalists. The clothes hanging in the closet that are never worn are thrown out or donated to charity. The books and DVDs sitting on the shelf that are gathering dust are given to a friend or recycled. The kids' toys piled up in the bedroom are passed on to other parents to occupy their little ones.

But being a minimalist is about more than just getting rid of your unwanted possessions. It is also about de-cluttering your mind, re-assessing your goals, and re-evaluating your ambitions. What are your priorities in life? What is important to you? Maybe it's time to try out the lifestyle of a minimalist and minimize your life!

換句話說 Retell

📌 Retell the text with the help of the words and expressions below.

minimalist, donate, recycle, pile up, pass on to, occupy, get rid of, clutter, assess, evaluate, ambition, priority, lifestyle, minimize

討論題目 Free Talk

📌 Talk on the following topic:

◆ Are you interested in becoming a minimalist? Why or why not?

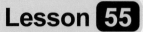

Don't Be a Bully
別當惡霸

搭配筆記聆聽會話 **Listen to the text with the help of the notes given**

bully	惡霸
nasty	惡劣的
protect	保護
tattletale	打小報告的人
tattle	打小報告，告狀

再次聆聽並回答問題 **Listen again and answer the questions below**

🔑 Questions for discussion:

1 Why did the boy's teacher call his mother?

2 Why were the boys fighting?

3 Why didn't the boy tell his teacher about the cause of the fight?

314

🅐 I'm not happy with you, son.

🅑 Why, Mom?

🅐 Your teacher called me today. She said you've been fighting with a younger boy.

🅑 But he started it!

🅐 Despite the fact that he started it, you shouldn't fight. He's younger and smaller than you. Don't be a bully.

🅑 I'm sorry, Mom.

🅐 What was the fight about?

🅑 He was calling Emma nasty names. When I told him to stop, he hit me.

🅐 So, you were protecting Emma? Did you tell your teacher about this?

315

B I didn't want to be a tattletale.

A In spite of the fact that you didn't want to tattle, you should always tell the truth to your teacher.

B OK, Mom.

A 兒子，我對你很不高興。

B 為什麼，媽媽？

A 今天你的老師打電話給我。她說你與一個年紀比你小的男孩打架。

B 可是他先動手的！

A 儘管他先動手，你不應該打架。他年紀比你小，身材也比你嬌小。別當惡霸。

B 對不起，媽媽。

A 打架的原因是什麼？

B 他罵艾瑪一些難聽的話。我叫他停止的時候，他打了我。

A 所以，你當時是在保護艾瑪？你把這件事告訴你的老師了嗎？

B 我不想當打小報告的人。

A 雖然你不想告狀，你應該都要將事實告訴你的老師。

B 好的，媽媽。

單字片語 Vocabulary and Phrases

1 **bully** [ˈbʊlɪ] *n.* 惡霸 & *vt.* 霸凌，欺負
（三態為：bully, bullied [ˈbʊlɪd], bullied）

Evan didn't enjoy high school because he was constantly bullied.
艾凡並不喜歡高中因為他經常受到霸凌。

2 **call sb names** 辱罵某人，取笑某人

Andy didn't like to wear glasses to school because he was afraid other students would call him names.
安迪以前不喜歡戴眼鏡上學，因為他怕其他學生會取笑他。

❸ **nasty** [`næstɪ] *a.* 惡劣的;令人反感的;糟糕的

Mark always makes nasty remarks about other people's appearance.

馬克總是會針對別人的外貌做出惡毒的評論。

The dish looks nasty, but it actually tastes great.

這道菜看起來很噁心,但它其實很好吃。

❹ **protect** [prə`tɛkt] *vt.* 保護

protect sb from / against...　　保護某人免於……

Simon was protecting Emma from the bully.

賽門當時是在保護艾瑪免受惡霸欺負。

口語新技能 **New Skills**

🔑 表示「打小報告的人」的說法

　　tattletale [`tætḷ͵tel] *n.* 打小報告的人,告密者 (美式用法)

= 　**telltale** [`tɛl͵tel] (英式用法)

= 　**snitch** [snɪtʃ]

　　注意

　　名詞 tattletale 與 telltale 通常是用來指小孩,而 snitch 則可以指任何告密的人,三者皆為非正式用語。

　　若要表示「打小報告」或「告密」則可用下列說法:

　　tattle [`tætḷ] (on sb)　　告 (某人的) 狀,打 (某人的) 小報告

= 　**tell tales (on sb)**

= 　**snitch (on sb)**

　　Holly tattled on Sam to the teacher for cheating.

= 　Holly told tales on Sam to the teacher for cheating.

= 　Holly snitched on Sam to the teacher for cheating.

　　荷莉將山姆作弊一事向老師告狀。

簡短對答 Quick Response

◆ Make quick responses to the sentences you hear.

討論題目 Free Talk

Talk on the following topic:

◆ Have you ever been a tattletale before?

Stereotypes
刻板印象

朗讀

搭配筆記聆聽短文 **Listen to the text with the help of the notes given**

supposedly	一般認為
a manual job	勞力工作
harmless	無害的
ignorance	無知
justify	使合理化

再次聆聽並回答問題 **Listen again and answer the questions below**

Questions for discussion:

1 What are stereotypes?

2 According to the speaker, why might stereotypes be dangerous?

3 According to the speaker, what is usually people's stereotype of an immigrant?

Stereotypes are widely held ideas about a particular type of person or thing. For example, if you see a car accident involving a male driver and a female driver, you might think the woman must have caused the accident because women are supposedly "bad drivers." Or, if you see someone working in a manual job, you might think that they cannot have had a good education.

Stereotypes can be harmless, but they can also be dangerous and rooted in ignorance of a culture or race. They are usually oversimplified and often incorrect. Some people use stereotypes—rather than facts—to justify their opinions. For example, if a crime was committed in a small town, some people might presume that the newly arrived immigrant must have done it. This is because the stereotype of an immigrant is often linked to crime. We must all unite to fight against and challenge stereotypes.

刻板印象意指對特定類型的人或事持廣泛的想法。舉例來說，如果你看到一起涉及男、女駕駛的車禍，你可能會認為一定是女子造成這起事故，因為一般都覺得女性是「差勁的駕駛」。又或者，假如你看到某人做勞力的工作，你可能會想他們不可能受過良好的教育。

刻板印象可能無傷大雅，但也可能相當危險，而且可能會從對文化、種族的無知中衍生出來。這些成見通常過於簡單化且大部分是不正確的。有些人會以刻板印象 —— 而非事實 —— 來合理化他們的想法。例如，假設在一個小鎮發生一起犯罪案，有些人可能會假定是新外來移民者的作為。這是因為對移民者的刻板印象常與犯罪聯想在一起。我們一定要團結起來對抗與質疑刻板印象。

單字片語　**Vocabulary and Phrases**

❶ stereotype [ˋstɛrɪəˏtaɪp] *n.* 刻板印象，成見
conform to the stereotype　符合刻板印象
= fit the stereotype

❷ particular [pəˋtɪkjələ / parˋtɪkjələ] *a.* 特定的

❸ supposedly [səˋpozɪdlɪ] *adv.* 一般認為，一般相信；據稱

❹ manual [ˋmænjʊəl] *a.* 勞力的；手工的；手動的
manual labor / jobs　勞力工作

❺ education [ˏɛdʒəˋkeʃən] *n.* 教育

❻ harmless [ˋharmləs] *a.* 無害的；無惡意的

❼ be rooted in...　根源於……
The city's traffic problems are rooted in poor planning.
該市的交通問題源自於規畫不當。

❽ ignorance [ˋɪgnərəns] *n.* 無知；愚昧 (不可數)

❾ oversimplify [ˏovəˋsɪmpləˏfaɪ] *vt.* 使……過於簡單化
(三態為：oversimplify, oversimplified [ˏovəˋsɪmpləˏfaɪd], oversimplified)

❿ justify [ˋdʒʌstəˏfaɪ] *vt.* 使合理化；證明……為正當
(三態為：justify, justified [ˋdʒʌstəˏfaɪd], justified)

Justin couldn't justify making everyone wait just for him.
賈斯汀無法提出讓大家乾等他一人的合理解釋。

⑪ **presume** [prɪˋzum] *vt.* 推測，猜想

I presume (that) you are tired after working so long and hard.
辛苦工作這麼久以後，我想你是累了。

⑫ **be linked to...**　　與……有關聯
= be linked with...

A diet high in sugar and starch is linked to many major diseases.
糖分與澱粉過多的飲食與許多重大疾病有關。

⑬ **unite** [juˋnaɪt] *vi.* & *vt.* (使) 聯合

實用詞句　Useful Expressions

🔑 表「對過去事物推論」的句構

　a　若為肯定推論，則可使用下列兩種句構：

　　1)　must have + 過去分詞　　一定曾經……
　　　Since I can't find my purse, I must have left it at the supermarket this morning.
　　　因為我找不到我的皮包，我一定是今天早上把它丟在超市了。
　　　It must have rained last night.
　　　昨晚一定下過雨。

　　2)　may have + 過去分詞　　可能曾經……
　　　The disease may have originated in the jungles of Africa.
　　　這種疾病可能源自於非洲叢林。
　　　Kent is an hour late. I'm afraid that he may have gotten lost.
　　　肯特遲到了一小時。他恐怕是迷路了。

　b　若為否定推論，則可使用下列句構：
　　cannot have + 過去分詞　　不可能曾……
　　You cannot have been to that restaurant; it hasn't opened yet.
　　你不可能去過那間餐廳；它還沒開張。

Scott can't have finished his assignment already.
史考特不可能已經寫完他的作業。

c 若為疑問句，則可使用下列句構：

Can + 主詞 + have + 過去分詞?　　有可能……嗎？

Can Daniel have lied to his friends?
丹尼爾有可能對他朋友說謊嗎？

Can Nora have gone bungee jumping?
諾拉有可能去玩高空彈跳嗎？

發音提示　**Pronunciation**

❶ **[aɪ]**	stereotype [ˈstɛrɪəˌtaɪp]	oversimplify [ˌovɚˈsɪmpləˌfaɪ]
	widely [ˈwaɪdlɪ]	justify [ˈdʒʌstəˌfaɪ]
	idea [aɪˈdiə]	crime [kraɪm]
	type [taɪp]	arrive [əˈraɪv]
	driver [ˈdraɪvɚ]	unite [juˈnaɪt]
	might [maɪt]	fight [faɪt]

❷ **[θ]**	thing [θɪŋ]
	think [θɪŋk]

朗讀短文　**Read aloud the text**

🎤 請特別注意 [aɪ]、[θ] 的發音。

　　Stereotypes are widely held ideas about a particular type of person or thing. For example, if you see a car accident involving a male driver and a female driver, you might think the woman must have caused the accident because women are supposedly "bad drivers." Or, if you see someone working in a manual job, you might think that they cannot have had a good education.

Stereotypes can be harmless, but they can also be dangerous and rooted in ignorance of a culture or race. They are usually oversimplified and often incorrect. Some people use stereotypes—rather than facts—to justify their opinions. For example, if a crime was committed in a small town, some people might presume that the newly arrived immigrant must have done it. This is because the stereotype of an immigrant is often linked to crime. We must all unite to fight against and challenge stereotypes.

換句話說 Retell

Retell the text with the help of the words and expressions below.

stereotype, particular, supposedly, manual, education, harmless, be rooted in, ignorance, oversimplify, justify, presume, be linked to, unite

討論題目 Free Talk

Talk on the following topic:

◆ Do you agree that all stereotypes are bad? Why or why not?

Lesson **57**

朗讀 ▶
Lesson 57

If I Were a Millionaire
假如我是百萬富翁的話

搭配筆記聆聽短文 **Listen to the text with the help of the notes given**

divide... into...	將……分為……
require maintenance	需要維護
make a difference	產生影響
war-torn	受戰爭摧殘的
cruise	遊輪

再次聆聽並回答問題 **Listen again and answer the questions below**

🔍 Questions for discussion:

1. How many parts would the speaker divide the money into?

2. Where would the speaker like to contribute the money to?

3. What does the speaker plan to do with the last part of the money?

CH
6

性格特點

If I were a millionaire, I would divide my money into three chunks. One third would go to my family, so they could live in comfort and wouldn't have to worry about money. I'd like to buy my mom and dad a smaller house, so it wouldn't require as much maintenance.

Another third would go to charity, so I could try to make a difference in this world. I'd like to contribute to heart and cancer research, and give money to charities that help children in war-torn regions.

And I would keep the other third for myself, so I could travel and buy nice things. I'd like to go on a round-the-world cruise and visit as many countries as possible. Hey, if I were a millionaire, I'd want to have some fun, too!

如果我是百萬富翁，我會將我的錢分為三個部分。三分之一會給我的家人，這樣他們可以過舒適的生活，也不用擔心金錢。我想買給我爸媽比較小的房子，如此一來不需要花太多精力去維護。

另外的三分之一會給慈善機構，這樣我能夠試著在世界上有點影響。我想捐獻給心臟疾病與癌症研究，也捐錢給幫助戰區孩童的慈善機構。

而最後三分之一我會留給自己，如此一來我可以旅遊並買好的東西。我想搭環遊世界的遊輪並盡可能地走訪愈多國家愈好。嘿，如果我是百萬富翁，我也想有點樂趣！

單字片語　Vocabulary and Phrases

1 millionaire [ˌmɪljənˋɛr] *n.* 百萬富翁
billionaire [ˌbɪljənˋɛr] *n.* 億萬富翁

2 divide [dəˋvaɪd] *vt.* 劃分；除以；把某物分為……
divide sth into...　把某物分為……

Mom divided the pizza into eight slices.
媽媽將披薩分成八片。

The pizza was divided into eight slices.
披薩被分成八片。

3 chunk [tʃʌŋk] *n.* 部分，一塊
a chunk of meat　一塊肉

A huge chunk of text is missing from this paper.
這篇文章裡有一大部分的文字不見了。

4 comfort [ˋkʌmfɚt] *n.* 舒適
in comfort　舒適地

My bedroom is the only place that I can relax in comfort.
我的臥房是唯一我可以舒適地放鬆的地方。

5 maintenance [ˋmentənəns] *n.* 維持；維修

6 contribute [kənˋtrɪbjut] *vi.* & *vt.* 捐獻，捐贈
contribute (sth) to...　將（某物）捐給……

John contributes to the local charity every month.
約翰每個月都會捐款給當地的慈善機構。

7 **war-torn** [`wɔrtɔrn] *a.* 受戰爭摧殘的
tear [tɛr] *vt.* 撕破，撕裂
（三態為：tear, tore [tɔr], torn [tɔrn]）

Several nations are offering long-term aid to
the war-torn country.
好幾個國家給予那受戰爭摧殘的國家長期的協助。

8 **region** [`ridʒən] *n.* 區域
= **area** [`ɛrɪə]

9 **cruise** [kruz] *n.* 航遊
cruiser [`kruzɚ] *n.* 遊輪

10 **as** + 形容詞 / 副詞 + **as possible**   盡可能地……
= **as** + 形容詞 / 副詞 + as one can

It is important to treat the illness as early as possible.
= It is important to treat the illness as early as one can.
儘早治療這個疾病是很重要的事。

實用詞句 Useful Expressions

📌 複合形容詞

◆ 複合形容詞為兩個或兩個以上的字詞，中間以連字號號相接所形成的形
容詞，用以修飾名詞。惟須注意的是，若複合形容詞中有可數名詞，則
一律以單數形表示。複合形容詞有下列幾種形成方式：

a 數量詞 + 名詞
　　a ten-day trip　　　　　十天的旅行
　　a three-year guarantee　三年的保固期

b 形容詞 + 名詞
　　a high-quality product　高品質的產品
　　a first-class wine　　　上等的葡萄酒

c 形容詞 / 名詞 + 名詞變成的過去分詞
　　a middle-aged couple　　中年夫婦
　　a heart-shaped card　　　心形的卡片

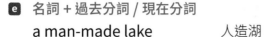

d 名詞 + 名詞

a name-brand product   名牌產品

e 名詞 + 過去分詞 / 現在分詞

a man-made lake   人造湖
a peace-loving people   愛好和平的民族

注意

本文中的 war-torn (受戰爭摧殘的) 即為「名詞 + 過去分詞」的複合形容詞。

f 形容詞 / 副詞 + 現在分詞

a good-looking guy   長得好看的男人
a never-ending task   永無止境的工作

g 形容詞 / 副詞 + 過去分詞

a ready-made meal   事先做好的一餐
a well-dressed woman   穿著得體的女子

h 名詞 + 形容詞

a world-famous actor   世界聞名的演員
a water-resistant watch 防水手錶

發音提示 [Pronunciation]

1 [ɔ]	war-torn [ˈwɔrtɔrn]

2 [ju]	contribute [kənˈtrɪbjut]

📌 請特別注意 [ɔ]、[ju] 的發音。

　　If I were a millionaire, I would divide my money into three chunks. One third would go to my family, so they could live in comfort and wouldn't have to worry about money. I'd like to buy my mom and dad a smaller house, so it wouldn't require as much maintenance.

　　Another third would go to charity, so I could try to make a difference in this world. I'd like to contribute to heart and cancer research, and give money to charities that help children in war-torn regions.

　　And I would keep the other third for myself, so I could travel and buy nice things. I'd like to go on a round-the-world cruise and visit as many countries as possible. Hey, if I were a millionaire, I'd want to have some fun, too!

換句話說 **Retell**

📌 Retell the text with the help of the words and expressions below.

millionaire, divide, chunk, comfort, maintenance, contribute, war-torn, region, cruise, as... as possible

討論題目 **Free Talk**

📌 Talk on the following topic:

◇ If you had some extra money to donate, what kind of charity or organization would you like to contribute to? Why?

Lesson 58

Don't Be a Grouch
別當愛發牢騷的人

搭配筆記聆聽會話 **Listen to the text with the help of the notes given**

I'm not in the mood.	我沒心情。
miserable	鬱鬱寡歡的
grouch	愛發牢騷的人
naturally	天生地
sociable	擅長社交的

再次聆聽並回答問題 **Listen again and answer the questions below**

Questions for discussion:

1. Is the man having fun at the party?
2. What does the woman say a beer will do to the man?
3. What will the man do?

CH
6

性格特點

Ⓐ What's wrong with you, Jeff? Aren't you enjoying the party?

Ⓑ Not really. It's boring, and I'm not in the mood.

Ⓐ Stop sitting in the corner, looking miserable. Come dance with me.

Ⓑ I don't like dancing.

Ⓐ Well, have a drink and talk to some people. Don't be a grouch!

Ⓑ OK, I'll have a beer.

Ⓐ Good choice. A beer will loosen you up and get you talking to people.

Ⓑ Oh, Tony's over there. He's standing by himself. I guess I could go talk to him.

Ⓐ See! Just relax and enjoy the party.

Ⓑ Not everyone's naturally sociable like you, you know.

Ⓐ And not everyone's naturally grouchy like you!

Ａ 傑夫，你怎麼了？你不喜歡這場派對嗎？

Ｂ 是不太喜歡。派對很無聊，而且我沒心情。

Ａ 別坐在角落看起來鬱鬱寡歡的。來跟我跳舞。

Ｂ 我不喜歡跳舞。

Ａ 嗯，那喝杯飲料跟一些人說說話。別當愛發牢騷的人！

Ｂ 好，我要喝杯啤酒。

Ａ 好選擇。啤酒可以讓你放鬆並也讓你去跟別人講話。

Ｂ 喔，東尼在那邊。他自己站著。我想我可以過去跟他聊天。

Ａ 你看！只要放鬆享受派對就好。

Ｂ 你知道，並不是每個人都像妳一樣天生善於社交。

Ａ 也不是每個人都像你一樣天生就愛發牢騷！

單字片語 Vocabulary and Phrases

1 **corner** [ˈkɔrnɚ] *n.* 角落
   in the corner　　（室內的）角落裡
   on the corner　　（戶外的）轉角處

2 **miserable** [ˈmɪzərəb]] *a.* 痛苦的；悲慘的
   Sam doesn't like to talk about his miserable childhood.
   山姆不喜歡談論他悲慘的童年。

3 **grouch** [graʊtʃ] *n.* 愛發牢騷的人，愛抱怨的人

4 **loosen sb up**　　使某人放鬆
   loosen [ˈlusn̩] *vt. & vi.* 鬆開

   Listening to music can help loosen you up.
   聽音樂可以讓你放鬆。

5 **naturally** [ˈnætʃərəlɪ] *adv.* 天生地；自然地
   Linda is a naturally outgoing person.
   琳達天生就是很外向的人。
   It is difficult to act naturally in front of cameras.
   要在攝影機前表現自然是很困難的事。

6 **sociable** [ˈsoʃəbl̩] *a.* 擅長社交的
social [ˈsoʃəl] *a.* 社交的；社會的

My neighbors are sociable people.
我的鄰居是很愛社交的人。

7 **grouchy** [ˈɡraʊtʃɪ] *a.* 滿腹牢騷的；易怒的
= grumpy [ˈɡrʌmpɪ]

The grouchy old man lives alone in the woods.
那位易怒的老人獨自住在森林裡。

口語新技能 New Skills

1 表示「沒心情做某事」的說法
be not in the mood (for sth) / to V　無心情 (做某事)
mood [mud] *n.* 心情
I'm not in the mood for a movie.
我沒心情看電影。

比較

be in a mood　心情煩悶 / 暴躁
= be in one of one's moods
I wouldn't talk to Ella if I were you. She's in a mood.
= I wouldn't talk to Ella if I were you. She's in one of her moods.
如果我是你，我不會跟艾拉攀談。她現在心情很暴躁。

2 Come dance with me.　來跟我跳舞。
動詞 come 或 go 若以原形出現，且其後有連接詞 and 與第二個動詞原形時，可省略 and，使 come 或 go 後面直接接第二個動詞，注意此為口語的說法。本句原為：

Come and dance with me.
→ Come dance with me.
同理，可造出下列句子：

Go and play with the other children.
→ Go play with the other children.
去和其他小孩玩。

簡短對答　Quick Response

◆ Make quick responses to the sentences you hear.

討論題目　Free Talk

🔍 Talk on the following topic:

◆ Do you consider yourself a sociable person?

Lesson 59

Cheaters Never Prosper
作弊的人永遠不會飛黃騰達

搭配筆記聆聽短文 Listen to the text with the help of the notes given

scholarship	獎學金
a prestigious college	享有盛譽的大學
smuggle	偷帶
disqualify	取消資格
a serious error of judgment	嚴重的錯誤判斷

再次聆聽並回答問題 Listen again and answer the questions below

Questions for discussion:

1 What had Alex planned to study in college?

2 Why did Alex fail the exam?

3 What did Alex learn from his experience?

336

短文聽讀 Text

Alex was so close to getting a scholarship to the college of his dreams. He had been preparing for years to study architecture in a prestigious college in the UK, and all he had to do was pass one final exam. However, Alex became nervous and started doubting his ability, so he decided to cheat by smuggling his smartphone into the exam hall. When one of the teachers saw him using his phone, he was immediately disqualified from the exam and given an automatic fail.

Alex was devastated. If he had believed in himself more, he might not have made such a serious error of judgment. If he hadn't cheated, he would have gotten the scholarship and would now be studying to be an architect. But he did learn one important lesson: Cheaters never prosper!

CH
6

性格特點

艾力克斯差點可以獲得夢想大學的獎學金。他已經準備許多年要在享有盛譽的英國某大學研讀建築學，而他唯一要做的是通過一個期末考。然而，艾力克斯變得很緊張，並開始懷疑自己的能力，所以他決定要偷帶他的智慧型手機進考試大廳。當其中一位老師看到他在用手機，他立即就被取消考試資格並自動給予不及格的成績。

　　艾力克斯悲傷欲絕。如果當時他更相信自己，或許就不會犯下如此嚴重的錯誤判斷了。如果他當時沒有作弊，或許就可以獲得獎學金且現在就在研讀怎麼當建築師。但他確實有學到重要的一課：作弊的人永遠不會飛黃騰達！

單字片語　**Vocabulary and Phrases**

1 prosper [ˋprɑspɚ] *vi.* 成功；興隆，繁榮
Business prospered under the new leadership.
在新的領導下生意變得興隆。

2 scholarship [ˋskɑlɚˏʃɪp] *n.* 獎學金

3 architecture [ˋɑrkəˏtɛktʃɚ] *n.* 建築學；建築風格 (不可數)

4 prestigious [prɛˋstɪdʒɪəs] *a.* 有名望的
prestige [prɛsˋtiʒ] *n.* 名望 (不可數)

5 doubt [daʊt] *vt. & n.* 懷疑
I don't doubt his abilities at all.
我一點也不懷疑他的能力。

IR Stone / Shutterstock.com

6 smuggle [ˋsmʌɡl] *vt.* 偷帶；走私
smuggle A into B　　把 A 走私到 B
The desperate man was arrested for smuggling drugs into Thailand.
那位走投無路的男子因走私毒品到泰國而被逮捕。

7 hall [hɔl] *n.* 大廳；走廊

8 disqualify [dɪsˋkwɑləˏfaɪ] *vt.* 取消資格
（三態為：disqualify, disqualified [dɪsˋkwɑləˏfaɪd], disqualified）
be disqualified from...　　取消……的資格
The athlete was disqualified from the competition.
那位運動員被取消比賽資格。

⑨ **automatic** [ˌɔtəˈmætɪk] *a.* 自動的

⑩ **fail** [fel] *n.* & *vt.* (考試) 不及格

⑪ **devastated** [ˈdɛvəsˌtetɪd] *a.* 悲傷欲絕的；極為震驚的

⑫ **error** [ˈɛrɚ] *n.* 錯誤，過失

⑬ **judgment** [ˈdʒʌdʒmənt] *n.* 判斷 (美式拼法)
= judgement (英式拼法)

⑭ **architect** [ˈɑrkəˌtɛkt] *n.* 建築師

實用詞句 **Useful Expressions**

🎙 All he had to do was pass one final exam.
他唯一要做的是通過一個期末考。

本句使用下列句型：

all sb has to do is (to) V　　某人唯一要做的是……
注意
本句型中的主詞 all sb has to do 原為 all that sb has to do，all 作代名詞，表示「全部」，that 引導形容詞子句修飾 all，而 that 通常會省略。be 動詞後的 to 可省略，直接接動詞原形作主詞補語。

All you have to do is (to) sit back and relax.
你唯一要做的是坐下來好好放鬆。

All we have to do is (to) wait.
我們唯一要做的就是等待。

發音提示 **Pronunciation**

❶ [aʊ]	doubt [daʊt]
	now [naʊ]

❷ [n] (置於母音後)	been [bin / bɪn]	phone [fon]
	in [ɪn]	given [ˋgɪvən]
	and [ænd]	an [æn]
	one [wʌn]	gotten [ˋgɑtən]
	smartphone [ˋsmɑrtfon]	important [ɪmˋpɔrtənt]
	into [ˋɪntu]	lesson [ˋlɛsən]
	when [(h)wɛn]	

朗讀短文 **Read aloud the text**

🔑 請特別注意 [aʊ]、[n]（置於母音後）的發音。

Alex was so close to getting a scholarship to the college of his dreams. He had been preparing for years to study architecture in a prestigious college in the UK, and all he had to do was pass one final exam. However, Alex became nervous and started doubting his ability, so he decided to cheat by smuggling his smartphone into the exam hall. When one of the teachers saw him using his phone, he was immediately disqualified from the exam and given an automatic fail.

Alex was devastated. If he had believed in himself more, he might not have made such a serious error of judgment. If he hadn't cheated, he would have gotten the scholarship and would now be studying to be an architect. But he did learn one important lesson: Cheaters never prosper!

換句話說 Retell

Retell the text "from the perspective of Alex" with the help of the words and expressions below.

scholarship, architecture, prestigious, doubt, smuggle, hall, disqualify, automatic, fail, devastated, error, judgment, architect, prosper

討論題目 Free Talk

Talk on the following topic:

◆ Have you ever felt stressful about an exam? How did you cope with the stress?

Lesson 60
A Modest Person Never Boasts
謙虛的人從不吹噓

搭配筆記聆聽短文 **Listen to the text with the help of the notes given**

talented	有才華的
swear	發誓
reincarnate	轉世
boast	吹噓
modest	謙虛的

再次聆聽並回答問題 **Listen again and answer the questions below**

🎙 Questions for discussion:

1️⃣ What is Lana good at?

2️⃣ What does the speaker think is the reason for Lana's popularity?

3️⃣ What might happen if Lana boasted about her talents?

My friend Lana is quite talented. She is an excellent pianist. If she were to play the piano for you, you'd swear Mozart had been reincarnated. She is also good at drawing and painting, and she is a wonderful cook. If she were to paint your portrait, you'd think it was a photograph. If she were to cook you a meal, you'd dream about that meal for an entire month.

Yet, she never boasts about her abilities like some people do. Perhaps that's why she is such a popular girl. Everyone likes her and wants to spend time with her because she is interested in people and actually listens to what other people say. If she were to boast about how talented she was, I'm sure some people would start to dislike her. But Lana would never do that. A modest person never boasts.

CH 6

性格特點

343

我的朋友拉娜十分有才華。她是很傑出的鋼琴家。假如她為你彈了鋼琴，你會發誓莫札特轉世了。她也擅長素描與畫畫，她的廚藝也很棒。她要是畫你的肖像畫，你會以為那是一張照片。她要是為你煮一頓飯，你整個月都會想著那頓飯。

然而，她從不像某些人一樣吹噓自己的能力。或許這是為什麼她是個如此受歡迎的女孩。所有人都喜歡她並想和她相處，因為她對人們感興趣，也真的會傾聽別人所說的話。如果她炫耀自己多有才華，我確信有些人會開始討厭她。但拉娜絕對不會這麼做。謙虛的人從不吹噓。

單字片語 Vocabulary and Phrases

❶ **talented** [ˋtæləntɪd] *a.* 有才華的；有天分的
talent [ˋtælənt] *n.* 才華，才能；天分
be talented in...　　在……方面有才華
= have a talent for...
Walter is talented in acting and performing.
= Walter has a talent for acting and performing.
華特在演戲與表演方面很有才華。

❷ **pianist** [ˋpɪənɪst / pɪˋænɪst] *n.* 鋼琴家

❸ **swear** [swɛr] *vt.* & *vi.* 發誓保證；發誓
（三態為：swear, swore [swɔr], sworn [swɔrn]）
swear to V　　發誓做……
I could have sworn there was a man following me.
我確信有個男子在跟蹤我。
The knight swore to protect the king and queen.
騎士發誓要保護國王與皇后。

❹ **reincarnate** [ˌriɪnˋkɑrnet] *vt.* 使投胎，轉世
reincarnation [ˌriɪnkɑrˋneʃən] *n.* 輪迴轉世

❺ **portrait** [ˋpɔrtret] *n.* 肖像，畫像

❻ **photograph** [ˋfotəˌɡræf] *n.* 照片
= photo [ˋfoto]
= picture [ˋpɪktʃɚ]

take a photograph / photo / picture　　拍照

The police took photographs of the crime scene.
警方拍了犯罪現場的照片。

7 **meal** [mil] *n.* 一餐

8 **boast** [bost] *vi.* 吹噓，自誇 & *vt.* 以擁有……自豪

boast about / of...　　吹噓 / 自誇……

= brag about / of...

Karen rarely boasts about her accomplishments.
凱倫很少炫耀自己的成就。

The Mediterranean country boasts amazing vacation spots.
那個地中海上的國家以擁有極佳的度假地點而自豪。

9 **modest** [ˈmɑdɪst] *a.* 謙虛的

= humble [ˈhʌmbl̩]

You're too modest!
你太謙虛了！

實用詞句　Useful Expressions

1 假設語氣 were to 的使用方法

If + 主詞 + were to...

本句型為假設語氣，可用於下列三個狀況：

a 強烈表示與真理或現在事實相反，使用時 were to 後應接動詞原形，主句採用過去式助動詞並接動詞原形。

If the sun were to rise in the west, I might believe you.
如果太陽打從西邊升起，我可能會相信你。
（本句使用 were to 強烈表示與真理相反，意即太陽不可能從西邊升起，故我不可能會相信你）

b 強烈表示未來不可能發生或發生機率極小的事。

If we were to miss the flight, we should call the insurance company.
假如我們錯過班機了，應該要打電話給保險公司。
（本句使用 were to 強烈表示在未來發生機率極小的事，意即我們不太可能會錯過班機）

CH 6 性格特點

345

c 強烈表示與過去事實相反，使用時 were to 後應接 "have + 過去分詞"，主句採用過去式助動詞並接 "have + 過去分詞"。

If our house were to have been destroyed by the fire, I would have been devastated.

如果我們的房子在大火中被燒毀了，我會傷心欲絕。

（本句使用 "were to have + 過去分詞" 強烈表示與過去事實相反，即我們的房子並沒有在大火中被燒毀）

2 Perhaps that's why she is such a popular girl.

或許這是為什麼她是個如此受歡迎的女孩。

本句使用關係副詞 why。why 只可用來修飾 the reason（理由）。若 the reason why 置於 be 動詞之後作主詞補語，the reason 可予以省略，保留關係副詞 why。由此可知本句原為：

Perhaps that's the reason why she is such a popular girl.

在限定修飾的關係子句中，亦可省略 why，保留 the reason，故本句亦可改寫如下：

Perhaps that's the reason she is such a popular girl.

發音提示 Pronunciation

1 [e]	play [ple]	portrait [ˈpɔrtret]
	reincarnate [ˌriɪnˈkɑrnet]	say [se]
	paint [pent]	

2 [m] （置於母音後）	dream [drim]
	some [sʌm]
	time [taɪm]

346

朗讀短文 Read aloud the text

📍 請特別注意 [e]、[m] (置於母音後) 的發音。

My friend Lana is quite talented. She is an excellent pianist. If she were to play the piano for you, you'd swear Mozart had been reincarnated. She is also good at drawing and painting, and she is a wonderful cook. If she were to paint your portrait, you'd think it was a photograph. If she were to cook you a meal, you'd dream about that meal for an entire month.

Yet, she never boasts about her abilities like some people do. Perhaps that's why she is such a popular girl. Everyone likes her and wants to spend time with her because she is interested in people and actually listens to what other people say. If she were to boast about how talented she was, I'm sure some people would start to dislike her. But Lana would never do that. A modest person never boasts.

換句話說 Retell

📍 Retell the text with the help of the words and expressions below.

talented, pianist, swear, reincarnate, portrait, photograph, meal, boast, modest

討論題目 Free Talk

📍 Talk on the following topic:

◆ Do you consider yourself a talented person?

CH
6

性格特點

347

Notes

參考答案

音檔 ▶

Lesson 01

🎤 再次聆聽並回答問題 **Listen again and answer the questions below**

1️⃣ Yes, old people can practice tai chi, too.

2️⃣ One benefit of tai chi is to reduce stress and anxiety.

3️⃣ No, it takes thousands of hours of training.

🎤 換句話說 **Retell**

Today, people of all ages around the world do tai chi as a form of exercise. Tai chi, an ancient Chinese martial art, is seen as having numerous physical and mental health benefits. Word has it that the slow movements and breathing can help to reduce stress and anxiety, improve mood, and promote better sleep.

There are versions of tai chi which place more emphasis on its combative side. Students learn how to use their own and their opponent's centers of gravity to their own advantage. However, it takes thousands of hours of training to master the ability to utilize tai chi as a form of self-defense.

🎤 討論題目 **Free Talk**

A friend of mine, Jerry, has been learning taekwondo for a few years. As a child, Jerry was skinny and weak. Other children often made fun of him because he never had the courage and strength to stand up for himself. One day, Jerry's father signed him up for a taekwondo class. At first, Jerry had no interest in learning taekwondo. Luckily, he had a good coach who was strict but patient. Under the guidance of his coach, Jerry eventually fell in love with the martial art. After practicing for a few years, Jerry is no longer the weak boy he once was. Now, he is strong and well-built, and more importantly, he is confident.

參考答案

Lesson 02

🎤 再次聆聽並回答問題 Listen again and answer the questions below

1 Brazilian jiu-jitsu is his favorite.

2 He recommends Brazilian jiu-jitsu.

3 No, he thinks she is small.

🎤 簡短對答 Quick Response

Q1 Have you ever taken a self-defense class before?

A1 No, I have never taken a self-defense class.

Q2 Do you consider yourself a strong person?

A2 No, I don't consider myself a strong person.

🎤 討論題目 Free Talk

Out of all the forms of martial arts, I would like to learn judo. Judo is a Japanese martial art that emphasizes flexibility and the use of leverage and balance instead of brute strength. It seems like the suitable option for me, since I'm neither tall nor strong. Judo teaches students how to respond to an attack safely, so the first thing that students learn in judo is how to fall without injuring themselves. Its focus on self-defense is also what interests me, because instead of fighting back against an attack, I would rather know how to protect myself. Judo also has many physical and mental health benefits. It helps build strong muscles, improve cardio health, and lower cholesterol. It also helps students increase concentration because judo mostly relies on techniques and timing.

Lesson 03

🎤 再次聆聽並回答問題 Listen again and answer the questions below

1 Bungee jumping is an activity that involves jumping from a tall structure while attached to a long elastic cord.

2 Yes, the speaker thinks there are few activities more thrilling than bungee jumping.

3 The key to bungee jumping is to not look down before jumping.

換句話說 Retell

Bungee jumping, an activity that involves jumping from a tall structure while attached to a long elastic cord, is an amazing experience that is on many people's bucket lists. It is one of the most thrilling activities. However, many people attempt to do it, but end up getting cold feet at the top. Therefore, it is necessary that you think about all aspects carefully.

Before jumping, it is essential that bungee jumping equipment be thoroughly checked. If you choose a reputable company, the safety record is likely to be good. Once you stand up there, the key to taking the leap is to not look down before you jump. It's also important that you not think too much about jumping. Just go for it! You won't regret it.

討論題目 Free Talk

I've never tried bungee jumping before, and I probably never will have the courage to do it. My brother, on the other hand, is an adrenaline junkie (腎上腺素狂 / 追求刺激狂). He loves doing all kinds of thrilling activities. Once, he went on a trip to New Zealand. Since New Zealand is known as the place to do extreme sports, my brother had to plan a trip to the country's most famous bungee jumping spot—the Kawarau Bridge in Queenstown. Once he arrived and stepped on the bridge and crossed over the railings, his heart pumped faster than ever. After taking a deep breath, he took the leap, with many people cheering for him. He said the jump itself was the most exciting thing he had ever done. And to go bungee jumping at one of the most famous sites made the experience even more unforgettable.

Lesson 04

🔖 再次聆聽並回答問題 Listen again and answer the questions below

① He has been going to the gym for a year now.

② Because she found it hard to stay motivated.

③ She will go to the gym with him tomorrow night.

🔖 簡短對答 Quick Response

Q1 Do you often do weightlifting?

A1 No, I seldom do weightlifting.

Q2 Would you like to look ripped?

A2 No, I don't want to look ripped.

🔖 討論題目 Free Talk

I prefer hitting the gym. To me, it is important to put myself in an environment where people are focused on working out. Seeing many people exercising helps me be more motivated and reminds me not to slack off. Also, in gyms, there are usually trainers that I can seek advice from. They can help correct my poses to make sure that I am training the right muscles and that I won't injure myself. Gyms also provide a wide variety of training equipment, and there is always equipment that best suits my training needs. I can use the dumbbells and heavy weights if I want to do weightlifting; I can use the treadmills and the bicycles if I want to do cardio training; and I can use the yoga mats if I feel like doing yoga or Pilates. Overall, hitting the gym is a more flexible and convenient option for me.

Lesson 05

🔖 再次聆聽並回答問題 Listen again and answer the questions below

① It is a race that consists of swimming, cycling, and running.

② You can start training for a triathlon.

3 Because the low-impact cycling and swimming compensate for the high-impact running.

換句話說 Retell

A triathlon is a multisport competition that consists of three distinctive events: swimming, cycling, and running. Although other variations exist, this is far and away the most popular combination. In the Olympic version of a triathlon, participants swim 1.5 km, cycle 40 km, and then run 10 km. All of these events are timed, and the transitions between the events are as well.

You can start training for a triathlon if you want to improve your physical fitness. Since it requires a persistent effort to improve in each of the three disciplines, it is a great way to get fit. Participants always try hard to surpass their previous personal record in each event. Triathlons also reduce the risk of injury to participants because the low-impact cycling and swimming compensate for the high-impact running.

討論題目 Free Talk

I would love to participate in the New York Marathon. Marathons are held all over the world. They are suitable for people of all ages as long as you are fit enough to run. As a person who runs daily, I have participated in several marathons before, including some of the most famous ones such as the Boston Marathon and the London Marathon. However, I've never had the chance to participate in the New York Marathon, which is widely regarded as the largest one. Even though I believe that I'll keep on running for the rest of my life, I might not be able to finish a marathon when I'm in my 40s or 50s. Since I'm not getting younger, I would love to have the chance to participate in this great event in my prime and run with some of the world's best marathon runners.

Lesson 06

🔖 再次聆聽並回答問題 Listen again and answer the questions below

1 She warns him about his smoking habit.

2 No, he finds it difficult to quit smoking.

3 She likes to go swimming.

🔖 簡短對答 Quick Response

Q1 Have you ever smoked before?

A1 No, I've never smoked before.

Q2 Do you keep a healthy lifestyle?

A2 Yes, I keep a healthy lifestyle.

🔖 討論題目 Free Talk

Personally, I prefer hiking to everything else. I have the habit of going hiking on a weekly basis. The thing that I look forward to every week is to go hiking on the weekend. There are various hiking trails around the city. The trails all have very distinctive scenery. Some overlook the city, some are near the coastline, and others are surrounded by mountains. What I love most about hiking is the moment when I finally arrive at the top of the mountain. It always gives me a satisfying feeling knowing that I've overcome the difficulties of climbing the mountain. And most of the time, the view is to die for, making the journey more worthwhile.

Lesson 07

🔖 再次聆聽並回答問題 Listen again and answer the questions below

1 The restaurant opened last week.

2 She is vegetarian.

3 He asked her not to use her cellphone while at the restaurant.

Q1 Have you ever tried venison before?

A1 No, I've never tried venison before.

Q2 Are you a vegetarian?

A2 No, I'm not a vegetarian.

🎈 討論題目 Free Talk

As a heavy user of my cellphone, I'm not really interested in dining at a "no cellphone" restaurant. I have the habit of taking photos of restaurants and the food while dining. It's a good way for me to make a record of all the restaurants that I've been to. Therefore, I would be frustrated if the restaurant didn't allow me to use my cellphone. However, I don't completely disagree with this policy. It is true that many people, including me, are too attached to our phones. There are even cases of people taking too much time taking photos of their food that the food has gone cold. From the restaurant owner's perspective, it might seem like the food was not fully appreciated. Perhaps I should go to these kinds of restaurants more often to break my habit of using my cellphone all the time.

Lesson 08

🎈 再次聆聽並回答問題 Listen again and answer the questions below

1 She realized that they contained too much sugar.

2 She wanted to eat a bar of chocolate.

3 She lost 3 kg.

🎈 換句話說 Retell

I used to drink a lot of soda and was continuously gaining weight. Wanting to stay fit, I thought that it was high time I kicked the habit of drinking soda. I also found that the afternoon snacks I fondly enjoyed contain too much sugar. For instance, my favorite chocolate cookies contained 17 g of sugar per "portion." Let's just say I never had only one portion! Therefore, I made up my mind to cut back on those, too.

It was very difficult for me at first: After every meal, I had sugar cravings and was desperate for a bar of chocolate! But, through willpower and determination, I successfully stayed away from junk food and began to lose weight. In the first week alone, I lost 3 kg. For those who drink too much soda and consume too much sugar, maybe it's about time they kicked the habit, too!

🔖 討論題目 Free Talk

Yes, I often crave snacks. I love eating all kinds of snacks, from chips and cookies to chocolate and candy. I usually have cravings for snacks at night, especially before I head to sleep. In my teenage years, I could eat as much as I wanted and did not gain weight at all because I exercised a lot and my metabolism was at its best. However, nowadays, I cannot afford to eat like that anymore. I have come up with a strict rule not to eat anything past 8 p.m. This is to help me stay fit and to avoid indigestion. And whenever I feel the desire to eat snacks at night, I drink water instead. This is a good way to fill my stomach and stay hydrated at the same time. I also try not to keep any snacks at home. There's no way I can eat snacks if I don't have any at home!

Lesson 09

🔖 再次聆聽並回答問題 Listen again and answer the questions below

1 No, he did not do well in the basketball game.

2 She forgot to bring her purse.

3 She suggests that they go out for pizza.

簡短對答 Quick Response

Q1 Have you ever tried to do something that was too hard for you?

A1 Yes, I've tried things that were too hard for me to do before.

Q2 Do you agree that we should always take things step by step?

A2 I think it's fine to challenge yourself once in a while.

討論題目 Free Talk

I have felt like a fish out of water before. It was when I moved to another country for a new job opportunity. I was unfamiliar with the culture and the environment, and I wasn't fluent in the local language. Although I tried very hard to blend in, I still couldn't help but feel like an outsider all the time. For a while, I was reluctant to interact with other people because I knew it would make me feel embarrassed. However, after a while, the situation became too inconvenient for me. I eventually decided to put an effort into learning the local language and began to talk to other people. I simply accepted the fact that I could not escape from the situation and I just had to find ways to cope. Being a fish out of water certainly felt awkward, but it helped me become more courageous.

Lesson 10

再次聆聽並回答問題 Listen again and answer the questions below

1 Because they wish to be healthier.

2 One of the health benefits is that it reduces the risk of heart disease.

3 There will be less climate-changing emissions.

換句話說 Retell

With a view to becoming healthier, more and more people are becoming vegetarian. For example, in the US, it is estimated that around 8% of adults are vegetarian. In some countries such as

357

Germany, the figure is higher. Being vegetarian comes with many benefits. It can lower the risk of heart disease and certain cancers, and type 2 diabetes as well.

Being vegetarian can also help the environment by reducing global warming. Although raising animals is a great source of food and income in developing countries, it could worsen climate change. The less meat we eat, the greater the reduction in climate-changing emissions. You could take these facts as food for thought when deciding whether to be a vegetarian or not.

討論題目 Free Talk

My mother is a vegetarian. Most people from her generation became vegetarian due to religious reasons. My mother, however, decided to be vegetarian because she wanted to help the planet. She became aware of the severity of global warming about 30 years ago, and thought that as a citizen of the world, she should make an effort to help reduce greenhouse gases. Therefore, she decided to become vegetarian. Although I completely support and admire her, I find it hard to follow in her footsteps. Simply put, I love eating meat! However, this doesn't stop me from loving my mom's homemade dishes. She is an amazing cook, and she can make vegetables taste as flavorful as meat. No wonder my father found it easy to become a vegetarian after he met my mother.

Lesson 11

再次聆聽並回答問題 Listen again and answer the questions below

❶ You should stay in cheap hostels to save more money.

❷ No, the speaker does not recommend dining at fancy restaurants.

❸ Yes, it is possible to travel on a low budget.

換句話說 Retell

Many people want to travel the world, but traveling can cost a lot of money. Flights, car rental, accommodations, entrance tickets to attractions, food and drink… The list of costly items can seem endless.

Have you ever wondered what you can do to make traveling more budget-friendly? Let me give you a few tips! You can travel on budget airlines instead of national carriers. You can take public transportation instead of renting a car. You can book rooms at affordable hostels instead of hotels. You can pre-book entrance tickets at cheaper prices. Instead of dining at fancy restaurants, you can eat street food. You can still travel the world whatever your budget is.

討論題目 Free Talk

I have traveled on a budget before. A few years ago, I flew abroad to Europe to visit my friend, who was living in Spain to study for her master's degree. From my past experience, I realized that the most expensive things when traveling are usually the flight tickets and accommodations. Therefore, I decided to fly with a low-cost airline instead of a traditional airline. As to accommodations, thankfully my friend let me stay at her dorm for free. And even when I traveled to other countries or cities, I stayed in hostels or couch surfed. I also saved money on other things as well, such as entrance tickets to tourist attractions and museums, by booking the tickets early online. Overall, my trip to Europe cost me less money than I had expected.

參考答案

📍 再次聆聽並回答問題 **Listen again and answer the questions below**

1 You should tip her $1 or $2.

2 No, tipping cultures vary in different countries.

3 No, you shouldn't give tips when traveling in Japan.

📍 換句話說 **Retell**

  Have you ever thought about how much you should tip when you travel abroad? Is tipping optional or mandatory? This is a dilemma faced by most travelers, who are unsure of the rules. So, let me give you a few general tips to make tipping less taxing!

  In the United States, the standard tip in most restaurants is 15%. It is customary to tip hotel staff $1 or $2, especially to those who help carry your luggage or clean your room. The tipping culture varies from country to country. For instance, in Australia and the UK, tipping is optional, while in Canada and Mexico, tips are expected. Meanwhile, in Japan, tipping is actually seen as an insult!

📍 討論題目 **Free Talk**

No, I don't think tipping should exist. I understand that in some countries, tipping is a good way for waiters and waitresses to gain extra income. In the United States, for instance, most restaurants only pay their staff at or slightly above the minimum wage, so waiters and waitresses have to rely on tips to make more money. However, I want to argue that instead of expecting customers to tip their employees, restaurant owners should just raise the wages. I also think that good restaurant service should be provided whether there's a tip or not. Customers shouldn't be punished with bad service when they can't or don't want to tip the staff.

Lesson 13

🖊 再次聆聽並回答問題 **Listen again and answer the questions below**

1 He drank a lot of vodka and got drunk.

2 The drinking tradition in Russia is to toast everyone and everything until the bottle is empty.

3 No, he does not remember how much he drank.

🖊 簡短對答 **Quick Response**

Q1 Have you ever drunk alcohol before?

A1 No, I've never drunk alcohol before.

Q2 Would you like to travel to Russia?

A2 Yes, I would like to travel to Russia.

🖊 討論題目 **Free Talk**

In my country, the drinking culture is much like many other countries. When everyone toasts together, you're expected to drink as well. If you don't feel like drinking, though, taking a small sip is also acceptable. And people who are younger or are of lower status should not hold their glasses higher than the others. When toasting, people usually yell in unison "Ganbei," which means "Cheers." Yelling this helps people get into the mood of drinking more easily and helps hype up everyone. Drinking also plays an important role in people's social lives. More and more people tend to meet friends at bars or nightclubs instead of only restaurants. Although excessive drinking can lead to many problems, it is undeniable that drinking is a great way to help people bond and to improve people's social lives.

參考答案

1 No, there are no sales assistants in a self-service store.

2 They need to use a smartphone to check out.

3 A downside is the risk of theft and fraud.

換句話說 Retell

Are you interested in shopping in a self-service store? In self-service stores, there are no sales assistants, and customers have to use their smartphones to check out. More and more stores, from EasyGo in China to Amazon Go in the US, are introducing this technology. Retailers like it because they can redirect resources from the repetitive checkout process to actual customer service, where they are most needed.

There are a couple of downsides to / of these self-service stores. For the retailer, there is the risk of theft and fraud, as well as the perception that the retailers are faceless entities. For the customer, especially those who are older or less tech-savvy, there is the risk of confusion and the possibility of making honest mistakes. Retailers need to strike the right balance between tech-driven efficiency and old-fashioned customer care.

討論題目 Free Talk

Yes, I would like to shop in a self-service store. It is impossible to deny that technology is developing fast. Sooner or later, technology will be able to replace human staff. And self-service stores are the perfect example. Nowadays, many supermarkets around the world have already installed self-service checkout counters, allowing customers to do the checkout process by themselves. I've had the chance to use this type of checkout counter before. I was shocked by how easy and convenient it was. If I'm not buying a lot of things, the checkout process can be done swiftly in less than two minutes.

And all I needed was my credit card. It makes me wonder, though, how a self-service store without any human staff at all would function.

Lesson **15**

🎙 再次聆聽並回答問題 Listen again and answer the questions below

1 People often seek help from the internet.

2 Usually, the first step is to work out a budget.

3 A way to earn more money is to get a part-time job.

🎙 換句話說 Retell

These days, many families and individuals find it hard to make ends meet, meaning they struggle to earn enough money to provide for their basic needs. Incomes often don't increase as fast as the cost of rent, gas, electricity, food, and many other household bills.

People often turn to the internet to search for ideas of how to save money. Usually, the first step is to figure out a budget. This way, you can see how much you should spend and know where to lower costs. There is another area you can focus on: earning more money. You could find a part-time job, request a raise or promotion at work, sell second-hand items online, or even become a dog walker!

🎙 討論題目 Free Talk

Before deciding where to reduce costs or how to increase my income, I usually start with making a budget. Keeping a budget helps me understand what I am spending the most on and which items are unnecessary. Based on this, I can decide what to cut down on. Normally, I restrict myself to dining out less than five times a month. However, if there are some special occasions that make me break the rule, I'll find some other areas to lower my spending. Overall, I try my best not to go over budget. Aside from reducing costs, I also invest money to increase my income. One of my investments is buying stocks. However, it's a very risky method. And sometimes I even lose money instead of earning more.

Lesson 16

🎙 再次聆聽並回答問題 **Listen again and answer the questions below**

❶ She says they need to reduce their monthly expenses.

❷ She suggests creating a budget.

❸ They will start making a budget next month.

🎙 簡短對答 **Quick Response**

Q1 Are you in the habit of saving money?

A1 Yes, I am in the habit of saving money.

Q2 Do you keep a budget every month?

A2 Yes, I keep a budget every month.

🎙 討論題目 **Free Talk**

I spend the most on food every month. To be more specific, dining out with my friends costs me the most money. I go out with my friends almost every week. Whenever we go out, we never just stay in one restaurant. After dinner at a fancy restaurant, we usually go to a pub, and then very likely a nightclub. The food at the restaurant and the drinks at the pub and nightclub all cost a considerable amount of money. I love going out with my friends, but judging from my budget, I doubt that I can afford to go on like this. Maybe it's the perfect opportunity for me to quit drinking and start saving more money.

🔖 再次聆聽並回答問題 **Listen again and answer the questions below**

1️⃣ They can sell whatever they want.

2️⃣ Yes, you can offer a cheaper price.

3️⃣ It was sold for $3 at first.

🔖 換句話說 **Retell**

At flea markets, people can buy and sell goods. Vendors can sell anything that they want to whomever they choose. It's a good place to get second-hand goods, antiques, collectibles, and cheap items. Most of the time, the prices are not fixed and you can haggle, which means you can offer whatever price you think is reasonable for the items you like.

There is also a slim possibility that you might get very lucky. For instance, a Chinese bowl sold for $3 in New York turned out to be 1,000 years old and was sold at an auction years later for $2.2 million! And an original copy of the US Declaration of Independence was discovered inside a $4 painting and was later sold for $2.4 million!

🔖 討論題目 **Free Talk**

Yes, I have been to a flea market before. The flea market I went to was full of vendors selling vintage clothes, homemade baked goods, and all sorts of second-hand items. I came across a vendor selling vintage clothing. The clothing items that the vendor was selling really caught my eye. There were university sweaters from the 1990s, some old leather bags that were made 20 years ago, and even several pieces of jewelry passed down from generation to generation. What I loved the most about these items was that they all had a story behind them. For instance, the vendor told me that one of the leather bags was his father's. His father always carried the bag with him all around the world on business trips. He had

參考答案

traveled to Europe, Asia, North America, and even the Middle East. The bag had been to more places than I have!

Lesson 18

再次聆聽並回答問題 Listen again and answer the questions below

1 He wants to sell it for $20 at first.

2 She pays $16.50 for it in the end.

3 She is looking for some good quality old vinyl records.

簡短對答 Quick Response

Q1 Have you ever haggled before?

A1 Yes, I have haggled before.

Q2 Do you enjoy going to flea markets?

A2 Yes, I enjoy going to flea markets.

討論題目 Free Talk

If I had the chance to be a vendor at a flea market, I would sell my clothes. As a person who loves fashion, it's important for me to keep up with the trends, so I'm always buying new clothes. My closet is full of clothes from last season that I barely wear now. It's a shame to see these clothes just hanging in the closet. Selling them to other people at a flea market would be a good chance for me to clean out my closet. And since I can also make some money out of selling my second-hand clothes, I would have more money to buy new ones! It sounds like such a good idea. Maybe I really should put this idea into practice.

Lesson 19

再次聆聽並回答問題 Listen again and answer the questions below

1 She loves the feelings of happiness and contentment that shopping provides.

2 Because they might spend more than they can afford.

3 Too much stress and depression might be the cause of excessive shopping.

換句話說 Retell

I'm a shopaholic. I can't go through a day without shopping. I love the feelings of happiness and contentment that shopping brings. Although my closet is crowded, I still think it's short of one more pair of shoes. Though my kitchen is packed, I always believe it needs one more appliance. Luckily, I earn enough money so that I can afford everything. And, even if I lose my job, I have plenty I can sell!

However, for some people, being a shopaholic is no laughing matter. While I earn enough money to cover my splurges, others might spend much more than they can afford. As high as their credit card bills are, they always add more to the balance. Shopaholics often shop as a way to cope with stressful situations, or to deal with depression. They are also prone to damage their personal relationships through their behavior—just like any other addict. Those who think shopping is taking over their lives should always seek help.

討論題目 Free Talk

No, I don't consider myself a shopaholic. However, before I learned to be more responsible with my money, I used to buy things constantly. I was always shopping for new clothes, new shoes, and new cosmetics. However, most of the stuff that I bought was only used once or twice. Some of it was never even opened. I wasn't aware of how much I was spending until I took a closer look at my credit card bills. Now, I always keep a budget and try not to buy things on impulse. After all, I don't come from money and my monthly salary is not exactly a great fortune. I do hope that one day,

參考答案

I will be so wealthy that I can buy whatever I want without checking the price tags, but I know that some dreams just won't come true.

Lesson 20

再次聆聽並回答問題 Listen again and answer the questions below

❶ He got 30% off in the end.

❷ No, the chairs don't go with the table.

❸ Yes, he will buy the chairs as well.

簡短對答 Quick Response

Q1 Do you enjoy shopping at a thrift store?

A1 Yes, I enjoy shopping at a thrift store.

Q2 Are you good at bargaining?

A2 No, I'm not good at bargaining.

討論題目 Free Talk

No, I've never bargained at a thrift shop before. However, my mother does it all the time, and not only in thrift shops but practically all other kinds of shops as well. Once, I went with her to a department store. Supposedly, in department stores, customers cannot bargain for a cheaper price and have to pay whatever price is listed on the price tags. However, my mother saw a jacket that she liked but thought was too expensive. She argued with the salesperson and said that she always shopped there and was a long-time customer of their store. She asked for a discount on the jacket even though there weren't any sales events at the moment. My mother refused to take no for an answer. In the end, the salesperson, not wanting to offend my mother, had no choice but to give her a discount. I felt sorry for the salesperson but was also impressed by my mother at the same time.

Lesson 21

再次聆聽並回答問題 Listen again and answer the questions below

1 Yes, he likes the town.

2 No, his family is not with him.

3 They will join him next week.

簡短對答 Quick Response

Q1 Do you live in a town or a city?

A1 I live in a city.

Q2 Have you ever invited friends over to your house?

A2 Yes, I have invited friends over before.

討論題目 Free Talk

I prefer living in a big city. I find living in the city more convenient because there are restaurants and supermarkets nearby. I rarely have to drive my car when I go out. And even if the destination is too far to walk to, I can just take the bus or the metro. I never have to worry about looking for a parking spot or paying the parking fee. Moreover, there are so many things to see and do in the city. We have a movie theater, a museum, and a department store. Another thing I love about living in the city is that the citizens are so diverse. We all come from different backgrounds and cultures, which helps shape all the different aspects of the city.

Lesson 22

再次聆聽並回答問題 Listen again and answer the questions below

1 They are in the woman's house.

2 She bought soil for the garden.

3 Yes, he will come again next week.

簡短對答 Quick Response

Q1 Do you have a garden?

A1 No, I don't have a garden.

Q2 Have you ever been to a housewarming party before?

A2 Yes, I've been to a housewarming party before.

討論題目 Free Talk

If I had a garden, I'd want it to be full of roses, which are my favorite flowers. In fact, I want there to be all different colors of roses: red, white, pink, yellow, blue, purple, and black. However, a garden with only flowers can be quite dull, so I also want to add some green and leafy plants. Herbs like mint and basil (羅勒；九層塔) would be a great choice. These green plants would be pleasing to the eye, and I could use their leaves for cooking as well! Succulents (多肉植物) would also be great additions to my garden. There are hundreds of varieties, and they are very easy to grow. There are so many flowers and plants that I would like to grow in my garden!

Lesson 23

再次聆聽並回答問題 Listen again and answer the questions below

1 It will be boiling hot tomorrow.

2 They should wear sunscreen lotion and avoid the midday sun.

3 No, it's too hot for him.

簡短對答 Quick Response

Q1 How is the weather today where you live?

A1 It's freezing cold today.

Q2 Do you always put on sunscreen lotion when you go out?

A2 Yes, I always put on sunscreen lotion when I go out.

討論題目 Free Talk

I prefer cold weather to hot weather. In the city that I live, it's always scorching hot in the summer. Sometimes, it gets so humid and uncomfortable that I don't want to step outside for even just one second. And whenever I'm at home, I always make sure that the air-conditioner is on. Because of this, during summertime, the bills for electricity are always very expensive. Therefore, I always look forward to winter. I don't mind the weather being cold. I actually enjoy chilly temperatures. There's nothing more comfortable than covering myself with a soft blanket and drinking a cup of hot chocolate on a winter day. And I can always put on more clothes if the weather becomes too cold.

Lesson 24

再次聆聽並回答問題 Listen again and answer the questions below

❶ Because his wife is feeling under the weather.

❷ The speaker received a parking ticket.

❸ No, the speaker does not regret it.

換句話說 Retell

A few days ago, my wife was feeling under the weather, so I took her to the doctor's. We were late for the appointment because the traffic was bad. We had to get to the back of the queue and wait for an hour.

To make matters worse, I received a parking ticket for parking illegally outside the clinic! Frankly, it was my fault. I knew I wasn't supposed to park there. There even was a sign that told drivers they would be fined for parking there. However, my wife's health will always be top priority, so I don't regret it at all.

参考答案

371

🔑 討論題目 **Free Talk**

Yes, I've been fined before. It was a ticket for jaywalking. I used to be an impatient person. I never liked waiting for the traffic light, especially when there were no cars on the street. One day, I wanted to walk to the post office, which was just across the street from my house. Normally, the street is busy with heavy traffic, but on that day, the traffic was pretty light, and there were only a few cars passing by. Therefore, I thought it seemed unnecessary to wait for the traffic light to turn green to cross the street. As I walked halfway across the street, I heard a man shouting at me. As it turned out, it was a police officer! In the end, I received a ticket and learned a valuable lesson.

Lesson 25

🔑 再次聆聽並回答問題 **Listen again and answer the questions below**

1 He got pickpocketed.

2 She suggests informing the police.

3 No, he doesn't want to report the crime.

🔑 簡短對答 **Quick Response**

Q1 Have you ever been pickpocketed before?

A1 No, I've never been pickpocketed before.

Q2 Have you ever reported a crime before?

A2 No, I've never reported a crime before.

🔑 討論題目 **Free Talk**

If I were the man, I would definitely report the crime to the police. Considering that I always keep important things such as my identification card, driver's license, and credit cards in my wallet, it would be a nightmare if my wallet were stolen from me. Moreover, I think you should go to the police even if you had simply misplaced your wallet. Informing the police is something we must do no matter how petty we think the matter might be. Even though there's a good chance that we won't recover what was stolen from us, it is still a way to protect ourselves from future troubles such as identity theft or somebody hacking into our accounts.

Lesson 26

🎙 再次聆聽並回答問題 Listen again and answer the questions below

1 No, it is not a clinical condition.

2 They might feel grief, loneliness, or loss of purpose.

3 A way to cope with empty nest syndrome is to join clubs and pursue new interests.

🎙 換句話說 Retell

　　You might feel down when your child leaves home and goes to university or moves out of the house. This phenomenon is called "empty nest syndrome." Even though it is not a clinical condition, people who experience it may be vulnerable to depression and marital conflicts. They may experience feelings of grief, loneliness, or loss of purpose.

　　You can join clubs and pursue new interests to avoid or cope with empty nest syndrome. Using it as an opportunity to spend some quality time with your partner is also a good way. When you and your child live apart, you can keep in touch with them on a regular basis. And whenever they come home to visit, you can treasure these moments even more.

🎙 討論題目 Free Talk

When I was a child, I lived in a village in the countryside. By the time I graduated from high school, I had no choice but to leave my hometown to pursue higher education. Even though life in the village was simple and tranquil, it could be dull and boring at times.

I was hoping to experience the hustle and bustle of the city. And for the first few weeks, I did enjoy the excitement and had a lot of fun. However, I started to feel homesick after a while. I missed the small village where everyone was so friendly and knew each other by name. In the city, on the other hand, people were indifferent and always suspicious of others. There were definitely times when I preferred country life to city life.

Lesson 27

🔑 再次聆聽並回答問題 **Listen again and answer the questions below**

1 No, this is not the first time he has lost his things.

2 She suggests that he should call his wife.

3 No, she doesn't want to lend him her phone.

🔑 簡短對答 **Quick Response**

Q1 Have you ever lost your keys before?

A1 No, I've never lost my keys before.

Q2 If you were the woman, would you lend the man your phone?

A2 Yes, I would lend him my phone.

🔑 討論題目 **Free Talk**

No, I seldom lose my things. However, when I lose something, it's always items that are very expensive. Once, I was taking the bus to school and I brought my laptop, which I had placed inside a bag. I fell asleep on the bus because I had stayed up all night writing a report. When I woke up, I saw that the bus had just arrived at my stop, so I quickly got off the bus. As soon as the bus set off, I noticed that I had left the bag with my laptop on the bus. Although I was on the verge of a breakdown, I tried my best to remain calm and called the bus company to tell them about the situation. To my delight, they informed me that another passenger saw the bag and gave it to the driver. Eventually, I got my bag and laptop back, and I couldn't have been more thankful.

Lesson 28

🔖 再次聆聽並回答問題 Listen again and answer the questions below

1 She tells him to tidy up his room.

2 Because he was getting changed.

3 He was pretending to be in a cave.

🔖 簡短對答 Quick Response

Q1 How often do you clean your room?

A1 I clean my room on a weekly basis.

Q2 Do you usually keep things in place or lying around in your room?

A2 Usually, my things are lying around in my room.

🔖 討論題目 Free Talk

Yes, I've talked back to my parents before. It was many years ago when I was a little girl. According to my mother, she wanted me to do some chores for her, but I was too occupied with my toys and didn't want to stop playing. She said that I even told her to do the chores herself. Since I was only 3 or 4 years old at that time, she was shocked to hear me talk back to her. She didn't know whether to laugh or cry. She mainly just wondered where I had learned to talk like that. My mother said she's thankful that I always help her with the chores now without much complaint. Perhaps that was the time when I was most rebellious.

Lesson 29

🔖 再次聆聽並回答問題 Listen again and answer the questions below

1 Because he needed to catch the train.

2 It can disrupt the body clock even more.

3 We should get straight out of bed.

換句話說 Retell

I was awoken from my deep sleep by my wife, Hannah. She told me that it was already 6 a.m., and that I had to get up now for fear of missing my train. I couldn't bring myself to leave my nice, warm bed, though, so I slept for another hour. As one would expect, I didn't catch my early train. Perhaps I should have booked a later train. Or perhaps I should have listened to my wife and gotten out of bed sooner!

It is not easy getting out of bed in the morning, especially when you're not a morning person. It can be tempting to keep pressing the snooze button so that you get a few more precious minutes under the covers. However, most sleep experts agree that going back to sleep can disrupt the body clock even more. That's why when the alarm goes off, you should get straight out of bed for fear that you'll fall back asleep!

討論題目 Free Talk

I don't consider myself a morning person. I love sleeping in and lying in my bed. It's always hard for me to get up in the morning, especially on cold winter days. There's nothing I enjoy more than being wrapped under warm covers when it's cold outside. And if I don't get enough sleep, I tend to be a bit moody. Since I love sleeping in so much, I'm always scared that I'll oversleep and be late for work. Therefore, I always have at least five alarm clocks set on my phone. My roommate often complains about my alarm clocks, but I don't know what else to do. I tend to fall back asleep as soon as I turn off the first alarm. Maybe I'll try to go to sleep earlier so that it won't be so hard for me to wake up in the morning.

🔖 再次聆聽並回答問題 Listen again and answer the questions below

1 They can volunteer for community cleanups.

2 No, he doesn't want to drink less coffee.

3 He should always take a reusable shopping bag before leaving the house.

🔖 簡短對答 Quick Response

Q1 Would you like to help save the planet?

A1 Yes, I would like to help save the planet.

Q2 Do you drink coffee every day?

A2 Yes, I drink coffee every day.

🔖 討論題目 Free Talk

Every weekday, I take public transportation to commute to and from work. I always bring my own lunch, which is stored in a reusable container, to work. This way, I can reduce consumption and waste. When I go out, I always take a reusable shopping bag and a set of utensils with me. At first, it was a bit inconvenient and odd using my own chopsticks and spoons when eating at a diner that only provides disposable ones. However, after picking up this habit, I realized that it's actually a lot cleaner because we never know what chemicals were used to make those disposable chopsticks or spoons. Aside from taking public transportation and using reusable items, I've picked up a few habits that can help save the planet. For instance, I turn off the light whenever I leave a room; I reduce my usage of hot water when I'm taking a shower; I also eat less meat in the hope of reducing greenhouse gases.

參考答案

Lesson 31

🔑 再次聆聽並回答問題 Listen again and answer the questions below

1. They say online dating allows you to meet people you never would have met in real life.
2. The speaker thinks people should take sensible precautions.
3. I should make sure I am comfortable with the situation.

🔑 換句話說 Retell

Recently, online dating has become widely accepted as a way of meeting new people. Indeed, one out of five relationships now begins through the internet. Those who are for online dating say it allows you to meet people you probably never would have met in reality. There are a wealth of dating apps available, including Tinder, with its well-known "swipe right" function.

No matter which app you choose, though, it is important to take sensible precautions, such as not revealing too much personal information. No matter what someone asks you to do or send, make sure you are comfortable with the situation. And whomever you choose to meet, make sure they are who they say they are!

🔑 討論題目 Free Talk

Yes, I am interested in using online dating apps. I think it's a good way for us to meet people outside our daily lives. These days, more and more people are afraid of stepping out of their comfort zones, making it harder for them to make new friends, not to mention start romantic relationships. Using online dating apps can give us plenty of opportunities to meet new people, increasing our chances of meeting "the one." However, it's wrong to ignore the fact that online dating apps can also be dangerous. After all, it's difficult to truly know another person until we've met them face to face. And there are some people who take advantage of these apps to cheat people out of money or commit other crimes. To sum up, I would love to try online dating apps, but I would also remember to be cautious when using them.

Lesson 32

🎙 再次聆聽並回答問題 Listen again and answer the questions below

❶ No, they have not met in person before.

❷ He suggests they go to a café for coffee, and then take a walk in the park.

❸ They will meet at 2 p.m. on Saturday.

🎙 簡短對答 Quick Response

Q1 Have you ever used an online dating app before?

A1 No, I have never used an online dating app before.

Q2 Do you have any online friends?

A2 No, I don't have any online friends.

🎙 討論題目 Free Talk

A friend of mine, Ted, met a girl on an online dating app. They have so much in common. They both like video games and comic books; they both like exercising and hitting the gym; they both are engineers working for large technology companies. From the moment they met, Ted couldn't stop talking about this girl. One day, he finally plucked up the courage and asked her out. And much to his delight, she agreed. On the long-awaited day, Ted made an effort to dress nice and even bought some flowers. When the girl showed up, he didn't know whether to laugh or cry. It was his colleague! They were shocked when they saw each other, but they found the situation quite funny. In the end, they talked more than they had ever talked while at work. Now, they are a lovely couple who have been together for years.

參考答案

Lesson 33

再次聆聽並回答問題 Listen again and answer the questions below

1. Over 3 billion people use social media around the world.
2. It can also be used as a source of news and information.
3. On average, a person spends almost two hours per day on social media.

換句話說 Retell

In spite of being less than twenty years old, social media now has more than 3 billion users around the globe. YouTube, WhatsApp, and WeChat are some of the most popular social media sites, with over 1 billion users. Nowadays, social media is used not only to share our photos and opinions, but as a source of news and information as well.

Despite the fact that most people lead busy lives, they still manage to find time to spend on social media. A person spends, on average, almost two hours a day on social media. Some of this is during the commute to and from work. And, in spite of the fact that many companies frown on social media use at the office, inevitably some of it is used during work time.

討論題目 Free Talk

Yes, I am a heavy user of social media. Although I don't like to post pictures or comments, I like to read other people's posts. I use social media probably more often than I should. I usually use it while I'm commuting to and from work, while I'm having a meal, and before I sleep at night. Overall, I probably spend more than four hours on it per day. However, most of the time, it's not that the posts on social media are that interesting; it's just that I sometimes feel anxious not knowing what is going on with other people. I feel a constant need to know everything, or else I won't be able to catch up with others.

This makes it hard for me to quit using social media. I realize that it has become an unhealthy influence on me, and I would like to break this habit more than anything.

Lesson 34

📍 再次聆聽並回答問題 **Listen again and answer the questions below**

1 She wants him to pick her up and take her to work.

2 He told her to fill up her car.

3 Because she thinks he had a bad attitude.

📍 簡短對答 **Quick Response**

Q1 Do you drive to work?

A1 No, I don't drive to work.

Q2 How do you usually commute to work?

A2 I take the bus to work.

📍 討論題目 **Free Talk**

If someone who was talking to me had a bad attitude, I would stop listening and walk away. It's natural to have negative emotions, but no one wants to talk to someone who is moody, annoyed, or irritated. Once, I was going on a trip and had to take the early train. I asked my brother to give me a ride to the train station. He probably got up on the wrong side of the bed and started talking to me in a bad tone. He asked me if he looked like a taxi driver and kept going on about how he was tired of driving me around all the time. Well, I would never force him to do anything for me, and all he needed to say was a simple no. Seeing that he was clearly in a bad mood at that time, I decided to walk away without saying anything, because anything that I said might have annoyed him and turned the conversation into a huge argument.

Lesson 35

🔑 再次聆聽並回答問題 Listen again and answer the questions below

1️⃣ It is an interactive computer-generated experience.

2️⃣ Children can use it to experience life in the past.

3️⃣ Surgeons can act as if they were in real-life situations.

🔑 換句話說 Retell

Virtual Reality (VR) is an interactive experience that is generated by computer. It takes place within a simulated environment. Generally, users wear a VR headset, which generates sounds and images that take them on a sensory journey. They can move around and interact with this new "world."

VR could become the future of gaming. Depending on the game you play, you can feel as though you are in a setting similar to the real world or a complete fantasy world. You can become anyone you want to be, and do anything you wish to do.

Besides gaming, VR also has many more practical applications. It can be used to train astronauts, making them feel as though they were in space. It can be used for education, helping children experience life in the past. And it can be used for medical training, allowing surgeons to act as if they were in real-life situations. The possibilities are endless.

🔑 討論題目 Free Talk

No, I've never experienced VR before. I would love to try it. I love playing video games, and I've seen VR applied in several games. It seems very cutting-edge and entertaining. It's also nice to see video game companies developing new ways to play that are very different from the traditional screen and controllers. With VR goggles, players can immerse themselves in any environment, and the experience will be more lifelike than ever. However, what has stopped me from trying VR is the price. To experience virtual reality, you need to have the equipment first. The headset and other gadgets cost a lot more than traditional controllers. I guess I'll just wait until the technology is more widely used so that the cost will lower to a more affordable price. Who knows, maybe by then there will be another new technology that'll surpass virtual reality!

Lesson 36

再次聆聽並回答問題 Listen again and answer the questions below

1. His girlfriend broke up with him.
2. She said he's not considerate enough.
3. He will try to be more considerate.

簡短對答 Quick Response

Q1. Do you consider yourself a considerate person?
A1. Yes, I consider myself a considerate person.
Q2. Have you ever been dumped before?
A2. No, I've never been dumped before.

討論題目 Free Talk

My friend Andy went through the worst break-up ever. He and his girlfriend had been together since middle school, so their relationship had been going on for ten years. Andy had never once thought about liking someone else or meeting another person. He always felt like his girlfriend was "the one." After they graduated from university, Andy thought it was about time they settled down and started a family. He had planned a surprise proposal with bouquets of roses and romantic candles. He had also invited all of their friends and family. However, as Andy knelt down on one knee and took out the ring, his girlfriend ran away, leaving everyone speechless. A few days later, we finally learned that his girlfriend was tired of their relationship and had met someone else. Poor Andy. He has been feeling down ever since.

Lesson 37

🔑 再次聆聽並回答問題 **Listen again and answer the questions below**

1 She is in London, England.

2 Because the flight tickets are expensive, and he doesn't have enough money.

3 Because she has a lot of coursework to do and doesn't have the time to travel.

🔑 簡短對答 **Quick Response**

Q1 Would you be willing to be in a long-distance relationship?

A1 No, I don't want to be in a long-distance relationship.

Q2 What do you dislike the most about long-distance relationships?

A2 I dislike the time difference the most.

🔑 討論題目 **Free Talk**

Yes, I believe I can maintain a long-distance relationship well. I'm not a clingy or needy person, and I rather enjoy being by myself. In relationships, I usually prefer to have some personal space and time. There are many things that I would rather do alone or with my friends than with my partner. Honestly, I don't mind not seeing my partner every day or not constantly being in touch with them. And look on the bright side: Being in a long-distance relationship would mean that I had more freedom to do whatever I wanted. Therefore, I believe I would be fine in a long-distance relationship. However, it doesn't mean that I actually want to be in a long-distance relationship. Just like everyone else, I still prefer getting to see my partner and being able to talk to them whenever I choose.

再次聆聽並回答問題 Listen again and answer the questions below

❶ Because the speaker thought she was pregnant.

❷ Stan told the speaker that he and his wife are expecting a baby.

❸ Most couples wait for 12 weeks until they reveal the news.

換句話說 Retell

I went for dinner with my friend, Dana, the other evening. Dana had a real glow about her and she ate plenty of food: two starters, a main course, and two desserts! I asked her if she was eating for two. Hardly had I said those words when I was overwhelmed with regret. Dana was deeply offended. She informed me that she was not pregnant. I guess she was just hungry. Me and my big mouth!

Last night, I went for a few drinks with Dana's husband, Stan. After a couple of beers, Stan became very talkative and let slip a secret: He and his wife are expecting a baby! So, Dana *is* pregnant! Hardly had he told me when I became very confused. Why did Dana keep her pregnancy a secret? Stan informed me that most couples wait until 12 weeks to reveal the big news. This is when the chance of miscarriage significantly decreases. At least now I don't feel that bad about me and my big mouth!

討論題目 Free Talk

Yes, I'm usually cautious about what I say. However, a few years ago, I used to always speak my mind. This got me in trouble several times. Once, during a meeting with my boss, he was introducing a new company policy, which required employees to work overtime if they could not finish their tasks on time. However, in my opinion, the reason why most employees could not finish their work on time was because of the heavy workload and mismanagement, not because the employees were lazy or inefficient. Being offended by the new company policy, I spoke up against it on the spot. The boss

參考答案

385

was obviously not happy with my objection. Although he couldn't fire me for not liking a company policy, he gave me a low score for my end-of-year assessment. In the end, I didn't receive any bonus. After that, I've learned that I shouldn't always act on impulse and I should be more cautious about what I say.

Lesson 39

再次聆聽並回答問題 Listen again and answer the questions below

1 She played Beethoven's *Moonlight Sonata*.

2 She can play the piano, the violin, and the flute.

3 He wants to know whether she is single.

簡短對答 Quick Response

Q1 What instrument would you like to learn to play?

A1 I would like to learn to play the drums.

Q2 What are some of your talents?

A2 I am good at singing and dancing.

討論題目 Free Talk

If I could choose to be talented in something, I would choose sports. I love watching sport games, and I've always admired athletes. If I could be talented in sports and become a professional athlete, then I could participate in sport events, too! I understand that it's a lot of hard work being a professional athlete, but I'm hardworking and dedicated. People always say, hard work beats talent when talent doesn't work hard. If I were talented in sports, I would make sure that I was 100% focused on my training and strive to become better every day. My goal would be to participate in the Olympics, which is the ultimate dream for most athletes. I'd love to compete with the people that I see on TV all the time. And it would be a great honor to represent my country.

🎙 再次聆聽並回答問題 **Listen again and answer the questions below**

1 He learned the skill from his own father.

2 His bike broke down.

3 He was proud and delighted.

🎙 換句話說 **Retell**

My father is a mechanic. I like to go to the garage when he is working there. Like father, like son, I enjoy playing with machines and tools. When my father picks up a wrench, so do I. When he checks a tire, so do I. I have learned a lot from him. My father had learned to be a mechanic from his own father as well.

One day, my bike broke down while I was cycling by the river. I studied what was wrong with the bike instead of calling my father, and I successfully fixed it. I was very proud of myself, and my father was, too. My grandfather was even prouder; he was delighted to see his trade being passed down to the next generation. We decided to form a partnership and set up Delgado & Sons Garage to serve the needs of the local community. The residents of the town loved seeing all three of us working hard. The business was immensely popular, and also profitable.

🎙 討論題目 **Free Talk**

Yes, I think my mother and I are alike. Many people have said that our personalities are similar. I used to be a bit offended when people said this because I had always thought my mother was stubborn and headstrong (任性的). We used to fight all the time about everything, and neither of us was willing to apologize first. It was always my father who came to sort the issue out for us. It wasn't until years later when I became an adult that my mother told me what she had thought about me. Apparently, she had always thought that I was stubborn and headstrong, too. And according to my father, he is often amazed by how similar my mother and I are. I guess "like mother, like daughter" is a phrase that is true in our family.

Lesson 41

🔑 再次聆聽並回答問題 Listen again and answer the questions below

1 He was looking for a job.

2 He should bring his advertising portfolio.

3 Yes, he wants to work at the company.

🔑 換句話說 Retell

Gordon was searching for a new job for a long period of time. He submitted many applications to numerous companies, but to no avail. Gordon was becoming desperate and was worried about how to pay his expenses.

That was until today! A large advertising company offered Gordon an interview. He received an e-mail requesting that he bring his advertising portfolio to show the account director. It's a famous advertising firm, and Gordon has always dreamed of working there. During the interview, Gordon impressed the account director so much that he was offered the job on the spot!

🔑 討論題目 Free Talk

My dream job is to become a fashion designer. I've always wanted to have a career in the fashion industry ever since I was a child. My favorite thing to do as a child was to dress up my dolls and make costumes for them. Now, I am studying fashion design at a prestigious university. I also have an internship at a world-renowned company. My manager said if I perform well during the internship, there's a good chance that they'll offer me a full-time position as a fashion designer. This sure gives me the motivation to go to work every day! I feel like I'm getting closer and closer to fulfilling my dream!

Lesson 42

再次聆聽並回答問題 **Listen again and answer the questions below**

1 Yes, he received the quote.

2 Yes, his boss is happy with the terms.

3 He will return the signed document to the woman.

簡短對答 **Quick Response**

Q1 Do you often have meetings at work?

A1 Yes, I often have meetings at work.

Q2 What are the meetings usually about?

A2 In the meetings, we usually report our projects' progress to our manager.

討論題目 **Free Talk**

Yes, I have been in a video conference before. Normally, we have meetings in person in the company's conference room. However, during the pandemic, most of the employees were working from home. We had no choice but to hold meetings online. Personally, I prefer video conferences. For me, it's less stressful than having meetings in person. I always get nervous when reporting to my boss face to face. In a video conference, however, I feel more at ease because I only have to look at the screen. There are several drawbacks to having meetings online, though. For instance, sometimes the internet connection at my house is so bad that no one can understand what I'm saying. It sure can be an awkward situation!

Lesson 43

🎙 再次聆聽並回答問題 Listen again and answer the questions below

1 No, she is not done with the report.

2 She went to the library.

3 They will arrive tomorrow.

🎙 簡短對答 Quick Response

Q1 Do you often go to the library?

A1 No, I seldom go to the library.

Q2 Have you ever handed in an assignment late?

A2 No, I've never handed in an assignment late.

🎙 討論題目 Free Talk

At work, I often have to meet deadlines. And of course, deadlines come with pressure. However, I have several ways to cope with the stress. First, when setting a deadline, I'm always realistic, meaning I'm aware of my capabilities and how much workload I can handle. Therefore, I always make sure that the deadline set is not an impossible one. Then, when undertaking tasks, I like to make a list of all the things I have to do and prioritize them. It gives me a clearer view of what is more important or urgent. Lastly, I'm not afraid to ask for help if the situation demands it. In most cases, it's better to receive help than to miss the deadline.

Lesson 44

🎙 再次聆聽並回答問題 Listen again and answer the questions below

1 She can speak English, French, Spanish, and Japanese fluently.

2 Because she can put her skills to good use.

3 She will travel to London, Toronto, and back to Detroit next week.

換句話說 Retell

I am multilingual and I am a translator. I can speak fluent English, French, Spanish, and Japanese. I work for a famous car manufacturer in Detroit, which exports cars all over the world. Despite just joining the company, I get to travel far and wide with my job. This is an ideal job for me because I can put my skills to good use.

When I was in Paris last week, I translated five important contracts in order to secure deals that are worth millions of dollars. Next week, I will be traveling to London, Toronto, and back to Detroit. Through my intelligence and diligence, I believe I have quickly made myself indispensable to the company.

討論題目 Free Talk

No, I'm not multilingual. I am fluent in Chinese since it's my mother tongue. And currently, I am learning English, which I hope to be fluent in one day. There are also other languages that I would like to learn. For instance, I would love to learn French. I've always loved French culture, and I'd love to visit the country someday. However, I want to at least know a few French words and phrases before I travel there so that I will be able to understand the culture better. Another language I would like to learn is Japanese, but it's not because I desperately want to travel to Japan. It's simply because I love watching Japanese animations and reading Japanese comic books. I want to be able to watch or read the stories in Japanese so that I can fully understand the punch lines or the wordplay in them.

Lesson 45

再次聆聽並回答問題 Listen again and answer the questions below

1 She is a marketing specialist now.

2 She was asked to plan an entire advertising campaign for a big client.

3 Because she didn't have the relevant experience.

換句話說 Retell

I was thrilled to be offered the job of a marketing specialist. I had been looking for work for a few months, and I had started to worry about how I was going to pay the bills. If it hadn't been for this new job, I might have had to ask my parents for money. Even better, the job proved to be exciting and challenging, and all my colleagues were nice.

During my second week on the job, I was asked to take on a very difficult assignment—plan a complete advertising campaign for a big client. I had never done that before, so I was worried that I didn't have the relevant experience to finish the task by the deadline. Thankfully, Amy, my coworker, was nice enough to assist me so that I could finish the work on schedule. If it hadn't been for Amy's timely help, I never would have finished it on time.

討論題目 Free Talk

I work as a project manager. The most challenging task I have been asked to do for my job was when I was assigned to oversee the development of a new product for the first time. I had only been with the company for a few months. Based on my work performance, my manager decided that I was capable of handling things independently. At first, I was overwhelmed by how many things I needed to coordinate. I had to deal with the research and development team, the design team, the material control team, and many others. Not wanting to mess anything up, I was extra careful and paid attention to every detail. I consulted my senior coworkers whenever I encountered a problem. I took the time to communicate whenever an issue was raised. I put in more effort and time than I did in other assignments. Even though it was challenging for me to take on the task by myself, fortunately, my manager was thrilled with my performance in the end.

Lesson 46

🎙 再次聆聽並回答問題 **Listen again and answer the questions below**

1 Her car won't start because the battery is dead.

2 He will take her mom to the hospital.

3 She sprained her ankle while dancing.

🎙 簡短對答 **Quick Response**

Q1 Do you often offer to help other people?

A1 Yes, I often offer to help others.

Q2 Are your parents healthy?

A2 Yes, my parents are as healthy as ever.

🎙 討論題目 **Free Talk**

Yes, I've once helped a friend in need. My friend, Josh, had to move out of his dorm when he finished studying his master's degree. At first, I only went to his dorm to help him pack his stuff. However, after we started packing, we realized that he had too many things! We ended up packing at least ten heavy boxes. Originally, he wanted to carry everything by himself and take the train, but after packing, we agreed that it was impossible. In the end, I offered to give him a ride. He thanked me and couldn't have been more relieved that he didn't have to carry all those boxes by himself. In the end, I not only helped him pack, I also gave him a ride and drove for four hours from the dorm back to his hometown. Helping a friend in need is something I would never hesitate to do.

Lesson 47

🎙 再次聆聽並回答問題 **Listen again and answer the questions below**

1 It is a phenomenon where certain groups of people cannot reach the top in an organization.

2 Women and minorities are affected the most.

3 One of the reasons is that women have more family commitments.

🎙 換句話說 **Retell**

The glass ceiling metaphor is used to describe the phenomenon where certain groups of people cannot reach the top in an organization. Usually, these people are women or minorities who can only reach the level of middle management in a company. They can see the top, hoping that they can reach it. But, in fact, there is an invisible barrier that stops them from getting there. We all wish that there were no glass ceiling; unfortunately, it's still quite common.

What causes it, though? One reason is that, since many senior management positions in companies are already occupied by men, there is an unconscious prejudice against women joining their "boys' club." Another likely reason is that women have more family commitments; therefore, they are less likely to compete for higher-paying jobs with better perks. We must all work together in the hope of shattering the glass ceiling soon!

🎙 討論題目 **Free Talk**

Yes, I agree that women can be good leaders. When I was in high school, the club I joined didn't allow girls to become club leaders. It was because the advisor of the club thought girls couldn't handle the pressure as well as boys. At that time, no one thought the idea was absurd; we simply did what we were told and chose a boy as the club's leader and a girl as the assistant. However, after a while, the boy realized that being the club leader was more complicated than he had thought. The leader had to arrange activities, communicate with club members, resolve issues, and perform many other tasks. In the end, not only did the boy slack off and refuse to do his job, but the girl stepped in to do everything in his place. In this case, having a girl as a leader was definitely a much better idea.

Lesson 48

再次聆聽並回答問題 Listen again and answer the questions below

1 Because he still has a few more hours' work to do.

2 No, he is not happy with his salary.

3 She suggests he tell his supervisors.

簡短對答 Quick Response

Q1 Do you often work overtime?

A1 No, I rarely work overtime.

Q2 Are you satisfied with your salary?

A2 Yes, I am satisfied with my salary.

討論題目 Free Talk

If I had a heavy workload at work, I would first assess which ones were more important or more urgent. After sorting out my priorities, I would review my work schedule to see if I had been working efficiently or if I needed to adjust anything. And then, if I were positive that I could not finish everything on schedule because the workload was too heavy, I would report the situation to my supervisor. Hopefully, they would help me lighten my workload. If not, I'd probably have no choice but to work overtime. However, if the situation continued for a long time, I'd probably start looking for a new job that had a lighter workload and didn't require employees to constantly work overtime.

Lesson 49

📌 再次聆聽並回答問題 Listen again and answer the questions below

❶ She is wearing bike shorts.

❷ Because there is too much congestion on the road.

❸ She suggests that he go cycling with her in the evenings.

📌 簡短對答 Quick Response

Q1 Do you often go cycling?

A1 Yes, I often go cycling.

Q2 Would you be interested in cycling to work?

A2 Yes, I would be interested in this idea.

📌 討論題目 Free Talk

I usually take the subway to commute to and from work. Recently, I'm considering cycling to work maybe once or twice a week. Although taking the subway is very convenient, it is always packed with people during rush hour. To be honest, I've always felt a bit uncomfortable being so close to strangers in such a compact space. These days, with a pandemic raging, I feel even more uncomfortable about the situation. This is the main reason why I want to change my method of commuting. Cycling seems like a good choice because I can keep my distance from other people and get plenty of exercise at the same time. However, it can be inconvenient, especially on rainy days. Therefore, cycling once or twice a week seems like a realistic plan. Maybe I'll start next week!

Lesson 50

📌 再次聆聽並回答問題 Listen again and answer the questions below

❶ It is a car that can drive without a human driver.

❷ The speaker says the industry is currently unregulated.

❸ Self-driving cars are vulnerable to hacking and computer malfunctions.

🔎 換句話說 **Retell**

A self-driving car is a car that can drive with little or no human input. This form of driving is so safe that it's estimated that thousands of lives would be saved each year if everyone used self-driving cars. However, companies need more investment to produce more self-driving cars. And the public needs to be convinced of their safety so that they are more willing to buy them.

No form of transport is completely safe, but what exactly are the concerns related to self-driving cars? The industry is currently unregulated, meaning there are no established safety standards. The transition from manual cars to self-driving cars could be chaotic, as there would be a mixture of vehicles on the road. Also, self-driving cars could be vulnerable to hacking and computer malfunctions. It is necessary to address these safety issues so that the potential safety benefits can be unleashed. Self-driving cars can only be the future of driving when this is done.

🔎 討論題目 **Free Talk**

No, I doubt that self-driving cars will be the future of driving. Although it is exciting to see new technology being developed, it is undeniable that there are still too many issues surrounding self-driving cars. Now, there are companies manufacturing electric cars with a self-driving mode. However, there have been many cases of accidents occurring due to the self-driving function. In the United States, federal investigations were even carried out to look into the self-driving function of these electric cars. Obviously, there is still a long way to go to reassure the public of the safety of self-driving technology, myself included. Another reason why I don't think self-driving cars will become the future of driving is that most of the time, drivers don't simply drive from one destination to another.

參考答案

There are times when drivers like to take a shortcut, make a quick stop, or pull over on the side of the road. My point is that driving manually gives us much more freedom, while with self-driving cars, it's uncertain whether computers will be able to keep up with all the sudden changes.

Lesson 51

🎙 再次聆聽並回答問題 **Listen again and answer the questions below**

1 Yes, she enjoyed his magic show.

2 She is curious about how he made the rabbit disappear.

3 No, he has an assistant.

🎙 簡短對答 **Quick Response**

Q1 Have you ever seen a magic show before?

A1 No, I have never seen a magic show before.

Q2 Do you believe in magic?

A2 No, I don't believe in magic.

🎙 討論題目 **Free Talk**

If I had a magic wand, rather than ask for wealth and success, the only thing I would like to do is make everyone I love healthy and well. A few years ago, my grandmother's health worsened and our family had to hire a caretaker to look after her. Throughout the years, she has been constantly in and out of the hospital. Her illness has made her and everyone in the family stressed and exhausted. Therefore, there's nothing I want more than good health for everyone that I love. If I had a magic wand, I would make sure that everyone would live a long, healthy, and happy life.

🎙 再次聆聽並回答問題 **Listen again and answer the questions below**

❶ Helicopter parents might coordinate their children's social events.

❷ These children might not know how to cope in the future.

❸ No, the speaker thinks helicopter parents are bad for children.

🎙 換句話說 **Retell**

I feel bad for children whose parents organize every aspect of their lives. Because these parents always "hover" over their children, they are called helicopter parents. They coordinate their children's social events, arrange endless extracurricular activities, and interfere in their educational life.

These parents are surely just expressing love for their children, and some children are undoubtedly happy with this situation. But having helicopter parents can actually leave children less able to cope when they grow up. Since their parents have always done everything for them, these children don't know how to manage their own time or make their own decisions. So, helicopter parents aren't really doing their children any favors by treating them like this.

🎙 討論題目 **Free Talk**

No, I don't think my parents are helicopter parents. In fact, they are quite open-minded and liberal. When I was growing up, they often let me decide many things, such as what club to join in high school, or what to study in university. There are times when they don't agree with my decisions. When this happens, we sit down and discuss things calmly. After they patiently listen to my opinions, they will express their thoughts rationally. Even though sometimes these discussions can lead to heated arguments, I never disrespect them and they always try their best to stand in my shoes. I'm

參考答案

thankful for their parenting style. It has helped me become as open-minded as them, and I'm not afraid to make my own decisions or speak my own mind.

Lesson 53

🎙 <u>再次聆聽並回答問題</u> **Listen again and answer the questions below**

1 She is making a vlog.

2 Her video is about her first day at university.

3 She will show him the video after she finishes editing it.

🎙 <u>簡短對答</u> **Quick Response**

Q1 Have you ever filmed a vlog before?

A1 No, I've never filmed a vlog before.

Q2 Do you know how to edit videos?

A2 No, I don't know how to edit videos.

🎙 <u>討論題目</u> **Free Talk**

I've always loved traveling and watching other people's travel vlogs. Therefore, if I were filming a vlog, I would like to make a travel vlog. I travel abroad at least once a year, and in my past travels, I only took photos. Even though pictures are worth a thousand words, they can only show a small part of the scenery or capture a specific moment at an event. With videos, I can record what people say and do, and even their emotions. I guess if I want to make a vlog, I should learn how to edit videos and even buy a decent camera first. That will surely cost me a lot of time and money. Maybe I should just stick to watching other people's vlogs.

Lesson 54

🎙 <u>再次聆聽並回答問題</u> **Listen again and answer the questions below**

1 They throw out the clothes or donate them to charity.

❷ They can pass the toys on to other parents.

❸ It can de-clutter your mind, help you re-assess your goals, and re-evaluate your ambitions.

🔑 換句話說 Retell

Many people become minimalists in order to seek a simpler life. The clothes hanging in the closet that are never worn are thrown out or donated to charity. The books and DVDs sitting on the shelf that are gathering dust are given to a friend or recycled. The kids' toys piled up in the bedroom are passed on to other parents to occupy their children.

Being a minimalist, though, is about more than just getting rid of your unwanted items. It is also about de-cluttering your mind, re-assessing your goals, and re-evaluating your ambitions. It can help you realize what your priorities in life are and what is important to you. Maybe it's about time to give the lifestyle of a minimalist a try and minimize your life!

🔑 討論題目 Free Talk

No, I'm not interested in becoming a minimalist. I love shopping and collecting things. I have collections of books, toys, mugs, and many other things. To my understanding, being a minimalist would mean that I have to throw these things away and keep only the necessities. However, I have put a lot of time and effort into my collections, so there is zero chance that I will ever dispose of them. It doesn't mean that I don't agree with minimalism, though. I do agree that clearing out your living space and getting rid of unnecessary items can help you have a clearer mind and a more comfortable living environment. And some of my friends have adopted the minimalist lifestyle and feel it is the best choice they have ever made. It is just not the right lifestyle for me.

Lesson 55

🔖 再次聆聽並回答問題 **Listen again and answer the questions below**

1. She called her because he got into a fight with another boy.

2. They were fighting because the other boy called Emma nasty names.

3. Because he didn't want to tattle.

🔖 簡短對答 **Quick Response**

Q1 Have you ever been in a fight before?

A1 No, I've never been in a fight before.

Q2 Would you protect your friend if he or she were bullied?

A2 Yes, I would protect my friend.

🔖 討論題目 **Free Talk**

Yes, I have been a tattletale before. I used to get in fights with my little brother all the time. And even now we are older, we still like to pick on each other. Although we seldom get into serious fights now, my brother still gets on my nerves sometimes with his pranks. Once, he pulled a prank on me by hiding my laptop. I was furious because all of my assignments and essays were in it. I ended up turning in one of the assignments late because of this stupid prank. I wanted to take revenge on him. At that time, our parents didn't allow us to date, and I had secretly found out he had a girlfriend. Being so mad at him, I told my parents about it. And of course he got some serious scolding for it. I had never known tattling on someone else would feel so good!

Lesson 56

🔖 再次聆聽並回答問題 **Listen again and answer the questions below**

1. Stereotypes are widely held ideas about a particular type of person or thing.

2 Because they are usually oversimplified and often incorrect.

3 Usually, people think immigrants are more likely to commit a crime.

換句話說 Retell

Stereotypes are widely held ideas about a particular type of person or thing. For instance, when seeing a car accident involving a male driver and a female driver, you might think the woman must have caused the accident because women are supposedly "bad drivers." Or, when seeing someone working in a manual job, you might think that they cannot have had a good education.

Stereotypes can be harmless, but they can also be dangerous and rooted in ignorance of a culture or race. Stereotypes are usually oversimplified and often incorrect. Some people use stereotypes instead of facts to justify their opinions. For example, if a crime was committed in a small town, some people might presume that it must have been done by the newly arrived immigrant. This is because the stereotype of an immigrant is often linked to crime. We must all unite to fight against and challenge stereotypes.

討論題目 Free Talk

No, I don't agree that all stereotypes are bad. I believe that stereotypes can help people have a general idea of what people from different cultural or racial backgrounds are like. Although they may not be completely true, stereotypes can still help us have a simple understanding. For instance, it's widely believed that the Japanese are efficient, the Spanish are laid-back, and the Germans are stern. Having these stereotypes might help us be more mentally prepared when meeting people from those countries for the first time. However, we should all still keep an open mind. Not everyone from the same cultural background or with the same skin color thinks or behaves the same. We should all take the time to learn more about individuals instead of presuming that they all act the same way.

Lesson 57

再次聆聽並回答問題 Listen again and answer the questions below

1 The speaker would divide the money into three parts.

2 The speaker would like to contribute the money to heart and cancer research and charities that help children in war-torn regions.

3 The speaker plans to keep it and use it for traveling and buying things.

換句話說 Retell

If I were a millionaire, I would divide my money into three chunks. I would give one third to my family, so they could live in comfort and wouldn't have to worry about money anymore. I'd like to buy my parents a smaller house, so it wouldn't need that much maintenance.

Another third would be given to charity, so I could make a difference in the world. I'd like to contribute to heart and cancer research, and give money to organizations that help children in war-torn regions.

Lastly, I would keep the other third for myself, so I could travel and buy nice things. I'd like to go on a round-the-world cruise and visit as many countries as possible. If I were a millionaire, I'd want to have some fun, too!

討論題目 Free Talk

If I had some money to donate, I would like to contribute to an organization that does research on Alzheimer's disease (阿茲海默症) and provides care for patients suffering from Alzheimer's. A few years ago, my grandfather was diagnosed with Alzheimer's, and it took a toll on him and the entire family. It was depressing seeing him turn into such a frail person. He started out forgetting bits and pieces, like where he put the keys or where the supermarket was. Then, he couldn't find his way home and couldn't recognize his children and grandchildren. In the end, it was extremely hard for him to do the simplest tasks such as going to the bathroom or turning the TV on. It was hard witnessing this happening. There is nothing that I want more than to have a cure for Alzheimer's. Therefore, helping organizations do more research on battling this disease would be my top choice.

Lesson 58

🎙 再次聆聽並回答問題 Listen again and answer the questions below

1 No, he is not having fun at the party.

2 She says a beer will loosen him up and get him talking to people.

3 He will go talk to Tony.

🎙 簡短對答 Quick Response

Q1 Do you often go to parties?

A1 No, I rarely go to parties.

Q2 When you are at a party, what do you usually do?

A2 I usually chat with my friends and eat plenty of food.

🎙 討論題目 Free Talk

I think I was more sociable when I was still a student. I used to love joining different clubs, meeting new people, and going to parties to socialize. I had a wide variety of friends, from international students and exchange students to students from different departments. When I walked around the campus, there was always someone waving at me. However, after I graduated and started working, it became harder and harder to keep in contact with everyone. The only people that I have constant contact with now are a couple of my closest friends. These days, I no longer want to be sociable and make a lot of friends. I still think it's important to be friendly, but meeting new people and becoming friends with every single person has become too exhausting for me.

Lesson 59

再次聆聽並回答問題 Listen again and answer the questions below

1 He had planned to study architecture.

2 He was caught cheating on the final exam.

3 He learned that cheaters never prosper.

換句話說 Retell

I was really close to getting a scholarship to the college of my dreams. I had been preparing for years to study architecture at a prestigious college in the UK, and all I needed to do was pass one final exam. However, I became nervous and started to doubt my ability. I decided to cheat by smuggling my smartphone into the exam hall. One of the teachers saw me using my phone, and I was disqualified from the exam and given an automatic fail on the spot.

I was devastated. I might not have made such a serious error of judgment if I had believed in myself more. If I hadn't cheated, I would have gotten the scholarship and would now be studying to become an architect. I did learn one important lesson, though: Cheaters never prosper!

討論題目 Free Talk

Yes, I've felt stressed about an exam before. I was in my third year of high school, and I was about to take my college entrance exam. I had been preparing for it ever since I entered high school. My goal was to excel in the exam so I could apply for a prestigious college that is famous for its engineering program. Even though

I usually got pretty good grades in mock exams, I still felt like my performance wasn't good enough. The pressure was building up as the day of the exam approached. At first, I felt so anxious that I had no appetite. As soon as my mother noticed that I wasn't eating anything, she came to me and asked about my feelings. After opening up to her, I felt relieved and less stressed. I guess the best way for me to cope with the stress was to have someone to talk to.

Lesson 60

🔑 再次聆聽並回答問題 Listen again and answer the questions below

❶ She is good at playing the piano, drawing and painting, and cooking.

❷ The speaker thinks it is because she never boasts about her abilities.

❸ Some people might dislike her.

🔑 換句話說 Retell

Lana, who is a friend of mine, is quite talented. She is a great pianist. If she were to play the piano for you, you'd swear Mozart had been reincarnated. Also, she excels in drawing and painting, and she is an incredible cook. If she were to paint a portrait for you, you'd think it was a photograph. If she were to cook a meal for you, you'd have dreams about that meal for an entire month.

However, she never boasts about her abilities like some people do. Maybe that's why she has so many friends. Everyone likes her and wants to spend time with her because she is interested in people and actually listens to what they say. If she were to boast about her talents, I'm certain some people would start to dislike her. But Lana would never do that because a modest person never boasts.

參考答案

💡 討論題目 Free Talk

No, I don't consider myself a talented person. I often like to try new things, but I never get to the point where I excel in them. For instance, I've learned French and Japanese before. Even though I enjoyed learning them, I somehow never continued the lessons to the next level. In the end, I'm still quite mediocre (中等的) in both languages. And since I haven't had much practice after I stopped taking classes, I've forgotten pretty much everything about French and Japanese. I also like to cook, but I'm definitely not the best cook in the world. I like to sing, but I haven't got the voice of an angel. I like to paint, but I've been told that my paintings look like they're done by a five-year-old. All in all, I have many hobbies, but not that many talents.

Notes

國家圖書館出版品預行編目（CIP）資料

英語輕鬆學：學好中級口語就靠這本！/
賴世雄作. -- 初版. -- 臺北市：常春藤有聲出版股
份有限公司, 2022.12　面；　公分.
--（常春藤英語輕鬆學系列；E68）
ISBN 978-626-7225-11-0（平裝）
1. CST：英語　2. CST：口語　3. CST：會話
805.188　　　　　　　　　111020666

常春藤英語輕鬆學系列【E68】
英語輕鬆學：學好中級口語就靠這本！

總 編 審	賴世雄
終　 審	陳宏瑋
執行編輯	許嘉華
編輯小組	鄭筠潔・陳筠汝・Nick Roden・Brian Foden
設計組長	王玥琦
封面設計	謝孟珊
排版設計	王穎緁・林桂旭
錄　 音	劉書吟・李鳳君
朗讀播音老師	Leah Zimmermann・Tom Brink
講解播音老師	奚永慧・呂佳馨
法律顧問	北辰著作權事務所蕭雄淋律師
出 版 者	常春藤有聲出版股份有限公司
地　 址	臺北市忠孝西路一段 33 號 5 樓
電　 話	(02) 2331-7600
傳　 真	(02) 2381-0918
網　 址	www.ivy.com.tw
電子信箱	service@ivy.com.tw
郵政劃撥	19714777
戶　 名	常春藤有聲出版股份有限公司
定　 價	559 元

© 常春藤有聲出版股份有限公司 (2022) All rights reserved.　　　　　V000121-5568
本書之封面、內文、編排等之著作財產權歸常春藤有聲出版股份有限公司所有。未經本公司書面同意，請勿翻印、
轉載或為一切著作權法上利用行為，否則依法追究。

如有缺頁、裝訂錯誤或破損，請寄回本公司更換。　　　　　　【版權所有　翻印必究】

郵票黏貼處

100009 臺北市忠孝西路一段 33 號 5 樓

常春藤有聲出版股份有限公司　行政組　啟

常春藤　www.ivy.com.tw　愛上英語的第一站

常春藤 英語集團 　　讀者問卷【E68】
英語輕鬆學：學好中級口語就靠這本！

感謝您購買本書！為使我們對讀者的服務能夠更加完善，請您詳細填寫本問卷各欄後，寄回本公司或傳真至（02）2381-0918，**或掃描 QR Code 填寫線上問卷**，我們將於收到後七個工作天內贈送「常春藤網路書城熊贈點 50 點（一點＝一元，使用期限 90 天）」給您（每書每人限贈一次），也懇請您繼續支持。若有任何疑問，請儘速與客服人員聯絡，客服電話：（02）2331-7600 分機 11～13，謝謝您！

線上填寫
免郵寄最環保

姓　　名：＿＿＿＿＿＿　性別：＿＿＿＿　生日：＿＿＿年　＿＿＿月　＿＿＿日
聯絡電話：＿＿＿＿＿＿　**E-mail**：＿＿＿＿＿＿＿＿＿＿＿＿＿＿＿
聯絡地址：□□□□□□＿＿＿＿＿＿＿＿＿＿＿＿＿＿＿＿＿＿＿＿＿
　　　　　＿＿＿＿＿＿＿＿＿＿＿＿＿＿＿＿＿＿＿＿＿＿＿＿＿＿＿

教育程度：□國小　□國中　□高中　□大專／大學　□研究所含以上
職　　業：**1** □學生
　　　　　2 社會人士：□工　□商　□服務業　□軍警公職　□教職　□其他＿＿＿＿

1 您從何處得知本書：□書店　□常春藤網路書城　□FB／IG／Line@ 社群平臺推薦
　　□學校購買　□親友推薦　□常春藤雜誌　□其他＿＿＿＿＿＿＿＿＿＿

2 您購得本書的管道：□書店　□常春藤網路書城　□博客來　□其他＿＿＿＿＿

3 最滿意本書的特點依序是(限定三項)：□試題演練　□字詞解析　□內容　□編排方式
　　□印刷　□音檔朗讀　□封面　□售價　□信任品牌　□其他＿＿＿＿＿＿＿

4 您對本書建議改進的三點依序是：□無（都很滿意）　□試題演練　□字詞解析　□內容
　　□編排方式　□印刷　□音檔朗讀　□封面　□售價　□其他＿＿＿＿＿＿＿
　　原因：＿＿＿＿＿＿＿＿＿＿＿＿＿＿＿＿＿＿＿＿＿＿＿＿＿＿＿＿＿＿
　　對本書的其他建議：＿＿＿＿＿＿＿＿＿＿＿＿＿＿＿＿＿＿＿＿＿＿＿＿

5 希望我們出版哪些主題的書籍：＿＿＿＿＿＿＿＿＿＿＿＿＿＿＿＿＿＿＿＿

6 若您發現本書誤植的部分，請告知在：書籍第＿＿＿＿＿頁，第＿＿＿＿＿行
　　有錯誤的部分是：＿＿＿＿＿＿＿＿＿＿＿＿＿＿＿＿＿＿＿＿＿＿＿＿＿

7 對我們的其他建議：＿＿＿＿＿＿＿＿＿＿＿＿＿＿＿＿＿＿＿＿＿＿＿＿

感謝您寶貴的意見，您的支持是我們的動力！　常春藤網路書城 **www.ivy.com.tw**